ALL DOWN THE LINE

A PEOPLE'S HISTORY OF THE ROLLING STONES 1972 NORTH AMERICAN TOUR

RICHARD HOUGHTON

Spenwood Books
Manchester, UK

BY THE SAME AUTHOR

The Beatles – I Was There

The Who – I Was There

Pink Floyd – I Was There

Jimi Hendrix – The Day I Was There

Led Zeppelin – The Day I Was There

The Smiths – The Day I Was There

The Jam – The Day I Was There (with Neil Cossar)

Black Sabbath – The Day I Was There

Rush – The Day I Was There

The Wedding Present – Sometimes These Words Just Don't Have To Be Said (with David Gedge)

Orchestral Manoeuvres in the Dark – Pretending To See The Future

Simple Minds – Heart of the Crowd

Shaun Ryder's Book of Mumbo Jumbo

Cream – A People's History

Queen – A People's History

Jethro Tull – Lend Me Your Ears

The Rolling Stones in the Sixties – A People's History

Gonna See All My Friends – A People's History of Fairport Convention

The Stranglers – Live (Excerpts)

ALL DOWN THE LINE: A PEOPLE'S HISTORY OF THE ROLLING STONES 1972 NORTH AMERICAN TOUR

Richard Houghton

Spenwood Books
Manchester, UK

ALL DOWN THE LINE

First published in Great Britain 2022
by Spenwood Books Ltd
2 College Street, Higham Ferrers, NN10 8DZ.

A CIP record for this book is available from the
British Library.

ISBN 978-1-9168896-6-8

Printed in the Czech Republic via Akcent Media Limited.

Design by Bruce Graham, The Night Owl.

Front cover design: Bruce Graham
Rear cover images: Daniel Teafoe, John Savesky, Gary Tufel
All other image copyrights: As captioned.

HEARD THE DIESEL DRUMMING

AcKNOWLEDGEMENTS

Bruce Graham for his design expertise; Dave Evely at Sound Performance; Charles Andrews, for permission to quote from his June 22, 1972, *Daily Lobo* review of the Rolling Stones at the University of New Mexico; Harvey Kubernik; Malcolm Wyatt; Bruce Koziarski; Robert Register; and Harold Colson, whose collection of press cuttings from the 1972 tour proved an invaluable resource.

And thank you to my lovely and supportive wife, Kate Sullivan.

INTRODUCTION

Will they tour the States again? Or is that it for the Rolling Stones? These questions are on the lips of Stones fans as I write, their *Sixty* European tour having just wrapped after 14 shows that grossed $120 million in the summer of 2022.

But those same questions were being asked at the beginning of 1972. 50 years ago, doubt hung like shadow over the future of the Stones. Sure, they had a new album in the shape of *Exile on Main St.* almost in the can (recorded at Keith's house in southern France, with Mick mixing and recording additional vocals in LA). And they needed the money a big tour would bring, as 1971's *Sticky Fingers* had done okay but Allen Klein had tied their back catalogue royalties in legal knots that wouldn't unravel for years.

But The Beatles had split up, Jimi Hendrix, Janis Joplin and Jim Morrison were all dead and the Stones still had the shadow of Altamont hanging over them, with a bounty rumored to have been placed on Mick Jagger's head by the Hell's Angels. No longer hanging together in and around London, the Stones were tax exiles scattered across Europe. Drugs were on the scene, and there was skepticism as to whether the Stones could properly function as a live outfit again. Plus the United States was coming to terms with 1970's Kent State massacre and still grappling with the Vietnam War, the draft and the civil rights movement. America was not necessarily going to embrace the Rolling Stones with open arms.

So it was that the band announced a 51 show coast-to-coast tour playing 32 cities in 54 days. With a groundbreaking new stage show, demand for tickets was high and the tour a sell-out. But was the time right for dancing in the streets? Or would it be fighting?

The Stones and their fans found themselves going head-to-head with the authorities from the outset. Concerts were marked by crowd riots in the clamour for tickets and many shows saw drug busts and tear gassings as a result of over-zealous cops. In Rhode Island, Mick Jagger and Keith Richards wound up in police custody when they should have been on stage in Boston.

The movie *Ladies and Gentlemen, the Rolling Stones* caught the Stones in action in Texas, and the insider's take on events was covered extensively by *Rolling Stone* magazine at the time and then by Robert Greenfield's 1974 book *STP: A Journey Through America with the Rolling Stones*. And Robert Frank captured some of the madness on celluloid in *Cocksucker Blues* (which the Stones prevented ever getting a full theatrical release). But the other story - the story from the viewpoint of the fans - has never been told before.

This is a journey through America with the fans of the Rolling Stones, taking in the highways and byways, the day trips to secure tickets, the anticipation in the lead up to shows, the drugs scored to enhance the concert experience, and the chaos, excitement and passion surrounding each show, both inside and outside the venue. It tells how the Stones touched teenage lives, sometimes changing them forever.

Excerpts from contemporaneous press reports give a flavor of the range of opinions reviewers had towards the band ('thank God for Rod Stewart') but also indicate just how big an event the 1972 tour was. In some cities – hey, most cities – the arrival of the Stones charabanc was the event of the summer.

If you had a time machine, would you go back to the summer of 1972 and pay no more than $6.50 to see the greatest rock 'n' roll band in their prime, playing tracks from their hot new release, *Exile on Main St.*? Well, until they invent that time machine, here's the next best thing. A journey across America in the company of over 300 fans and one or two other friends and associates. Ladies and gentlemen, the Rolling Stones….

Richard Houghton
Manchester, UK
October 2022

MICK JAGGER

I don't want high-priced tickets, delays, riots or any of that crap. We're going out there to make a lot of money and win a lot of friends.

KEITH RICHARDS

The point is that the Stones had reached a point where we no longer had to do what we were told to do.

ROLLING STONES
STONES TOURING PARTY
1972 NORTH AMERICAN TOUR

3 June	Pacific Coliseum, Vancouver, Canada
4 June	Seattle Center Coliseum, Seattle, Washington (2 shows)
6 June	Winterland Ballroom, San Francisco, California (2 shows)
8 June	Winterland Ballroom, San Francisco, California (2 shows)
9 June	Hollywood Palladium, Los Angeles, California
10 June	Long Beach Arena, Long Beach, California
11 June	The Forum, Inglewood, California (2 shows)
13 June	International Sports Arena, San Diego, California
14 June	Tucson Convention Center, Tucson, Arizona
15 June	University Arena, Albuquerque, New Mexico
16 June	Denver Coliseum, Denver, Colorado (2 shows)
18 June	Metropolitan Sports Center, Bloomington, Minnesota
19 June	International Amphitheatre, Chicago, Illinois
20 June	International Amphitheatre, Chicago, Illinois (2 shows)
22 June	Municipal Auditorium, Kansas City, Missouri
24 June	Tarrant County Convention Center, Fort Worth, Texas (2 shows)
25 June	Hofheinz Pavilion, Houston, Texas (2 shows)
27 June	Mobile Civic Center, Mobile, Alabama
28 June	Memorial Coliseum, Tuscaloosa, Alabama
29 June	Municipal Auditorium, Nashville, Tennessee

ALL DOWN THE LINE

4 July	Robert F Kennedy Memorial Stadium, Washington DC
5 July	Norfolk Scope, Norfolk, Virginia
6 July	Charlotte Coliseum, Charlotte, North Carolina
7 July	Civic Arena, Knoxville, Tennessee
9 July	Kiel Convention Hall, St Louis
	(2 shows)
11 July	Rubber Bowl, Akron, Ohio
12 July	Indiana Convention-Exposition Center, Indianapolis, Indiana
13 July	Cobo Hall, Detroit
14 July	Cobo Hall, Detroit
15 July	Maple Leaf Gardens, Toronto, Canada
	(2 shows)
17 July	Montreal Forum, Montreal, Canada
18 July	Boston Garden, Boston, Massachusetts
19 July	Boston Garden, Boston, Massachusetts
20 July	The Spectrum, Philadelphia, Pennsylvania
21 July	The Spectrum, Philadelphia, Pennsylvania
	(2 shows)
22 July	Civic Arena, Pittsburgh
24 July	Madison Square Garden, New York City, New York
25 July	Madison Square Garden, New York City, New York
	(2 shows)
26 July	Madison Square Garden, New York City, New York

The tour kicked off in Vancouver. 2,000 ticketless fans tried to crash the gates of the Pacific Coliseum, resulting in injuries to 31 police officers.

PACIFIC COLISEUM
JUNE 3, 1972, VANCOUVER, CANADA

VENUE CAPACITY	15,570
PERFORMANCES	1
ARRESTS	13

RODNEY HELMS,

AGE 21

I first saw the Stones on *The Ed Sullivan Show* in 1964. In 1967, when they were back on the show, Ed Sullivan tried to get them to change the lyrics to the song, 'Let's Spend the Night Together', to 'let's spend some time together'. They must've been pissed that he even approached them to ask them to do that. He was an old man even in the mid-Sixties, and old-fashioned in his values by mid-Sixties standards. He was erring on the side of conservatism

Rodney Helms was only 15 feet from the stage in Vancouver

almost to a fault. In my sophomore year of high school, we had a contest to sell magazine subscriptions. I sold subscriptions to relatives and sold so many I won a prise. My prise was a copy of *Between the Buttons*, which was great as I didn't have much pocket change to buy LP records in those days. That was the first Stones album I owned.

I saw the Stones in Vancouver in '72. They flew into Seattle, Washington and then took a stretch limo all the way up to Vancouver, BC. I wouldn't wanna have to pay the gas bill for that! Canadian TV had footage of the Stones talking to a couple of the Canadian customs officers. They didn't show it in the clip, but they probably asked them, 'Do you have anything to declare?', and then the obvious question, 'Do you have any drugs on you?'. Which they didn't have, so they had no problem getting through customs.

There was only one place where you could buy tickets for that concert. You couldn't buy them by phone and you couldn't buy them in Seattle, Washington. They were only on sale in Canada at one outdoor ticket booth at the stadium, which is kind of unusual. The ticket was only six dollars. Even a candy bar costs six dollars now! I wanted to make sure I could be near the first in line, so I took my sleeping bag with me and camped out at the outdoor ticket booth. They started selling tickets at nine or ten o'clock the next morning. There were about 20 people waiting in line in front of me. The tickets sold out in something like two hours, and a lot of people were pissed off that they didn't get tickets.

On the evening of the concert, there were some people who were very upset that they couldn't get in. They had picked up some small rocks and were throwing these across the parking lot at the PNE. Later in the evening, I heard a car had been set on fire outside the stadium by the people who were upset that they couldn't get in. But there were people buying tickets off scalpers, I'm sure. I talked to people as I was going into the stadium and they said they were amongst the last people to buy tickets before it sold out. This was the beginning of the tour, so it was an important concert inasmuch as a lot of people wanted to go to it.

The PNE Coliseum was a hockey rink. It held about 15,000 people and it still exists. It was festival seating. I was amongst the first 200 people to get in. Rather than sit where the seats were, far from the stage, they let people stand near the stage, so I was maybe 15 feet from the stage itself. A lot of stadiums wouldn't allow you to do that. They didn't advertise it in advance that they were going to have Billy Preston there playing the piano or keyboard, and they also had a surprise performance by Stevie Wonder. It blew my mind. It was quite a shock to see both those performers, and quite the treat.

The Stones played close to an hour and a half. They played around 12 to 15 songs, including 'Satisfaction' and 'Midnight Rambler'. A lot of people were smoking grass and it created a little bit of a cloud inside the stadium. After a while, you could smell the aroma and it was quite pervasive. It was warm at that time of year, and it was warm inside the stadium too. If you've got enough people together like that, the body heat warms everything up as well. Quite a lot of people were standing, but we weren't packed in like sardines. Quite a few people chose to stand like I did to get near the stage.

I have a copy of *Life* magazine with two or three pages of content and with Mick Jagger on the front, in the white or tan-colored jumpsuit that he wore. I treasure that. I wish there was a video of the show but videotape was in its infancy in those days. If there's any footage it will be 16 millimetre. The show has to rank as being the best I ever saw, because I was able to get so close to the stage. That's what makes it stand out from any of the other concerts that I saw. I wasn't the kind of fan that went to a lot of concerts. In hindsight, I wish I'd attended more. But you can't go back in a time machine and make that happen.

HOWARD MARKSON

I first saw the Stones in Winnipeg in July 1966. I was already 19 and I went with my buddy Billy. Our seats were pretty decent. The big buzz was how the group could be rowdy and egg on their fans, so I watched not only the show but how it played out. I remember Mick wore a tight pair of white pants, and shook his butt impishly and provocatively. One male fan jumped from the balcony onto a curtain behind the group. He crawled down onto the stage, only to be greeted by security. For years I considered this the greatest concert I had ever been to.

But in June 1972, I drove 1,500 miles

Howard Markson had already seen the Stones in '66

from Winnipeg to Vancouver to see the Stones again, this time with my
fiancée, who I was marrying later that month, and our friends Rhea and
(a different) Billy. The buzz beforehand was all about the potential for
violence and we were a bit nervous about attending the show. We were also
conscious of the fact that Vancouver was hosting the start of the tour.

Many of the tunes were being played live for the first time ever. 'Tumbling
Dice' got my rocks off. But I most remember 'Midnight Rambler'. Mick had
some sort of strap or whip, which he would strike dramatically on the stage.
It's the slow part where he sings, 'You've heard about the Boston Strangler...',
at which point he whacked the stage. It was quite awesome. When we left
the Coliseum, there were lots of horse-mounted cops and we could see that
there had been some sort of crowd riot. But we were able to leave peacefully
and it was no problem getting home.

JACQUELYN HARDING

I went with my boyfriend, who I later married. It was our first date. I
will always remember the excitement and all the songs and seeing Mick
and the band. Little Stevie Wonder opened for them and he was pretty
awesome too. I could not believe I was actually there, and the concert
was wonderful except the Stones did not do an encore and would not
come back out on stage, which I thought was pretty stinky. When I got
home, my mom was worried because she heard that there was a riot after
the concert. Well, I did not see any riot.

PHILIP J NIELSEN

It was the first time people had to line up a week early to buy tickets, and
many people slept outside of the Empire Stadium overnight to get tickets.
We did not. We were only allowed to buy four tickets per person, which
was supposed to keep scalpers from buying the bulk of tickets ahead of the
general public. Tickets were six dollars apiece and they were resold for up
to $150, so it didn't keep scalpers from selling them. I sold my two extra
tickets for seven dollars each just so I could cover my gas.

We were excited on the day of the concert and got to the Pacific
Coliseum pretty much as soon as the doors were opened. Stevie Wonder
put on a hell of a show and we figured that the Stones would be at least
as good. Unbeknownst to us, there was a riot going on outside while the

Stones were playing. Some of my friends now say they really enjoyed the concert, but I was disappointed. The Stones seemed so bored and disinterested. It felt like they were mailing it in. This may have been because they knew about the riot outside. We were not the only city to have riots – the entire tour was marred by riots and major disturbances. As we left the Coliseum, we noticed that every glass entrance door had been smashed in and cops were everywhere. That was the first inkling that something had gone on while the concert was happening.

YESTERDAY'S PAPERS

CHRIS BIRD & ROB TURNER
THE PROVINCE, JUNE 5, 1972

The Rolling Stones kept 17,000 young fans happy on Saturday night while more than 200 police battled rock, bottle and fire bomb throwers outside the Pacific Coliseum. About 30 policeman suffered injuries ranging from cuts and bruises to concussion and broken bones. Eight were admitted to hospital and released after treatment. Police estimated that more than 2,500 persons were involved in a two hour battle. Damage to the Coliseum was confined to broken windows. 13 persons were arrested by Sunday and eleven had been charged with offenses ranging from possession of explosives to assaulting police.

JEANI READ
THE PROVINCE, JUNE 5, 1972

Saturday night at the Coliseum, the self-proclaimed greatest rock and roll band in the world played their first North American concert since Altamont in December 1969. And no matter how hard they humped it - and they did for a solid (yawn) 90 minutes - it never quite happened.

Once there was only one Jagger, only one strutting, lewd, brilliantly vile Jagger, the venomous grimace in the voice striking an impact that could not possibly be compared to anything else. But now Jagger has competition and is losing out, not possessed by the music or by the audience, a pale imitation. It was lazy, and it didn't ring, true, losing momentum and becoming form. Thank God for Rod Stewart.

The Seattle show was the first performance by the Rolling Stones in the United States since the ill-fated Altamont free concert in California in December 1969.

SEATTLE CENTER COLISEUM
JUNE 4, 1972, SEATTLE, WASHINGTON

VENUE CAPACITY	17,200
PERFORMANCES	2
ARRESTS	8

DENNIS KOESSEL

We camped overnight in the parking lot for tickets, which turned into a free for all when they went on sale. We did the same for the concert. Stevie Wonder opened and that was a spectacle in itself. The Stones were

Dennis Koessel kept his tour ad

awesome and played a good long set. It was a nice hardcore Stones show.

ERIC SNYDER, AGE 14

It was so amazing and still the best concert I've ever seen. The Rolling Stones were in their prime and, oh my god, Stevie Wonder was awesome. I stood in awe watching my rock gods perform. It had a lifelong impact on me.

DAVID WADE

I was just a youngin when I bought their first record and then bought all the rest through time. I love The Beatles but the Stones' blues influence in their music was my favorite. Eight of us went to the show together. We dropped acid and took the bus downtown. We were happy to see Stevie but much more anxious for the Stones, and they did not disappoint. It was a rock and roll party like no other. The place was packed and the sound was splendid. It was good in-yer-face rock and roll and a great show. We missed the last bus home and spent the night downtown until 6am, when the buses ran again. I saw Led Zeppelin at the same place not long after, but the Stones show was the best. There were no seats, just wall-to-wall people. And everyone was high…

LLOYD BARDE, AGE 22

I had seen The Beatles when I was 14. My early albums were Bob Dylan and the Dave Clark Five, and the Rolling Stones in 1966 was when I got on board. But 1972 is when it really opened up. I had no idea what was going to happen when I walked into the Seattle Coliseum.

When I went to college, I moved from Seattle to meet up with my cousin in Greeley, Colorado. We put our record album collections together, took the 500 duplicates and started a little record store. I was in the store one day when I got a call from a friend in Seattle who said, 'Hey Lloyd, do you want to come up and see the Rolling Stones? I can get your tickets right now.' I said, 'Definitely,' and I turned to my partner, Glenn, and the four other people in the store and I said, 'Hey guys, do you wanna go and see the Rolling Stones in Seattle?' Everyone said 'yes'.

So now we had a group of six people who took off late at night, driving across Wyoming to go to see Yellowstone and then on to see the Rolling Stones. It was the *Exile* tour and we knew all the songs, because we played them all the way to Seattle. We were a wild and loose group. We made it to Seattle and met up with my friend. We were very excited. We took many different substances and went off to the Seattle Coliseum for the afternoon show.

We walked in. It was a big crowd. Stevie Wonder was the opening act. That was incidental but it was cool. As the Stones came out on stage, Glenn pulled out a cassette tape recorder he had snuck in so we recorded

17

it all. We were very, very high and in a completely alternate reality. We got pretty close to the front of the stage. There were things going into the tape recorder, like, 'Oh my God, they got too much fucking make up on!' I hadn't seen Keith Richards do his thing. And Mick? Mick was just strutting at his peak. This was also the introduction to Mick Taylor. Although he'd been on the '69 tour, this is where he took over. One of my main memories is Mick Taylor's guitar just cutting through everything. It was an incredible show – Bobby Keys, Nicky Hopkins, the works. It was mind blowing.

We went out of there and drove down the freeway in one of those little Toyota pick ups. Someone was standing in the back of the truck, yelling at every car that we passed, 'You have to go see the Rolling Stones! See the Rolling Stones!' We were completely out of our heads.

We got back to my friend's place. One of our guys' nickname was The Ace (we all had nicknames). The Ace said, 'We got to go back to the next show.' Because there was an evening show. I said, 'We don't have tickets. We can't get tickets.' And another one of the guys, whose name was Granny, said, 'Well let's go anyway. We'll figure it out.'

It was completely sold out, 14,000 people. There was a kind of all-the-way-around gate around the Coliseum with a few entrances. We were watching carefully, navigating our chances, and all of a sudden one of our guys goes, 'Look, there's a door open.' Someone had gone in or out and the door hadn't closed behind them.

The Ace somehow scaled this fence and went running across the courtyard to the open door. The rest of us started following suit. The Ace was about 20 feet from the door when some security guy came running towards him to make sure he didn't get to the door. But another one of our guys managed to put a cross-body block on the security guard and literally took him out. The rest of us were hot on The Ace's trail, and we got in. I think we were in for the third song, 'All Down the Line'. The rest ended up in close proximity but I stuck with The Ace because I knew he was going to take me all the way there to the stage.

So we got to see the second show from a different vantage point and practically had our hands on the stage. To see the show a second time completely sealed the deal. 'See the Rolling Stones' became the legendary motto. And as I'm telling the story I'm having a sense of running across the courtyard following The Ace.

STEVE GAYDICH

I was at the second show. My friend and I recorded it. Stevie Wonder blew 'em off stage. I remember the power going out when the Stones were playing. It could have been an off night. However, Charlie was rocking.

YESTERDAY'S PAPERS

JOHN HINTERBERGER
SEATTLE TIMES, JUNE 5, 1972

Mick Jagger, the Stones lead singer, bounded into the air for a few trial leaps, then howled and scolded into 90 minutes of hammering rock and roll. He gyrated, pumped, ground, tousled his hair with his tossing hands, and eventually worked at his costume until all that was left was a pair of skin-tight green trousers, white shoes, and a black under shirt decorated in gold sequins. He closed his afternoon show chanting the anarchic lines of 'Street Fighting Man' while spinning a British flag over his shoulders – before contemptuously, dropping it in the heap – at the same time twirling a hand microphone like a yo-yo. The crowd roared back volleys of approval.

MICK TAYLOR, THE ROLLING STONES

I nearly saw Mick and Keith have a fight in a seafood restaurant in Seattle. Keith was really pissed off 'cause Jagger had thrown this beautiful leather jacket into the audience at the end of the gig. At the dinner table they were yelling across at each other. After that I don't think Keith lent Mick anything to wear onstage.

From Seattle the Stones moved down the Pacific coast to San Francisco, where they played four shows at the Winterland Ballroom for legendary US promoter, Bill Graham, two on June 6th and two more on June 8th.

WINTERLAND
JUNE 6 & 8, 1972,
SAN FRANCISCO, CALIFORNIA

VENUE CAPACITY	4,500
PERFORMANCES	4
ARRESTS:	0

MIKE WISEMAN

The first time I heard the Stones was on the radio, when 'Not Fade Away' was getting air play in 1964. I knew very little about Brits or British youth culture and I had not been impressed by The Beatles with their Captain Kangaroo haircuts. It just seemed calculated to appeal to pre-teenage girls. I was experiencing puberty and I was more interested in other things than holding hands; not much, but a little bit more than that. What I liked about 'Not Fade Away' was that it sounded more ethereal than The Beatles sound. In fact, with the maracas and the acoustic rhythm guitar, I actually liked it better than Buddy Holly's version.

Mick's vocals had a sound that was like me or any other American person. The Beatles had that to some degree, but not as good as the Stones. I wasn't a fan of the Stones yet, but I was pretty interested in seeing them. They appeared on *The Dean Martin Show*, and I liked the way they looked. They weren't all in the same suits, and they looked kind of casually dressed, like five guys who just came to play music. It seemed very unpretentious and they didn't give the impression that they were trying to sell themselves to anybody. I was in a musical group myself and we didn't do that.

Time went on. At first, I didn't like their single 'Tell Me', but I gradually got to appreciate it more. I liked it more than other stuff that was on the radio so it was okay. On May 9th, 1965, a school friend of mine named Bud asked me if I wanted to come along with him that night over to the San Francisco Civic Auditorium to see the Rolling Stones. I really wasn't that interested. I asked who else was playing and he said, 'Paul Revere and the Raiders', who were one of my favorite groups. By this time, I was playing drums in a group with my friends and I wanted to see how their drummer played. There was another group on the bill named the Mojo Men. They had a single that was doing well on the local charts and I kind of liked them also, so I went along with Bud that night. (Bud said the reason he wanted to go was because he wanted to stand in the middle of a bunch of girls pushing towards the stage and hold his arms out to the side and feel tits!)

When we got to the San Francisco Civic Auditorium (now call The Bill Graham Civic Auditorium), there was no line for tickets. It's a fairly small auditorium, holding about 5,000 people. The main floor is only maybe 50 feet longer than a basketball court and the same width. There is a balcony all around it and the stage was at one end.

I wanted to sit where I could get a better view of what the drummer was doing, so despite the fact that the crowd was very small, with maybe only two or three hundred people at the most, we sat in the balcony at an angle where I could see the drummers.

We enjoyed the first two acts and then the Stones came on and there was a swarm of girls to the stage. There weren't enough so Bud could make his dream come true, but you could see that they were crying and screaming and jumping up and down and trying to get up on the stage with Mick. We learned, I think from the announcer, that Keith Richard had been knocked out from an electrical shock the previous night when they played at Sacramento and that the concert had almost been cancelled for that reason.

They started their set off with a medley, beginning with 'Everybody Needs Somebody to Love' and segued into 'Pain in My Heart' and followed that with 'Off the Hook'. I can't remember where it went from there, but I was a believer from that point. I bought the album *The Rolling Stones, Now!* and loved it. I started to get into blues. I had always liked Chuck Berry a lot better than Elvis - he was rock and roll - and I really enjoyed the Rolling Stones covers of his songs. Later that summer, I also bought *England's Newest Hitmakers* and *12x5*.

I saw the Stones in 1969 when they played at the Oakland Coliseum. I went with my girlfriend, who is now my wife, and we saw them with Ike and Tina Turner. When Mick asked the stage crew to turn the lights on in the hall and invited the crowd to come down to the front of the stage, hundreds of people mobbed the stage and started jumping up on it and had to be taken off by security guards, just like at the 1965 concert. There was a fight between Bill Graham and the Stones road manager on stage.

Bay area audiences who were fans of the Stones didn't usually act like this. They usually showed up at the Fillmore and Winterland and were very calm listeners. They just didn't get all excited like the teeny boppers did. When Mick invited them to come down front, all that changed. Little did we know that this would be a portent of things to come which were not so good.

Shortly after the Stones appeared at the Oakland Coliseum Arena, I was riding home across the San Mateo Bridge when I heard The Beatles had broken up. This was right around the end of November in 1969. Shortly after that, I heard that the Rolling Stones were thinking of presenting a free concert in the Bay area. I can't think the two events were unrelated. Here were the Stones, the last group standing from the British Invasion, and it seemed only natural that they would want to celebrate their being the last of the two rock groups who could be considered the best.

At first, the concert was scheduled for Sears Point Raceway, a place up above the Bay area kind of close to Santa Rosa, but then a few hours later it was said that the planned concert was rejected by the county in that area. I stayed tuned to the radio to listen for updates. Shortly after that, it was rescheduled for the Altamont raceway, which was about 20 miles from the greater Bay area, closer to Tracy, California than the San Francisco and Oakland urban area.

My girlfriend and some of my closest friends attended the Altamont concert with me. We sat back about a hundred yards from the stage and we had no problems. But we could see that there were constant interruptions from the crowd near the stage, which kept on pushing forward. This was not a crowd that was willing to be peaceful and loving and compromise. This was a crowd of people that thought that they were entitled to sit closer to the stage than you, and they were willing to push their way in to do it. Unfortunately, they also pushed over the Hell's Angels bikes repeatedly and got beat up for doing it. By the end of the day, the Hell's Angels were clearly pissed off at the crowd and they were unable to keep the crowd under control while the performers were on stage.

When the Stones finally came on, the Hell's Angels were still doing their job. Meredith Hunter pulled a gun and waved it in the direction of the stage. One of the Hell's Angels, Alan Passaro, stabbed him and killed him. I can't believe that Passaro did not save somebody's life by doing that.

We heard all kinds of negative press blaming the Stones and the Hell's Angels, and everybody but those that I thought were responsible, which was the crowd itself. I can't imagine what would have happened if the Hell's Angels hadn't been there. Regular uniformed security guards would have been overrun and the stage would have been torn down. The Hell's Angels actually did a great job of containing that audience.

Flash forward three years. The Stones put on a show at Winterland, and when that sold out, they scheduled another show for Winterland. It was the best I had ever heard the Stones. Nicky Hopkins was with them, along with Bobby Keys and Jim Price. It was the best rock and roll show I've ever seen.

SARALINDA SPINNER
I lived next door to Bob McClay, a DJ for FM Radio KTIM in San Rafael, Marin County. We lived in Sleepy Hollow, on the same street that Peter Tork of The Monkees rented. I babysat for Bob and he gave me tickets to this concert in return. I was in my senior year of high school. Stevie Wonder opened and then the Stones. Mick came out wearing a light blue work shirt that was in style at that time, and then stripped down to his white jump suit. That was amazing. I had gone to Altamont but left early and didn't see the Stones play. I left before dark.

MICHAEL LAZARUS SCOTT
On June 6, 1972, I saw the Rolling Stones and Stevie Wonder at Winterland in San Francisco. It was the best concert I ever saw.

The last time I had seen the Stones was at the infamous Altamont show at the tail end of the Sixties. Now they were back, playing the relatively small (for them) Winterland Arena, as a kind of goodwill gesture to the Bay Area. My girlfriend, Marlene, burned some photographer guy for tickets to the first afternoon concert. She left early to get a spot in line and I left work at noon, telling my boss I had to go vote. We were in the first ten groups of folk, and when the doors opened everyone in front of us ran for the front of the stage. I had a plan, and headed for the balcony and procured seats right behind the soundboard, looking right down on the stage. Fuck sitting on the floor!

First up, they aired a screening of the *TAMI Show*, culminating in performances by James Brown and the very young Stones. The sound people and folk all around us shared our smoke and, at some point, a Dixie cup was passed to me, filled with tabs of Orange Sunshine. The sound dude said, 'Take one and pass it on. Compliments of the Stones.' How thoughtful indeed!

Just as I noticed everyone around me was grinning like Cheshire cats, Stevie Wonder and Wonderlove took the stage. Stevie had recently left Motown and was doing his own thing. Dressed in a long African dashiki, he commandeered a cockpit of keyboards, sometimes having three going at once. He made his way to the drums and played with a rhythm unlike anything I had ever heard. At one point, he got up to dance and play his harmonica, with the aid of two big-hipped backup singers on each side, that bumped him out of harm's way. I remember thinking his act would be hard to follow, but I should have known better!

Before the Stones began, out ran a guy who jumped higher than I thought possible, kicking his legs out and touching his outstretched hands to his feet. Everyone gasped, thinking it was Mick, but when he landed my girlfriend called out that it was Robert Shields, the mime artist, who went through his entertaining routine.

Finally, Bill Graham said, 'From England, the greatest rock and roll band in the world, the Rolling Stones,' and with a wallop they were into 'Brown Sugar' and then, without stopping, they were straight into 'Bitch'. I think 'Rocks Off' was next, then 'All Down the Line', 'Rip This Joint' and it was on…

They were augmented for the first time by Nicky Hopkins on keys, Jim Price on trumpet and Bobby Keys just murdering it on sax. This was the smallest venue I'd seen them play and they were deafeningly loud. Mick was dressed in lime satin trousers and an orange satin coat and looked like a popsicle. Keith had a blond streak in his rooster shag and was wearing a white satin pirate shirt, patched jeans and high-heeled snakeskin boots. While playing his clear Dan Armstrong guitar, he stood perilously on the edge of the stage, seeming to swoon out over the audience – elegantly wasted for sure. Meanwhile, Mick had not stopped dancing since he hit the stage; climbing high up on the PA speakers, he was a combination of James Brown and Rudolph Nureyev.

The band slowed down for 'Sweet Virginia' and (I think) 'Dead Flowers'. In between songs, someone in the audience offered up a joint to Bill, who took a toke and then passed it to Keith who stuck it between his lips, propped a leg up on Charlie's drum riser and went into 'Midnight Rambler'. Neither Keith nor the joint moved, but Jagger crawled around the stage, whipping it with his wide, gold lame belt, muttering and testifying like a deranged 70-year-old black man. This is Fucking Rock and Roll!

They pull out the hits – 'Tumbling Dice', 'Sympathy for the Devil', 'Jumpin' Jack Flash', 'Satisfaction' – and somewhere along the line, in my enlightened state, old Winterland seems to be spinning and it looked to me like the inside of some crazy flying saucer that had abducted all us freaks and that we were hurtling through time and space. The band was our engine and Mick our gallant captain. I wished we had never had to return to earth, but be that as it may, I'm sure glad I got to make that voyage!

JO BUMGARNER DEMPSEY

My boyfriend at the time remembers us sitting on the sidewalk smoking pot and being in line waiting for the doors to open, and the cops strolling around us, not bothering to harass us for smoking that illegal (at the time) stuff. He also remembered that we were sitting in a balcony on the side, right above the stage and drug deals going on in the men's room. But so many of us were pretty stoned at the concert and my memories are fuzzy!

ROBERT HAWKS

I saw the second show at Winterland. Having been born in Chicago's South Side Hospital in 1952 and growing up listening to Hank Williams and Muddy Waters, my father having joined the Great Northward Migration from Tennessee, 'their' music was already mine. They did, however, give it legitimacy when it came to girls. Instead of being cute like Paul McCartney, you could/would likely resemble Keith. My first Stones encounter was 1964 in Sacramento, California. Totally unaware of them, I witnessed an odd group being escorted through the historic tourist site of Sutter's Fort. I recognized the accents as British but they looked like they had never seen sunlight. Later, at school, I learned it was this group Rolling Stones, and girls either loved or hated them. However, most of the girls that I fancied liked them.

TERESA JOHNSON (GYPSY ROSE)

I purchased a ticket well in advance and asked my friend to babysit my three-year-old daughter, Celeste. My friend cancelled at the last minute so I took Celeste with me. At the door, I explained the situation and they let her in, free of charge. Yay! There was no seating. We all sat on the floor. They showed the movie *Reefer Madness* and everyone had a hearty laugh. Stevie Wonder opened and the large balloons bounced all around the audience. He was astounding and I fell in love with him forever. When the Stones came on, the crowd went wild. Everyone jumped up on their feet and Celeste and I could no longer see. So I put my little girl on the floor and told her to go 'thataway!' We crawled through a sea of legs. The people, seeing a baby, moved aside and let us through. When we reached the stage, I picked her up and put her on my shoulders. Mick came over and sang right to her. It was thrilling! She is 50 years old now. She doesn't remember it. But I will remember that concert for the rest of my life.

CHARLIE GREENE

The summer of 1966 is where it all began. I had just graduated from Catholic grammar school and was ready to rock at 14 years old. I was introduced to rock 'n' roll, like everyone else, when The Beatles hit *Ed Sullivan*. A band on a later show then caught my eye. Their music was R&B and they weren't dressed in suits like The Beatles and all the other British bands. They were the Rolling Stones, which I thought was a tres cool name. I found out later that Brian got it from a Muddy Waters song, 'I'm a Man'. I could tell they were rebels.

In 1966, my best friend and I would hang out at the Matrix, which was in my neighborhood in San Francisco. Marty Balin started the club with his band, the Jefferson Airplane. All the SF bands played there, including the Grateful Dead, Big Brother (Janis) and the Holding Company, Steppenwolf (who were called Sparrow at the time) and the Steve Miller Blues Band. I also used to see them all play for free at Golden Gate Park, and I saw the Jimi Hendrix Experience play there in 1967.

On July 26, 1966, my older sister and I saw the Rolling Stones at the Cow Palace. It was Mick's 23rd birthday. It was an awesome gig but the sound was like the *Got Live If You Want It!* LP, with the girls all screaming. Brian played his red 12-string Rickenbacker guitar and he also played sitar on 'Lady Jane'. The coolest thing I remember about the gig was Mick swinging his jacket towards the audience over and over, like he was going to throw it to them moving forward with every swing. He eventually swung it over his shoulder and took off dancing. Tres cool, Mick.

On June 6 and 8, 1972, the Rolling Stones were playing Winterland. My good friend and I stood in line for hours outside Winterland, waiting to buy tickets for the four shows. We got four tickets for each show and I attended the Tuesday afternoon and Thursday night gigs. What I really liked about the gigs was that Bill Graham sold only 75 per cent of capacity so you could walk around the ballroom.

Stevie Wonder opened playing drums. I remember Stevie rocked the house with his Master Blaster when he played 'Superstition'! The Stones came on and pretty much stuck to the *Exile on Main St.* songs. I feel the band's chemistry is what makes them so good. Being a former drummer, I focused on Charlie playing on his kit. The horn section (Bobby and Jim) seemed new to me but made the band even more complete. It was a small stage but Mick took it over with his dancing. My favorite song was when Keith sang 'Happy' with Mick on chorus. That was epic!

A friend of mine was the manager at the Trident restaurant in Sausalito. I didn't go but he told me numerous stories about when the Stones went there on Wednesday between the two gig dates. Tequila Sunrises and mirrors were part of the subject matter.

I went to numerous Stones gigs after that, ending with the *Bigger Bang* gig in 2005 at SBC Park. That was a cool gig, opening with 'Start Me Up'. What a transition from that small stage at Winterland to the arena and stadium tours. That's the reason I stopped going to more Stones concerts. I was so used to seeing bands in clubs and auditoriums like the

Fillmore Auditorium, Avalon Ballroom, Matrix and Winterland. Arenas just don't do it for this 14-year-old kid.

PAUL HILER

My buddy and I used to get high together and we would sit in his room and drop acid and stuff and listen to his older brother's Stones records. I was about 15 years old.

The first time I saw the Stones was '69 at the Oakland Coliseum. It was quite the deal when I saw them in '69. I'd taken some LSD and stuff. Some points I remember more clearly than others. They did two shows at the Oakland Coliseum.

And I saw them twice at Winterland in 1972. Winterland was an ice skating palace. When the Stones came to town it was a big deal. It didn't matter what was going on and what you were doing, you were going to be there. I worked with a guy named Bucky Lyle at a furniture factory, making sofas, and tickets went on sale that day at noon. When that was announced, we just said 'fuck the job' and went up to the little music store where we bought tickets. I got tickets for both shows. I took a girlfriend one of the nights, although you should never take women to shows. There was a saying I used to have - never take sand to the beach.

It was a fantastic show. We were all just hyped up for it big time. That night I turned 18 and that day I graduated from high school. The Stones played the first show about 6 o'clock. It was crowded. It was so much better than those shows they have nowadays. '72 was a bigger show than '69, with more people on stage. It was a bigger production. I still got right up in front. I was probably 25 yards to Keith Richards. Back then you could push and weasel your way up to the front. I did the same in '69. But that show was nice and small.

'69 was probably the better of the two shows. *Let It Bleed* had just come out and the material was still new. And they really, really, really had it down. The show I saw in '69 was very much like it was on *Get Your Ya-Ya's Out!*, even though that was recorded at Madison Square Garden. Mick Taylor was just so good. Keith could bang out those chords, but it was so much Mick Taylor. He really carried them. I don't think they were really ever the same again after he left. It just didn't have the stylish punch to it any more. And it was an incredible line-up, with Nicky Hopkins. It's like

28

Miles Davis when he recorded *Kind of Blue* with everybody who was in that session. Mick Taylor didn't have anything else to prove after he had been in the Stones.

The Stones were the cream of the crop. To go to a Stones show was like your birthday, Christmas, New Year's Eve and Hallowe'en all rolled into one night. It was a big deal. The electricity in the air was unbelievable. I probably got a little too stoned in '72. We smoked some PCP. You'd go to these things and everybody was getting high.

Things just got bigger and bigger, bands wanted more money and everything got to be such a big production. I went to every show the Stones ever did in San Francisco until 1981. I saw the last one at Candlestick Park, in '81. But then they just got too big. They weren't the Stones anymore. They were like little caricatures on a cartoon stage. I wouldn't go and see them now. And I wouldn't pay what they want for tickets anyway.

CURT ANGELEDES

The very first time I heard the Rolling Stones on the radio at home, the first few bars stopped me dead in my tracks. From there I did two things I had never done before. The first was to turn up the family radio and the second was to stop performing the chore I was involved in. What I heard was so full of energy, color and joy that it blew away any thoughts of maintaining a stance within the gray, quiet, old world that up until that point in time was what appeared to be all that the world had to offer. Sure, there were The Beatles and Bob Dylan, but the Rolling Stones said it all so much better than anybody else...

A few years later I had the good fortune of being in the right place at the right time. I was buying a Stones LP and the store owner was able to point me in the right direction for getting a ticket for the Stones concert at Forrest Hills Stadium and on June 2, 1966 I had the most exciting experience of hearing the Stones live for the first time.

Three more years passed and this time tickets for the shows at Madison Square Garden in '69 were less of a roundabout issue than in '66 and just for the fun of it, and because the travel bug had really sunk its teeth into me, I followed up these shows with a trip to California to see the band at Altamont.

Luck played a dual role here: I hitchhiked from New York in just barely enough time to see only the Rolling Stones that night, and I managed to be blissfully unaware of the mayhem that went on apace only a few hundred feet away, because my late arrival only allowed me to enjoy the music at quite a distance from the stage.

Three more years went by and when the '72 tour was announced, many folks I knew went into a frenzy in back of getting tickets. I simply spent an entire 24 hour period at a place called Stonestown (a mall in the San Francisco Bay area, near the community college) waiting for the tickets to go on sale.

I don't recall the date of the tour announcement, but I do remember that in the early morning hours of May 14th, I heard on the radio that tickets for the four Rolling Stones shows in the Bay Area would go on sale the next day. Upon hearing that broadcast, I put together a small bag with a radio, food, smokes, etc. and took off walking from the campus at SFU to the Ticketron outlet inside Sears at the mall.

While walking to the place I thought I might be first in line, but upon arrival I discovered that I was sixth in line. These few of us spent our time imbibing various substances and calculating exactly where in the line the tickets would run out. I opined that if you were number 24 in line you would not get both nights in pairs if such was your desire. I was right. The individual who surmised that if you were number 47 in line you would be totally out of luck was also correct. Tickets ran out at number 46 in the line. All of this came from the fact that a computerised system of ticket sales, along with a four ticket maximum per person, factored against a set number of outlets and the venue seating capacity seemed to produce the numbers we spent our time considering.

As the hours went by, ever more people showed up to buy tickets. First in ones and twos, and then in larger groups. By the time the ticket windows opened 24 hours later, there could have easily been as many people at that one outlet as could legally attend any of the shows. The small group that was present when I got there decided not to share our calculations, as acquiring a ticket was highly competitive and the situation had the potential to become rather riotous.

Eleven days later, when the new record, *Exile on Main St.* became available, I walked back to the Stonestown Mall to get it. For the days between then and the show, it was played many times a day as well as late into the night. This new album was quite a diverse offering and, to boot, it was a double album that, when played from beginning to end, could occupy a fair amount of time enjoying it.

When June 6th arrived, my girlfriend and I, along with our friend from SFU, dressed up in festive attire, made certain that our tickets were securely carried, smoked about a gram of hash apiece and headed out. We expected that the concert would be a huge party with a few thousand like-minded music fans and we were not disappointed.

We went from the campus at San Francisco State University to the Winterland Ballroom by public transit. A couple of buses and about an hour or so later, we got to the corner of Post and Steiner where we encountered a large and festive crowd waiting to get in. San Francisco was, at this point in time a very colorful and diverse place and this was shown by the many, many different styles of dress as well as many different means of being under the influence.

The police were present in full force with some traffic division, some undercover and some riot cops just in case. I only saw minor confrontations between the man in blue and some of the unfortunate unticketed, the hopelessly drunk or the too-stoned folks who seem to be at almost every Rolling Stones show. There were people selling t-shirts, buttons, posters and 'extra tickets' for as much as ten times face value.

After some more waiting time, we got in the venue and made a beeline for our chosen spot in the center of the first row of the balcony. The seating was selected on the basis that it would provide a view of the entire proceedings without any obstruction and because so many people wanted to be as close as possible on the floor, there would be very little competition for these seats in the balcony. That's not to say that it was unnecessary to move with some haste from the front door to the seats, as the entire house was general admission.

Shortly after getting to our seats and getting comfortable, Stevie Wonder performed as the opening act, then a rather skilful mime entertained for a spell. Finally, the Rolling Stones bounded onto the stage and delivered a blistering fifteen song set list. It was an energetic and exciting mix of four songs I had heard live before and eleven songs that I heard live that night for the first time, six of them from the new *Exile on Main St.* album.

31

This tour was when the band really started to get a handle on stage craft for the sake of a better presentation. Their own sound system delivered sound of high quality, high volume and high fidelity. The lighting system was something else they brought along which enhanced the whole experience. The stage decor, with the serpents on the floor, was also a nice touch.

The end of the show was not the end of the party. We carried on for some time in the near vicinity of the venue hanging out with other people who had just seen the concert. After that, we went to some cafe or other and had a meal and some drinks. Even after arriving back at where we stayed, the party continued until the wee hours of the morning, to the music of the Rolling Stones.

KEVIN O'NEIL, AGE 15

I saw the Tuesday after school $5 matinee show. It was my first Stones show and my first time at Winterland. Robert Shields, the San Francisco street mime, did his act between Stevie and the Stones coming on stage. This was a general admission show and a smaller (5,000) capacity venue was rare for that time. But Uncle Bill Graham had the influence to get the Stones to play more intimate shows in the Bay Area. It was kind of an apology series of make-up shows for the disaster at Altamont. I live down the hill from Altamont Pass now, in the Livermore Valley wine country.

Kevin O'Neil saw the matinee show

TOM SCHUTZ

It was June, the end of school year and the Stones were coming to town. My friend Mark Stoner (true!) and I decided to skip high school grade graduation as it wasn't graduating year to go see the Rolling Stones five times on the West Coast on their 1972 tour. At that time, they were the biggest show on earth and seeing them meant a lot more than high school graduating processions, so for $6.50 per ticket we needed $32.50

to see the five West Coast shows! Funded, and hitting up Grandma in Long Beach as a safe haven between shows, we got a ride from a neighbor who had a trucking business and who added us to his cargo to San Francisco.

We saw the first show in San Francisco on June 8. We got the tickets from Ticketron at our local Sears. The tour was open seating and we ended up in the bottom section, third row on Keith's side… Stevie Wonder opened all the shows, and not knowing too much about him in 1972 we only recognized a couple of songs. Mark, not knowing Stevie was blind, thought he was being led out by his hand like royalty!

The Stones came out to the ever famous 'Ladies and Gentlemen, the Rolling Stones!', with Mick jumping out in a silver sparkling jacket and purple jump suit. The opening chords of 'Brown Sugar' from a grinning Keith blared, and midway through the song a huge tongue banner unfurled above the stage where the flag usually was. It was Stones Nation! 'Bitch' followed and the Stones were rocking. The third song was 'Rocks Off', which was cool, new and rocking, and 'Dead Flowers' had Mick and Keith sharing mics and vocals. Both songs were a treat. I remember the crowd on the floor was surging back and forth, three feet in either direction, like a wave in a sea of people.

AL ONSTEAD, AGE 22

We lived in an apartment in an area with little individual huts in, at Point Richmond. We went to Sears in Oakland for tickets, got there at 1am and got the last ticket in line at 10.20am. Four shows sold out in 20 minutes. I was on the floor, ten feet back, and what amazed me was how Stevie Wonder played every instrument. When the Stones came on, both Bill and Keith had see-through guitars. I've seen the Stones six times. On the *40 Licks* tour, where they were on a removable stage, they came and played three songs right in front of me, on row 1.

RICH TROTTO, AGE 25

I first heard the Rolling Stones on the radio, like a lot of people in '64-'65 along with a lot of other British groups and I liked them, but not any more than the others, especially The Beatles. The turning point came sometime around '67 when I bought a bundle of four albums at Costco;

Out of Our Heads, Aftermath, December's Children and *Between the Buttons*. Listening to those albums made me realise that the Stones were a cut above most of the other groups. I still think that was some of the best music they put out in their career.

Beggars Banquet came out about the same time as The Beatles' *White Album*. When payday came, I bought both albums, and one of my friends and I took the albums and a bunch of acid up to another friend's apartment. They didn't have a phone so they didn't know we were coming and when we got there, they were on their way out to a concert, but they said we could stay and they would join us when it was over. So, my friend and I dropped some acid and put on the first side of *Beggars Banquet* and it was still playing when my friends got back from their show hours later. We couldn't bring ourselves to stop it, because every time 'Sympathy for the Devil' started up, it was too great to cut off and we would let the side of the album play on.

The only other Rolling Stones show I attended was on Thanksgiving 1969 at Madison Square Garden. It was an amazing night. The Stones seemed a little rough following BB King and then Ike and Tina Turner, but that didn't last long. They really jelled on 'Sympathy for the Devil', and after that they tore the place up. The other song that I remember being a standout over 50 years later was 'Midnight Rambler'. Living in New York, I spent weekends at the Filmore East and saw many of the major bands at the time, Cream, Traffic, Jefferson Airplane, Grateful Dead, The Band, Janis, Chuck Berry, The Who, early Fleetwood Mac…

I moved from New York to San Francisco in 1970. In 1972 rumors were going around that, following Altamont, the Stones wanted to do something special in San Francisco. (Doing a free show in San Francisco was the original intent of what became the Altamont show. The Stones originally planned to do a free show in Golden Gate Park in San Francisco, not on some Godforsaken East Bay raceway after the city denied a permit. Neither I nor any of my friends went to Altamont)

In '72, the Stones went to Bill Graham instead and he suggested four shows at Winterland with limited ticket sales, and price (the lowest of the tour), and preference for San Francisco residents to get tickets. That was accomplished by selling a good percentage of tickets at the Winterland box office, which is where we got ours. Thank goodness, because the Ticketron sales were a complete mess.

I went with a bunch of friends who regularly went to shows together, in particular Grateful Dead shows and most of the other San Francisco bands. The thing about Winterland is that it was an old ice rink. It maybe held 4,500 people when Graham really packed us in. It was the home of the Ice Capades for many years and was also used for hockey games. If you can imagine a hockey rink, the stage at Winterland was normally placed at the far end where one of the hockey goals would be. However, for some concerts, including the Stones, the stage was placed at mid-court against one side, corresponding to where one of the team's benches would be. This made for less seating, but lots of open space around the sides of the stage for dancing, which there was plenty of room for since not that many tickets were sold. There was so much room that the people on the floor could just wander right up close to the stage to get a better look. In fact, one of my friends handed Keith Richards a joint. At the time I had the feeling that it was like the Stones were playing at a high school dance. Given all of the trouble that followed the Stones on the tour, it was a testament to San Francisco concertgoers that they could play a show in such a mellow personal setting.

I thought they were great. They seemed to be really enjoying themselves and getting into the music. Looking back, the songs that stood out were 'Tumbling Dice' and pretty much anything they played off of *Exile on Main St.*, which I think is musically their finest album, along with 'You Can't Always Get What You Want', and, as in '69, 'Midnight Rambler'. It's curious. The studio version of that song is okay, but they seemed to really get into it live.

I don't have one particular moment that stands out in my memory, just that it was a great show. Stevie Wonder was wonderful. I remember it being the first time I heard 'Superstition', which was memorable. The Stones seemed to be closer to a bar band than a big venue show. I don't remember them even dressing that flashy (for San Francisco). They kind of fit right in.

The Winterland show was wonderful and it was a special day. However, it seemed a little short time-wise and that makes it hard to stand it up to say, Springsteen on New Year's Eve in 1980, or a four-hour long Grateful Dead or Crosby, Stills, Nash & Young show, but as far as access to the band, the atmosphere and the quality of the music? The Stones at Winterland was as good as any.

CATHERINE GRAY, AGE 17

I was gifted a ticket to see the Stones and went by myself, I was up against the stage and had borrowed a beautiful marabou jacket, which got ruined. But it was awesome, and the Stones were amazing.

JANET EVANS

We drove over the Oakland Bay bridge in a VW bus and parked right next to Winterland. It was an awesome small venue, and an awesome concert.

MARC ROSE

I wasn't a Stones fan. I've always landed on the bright side not the dark – The Beatles and Beach Boys versus the Stones, the Grateful Dead versus The Doors. I camped out on Bascom Avenue in San Jose, California in front of the Record Factory for three days to get tickets. Then it was general admission at Winterland, so I camped out there for two days. And they had the audacity to play for 45 minutes. I was pissed off.

RANDY STANLEY

I was born and grew up in the Bay Area, about 30 miles south of San Francisco, now the heart of Silicon Valley. Occasionally, I'd hear my sister playing her copy of *Meet The Beatles*. It was okay, but I was not moved. I had two cousins, one of whom was four years older, the other a year older. They would often rough me up, in a cousin-loving way. It helped me toughen up. I grew to be a good size, but the younger one ended up at six foot six and 300 pounds, so I 'looked up' to them both. Visiting their house in the middle of 1965, they were playing music that was definitely not The Beatles. I asked, 'What is that?' I was moved. It was *The Rolling Stones, Now!* and it was much rougher and raw than The Beatles. For me it was like, 'Holy crap, I've got to have more of this.' From then on, I was hooked and it was the Stones only for me.

I saw them for the first time on July 26, 1966, Mick's 23rd birthday. My dad took me and three of my friends. The venue was the Cow Palace in Daly City, the town just south of San Francisco. I was 13. It's the only time I saw Brian Jones, but it's a great memory. I saw them again in '69 at the Oakland Arena. There were no more screaming girls after three years - the audience was just enjoying the music - and they played for an hour as opposed to the half hour in '66. I remember 'Midnight Rambler', Mick on his knees slapping the stage with his belt in time with Charlie hitting the drums with a big bang. It may be my favorite song to see them play live, although that's like asking which is my favorite kid. I can't choose.

In 1972, I was in my second year of junior college. My first was mostly wasted as I just went to look at 'college' girls and sleep in my car. By this time, I was full-blown Stones every time, all the time. To this day if it's just me I only listen to the Stones. It drives my family crazy.

Altamont in '69 wasn't a great experience for many. I wanted to go but my mom put an end to that. It's been written the Stones wanted to maybe 'repay' the area so they did four shows at the Winterland Ballroom in San Francisco. Winterland is a relatively small venue so it was a coveted ticket. I don't remember the details, but I was somehow able to stand in line, probably at Sears, at the Ticketron site and get four tickets.

I went with a couple of friends from high school and my girlfriend. She was a little younger than me, and I remember her dad wasn't thrilled about her going as it wasn't in the best part of SF. We attended the first show on the 8th. I remember it taking a while to get in as there were only a couple of doors open and they were physically searching everyone. Winterland had an open floor at stage level and a balcony all around upstairs. We were on the floor, probably 20 to 30 feet from the stage.

Stevie Wonder was the opening act. The Stones played for an hour and 20 minutes, a great show with great energy. I remember there was a bottle of Wild Turkey on the amps that Mick and Keith were sharing. Mick would take a drink and put it in one spot, then Keith would go back to where it was before Mick moved it. After Keith took a swig he would place it in a different location, and Mick would have to hunt it down, take a drink and put it back in his spot. This went on the entire show.

I don't know the entire set list, but I do remember 'Midnight Rambler', as well as 'Brown Sugar', 'You Can't Always Get What You Want', 'Gimme Shelter' and 'Jumpin' Jack Flash'. and several from *Exile*. It was great being so close; this was easily the closest I had been to the stage. At one point, Mick and I made eye contact for maybe a second or more, at least it seemed like it at the time. I realise he could have been looking at some other idiot as well, but I'm sticking to my story!

It was a great experience, and maybe the Stones at their peak, although having seen them now in seven decades, I don't want to make that statement. I didn't know I was seeing Mick Taylor for the last time as a Rolling Stone.

Starting in '81, I began seeing them multiple times when they toured the US. In '94, on the *Voodoo Lounge* tour, my brother and I had purchased several tickets and we had some extras which we advertised. A couple from the UK were looking for tickets so we sold them two for at least one of the Oakland Coliseum shows, and I gave them a ride to the concert. We kept in touch, and they came back over in '97 for the *Bridges to Babylon* tour and stayed at my parents' home. In '99, I helped them organize and collect money for folks going to Wembley from the US. They rented a bus to take folks to the concert. I stayed with them while in London and saw two concerts at Wembley and one at Shepherds Bush, all great times.

I've now seen the Rolling Stones 74 times, the last three, unfortunately, without Charlie. That hit me harder than I thought it would.

VERONICA SNYDER SPICKLER, AGE 15

I guess I've always been a Stones fan. We moved to the Monterey peninsula in '65 after my father retired from the service. I shared a room with my sister who is five years older and of course I grew up on her shirt tails. Monterey is about a two hour drive south of San Francisco. We arrived just in time for Monterey Pop and the Summer of Love. You could actually hear the music festival from our house! Rumor has it that Brian Jones was there with some girl. And I remember my sister had a life-size poster of Mick Jagger on the back of our bedroom door for the longest time. But I digress...

It was probably May in 1972 when I was working at an ice cream parlour in Monterey. I was pretty close to the family that owned two Swensen's at the time, one in Monterey and one in Carmel. One evening these two guys came in and we got to talking over ice cream and it came up that they had two extra tickets to the Stones that June. I was frantically trying to buy the tickets off them, but one of the guys looked up at this framed lithograph of this cartoonish character eating an ice cream cone – well, he was actually pressing it to his head – and said that they would

38

trade the tickets for that. Thus began a flurry of phone calls to track down the owner's son since the lithograph didn't belong to me. Somehow, I was able to finagle that picture to trade for the tickets. (Decades later, I found out that the litho was the future cover of a Grateful Dead album that came out later that year by an artist named Stanley Mouse. We have some of his artwork hanging in our hallway to date since my husband is kinda a Deadhead, although I am missing that gene.)

I was trying to figure out how I was going to get away with going to San Francisco with my friend Steve when I was barely 15. My mother had just had a baby who was still a toddler at the time, so her attention was focused elsewhere other than on my escapades. And Steve was just a really nice guy and knew some people that had a flat in the city, which was our jumping off point.

We got to Winterland and it was still dark. It must've been like three or four in the morning. I tried to get some shut eye but it was kind of loud and uncomfortable. After the sun came up it started getting really busy. I remember there were lots of bikers there and it seemed a little rough, crowd-wise, and it was still hours before they would open the doors. By the time we got in, we were very close to the stage – like right at the stage – but quite exhausted. It was very different from other concerts that I attended over the years, because there was no barrier in front of the stage and I don't recall anybody asking us to move away or anything like that.

I couldn't tell you the playlist unless I looked it up. I wish I could remember what Mick was wearing and all that stuff, because later down the road I enjoyed wearing one of Mick's jackets to another Stones concert in Oakland. A friend of a friend did his wardrobe, and no one else could fit in it. Mick's kind of a little guy. And one of a kind!

STEVEN JACKSON

I was one year out of the military. I had an older sister that was living in a hippie commune in the Haight-Ashbury called The Good Earth so naturally I went down there to live. It was about a year after that when the '72 concert happened. A real good friend of mine was an employee of the promoter Bill Graham, and he got his tickets and got us in the front door past the line, which was a block long.

The show was tremendous. Stevie Wonder is a national icon and he was at his peak back then. And the Stones? What can you say about the Rolling Stones? Man, I mean, they had the *Sticky Fingers* album with 'Brown Sugar' on it and all the other great hits. And *Exile* had just come out, so they were doing all those songs, and Mick was just prancing and dancing and being Mick Jagger. It was auditorium seating but everybody was standing on their seats and in the aisles in order to see the show. The Stones were always my favorite bad boys of rock and roll. It's the best show I've ever been to.

SUSAN CONWAY DEROSA

The show I went to opened with Stevie Wonder and had mimes Shields and Yarnell at intermission. My brother had camped out before the box office opened and surprised me and my roommate with tickets.

EDIE MONICA

I remember how the rowdy crowd fell silent when they came on stage and surprised everyone with how good they were. Good times!

CHIP MONCK

I was lighting and production manager on the '72 tour. The one thing that was a gift about that tour was that the design of it was certainly not traditional. That would ruffle local crews, which one could expect, and usually the answer was, 'We had no idea this was as complex (ie. fuckin' different…). We'll need a few more hands.' Typically, that was four to six more. The mirror just grew from me wanting to try and get more out of the band.

I got into lighting and stage production thanks to my mother. My mother had a fucked marriage and she was always into musical comedy. I didn't want to do much more school so the school was given a doctor's letter saying that if I didn't go with my mother to see a doctor in New York on the first Wednesday of every month, I was going to have serious problems in my future life. At the ages of 11 and 12, I was woken on the first Wednesday of every month at 5am to make a 7am train from Wellesley to Boston and then on to New York. A doctor's certificate was filed at the school, like clockwork, and we'd check into the Biltmore Hotel in New York, have lunch and then go off to a Broadway matinee at 2pm, followed by a mini supper and then we'd be off to a 7.30pm evening show. In the space of two years, I saw *Carousel, Paint Your Wagon, South Pacific, Guys and Dolls, Peter Pan* and 39 more shows. Then we'd get on the train from New York back to Boston and on home to Wellesley and I'd make school on the Thursday.

By about the second trip and second month, it was magic. It became my escape. I loved the passion, the color, the movement, the make believe, the choreography, the precision, the timing, the production. This was far more important than the usual Wednesday lessons… I was hooked. How did Carroll, my mum, know?

My mother never suggested this was something I ought to be interested in. She said, 'This is just fun for me and I want to share it with you.' She was very chatty. She was a dancer at one point for the Russian ballet. We'd go back stage after a performance and it was there I met Ralph Alswang, Peggy Eisenhower, Abe Feder, Jeanie Rosenthal and all the major lighting and staging designers, who were working the tools I would soon become familiar with, and we'd all have coffee.

About halfway through all of this, Abe Feder said to me, 'You should go to Yonkers and see Charlie, he's starting a new company.' My mother gave me 250 bucks. She said, 'You know the subways, you know the trains. You can get back to Wellesley – go and find Charlie.' I found the address in the phonebook. I went and knocked on the four garage doors that said 'Altman' and I found him and he said, 'Okay, well I've got things to do but you can gel up these 942s for me, and the rest of them if you can, and don't forget to bend the clips so the gel frame doesn't fail when you put in the next one.' I said, 'Yes sir,' and I did that and he came back in about five hours and said, 'That's neat. Tomorrow, if you're not doing anything, come up to the shop and meet the guys.' I said, 'All I want to know is how it's built and why, and then I'll figure out how to use it.'

I was 15 years old and it was 1954. I joined Charlie Altman and it all started from there. I was concerned about folk music because this was pre-rock 'n' roll. How could I take all of this glitz and glamour and wonderful costumes and great orchestration and use it to present folk music as these folks are doing with the music of the past? It just fell into my lap.

I moved to New York and started working at the Village Gate. It turned out to be great fun and I learned a lot. The list of attendees was magnificent. Sam Shepard was my reading assistant for two days. He and Charlie Mingus's son were busboys there.

I first worked with the Stones at Altamont. Jo Bergman, Mick's PA, saw CSNY at the Greek Theatre in Los Angeles, called Mick in Mount Fairy, Australia, where he was filming *Ned Kelly*, and said, 'I found ya your lightman.' So I started with them for the 1969 US tour. I was in charge of lighting and production management. Sam Cutler was the tour manager in '69, but I successfully got rid of him after Altamont.

Altamont is a story of total failure and everybody thinking about their own little position – Rock Scully, Sam Cutler, Alan Rogan and the Angels. Everybody wanted to get done what they wanted to get done. So there's no facilities, no toilets, no food and 300,000 people. I presented all my plans to Mick and they blew into the pool in the middle of the presentation and he said, 'Oh, fuck it – just do it.' That was generally the way he looked at tech and organization. His eyes glaze over and he'd say, 'Fuck it – do it.' That's the answer I often got, so I just did it.

The 1970 European shows were designed to capture Europe and bury '69. It was simply something stunning, and best done in Europe. The '72 tour put the Stones in the position they then owned, and buried the taste of Altamont. It was quite simply a very well-planned tour, a mechanical delight of simplicity. They, starting with Charlie, picked up the gauntlet. The idea was to challenge MPJ at every opportunity. That was the game. Playing out of the way places at smaller venues that weren't used to big rock'n'roll acts, such as Mobile and Tuscaloosa, didn't present particular challenges. Everything was designed to be enlarged or compressed to suit the venue.

I never had a budget. I just built it and found two or three different ways to pay for it. One way was by going directly to the accountants who would say, 'Okay, what else do you need?' Or I went through Peter Roach, when he became management after Ronnie Schneider. He was a little more cautious but he had the ability to judge what was necessary, what was folly and where not to go. He was just bright and that was a pleasure. Ronnie was more money than anything else but I never got stopped. So we started building.

DANA BEST

I never saw the Stones. Although I went with some friends to the Winterland, my friends bought tickets from a scalper and left me alone outside. I almost snuck in when a side door opened up just a few feet away, but I froze because cops and security were busting heads everywhere. I decided to go home.

YESTERDAY'S PAPERS

CRAIG MODDERNO
DAILY CALIFORNIAN, JUNE 22, 1972

Jagger tried climbing on a huge amplifier only to look over at Bill Graham and have the master nod his disapproval. Like a child who instinctively knows when to leave well enough alone, Jagger abandoned his plans for a human high rise and concentrated on dancing on a huge dragon colorfully drawn onstage...

JOHN WASSERMAN
SAN FRANCISCO CHRONICLE, JUNE 9, 1972

Jagger is one of the experiences of our time, like him or not. There is a lot more involved than flinging oneself about... Bill Wyman, who has not been seen to move since 1967, somehow managed to produce notes from his bass despite this handicap, and Charlie Watts was solid as always.

JOHN BURKS
SAN FRANCISCO EXAMINER, JUNE 9, 1972

Their final set on the San Francisco leg of their 31-city American tour built from an okay start last night to a triumphant encore, an hour and a half later, on 'Honky Tonk Women'. If there was any doubt about the Stones' continuing hold on their San Francisco devotees, it was utterly swept away by the ecstatic whoop that greeted the band when they returned onstage to play that encore. That whoop was louder, more explosive than any of the music played at Winterland the whole evening. And that's not only some tribute, it's a victory for raw lung power over the most advanced electronic technology in the realm of amplified music.

The tour headed south from San Francisco to Los Angeles. First up was the Hollywood Palladium, one of the smaller venues on the tour.

HOLLYWOOD PALLADIUM
JUNE 9, 1972, LOS ANGELES, CALIFORNIA

CAPACITY	4,500
SHOWS	1
ARRESTS	0

MICHAEL PHILIPS

The Stones wanted to play some smaller venues, so they played the Hollywood Palladium. Earlier in the year, I went to the Hollywood Palladium to see Chuck Berry, who was opening for Black Oak Arkansas. Chuck always toured by himself and each venue or headliner would arrange for a rhythm section to back him up. Jim 'Dandy' Mangrum, the lead singer for BOA, knew the Stones were rehearsing for their tour in LA and thought it would be cool if members of the Stones backed up Chuck. So he asked them if they wanted to do it and Keith said yes and he brought bassist Carl Radle and drummer Jim Gordon from Derek and the Dominoes, along with a pianist who looked to me like Ian Stewart but has since been reported to be Nicky Hopkins, even though the two of them looked nothing alike.

From my position in front near stage left, I could see Mick and Bianca standing and watching the show from backstage, occasionally dancing together. When Chuck was introduced, he and the band came out and none of them were ever introduced to the audience. You just had to know who they were. Keith was pretty recognizable, but I don't think most people knew who the others were. Part way through the set, Chuck kicked Keith off the stage. I don't know what happened, but Chuck had appeared to be irrititated with him. Keith wasn't showboating or anything, so I don't know what the problem was. Maybe Chuck just wanted to be the only guitarist on the stage. Nevertheless, it was a great show, full of energy, and the crowd loved it. I'm told that that experience seeing a show at the Palladium was what made Mick and Keith decide to add the venue to the tour.

KEN OLLIE CRAMER

Shortly after releasing *Exile on Main St.*, the Stones announced a series of shows in the Los Angeles area. They would be playing at the Forum, in Inglewood, an arena that held over 17,000. Another night they would be playing the Long Beach Arena which held a little over 13,000, and opening night would be held at the relatively small Hollywood Palladium, which holds less than 4,000. The Hollywood Palladium had been built in 1940 as a showcase for the big bands of the day. The big band leader Lawrence Welk had called the Palladium 'home', producing his TV show from there for years. During the Sixties, rock and roll took over this Hollywood hall. The Stones had played at a 'Battle of the Bands' show at this venue in '64 or '65 and had fond memories of playing in this fabled concert hall.

In '72, the Hollywood show was the hot ticket. The arena shows tickets could be bought at the regular ticket outlets. The Palladium show would be mail order only, due to the historical nature of the Rolling Stones playing this icon of a theater on Sunset Boulevard. The address for this mail order would be published in the calendar section of the *Los Angeles Times* Sunday edition. My girlfriend's brother-in-law worked for the *Times* and was able to bring home that week's calendar section on Thursday, days before everyone else could get a hold of the secret address. Mailing away days before the masses did assured of us tickets.

Through the years I have been lucky enough to have seen many of the greats. My first rock and roll was The Beatles playing their second-to-last venue concert, at Dodger Stadium, Their final concert a couple of nights later was in San Francisco. I have seen Jerry Lee Lewis pound his piano, Pete Townshend windmill while playing his guitar, and I even saw Ray Davies fall into the crowd while doing an encore at the Hollywood Palladium. I've been a Deadhead for over 50 years. (I quit counting shows when Jerry Garcia passed; my total at that point was 127 Grateful Dead shows.) Out of hundreds of concerts I have seen through the years I would have to rate that Rolling Stones concert at the Hollywood Palladium back in '72 right at the top.

TONY DEAN

It was Thursday June 8 1972 and my ninth grade English teacher told me to go home and come back with a new shirt. My friend Gary and I were wearing funky homemade Stones tongue t-shirts. We never went back to school that Thursday. We were busy worrying about getting our Stones tickets through the US Mail.

That afternoon, we were listening in disgust to Wolfman Jack on KDAY replaying *Exile* tracks all day, with callers with tickets screaming over the radio about their stupid Rolling Stones tickets arriving in the bloody mail. Me and Gary sat there staring at the radio in envy, weeping. I went home and worried myself to sleep.

Back in the day, the mail usually arrived between 8am and 9am. I was waiting for that sucker. Finally, I spotted that ridiculous son of a bitch mail truck dithering back and forth, zigzagging across the block and waddling closer, dropping off mail. I decided to greet him. He looked confused and frightened at a chubby ninth grader wearing a homemade Rolling Stones tongue t-shirt and foaming at the mouth.

Gary and I cut class. Standing at the bus stop in north Hollywood, by coincidence my father drove by, saw us and busted me. I told him we needed to go see the Stones today, not go to school. I remember he laughed and gave me ten bucks. And he picked us up after the show!

It was my first rock concert. We got there close to ten in the morning. There were already many people waiting in line, so we hung out with the freaks and hippies, playing cards, getting high and checking out the babes. I remember the media snooping around the place and the crowd outside, queuing around the Palladium block. Afterwards, my ears were ringing and I was drenched in sweat, thirsty as hell and high as a kite. It was a beautiful buzz.

TOM SCHUTZ

It took us all day to hitch our way down to Los Angeles for the Hollywood Palladium show on June 9th. The Stones were playing two shows at this small venue, and we had tickets for the evening show. My uncle had gotten them; he went to UCLA at the time and it was relatively close for him to go to the box office. We arrived in time to stand in line and push ourselves to about three heads in front of us.

Mick rocked the white jump suit, with litter sprinkled on his chest, and everyone was yelling 'Keith! Keith!' He bent down and showed us his teeth, at the time not the model smile, but the image is forever burned into my brain!

That show was the best Rolling Stones show I've ever seen, before or since. It was pure sweaty rock 'n' roll. Against the famous curtain, they played the set like it was a smoky bar room. 'Midnight Rambler' slinked, I remember 'All Down the Line' as one of the fastest nastiest songs I'd ever seen live… Mick just snarled the songs that night!

On the 'Jumpin' Jack Flash'/'Street Fighting Man' ending, they hit a groove and went on forever. Mick drenched everybody in water before pouring the bucket all over himself. The water beads when he was shaking his head looked like diamonds in the lights… still no encores.

FRANK CHRONIS, AGE 17

You had to show the cops your ticket to get to within a mile of the venue because the streets were blocked off. It was very intense for me as I was afraid to miss a single note or moment. I remember 'Midnight Rambler' and Mick sitting on the stage, whipping it with his belt.

BRAD WALKER

It's 1972 and the Rolling Stones are to tour America once again. I had seen them in 1969 at the LA Forum, their first paying gig in America for a while. The first time I saw them was on their second US tour, at the LA Sports Arena in December 1965 and I don't remember if they had been to town since. At any rate, I would see them in 1969 at the Forum and then close out the decade with them at the ill-fated Altamont free concert, where one of the Hell's Angels, hired to secure the stage area of the show, would kill a person who waved a starting pistol around, mostly because he was obviously very stoned and the vibe near the front was bad. But the band, despite many interruptions and the very unfortunate death of the audience member, showed themselves to be excellent purveyors of their own unique brand of hard rock 'n' roll, much better and tighter than the show I had seen some months before in LA.

So how would they be in 1972? *Exile on Main St.* had hit the stores and I was already ranking it with *Sticky Fingers* as one of their very best and I sure wanted to know just how the '72 version of the 'Greatest Rock and Roll Band in the World' would perform. I secured tickets for their Long Beach Arena show of that year. But there were rumors of a show to be held in the small – 3,000 capacity – Hollywood Palladium. These rumors turned out to be true and, as the demand would obviously outstrip the ticket supply, I had to make sure I was one of the lucky ones who got a ticket and not one of the many who would be disappointed. So here is what I did.

I found out, via radio, that the mailing address for the tickets would be printed in the Sunday *LA Times* Calendar section. So I called the *Times* and asked when the Calendar section would hit the street. '4am' was the answer and I was there to get one of the first papers that came off the press. The ticket address was a post office box! Oh no! The post office was not open on Sunday! I was going to have to find the particular post office that had that box number and bring my ticket order to the box on Monday. I was waiting at the post office when it opened the next day. It was somewhere in Santa Monica and, when they opened the doors that morning, I was there, ticket order and check (it was $8.00 for two tickets) inside a stamped envelope and, 'Would you hand-cancel this, please, with the time of day.' It would turn out that there were 50,000 ticket requests mailed in. I got tickets numbered 007 and 008, the fourth request to be filled. I was majorly jazzed!

The days leading up to the show were like waiting for Christmas as a kid. I decided to not bring a date but rather to bring half-pints of Jack Daniels in my cowboy boots and get there early. I arrived at the show at 10am – the show was scheduled for 7pm – and scalped the other ticket for a twenty. Now I had money, booze and a ticket. Was I set, or what?

Once we were finally let into the venue, I proceed to befriend the security guy who was stationed next to me (I had secured a spot stage-front between the vocal monitors) and this gentleman would keep people from getting close to the stage. All except for me. I was allowed to not just lean on the stage, I could almost lay between Jagger's vocal monitors. If you ever want to have a concert experience, this is better than being backstage. I talked with Mick throughout the show and offered him some of my Jack. He politely refused, before taking a big pull on a quart bottle of the same brand!

If I have to tell you that they were killer, you probably aren't paying attention. They were completely outstanding in every way. From 'opener' Stevie Wonder through to two or three Stones encores, it was definitely a night I will never forget. As indeed I haven't, 50 years later.

GARY TUFEL, AGE 26

Despite the fact that it was 50 years ago and I was tripping on acid at the show in honour of the occasion, I think (hope) my memories are at least partly reliable. I was 26 years old and living in Los Angeles, in Hollywood, but not the glamorous part. This was an exciting, wild and crazy time in LA and every rock band, famous and obscure, played there sooner or later – paradise for a rock and roll addict like myself. The Stones, whose opening act on the entire tour was Stevie Wonder, played three or four LA venues, including the historic Hollywood Palladium, where I saw them. There were several reasons that venue was preferable to, say, the massive Los Angeles Forum, which was an indoor sports arena, including that it was near where I lived. More importantly, the Palladium had festival seating, meaning that the main floor of the theatre had no actual seats, just a big wide-open space that the audience could dance on and walk around freely, including right up to the lip of the elevated stage. There was seating in the balconies.

I'd been a Stones fan from when they'd first come to the States around 1964, but I'd never been lucky enough to see them live – only on television. I'd seen Stevie Wonder live before though, also around 1964 on the Motortown Revue in Lansing, Michigan. That was an incredible touring show that featured every act in the Motown-Tamla-Gordy labels' stable, including Marvin Gaye, the Four Tops, the Supremes, the Temptations, and Stevie Wonder.

My friend Sharlene heard about a lottery for tickets to the show on her way home from work, so she collected me and our friend Toots, we raced out to buy money orders and mailed them in. It was a lottery for the tickets, and we got them. Tickets for the Stones show were $10 and I had some LSD for myself and my friend Linda to take as part of the 'experience' that night. How I got tickets for us considering what had to have been thousands of requests is lost in the mists of time, but I do remember the anticipation building in the weeks and days leading up to the concert.

The Palladium was packed on show night but it was still easy for us to position ourselves right in front of and slightly below center stage, and the show was everything we'd expected. The band were very tight and Stevie Wonder was a very hard act to follow, but the Stones did not disappoint. My most vivid memory is of Mick performing 'Midnight Rambler' just a couple of feet or less in front of us. When he got to the line about the Boston Strangler, I remember him whacking the stage floor right on cue with his belt (which he'd already removed). I have no idea why that image has stuck in my mind for the past 50 years, but at the time it brought the house down in a very good way. I've lost track of the number of rock concerts I've been to over all these years but this one was certainly one of the most memorable of all.

ROBERT STAPLETON

I worked for Tower Records on Sunset Boulevard at the time and a bunch of us from the store got tickets and passes. The passes only got us into the private bar/club at the side of the bar and the upstairs reserved seating area. I got to the Palladium around three or four o'clock. About 300 to 500 hundred fans sat on the floor while they showed the original *Dracula* and *Frankenstein* movies on a screen on the stage. Around five or 6pm, we all stood up as the venue was beginning to fill up. I started out on stage right, about ten people from the front, and by the time the Stones came on I was two people away from the stage.

The crowd kind of moved and swayed on its own. Stevie Wonder came on and killed it but we were all there to see the Stones. They started with 'Brown Sugar', ended with 'Uptight'/'Satisfaction' and you know the rest. I

Robert Stapleton was at the Palladium show

never got to use the bar pass as I was never able to leave where I was. After it was all over, we all knew we had seen something special. I saw them again the next night at Long Beach, and then two shows at the Forum. But I must say this show is in the top five of my all-time list of shows seen.

HARVEY KUBERNIK

I saw two shows by the Stones in 1969 at the Forum in Inglewood. My mind was blown but I realized I could never really be in a band like them. I was happy to dig the sound and the pound.

I was ready for the 1972 tour. I slept with my brother and friends, all '69 veterans, at a ticket outlet in downtown Los Angeles and somehow was able to purchase ducats for four concerts – in Inglewood (both shows), Long Beach and San Diego. I also sent in to purchase tickets for the Hollywood Palladium gig and got in, two standing rows from the front where Mick Taylor weaved.

Stevie Wonder as opening act was the perfect appetizer for the real meal deal. He played drums on one number and it was funky and sexy, like his repertoire. I remember seeing Rodney Bingenheimer in the lobby afterwards. He told me the windows of the venue had to be boarded up as promoters feared possible stampede, chaos and vandalism. I never have recovered from this week of peak live music experiences. I did not look at one girl at these gigs, let alone think about getting a phone number. My focus was on the ticket in my pocket and waiting for the goods to be delivered.

Maybe it was the fact that *Exile* was overdubbed, mixed and mastered locally at Sunset Sound studios. Regional flavor and beat heat that added to the band's cosmic performances. It was louder than the '69 bookings, the mix was fantastic and the horns and piano really tossed the action at us. I thought at times that the collective on stage and the music being created by the band and devoured by our eyes and ears was a subject specific Los Angeles and Hollywood sonic brew and we were also captives inside an exiled outfit singing and telling us about our local environs. The *Exile* LP clarified and fortified many moments from these five recitals.

After those seismic appearances, I mulled over the idea of writing about rock music. I felt the pull of the bull. I was buzzed for a couple of months, and then I saw David Bowie in October of '72 at the Santa Monica Civic Auditorium, where I was further convinced that the year of 1972 music and concerts I had witnessed by the Stones and Bowie could somehow transport me to a future I had to trust beyond buying records.

50 years later, blessed and grateful, I've published hundreds of articles and 20 books. And a slew of articles on the Stones. Over the decades I've met the band, and attended some *Bridges to Babylon* recording sessions and a rehearsal in 2016. I've interviewed Bill and Keith and I knew Charlie. However, I never met a girl named 'Sweet Virginia'.

YESTERDAY'S PAPERS

CHRIS VAN NESS
LA FREE PRESS, JUNE 16, 1972

Nobody bothered to tell Taylor and Richard that guitars occasionally have to be retuned between songs… The vast majority of the audience left feeling satisfied – they had, after all, seen the Rolling Stones in person. Somehow, seeing the Rolling Stones in person was all that mattered…

From the Palladium, the Stones moved to Long Beach Arena, which they had first played in November 1964 on their second ever US tour.

LONG BEACH ARENA
JUNE 10, 1972, LONG BEACH, CALIFORNIA

CAPACITY	13,500
SHOWS	1
ARRESTS	61

TOM SCHUTZ

We got to this show late because of transportation problems. While waiting in all kinds of lines, my friend Mark Stoner would say his name when asked, and when he said 'Stoner', no one believed him. 'So,' he said, 'for a joint if I can prove it?' 'Sure.' He'd show his ID, which said Mark Stoner, and that's how we stayed high the whole tour! We sat midway back and saw the classic motorhome pull in with the Stones tongue on each side… very cool. Stevie Wonder was late and his set caused the Stones show to be late. They came on at 11pm and Mick jumped through a tongue on his way on stage as an entrance. I remember Mick Taylor was wearing a white hat. 'Dead Flowers' was a great vocal exchange – the crowd were super into it. And the first encore! 'Honky Tonk Women'!

STEVE BUTCHER, AGE 14

It was right before my 15th birthday. My next door neighbor was a kid called Frank. We were four months apart in age and like brothers. Frank was a huge music fan and we were rock 'n' roll kids. I'd go over to his house and listen to records and we would swap records. We heard the Stones were coming and we had a plan to cut school to get tickets. I think tickets went on sale in late May. We went over to the Broadway department store where there was a Ticketron outlet in the basement. We planned that we would get there an hour early.

We got there a little early and noticed that people were already at the front door of the store before it opened. We were fourth in line. We were little hellraisers back then. They opened the door and people began running down the stairs to the basement. But the Ticketron machine was an old dot matrix printer and it wasn't working. They were trying to get it to work. The two people in front of us got tickets, and then it broke down. And then it started working again and started printing out these tickets. Me and Frank were the last ones to get tickets. Only four

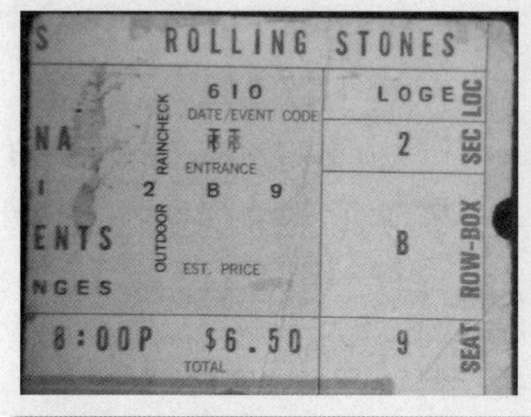

Steve Butcher was at Long Beach Arena

people got tickets, and the people in the line behind us were pretty upset that they weren't able to get tickets. I don't know if the show was sold out or if it was because the person operating the machine didn't know what to do and the machine was overloading.

I'd been to maybe three or four concerts before the Stones show. My very first one was Black Sabbath at the Long Beach Arena maybe a year before that. My folks didn't approve of it because of all the hippies and drugs that were supposedly there, so I couldn't tell them when I was going to concerts. They were good parents and didn't want me getting in trouble. But I wasn't a druggie at that point – or later.

There was one big black and white screen. It was the first time I've ever seen a big screen. It was like a video board and it was probably close circuit TV. Stevie Wonder was towards the upper right on the stage. I was in section two in the loge. The low numbers started in the back, and we were straight back, looking head-on from the loge. So I think the show did sell out right after we got our tickets.

I remember hearing the song 'Bitch' and it being the second song they played. I had a cassette recorder and I made a home-made shoulder strap and smuggled the cassette player in. I recorded most of the concert. It was a terrible quality recording. The volume was modulating in and out, and I have no idea what happened to that tape.

I saw Zeppelin that same month maybe two weeks later, at Long Beach Arena. It was just huge speaker cabinets stacked on the stage and it was just blasting out. It was very loud. I love live music and live concerts. I love concerts that sound like the live albums, like *Ya-Ya's*. A lot of people just go to concerts for the experience, but I wanted to pay attention to the band. Some people couldn't care less about the band. I was just listening to the music and staring at every member of the band.

Frank went on to radio announcing school and actually became a DJ in New York City with his buddy, Marc Coppola, who is Francis Ford Coppola's nephew and Nicholas Cage's brother. We all grew up on the same street. Marc and Frank had a morning show in New York on either WBAB or WPLJ. The Stones were coming to New York and the station was doing a little radio event the night before the concert.

Frank said he was standing at the back of the room and getting ready to leave and as he started to walk out, he looked to his right and here comes Mick Jagger, walking right towards him, by himself with no security. Frank was the first person that Mick came to and he put out his hand and shook Frank's hand. Frank said his jaw dropped. And I can picture him doing this, because whenever he freaked out, Frank's jaw just hit the floor. He found a piece of paper and got Mick's autograph. He said that's the only time he ever asked anybody for their autograph. He couldn't believe it. The Stones were his idols.

IRA KNOPF

There was no sloppiness in their music or stage presentation. When the Stones came out, Jagger strutted across the stage from one end to another, waving at everyone. The additional musicians were Nicky Hopkins on piano, Bobby Keys on sax and Jim Price on trumpet. Charlie Watts on drums and Bill Wyman on bass were comfortable with their instruments, while Mick Taylor was playing a sunburst Les Paul Standard, only switching to an acoustic guitar on 'Sweet Virginia'. Keith Richards went through numerous guitars on almost every song. The band was tight and the sound was clean and clear, with no glitches in the music and no tech problems. There was no encore or jam with Stevie Wonder. They finished the set and off they went. Great show!

YESTERDAY'S PAPERS

PRESTON REESE
LONG BEACH PRESS TELEGRAM, JUNE 12, 1972

Wearing what looked like a silver sequined suit, Jagger opened this hour and a half long set with 'Brown Sugar'. It was the same voice that radio and record player speakers blared forth, but frail now, struggling to overcome the heavy amplification of his five piece all-electric band.

The Forum in Inglewood, Los Angeles was the next stop off on the tour, where the Stones played two shows.

THE FORUM
JUNE 11, 1972, LOS ANGELES, CALIFORNIA

CAPACITY	17,500
SHOWS	2
ARRESTS	0

MICHAEL PHILIPS, AGE 18

I saw the Stones' 1972 tour at the LA Forum. I also had highly sought-after tickets to the show at the Hollywood Palladium, which only holds about 3,000 to 4,000 people, but I couldn't afford to go to both concerts and so sold my Palladium tickets. I also saw the 1975 tour there, but the 1972 show was more exciting to me, as it was the first time I'd ever seen the Stones and also Mick Taylor was in the band. And the lighting was very cool, with spotlights located behind the stage that were directed at a giant mirror above the front of the stage, so the light was reflected down on the band – a novel and cool effect.

I was a senior in high school. I first discovered the Stones in about 1966, when 'Out of Time' was released. I was home from school, sick in bed, and listening to the radio. That song was in heavy rotation. I can't say I fell in love with it, but I was intrigued by the xylophone, by Mick's voice, and by the whole vibe of the song. It wasn't until 'Jumpin' Jack Flash' came out a few years later that I was smitten. Someone played it at a dance party and I was instantly entranced and became a big fan of the band.

The '72 show at the Forum was crazy exciting. Stevie Wonder was the opening act but I didn't appreciate him at the time. When the Stones came out, I remember there was pandemonium. This was obviously before MTV and staring at screens, so the audience didn't just sit there. The ushers and security people had a thankless job of trying to keep people out of the aisles. I don't remember what the Stones played, but it was a lot of the songs they still play today. I do remember the dramatic, slow part of 'Midnight Rambler', when Mick sings, 'Well you heard about the Boston –' wham! I think he was swinging a big belt on the floor during the 'wham', and the house lights flashed in synchrony. That was very cool.

TOM SCHUTZ

At the LA Forum, they played another two shows, one in the afternoon and one in the evening. They were coming at a crazy pace. We were sat on the first row at the side of the stage for the evening show. Mick was in a purple denim jacket. They seemed sluggish to start with but hit their stride with 'Midnight Rambler'. Mick twirled, scattering red roses across the stage.

That night we slept at Grandma's…

CATHY McDONNELL ARDANS

I was a huge early Stones fan, being the vice president of the San Diego, California Rolling Stones Fan Club from 1964 on. But I felt like they were going through the motions that night. Between songs Mick and Keith would disappear and it seemed to me that they were running backstage for hits of cocaine. That's just my opinion, of course, based on the popularity of cocaine at the time. I was quite disappointed in them, maybe because Stevie rocked the place so hard that he was a difficult act to follow. He was just amazing. My enthusiasm for the Stones had waned since they kicked Brian out of the band. It was a lackluster performance that was missing the usual excitement of a Stones concert. I saw them again several times later, the last being the *Steel Wheels* tour, which did have the excitement and power of a real Stones concert.

RANDY WOOLEY

At the time, the Stones hadn't toured because of marijuana-related legal problems. Stevie Wonder and Martha and the Vandellas opened for them. It was a great show.

STEVE VAN BOOVEN, AGE 14

My Uncle Gary took me to my first Rolling Stones concert, 50 years ago. In January of '72, he took me to a friend's house he was house-sitting for at the time; this house was amazing. It was in the hills above Ventura Boulevard in Encino, California. I remember walking down the hall of this house, looking at all of the gold and platinum records that were hanging on the wall, and the view this house had overlooking the entire San Fernando Valley and the massive pool in the backyard. It turned out my uncle was house-sitting for a college buddy of his who was now a big-time producer. I only remember his first name was Don. As a gift, Don gave my uncle three tickets to see the Rolling Stones with backstage passes, where Don would be.

Our seats were to the right of the stage where Keith Richard stood. It was a fantastic experience to see the greatest rock 'n' roll band ever. We went backstage for about 30 minutes, and I remember that I spotted Mick walking down the hall out of the corner of my eye. He stopped and talked to Don for a few minutes, and he rubbed my head and said, 'Hello, how are you? I hope you enjoyed the show,' and walked off! The minute the Stones hit the stage; I was blown away by Mick's intense energy. They were fantastic, and I was forever a Rolling Stones fan for life.

CAROLYN REED CHAPMAN

There's really nothing to remember. My seat was so far back that I decided I would never again go to such a big venue. My favorite memories of the Stones are from the *TAMI Show* in 1964, when I had a great seat both nights in a relatively small venue, the sadly now demolished Santa Monica Civic Auditorium.

TIM GROBATY

I was into them from the beginning. I was pretty precocious musically. I listened to a lot of bands when I was ten, eleven and twelve years old, bands that other people hadn't heard of. I bought *Got Live If You Want It!* at the grocery store. I I liked all their early stuff, the London stuff, and I got *Flowers* when I was pretty young. 'Satisfaction' was ubiquitous, of course. It was the number one song of the year and then the decade.

Sticky Fingers and *Exile* are pretty inseparable for me. I often get confused as to which one has which songs on it, because they're almost like a *Rubber Soul/Revolver* pairing. I saw them at the Forum on June 11. They did two shows that day. I went to the early one. I bought tickets when I was in high school. I don't remember when tickets went on sale, but me and my friends stayed up all night at a chain clothing store called The Broadway which had a Ticketron machine in the basement, which was a precursor to Ticketmaster, waiting and waiting for them to open, so that we could run downstairs to get the tickets. When the doors opened, there was a stampede down the stairs to the basement, with people falling over one another

The ticket machine was slow but we were second or third in line and we ended up scoring tickets. I got into trouble for missing school and was called into the Vice Principal's office. He gave me a long speech and asked me if I'd learned my lesson and if I was going to do that again. I said, 'If the Stones come back? I will!'

It was a big event. Stevie Wonder opened for them and he was an extra bonus. He put on a great show. He was pretty big on his own right by then. I think he was touring *Talking Book*. The Stones show was pretty much classics – 'Brown Sugar', 'Tumbling Dice' and 'Jumpin' Jack Flash' – the stuff they've played a million times. I saw Led Zeppelin 17

59

days later in Long Beach, and that was captured on the album *How the West was Won*. It was the best time for rock shows. It was a great time for music and it was relatively cheap. I think I paid maybe $12 to $14 for the tickets to see both the Rolling Stones and Led Zeppelin. That was real money back in those days, but it wasn't the kind of thing that was gonna break you like it does now.

The Stones show was a typical concert, a pretty festive atmosphere. I don't remember it being rowdy or anything. It seemed fairly respectful. Stevie Wonder set the place up. There was probably a lot of dope smoking going on back in those days. Joints would be going up and down the rows. Dope was cheap and everyone would just light one up and pass it down. The cops were turning a blind eye to it. They had to. I remember walking up and down the aisle at one concert when I found a bag of weed. I waved to my friend and said, 'Hey, look what I found!' In the second I waved it around, a cop grabbed it out of my hand. Easy come, easy go. But generally the police didn't do anything about marijuana at concerts. They were just too far outnumbered.

I saw Dylan with The Band. That was a great show. Bob had been gone for so long and had stopped touring, and possibly wasn't going to do anything again after that. I just remember trying to soak up every note that I heard. But the Stones in '72? That was right up there with that. It was just a collection of anthems. They're just part of the musical consciousness. You've heard all those songs so many times. Even something like 'Sweet Virginia' is a treat, something they will drop into the set that you might not have expected.

I saw them a few times since but '72 was the best. And I never came to terms with Ron Wood being in the Rolling Stones. He always seemed like a poser to me, playing the role of rock 'n' roll guitarist. I just never rated him that much as a guitarist. I thought he should be a bass player, which is where he started. I'm a Mick Taylor fan.

The last time I saw them was when Prince opened for them in 1981. I didn't wanna see them this time around (in 2021). When you've seen them in their prime, it's pretty hard to keep going back.

JULIE HOLLANDER, AGE 15

I got into rock 'n' roll at a very young age. I was a big AM radio listener. I remember The Beatles on *Ed Sullivan*. I started out as a Beatles fan because they hit here in the US first. I don't remember when I made the connection with the Stones but I was listening to them from a young age too. I had a lot of friends that were older kids in the neighborhood who were turned onto a lot of music, especially British music, and friends with older sisters.

Julie Hollander was at the LA Forum

The Stones in '72 was my second concert ever. Before that I had only seen Grand Funk Railroad in 1971. I think my neighbor got the Stones tickets because her father was a season ticket holder for the Lakers basketball team and they played at the Forum, where the show was held, so maybe season ticket holders got access to tickets first. I still have my ticket stub. I believe the ticket price was six dollars and fifty cents.

Three of us went. My friend was a little bit older, 16 or 17, and dating a guy who had a car so that's how we got there. I didn't drive yet. Stevie Wonder was the opening act. I knew who Stevie was. It was a big deal, looking back. The Stones were so influenced by soul music and by black music at the time, so I thought it was pretty cool that they did that.

My most vivid memory of the concert is of 'Midnight Rambler'. At the end, where they stop the music in the song, Mick took his scarf off and was using it as a whip. Every time the drum would hit, he would slap his scarf. I can still see that in my mind's eye. Jim Marshall's estate posted a picture from that show of Mick on Facebook, in a jumpsuit and with a big scarf around his neck. That's what struck me about that photo when I saw it. I have carried that memory for ever.

I can't tell you how many shows I've seen, because I've worked in the music business now since I was 27. I've seen a lot of shows. I've seen a lot of Stones shows since then and that one stands out. We had good seats. They didn't have video screens at that time so we must have been close enough, which would make sense, her dad having had season tickets and so having first call on the really great sections close to the stage. After the show, we went to a famous hamburger place that I'd never been to before called Tommy's Burgers. That was another first for me.

Flash forward and I work for the company that is doing the current (2021) tour. I've worked for two promoters during my career and both of those have worked very closely with the Stones. I've probably worked at as many Stones shows as I've attended over the years. They played a small club here called the Echoplex, as they have done on tours over time, and so I had the privilege of being able to see them in a club that held perhaps 500 people. I've had some great experiences in my life and that's definitely in the top five. Mick still works the part of the stage that he's got when he's playing to 500 people, just the same as he would if he was playing to a football stadium filled with 50,000 people. He's gonna have that swagger and move those hips whether he's in a rehearsal room or on a giant stage.

MICHAEL POPOV

Photos: Michael Popov

My first Stones show and probably my all-time favorite concert was the matinee show I saw on the 1972 *Exile* tour at the Forum in Inglewood. I think they called it the Stones Touring Party. I had to mail into a lottery and was luckily picked and sent four tickets at $7.50 apiece. How times have changed. I took Cindy who was my best girl at the time (even if she didn't know it!) and another couple. We had the greatest time. Stevie Wonder opened the show and was just phenomenal, as if we expected anything else.

The Stones then took the stage and I was floored the minute Keith started 'Brown Sugar' and Mick started moving. I had no idea he could move like that. Mick Taylor had firmly taken over from Brian, Bill and Charlie held the rhythm together and we were off on a rock and roll extravaganza. They were showcasing the *Exile on Main St.* album, of course, and they played songs from *Sticky Fingers*, *Let It Bleed* and *Beggars Banquet* with some oldies mixed in. The guitar chemistry between Keith and Mick Taylor was awesome. Taylor played a strong yet very melodious lead. It was at this time that the Stones became my all-time favorite rock and roll band. We took some photographs from our seats.

Michael Popov was at the Forum

JILL LEWIS

I camped out the night before to get good seats and ended up in the third row. Not too shabby.

SHARON RENNIER

My best friend and I had tickets to see the Rolling Stones in 1966 at the Swing Auditorium in San Bernardino but we couldn't drive and a ride never showed up so we missed that show. The next Rolling Stones show that I missed was 1969. I was nine months pregnant and wasn't allowed to go. Then came the '72 show at The Forum in Inglewood, California. Tickets were sold by mail order and I attended the matinee show with my husband. Stevie Wonder was the opening act. I remember Keith singing 'Happy', the first time he ever performed his own solo song, and the rose petals that Mick threw at the end of the show. If I close my eyes, I can see the whole concert play in my mind. My daughter is a huge Rolling Stones fan, and has never forgiven me for not taking her.

YESTERDAY'S PAPERS

ROBERT HILBURN
LA TIMES, JUNE 10, 1972

The way Bobby Keys, Jim Price and Nicky Hopkins have been integrated into the band, the new material provides some of the concert's best moments. But it helps to be familiar with the new songs. That's why *Exile on Main St.* is a rather important concert companion piece.

Having completed their Los Angeles-area shows, the Stones Touring Party headed south to San Diego.

INTERNATIONAL SPORTS ARENA
JUNE 13, 1972, SAN DIEGO, CALIFORNIA

CAPACITY	16,000
SHOWS	1
ARRESTS	60

MICHAEL TUCKER, AGE 26

It was a Tuesday night. For some reason I thought it was a Saturday, but you lose track of time and days as you get older and 50 years was many years and many days ago. I asked my ex-wife what she remembered about the concert and she said she doesn't remember going to it. Since it was a Tuesday, we didn't have a lot of time to party before the concert and so my memory is pretty good. I was 26 years old and had been in San Diego for three years. We went with a bunch of our neighbors. There were probably six of us. We got to the Sports Arena about six or so. That gave us some time to get primed for the concert. It wasn't too hazy when we went inside but after the lights went down it sure did. I was in awe as we got seated and a number of blank, tall rectangular screens were hanging about halfway around the arena. They started showing old black-and-white *Dragnet* TV shows. Are you kidding me? I knew it was going to be a good concert. I didn't have any idea who the opening acts were. I can't remember who the first act was but I know it was either Stevie Wonder or Jo Jo Gunne. Little Stevie Wonder had grown up since I first heard him sing 'Fingertips' in the early '60s. Jo Jo Gunne did 'Run Run Run' and kinda set the stage for the Stones. I remember Jay Ferguson's outfit for some reason. I think he was wearing platform boots and standing while he was banging away on the piano.

I was so into the music I can't tell you all the songs the Stones played but I was really enjoying the concert and then the concert ended, the lights came on and we made our way back to the car. By then I was just following whoever was in front of me. It was better than the Led Zeppelin concert in 1970 when the opening act was Black Sabbath. Unfortunately, that concert was constantly being interrupted by a bunch of rowdy concert goers who didn't like the songs being played. They only wanted to hear 'Communication Breakdown' and 'Whole Lotta Love'. Sad.

TOM SCHUTZ

We headed from Grandma's to San Diego via a ride from my uncle in his yellow VW. We got there early and bought tickets, which was easier because it was open seating. The crowd was huge. It spilled into the street, overflowing into Tower Records. There was no line as such, just a mass of people milling around all the way up to the entrance doors. Police were trying to keep everyone out of the street but traffic was blocked because of all the bodies. And the going in was slow. We ended up a quarter of the way back in the middle section.

Outside, there were incidences of people trying to force their way in with no tickets. There was tear gas… arrests being made… But inside we had no idea.

The crowd was roaring, Stevie Wonder seemed enthusiastic… and the Stones hit the stage, Mick in purple and a denim jacket. The crowd was loud! Keith waved and then did the best start to 'Brown Sugar' – it rocked!

The crowd was going mad. 'Rocks Off' sounded exactly like on *Exile*. They were tight! By the time 'Midnight Rambler' came on, the crowd was swaying as one, everyone was on their feet the whole show. You could feel the Stones feed off it. They must have too, because we got an encore with 'Honky Tonk Women'. I remember Keith tuning up mid-guitar solo.

LARRY JOHNSON, AGE 20

The Rolling Stones in '72 was my first concert. The tickets were $6.50. I went with my girlfriend at the time, who was later my wife, who was later my ex-wife! I was blown away by the event. Back then it was open seating, but I still got pretty good seats. The atmosphere, the crowd and the energy were intoxicating. I was immediately hooked on concerts. Someone had printed a bunch of bogus tickets and sold them outside, and when the people were turned away at the door a riot started. They broke out all the windows to the Sports Arena and went across the street and destroyed a Tower Records store and a couple more stores. I was inside enjoying the concert and had no idea what was going on outside. When the concert was over, we were walking out and there was glass everywhere. The police had already dispersed the crowd. My brand new car was damaged that night, the driver's door and front fender were dented.

The Stones were banned from San Diego for several years because of events that night even though they had nothing to do with it. They did play in San Diego in 1981. I had to go to LA for them in '75 and '78. And I saw them again in LA in 2021.

PETER NOWELL

I was 10 in Christmas 1966 when my parents got me a cheap plastic table top General Electric AM/FM radio. That was the heyday of Top

40 in America and I would listen to it fairly religiously. Around that time, *Between the Buttons* came out and we would have gotten the singles, so 'Let's Spend the Night Together' and 'Ruby Tuesday'. They clicked a little bit. The radio stations occasionally threw in 'The Last Time', '19th Nervous Breakdown' and 'Satisfaction', and I enjoyed all their stuff along with everything else that was happening.

What really kicked in with the Stones, and really made me focus on them, was hearing the opening licks of 'Jumpin' Jack Flash' for the first time, with that guitar tone and that riff. I just said, 'What the hell is this?' I became supremely interested, and then I got *Get Your Ya-Ya's Out!* for Christmas and played that to death. From then on, every time I got a bit of extra money I went back and bought old catalogue, so I pretty much was up to date in 1972. The Stones rebellion thing appealed to me at the height of my teenage angst. They really connected on that level.

The tickets for the San Diego show were mail order. I sent in my six dollars and fifty cents in January or February and was shocked when I got a ticket back a couple of weeks later. I put that in a safe place. I would have been a sophomore in high school. It was finals week. I had one final the next day, which I did no studying for. My folks sort of indulged my music thing. I was a pretty discreet kid. All the naughty things I did they had no idea about, and I rarely got caught.

It was before I had my driver's license. I didn't go with anybody because I didn't have a whole lot of friends. I was pretty much a loner. I don't know if I even knew of anybody who was even going to the show. I had my mom drive me to San Diego Sports Arena but made sure I had her drop me off about five or six blocks away, so nobody saw me in front of the midway drive in. I just hoofed it the rest of the way.

This was the very first show I'd ever been to. I'd never ever gone to a concert before. This was a new experience for me on a number of different levels. I got there and the adrenaline was running. It was festival seating which was catch-as-catch-can in those days, so I was really excited because I got down on the floor. And I thought I was pretty close. Every once in a while, there'd be some rustling on the stage and everyone sitting on the floor would get up and rush to the stage and I followed along and I sat down. We were slowly compacting ourselves. Before the show started, I was sitting on the ground and I had this guy sort of sitting between my legs and his girlfriend sitting between his legs so they had me pinned to the ground and I couldn't move.

The other thing I remember is they had really big and advanced for the time – but prehistoric these days – big rear projection screens on each side of the stage. They were monitoring a local TV station and one of the shows they were showing was an episode of *Dragnet* with Jack Webb. It was one of his classic anti-drug ones. Not knowing the audience, it was pretty funny. People were just laughing at it.

The show started and it was Stevie Wonder, who I was not a big fan of other than a couple of his early Motown singles, and then the Stones came on. I've never been in an environment that was that electric. It was stunning. I was just in awe. After 50 years it's tough to remember a whole lot about it, but I do remember that they came out and did an encore of 'Honky Tonk Women' and I did a 360 and looked up at the crowd and saw 15,000 people in rapture. They were just bouncing up and down. The look on their faces was something I'd never seen before and really haven't seen since.

It was a great night. I went outside in a daze and walked back the five or six blocks to the rendezvous point for my ride home. I passed through the parking lot and didn't see anything. I met my mom and told her, 'Yeah, it's all good.' Then I got the paper the next day and found out that there had been a quasi-riot in the parking lot with cars set on fire and people arrested and some people hurt. Eventually a San Diego cop got disciplined – I don't know what the ultimate outcome was, whether he was fired or what – for beating up some teenage girl. And I was, 'Jeez, I missed all of that!'

And that was the story of my San Diego concert. No drugs involved. I didn't see anybody I knew. But it was my first show and still the best one I've ever seen. And I've been to a lot.

I haven't followed the Stones since. When it got to *Goat's Head Soup* I said, 'No, this isn't working.' Jagger started singing in this exaggerated style, an endless self-parody. And the follow up was *Black and Blue*, and for me it was, 'Man, this is not working.' *Some Girls* and *It's Only Rock 'n' Roll* were okay, but I just lost interest after that. I became much more interested in the Ramones and the Clash. The punk thing picked up where the Stones left off. I saw them in '75 at the LA Forum and enjoyed that show a lot too – they still connected with me – but the new material just didn't work. And now I've got a problem with an 80-year-old man prancing around like it's 1964. It's a little unseemly.

BILL YOGGERST

I was at the Rolling Stones concert at the San Diego Sports Arena. The only memory I have is the opening song, 'Brown Sugar'. Mick was twirling a big, feather boa.

JOHN ZAVESKY, AGE 20

I got a solo ticket for the show as I knew it would be easier to score a decent seat and I was 20 and single at the time. The Sports Arena was a huge round building with a massive flat parking lot. There were hundreds of folks in the parking lot when I arrived which wasn't unusual. I can't recall the opening act, as I got to the Sports Arena late and only caught the final song before the lights went on.

Everybody was waiting with great anticipation for the Stones. The Stones went on. I believe they opened with 'Jumpin' Jack Flash'. I was seated in the second section off the floor, stage right. Approximately 30 minutes into the show, there was a loud crash sound and then loads of people charged the floor and arena. The band stopped playing. The lights went on. Security was trying to deal with the crashers. I sat like others, thinking the show would resume. That didn't happen. They announced the show was over.

The section I exited was not damaged. I walked around to another entrance and there was glass everywhere. It looked like the doors had either been pushed or kicked in. There were hundreds of people in the parking lot. Loads of cops. People getting arrested. I ended up going

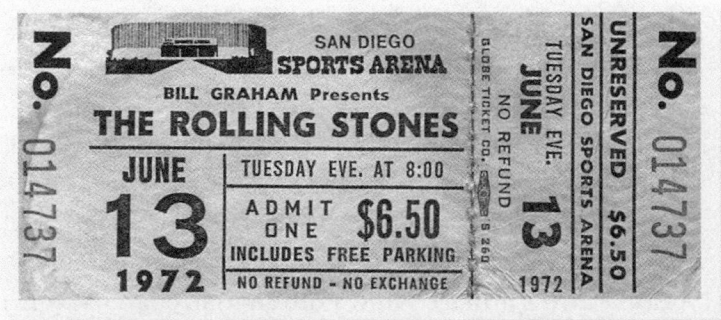

John Zavesky was at the San Diego show

to my car and just sitting in it for a long time until the line to the exit thinned and thinking that this really sucked, but it couldn't have been as bad as Altamont.

While I have every Stones album and love the band, I never went to see another Stones concert. I still have the cardboard promo poster for the show. They put one up in the record store I worked at.

MICHAEL MENDELL, AGE 18

I became a Stones fan after hearing them on the radio and listening to them on my best friend's Fisher stereo. I was a wannabe hippie in junior high, aged 12 to 14, and hit a joint with an older cousin in the river bed near my home at the age of 15. In 1972, I was 18 and graduating from high school. I saw the tour with my best friend Rudy. Tickets were $15, I believe, and the show was put on by Bill Silva Productions. We started out in our seats on the left side of the stage but moved to the floor when Mick Jagger came on. I was less than 20 feet from his wiry ass! They played all songs from the *Sticky Fingers* album. I'm still a fan.

JOE HUGHES

The waiting, the camping out, the riots were over as Mick Jagger and his Rolling Stones gathered themselves in a van outside the Sports Arena early today and headed back to Los Angeles. Jagger's flamboyant purple pyjama-like trousers and denim jacket were drenched with perspiration, evidence of a hard day's night, but the headstone seemed to glow in the aftermath. 'San Diego's a groove, they're hip here,' he said to guitarist Mick Taylor as the van sped off, bringing San Diego's concert of the year to a peaceful conclusion. Jagger had heard of the problems outside the arena while he was on stage last night, performing before more than 16,000 wildly enthusiastic persons. But he couldn't muster up any sympathy for the events. Wherever Jagger and the Stones roll, trouble is sure to follow. It has become a part of their repertoire. And it fits their image well. The Stones are not apotheosised by magazines. Nobody calls them adorable, sweet, funny or nice. They have been described as 'every mother's nightmare', and nothing has changed much since 1962 when they evolved on the scene.

The Stones were hustled into San Diego late yesterday amid security precautions fit for president. Their arrival by charter jet at Lindbergh Field was a top level, hush-hush secret as was their whereabouts a few hours before the concert. 'We just don't want any incidents,' is the way one of Mick Jagger's phalanx of musclebound bodyguards explained the atmosphere upon deplaning with the rest of the Stones entourage – complete with aides, hangers on and groupies in tow – at the airport. Such 'incidents' – mainly death, dope and destruction – stalk the Stones.

TERRI STEAGALL MADDOX

I didn't make it in as there was a riot outside. Hell's Angels were doing security and I was so close to Mick and all three women he was with that I could have touched them.

YESTERDAY'S PAPERS

CAROL OLTEN
SAN DIEGO UNION, JUNE 14, 1972

Step right up, folks! Welcome to the carnival! Buy your shirt, with a phantom red blot on the front – the mark of the Rolling Stones – and see the Rolling Stones live and in person! And on a monitor television at the same time! See Mick Jagger jump, pout, stagger, fall. See windows broken by an angry mob. People arrested. See them packed up on stretchers in a police ambulance. That's the Stones concert last night in the Sports Arena, where a sold-out house of 16,000 reflected a huge carnival of life with the Stones as master ringleaders. And, despite the rip-off, the big hype, and everything else, they were brilliant.

Keeping LA as their base, the Stones commuted by plane to the next few shows.

TUCSON CONVENTION CENTER
JUNE 14, 1972, TUCSON, ARIZONA

CAPACITY	**8,962**
SHOWS	**1**
ARRESTS	**6**

MANUEL BARREDO

I almost got hit by a limousine that they were in on by the University of Arizona, on University Boulevard and Park Avenue. I was crossing a street there after my class and was going to find my parked car. I recognized them inside the limousine. They were in Tucson to perform in a concert at the TCC. I was on the crosswalk. The driver did not stop and I had to run quickly so as not to get hit. I remember yelling at the limousine with a few choice words. They were probably cruising and looking at chicks.

ALEX WADDELL, AGE 16

I went with my friend Mike. I had been a Stones fan since the mid-60s and thought that this might be my last chance to see them! One of my class mates cut class at Saguaro High School to buy the tickets, which cost $6.75. I still have the ticket stub. As a 16-year-old boy, seeing a woman wearing a see-through dress while waiting to go in left an impression on me. I had not been a Stevie Wonder fan previously but I really thought he was great and started my continued appreciation of him. As always at concerts back then, you could only see the bands through a cloud of marijuana smoke. Unfortunately, we didn't have any, so I was straight for the concert. I also remember seeing the riot police when we were leaving the concert. I believe that a bunch of people tried to break in to see the concert.

HERB WAGNER

It was a sold-out show. Some people tried to bumrush the doors and police used tear gas to dispel the crowd outside. It was a good show.

KAREN MARKS, AGE 20

I remember dancing on my seat to 'Brown Sugar'. Tickets were $12, which seemed high, but that was a different time. And there was a good energy to the show.

BILL CLIFFORD

Stevie Wonder stole the show. The Stones played for an hour and left. There was no encore.

LINDA BEIMERS

Stevie Wonder stole the show. The Stones only played for 45 minutes and no encore! The terrible part was that the police and security people beat the shit out of people trying to get in. Big downer. Plus the tickets were twice as much as usual. I have my ticket stub - $9.50!

JUDY ZIMBERT

I distinctly remember Mick came to the front of the stage before the concert to meet a young girl in a wheelchair. That memory is more vivid than the concert.

KOREY KRUCKMEYER

The venue capacity was just shy of 10,000, and our seats were center on the floor, about ten rows back.

FELIPE SOUTHARD, AGE 13

I was there. I was 13 years old with a baggy full of joints!

MARGO WARREN, AGE 17

I was 17 years old and a high school senior. Several of my friends also attended. It was festival-style, so no seating on the floor. I was able to find my journal entry about the concert. Here it is:

Left my house at 4pm for the concert. 'They (Tucson Community Center? Police?) were worried since they'd had trouble the night before in LA with people trying to break into Rolling Stones.

I was fascinated by everything, seeing Bill Graham in person, seeing guys so cute – you see how easy it would be to want to be a groupie, meeting people, flirting… [smoked some pot with some girlfriends]. Then the Stones came out and I was way up front. There is nothing to compare to the sex and grossness that comes off Mike Jagger. His movements are unreal. His face is unreal, his lips. He didn't wear undies. And God he just makes all these faces and mouths 'shit' and 'fuck' the whole song. And then when it's between songs he just sounds so sweet by saying 'it's so nice to be in Tucson' in this sweet little innocent boy English accent.'

I am not sure what I meant by the 'grossness' that comes off Mick Jagger. Overall, it sounds like a positive to me!

MEL HANNAMAN

I was a Beatles fan, grudgingly singing along with the Stones. In '72 I was a junior in high school, and went to the concert with my boyfriend, a senior and a Stones fan.

The weather was hot and the crowd was huge and unruly. Waiting to get in is when I saw several groups of young men dressed in hot pants, tank tops and clogs. What a shock. I was in drama and have always had pretty good 'gaydar', but that was a surprise to me. We figured they were fans from California. My first concert was TCC's opening, and featured Three Dog Night. We dressed up to go. The Stones concert was my second, and by then regular looking hippie types prevailed. Once we got inside it was packed, and thick with smoke. I remember joints being passed the whole time. That's probably why I don't remember much of the music or even Stevie Wonder as the opening act.

I do remember there being no encore by the Stones but waiting just in case, and just as much of a crowd leaving. I enjoyed it, eventually became a huge Stones fan, and had a couple posters of Mick up in my barracks area once I joined the Army. I still love their music today.

I saw them again in 2002 in Atlanta, a treat from my son. 40 years later and I was still so happy to see them live. My ten seconds of fame happened then when I was shown on the Jumbotron, rocking out to

'Mustang Sally'. I wore a lime green sweater and purple cords. I was asked to go on stage, but between my imbibing and the two-inch heels on my Harley boots I couldn't navigate the steps from the nosebleed section seats. I regret that to this day. I'm so very glad they are still rockin' it.

SHARON CURTIS

It was the Seventies and most of it is a blur. I was living in the University of Arizona dorm and my roomie was a Phoenix gal. I remember that Tina Turner stole the show. We, the audience, were too exhausted for the Stones after Tina. I remember reading that Mick Jagger said 'never again' with Tina.

SUSAN WORTMAN

I went to that concert. We had close floor seats, the arena was filled with the aroma of marijuana and everyone freely shared joints. We stood on our chairs, screaming and dancing.

WAYNE GADDY

It was a huge deal, definitely the biggest concert to hit Tucson up to that time. The fact that they skipped Phoenix to play Tucson made it more special. I showed up at 4am for the 10am ticket sale. (Those were the days when you could get great seats for your hometown concerts.) By 6am, there were well over 100 fans in line. Close to 10am, a couple of guys tried to bull their way in to the front of the line and were summarily thrown on their asses by the nearest line members.

I got tickets on the lower side loge, even with the front of the stage and slightly above it, which provided a great view of everything that happened onstage. I was close enough to see Jagger's makeup, including a star he had painted on his face. The funniest moment was in the instrumental break during 'Midnight Rambler'. There were several adolescent girls in the center, front row. Jagger got on his knees, leaned over and gave them the finger right in front of their faces. The girls were besides themselves, probably with joy at Jagger singling them out!

When we got out of the arena, we found a police presence and heard there had been a riot of a fairly substantial crowd who tried to break into the center during the concert. I also remember it being covered either by the *Daily Star* newspaper or local TV news the next day or the day after that.

LEN HOLMES

I was there. A riot broke out. Gate crashers tried to get in but cops with tear gas said no!

PHILIP T BURRIS, AGE 16

A buddy of mine and I were sitting in my truck at his girlfriend's house. She lived about six or seven blocks south of the Convention Center. At some point, it sounded like hell broke loose. The next day I read in the paper that people without tickets charged the gates and a full-blown riot started. They tore up a bunch of stuff and quite a few people got arrested. It was big news in Tucson at the time.

YESTERDAY'S PAPERS

JOHN HENRY
ARIZONA DAILY STAR, JUNE 15, 1972

Before Stevie Wonder's set was over, there was some question whether the Stones could top it but the Stones proved equal to the task, thanks mainly to the gyrations of Jagger, who teased the audience with his hips shaking, head bobbing and feet shuffling as the band, with horns added, blew the crowd into a frenzy. By the time the group… got into the final three numbers, the audience was on its feet and dancing in the aisles. The Stones may get bigger audiences elsewhere on their tour, which ends in July in New York, but nowhere will have had a more appreciative audience than the 8,000 plus at the Community Center last night.

The Stones flew in to Albuquerque on the day of the show, played and flew out again.

UNIVERSITY ARENA
JUNE 15, 1972, ALBUQUERQUE, NEW MEXICO

CAPACITY 14,000
SHOWS 1
ARRESTS 0

Rebecca Lowry was known as 'the Ticket Lady'

REBECCA LOWRY

The Albuquerque show sold out in less than 90 minutes. I say that with certainty because my best female friend Debbie and I worked our way through college as the University of New Mexico Popular Entertainment Committee's 'ticketladies'. It was a title that had been bestowed upon us, and people preferred using it instead of our names. 'Hey, Ticketlady! When does Led Zep go on sale?' 'Hey, Ticketlady! Where should we unload the Super Troupers?' We may have only earned $1.93 an hour, but what the job lacked in salary, it made up for with a kind of prestige. And that meant we were amongst only a handful of people who were the first to know the Stones were coming to our little town, a sleepy, conservative little town that we were inclined to refer not-so-lovingly to as Badgerfang, New Mexico.

There is absolutely no way Albuquerque would have been chosen as a venue for the Stones if it weren't for the UNM Arena. It seated about 14,000 at the time. The arena would later be nicknamed 'The Pit' because of its construct; the street level you entered on was actually at the summit of all that seating. The arena had been sunk into the sand by local architect Joe Boehning six or seven years pre-Stones; an enormous 40-foot chasm that actually does take your breath away as you edge toward the concrete steps that you must descend to reach your seats. Excavating the earth to create The Pit had been pretty much the same thing as creating a hole that could accommodate an upside-down pyramid. It was far from an ideal venue for concerts, because access to the floor required the band's crew to navigate a steep ramp with speakers, sound towers and any staging. We'd seen more than one speaker get away from sound guys as they brought them in from the semis parked out back. And that ramp would also be where the Stones would enter in order to access the stage.

In addition to the physical challenge The Pit posed, the UNM Athletic Department didn't want us there to begin with. Crazy music. Crazy hippies. Crazy dope-smoking. Crazy amounts of potential damage to The Pit. (Basketball, you see, was the university's cash-cow.)

Sports Illustrated had sources who had gauged the sound level produced by basketball fans in The Pit at 125 – 130 decibels. It would get so loud that sometimes, squooshy, fibrous puffs of insulation would actually float down from the ceiling during a game. 130 decibels is pain-level, so not all that surprising that floofs of insulation would dislodge from the ceiling and float down on the audience below when a game got especially tense. But if that was what happened during a basketball game, what weirdness was the World's Greatest Rock and Roll Band capable of generating?

New Mexico prides itself on remaining part of the Wild West. Little wonder, then, that the Stones show carried with it some Old West-style romance and intrigue of its own. Rumors were rampant that the West Texas branch of Hell's Angels was planning to ride into town and tear the place apart. I'm not sure there is or ever was a West Texas branch of the Angels, but with all the craziness surrounding the concert, it seemed kind of plausible. Everybody remembered Altamont and what happened there. No one at UNM was taking any chances that a crew of bikers might show up, overexcite themselves and murder somebody, or at least break some windows in the Pit. This show couldn't be jeopardized.

The Popular Entertainment Committee (PEC) took hosting the show as a rite of passage and an honor - kind of like being knighted. Security was tighter than any show that had gone before. There was a huge police presence and zero tolerance for scalpers. Even our ticket-takers were soon to learn there would be more to their job than ripping a piece of cardstock in half.

The year of 1972 preceded the advent of Ticketmaster and the 'uncounterfeitable' ticket. The tickets PEC used for this and other Fillmore-seating shows were solid color, made of a cardstock consisting of multi-colored paper pressed together into a thin cardboard. That way, if the ticket-takers tore the ticket at an angle, they could see fairly quickly the various colors and verify the ticket was real.

And the Stones show drew more than its share of counterfeit tickets. One ticket-taker presented us with a fake he'd confiscated that was made from plain white art paper with the printed information free-handed with a ball-point pen. To replicate the color of a real Stones ticket, the counterfeiter had colored it painstakingly with a blend of Crayola crayons. My boss liked that counterfeit ticket so much, he kept it.

Since there were no 'Day of Show' tickets for us to sell, our boss sent us outside, armed with walkie-talkies to make us official-looking, to help marshal the crowd lining up outside the arena. New Mexico heat is oppressive in June, and 1972 was no different. The crowds that we queued up in snaky lines around the arena were wearing cut-offs, tanks, halter tops, no shirts at all, sandals. Some people stuck it out as long as they could, but eventually gave up their place in line and sought what little shade the north side of the arena was casting.

The Athletic Department had made it clear they didn't want broken beer bottles uglying up their flagship facility, so people coming on premises with containers, even if filled only with water, were told to toss them. Slightly before sunblock was invented, or at least before it was to become a mainstay, 1972 crowds were opting to let themselves be cooked for the sake of a good view of Mick's lips. People were being broiled alive right in front of us.

That's why the guy dressed in a full-blown Henry VIII costume (velvet doublet, Tudor bonnet, tights, little curly-toed slippers, brocade cloak) stood out so readily. Sitting out there in The Pit parking lot with his tights-clad butt crisping up on the asphalt, baking in the New Mexico gunfighter sunlight. Later that night when we opened the doors, we'd see that guy again, catapulting himself over the concourse railing and bounding down 23 rows of bleacher seats to secure his place on the main floor.

By about noon, we abandoned marshalling the lines outside and headed indoors, desperate for refrigerated air, and we'd heard there were soft drinks. Besides, there was no danger of anyone doing anything crazy as they waited outside to be let in. It was too hot for anybody to want to attack or fight anybody else.

The lighting set-up for the show was amazing. Knowing how the Athletic Department felt about anything screwing up any of their facilities - but especially their beloved Pit - I couldn't figure how Stones-caliber lights were going to be installed. Chip Monck was the lighting guy for the '72 tour, and he had come up with some weird, mirrored set-up that projected light from behind the stage and bounced it back onto the stage from the mirrors down front.

The stage itself is still one of the most vivid memories I have of the show. It was white with a huge Chinese dragon emblazoned across it, and it was assembled in pieces. I was chatting with Tommy, one of the riggers, during set-up, as stagehands mopped the dragon stage with a mixture of 7-Up and warm water. Tommy said they did it so the stage would be tacky. 'That way,' he said, 'when Mick starts dancing, he won't slip and dance overboard into the security pit.'

You didn't see the regular strap-hangers wandering around backstage at this show like they usually did at other Albuquerque concerts. For the Stones, there were various levels of passes required to access the different 'regions' of the venue. Although that's pretty typical now, it wasn't back in the day, at least not in Albuquerque. Back then, you either had a pass or you didn't. Just one pass. One size fits all. An adhesive-backed satin patch you stuck to your thigh or butt to make your friends jealous.

Passes for the Stones inner sanctum (green room, stage, dressing room, etc.) were even stamped with tour manager Peter Rudge's signature. Some passes were changed out several times over the course of the day, apparently as an added level of security. The Ticketladies were definitely not going to be privy to those.

But the hysteria of the day had gotten to us. We weren't content with being able to enter The Pit several hours early and have our choice of seats before the general population stormed the doors. We were determined to get close enough to see those Rolling Stones at arm's length.

Several months before, at a different concert, the local promoter had failed to order backstage passes. He tasked us with coming up with some kind of pass that concert-lurkers wouldn't be able to replicate. We'd dug around the box office and found an old rubber stamp someone had left behind. It was a big, stylized number one. Someone had said Hell's Angels used something similar for their One Percenter tattoos. (Now, there's a cosmic sign for you.) I didn't know anything about that. To me, the stamp looked more like the old logo for One-a-Day Vitamins I'd seen in a magazine. Since we sure weren't going to be a part of the Stones' inner circle, we decided to give that old rubber stamp one more try. We'd make our own passes and pray to God no one was paying that much attention.

Truthfully, I don't think our little homemade passes had anything to do with our eventually scoring standing room on the ramp where the Stones would pass by. I think our faces were, after working many, many shows, familiar enough to the local security folks, stagehands, riggers, spot operators, etc., that they just naturally assumed we were *supposed* to be there. So everybody from the Stones Touring Party assumed so too. We clustered along with all the other pathetic concert-lurkers and ramp-leeches down the ramp from The Pit's team dressing rooms, trying not to make prolonged eye contact with anybody.

Original opening act Martha and the Vandellas were a no-show. (To this day, I don't know why they didn't show up.) Stevie Wonder opened instead, and completely tore it up. Beachballs and frisbees and pungent smoke were floating above the audience, and when a beachball smacked Stevie, he fished around for it and kicked it back into the crowd. It was a regular Mardi Gras.

At the end of his set, there was a quick break and then the houselights dimmed, except for one follow-spot trained on lighting guy Chip Monck. That, of course, was when we all began the process of going temporarily deaf. But before I had the chance to say, 'I can't hear a damned thing over this crowd,' the headliners appeared on the ramp. Mick Jagger was wearing the purple jumpsuit (all STP shows got either the purple or the white jumpsuit) and an outrageously long peach-colored scarf. And he was sucking a lemon.

The ramp lights dimmed, replaced by crew members with penlights, marking the floor in front of the band, leading them to the stage. As Mick bounced up and down on his toes, getting ready to exit the ramp for the stage, he took a bite out of that lemon and spat it out on the rubber-matted floor, coincidentally close to my foot. Debbie, my best female friend, saw me watching him and that discarded chunk of lemon, and even though I couldn't hear her, I could read her lips: 'Oh, my God - you're actually thinking of picking that up, aren't you?'

A fly-mic dropped from the support beams in the ceiling and lighting guy Chip Monck grabbed it, just like the tuxedo-wearing guy who announces prize-fights: 'Ladies and gentlemen, the World's Greatest Rock and Roll Band, the Ro —' Totally deaf at that point. It felt like having your head inside a giant conch shell. But not in a pleasant way.

The other Stones went onstage first, like Mick's bridesmaids. Charlie had on a t-shirt with a silk-screened WWII plane dropping a string of bombs, over which he wore a mambo shirt that looked like something Ricky Ricardo would have worn while playing maracas. Yellow with red trim, it had huge conga drum-player sleeves built from ruffle upon ruffle upon ruffle.

They opened with 'Brown Sugar' and ended with 'Street Fighting Man' and 'Jumpin' Jack Flash'. Puffs of the fibrous ceiling insulation wafted down over the audience who, in their euphoric trance, most likely never even realized it.

Probably everybody who attended can still recite the set list by heart, even now, a half-century later. But something very few people ever mention and may not even remember is that during those last two songs, the lighting crew turned up the houselights and we all saw each other for the first time, joyous and celebrating, together down in that 40-foot-deep hole. It was like a positive, freeing, harmless version of *Lord of the Flies*. At 130 decibels.

I regained full hearing right before we hosted the Jethro Tull *Thick as a Brick* tour at the exact same venue, exactly one week after the Stones' plane, emblazoned with that lips and tongue logo, vanished into the sky. (But Jethro Tull was just a concert.)

DAVE MARTIN

It was general admission and I was in line at 3am. I waited all day and wound up thirteen rows from the stage, dead center. It was well worth the wait. It was the best show ever.

SUSAN LARGENT, AGE 17

I was in fourth grade when my older sister started bringing home Rolling Stones records. I saw them on *Ed Sullivan* and wasn't too impressed. But I started really liking the group when I was in junior high; they all were so adorable. When my sister moved out, she left several of their early albums and I added a few to the collection.

I was 17 when the Stones came to town in 1972. Tickets were only $7.00. I went with my best girlfriend and we got there early. The fans started showing up and the crowd kept growing. People were passing joints around and – of course – I indulged. Those were fun times – smoking pot was more of a social event, but it was very hot, I was very high and we were in the middle of this huge crowd. I thought I was going to pass out. Finally, they opened the doors and this mob-like crowd started rushing the entrance.

We found our seats and the concert started. I wasn't a big Stevie Wonder fan. I do remember a few songs he sang, but I had come to see the Stones. I remember them playing 'Brown Sugar' and 'Bitch', and Keith singing 'Happy'. Other than that, I don't recall much. When I think about the great groups we were privileged to see in person, and that it didn't cost $400 or more, I realise I was very lucky.

HELEN HORNE CANTWELL

I had just graduated high school. I invited my two male cousins from Arkansas to come to Albuquerque to go with my friend and me to the Stones. I had on an embroidered muslin top with jeans, Indian jewelry and a bandana. We got primed on the way. We were in line and it was pretty warm and there was a blinding sun from the West. We were all excited! I can't say I remember much, but what I do remember is how the music made me feel. And what's crazy is that this summer I put *Exile on Main St.* on and I felt the exact emotions. It just took me back. That feeling has never died

Helen Horne Cantwell went with her cousins

and is probably why I've seen the Stones eight times. Friends we knew lived in Hobbs, New Mexico and they knew Bobby Keys. He just makes that album.

RHONDA BYRUM, AGE 16

My escape was concerts and acid. I was really excited to see the Rolling Stones. I had started going to concerts at 12 years old and loved rock and roll. I have seen so many of the greats – and so many acts that nobody remembers! Before getting in line, there was the ritual of stashing the weed and hiding the wine pouch (over the shoulder but inside my shirt under my arm) and taking a hit of acid. I remember walking up and seeing this super long line that was moving at a snail's pace, because they were letting in one person at a time. I had never seen this at any of the concerts I had been to, even at The Pit (which is what we call the basketball arena).

We were in line forever. Stevie Wonder started playing and we still had such a long ways to go, but at least we could hear him – and we were high. As we got close to the front of the line, you could see they were searching people, purses and bags. The trash cans were full of booze, and some drugs. Walking through the doors you knew they didn't get all the drugs. You could get high on the air. We finally got inside to see Stevie Wonder play his last two songs. Then it all becomes pretty foggy…

Mick Jagger was fascinating to watch. I wanted to hear more of the older music, but it was all good.

CAM KING

I was in my sophomore year at the University of New Mexico when the Rolling Stones were initiating their tour for 1972. Dates were still being filled in during the early spring, and the campus buzz was that there might be a chance they would play in Albuquerque. The campus paper, *The Lobo*, blazed out a full-page headline before the end of spring semester, 'Sympathy for the Devil, June 15.' I don't recall exactly by what means I bought my ticket, but I did so as soon as I could. The venue was The Pit, the subterranean excavation that served as the UNM basketball arena.

I have never been comfortable being part of a mob, so I was a bit nervous as I gathered with a fairly unorganized group at the north end of the arena on the late afternoon of the concert. There may have been access points at the other three sides, but I remember being told that this was the official entry point. It was an hour before showtime, and the crowd was as polite and accommodating as an anxious crowd of 1970s rock fans could be, when all of a sudden there was a hue and cry as a gang of young toughs tried to cut into the front of the crowd. They were soundly rebuked and pushed aside, and I remember the looks on their faces, as if they had made their best shot and it didn't work. The one thing that permeated the post-hippie years of New Mexico was the feeling that there was always a dissipated group of ne'er-do-wells who constantly tried to exploit the good natures of those around them, and on this occasion they failed.

I had somehow been able to smuggle in my father's Bell & Howell Super 8 movie camera, with the Ektachrome film that had the highest ASA for such an environment. Once I got inside, I was a bit disappointed, but not surprised, to see that at least 200 people had already gained access to the front rows from the stage to a third of the way back from the stage. And another thing struck me as strange – Stevie Wonder was being introduced, even as masses of people were still pouring through the gates. By any measure, this was a classic Albuquerque SNAFU.

I was situated high up on the north side, and I was pretty much by myself. This concert was not a sell out. It had been announced late, promoted poorly and managed even worse. But the Stones had a stage and they did not attenuate their performance simply because it was a low profile gig. They were pros and did their thing, but I honestly do not remember anything that rose above a competent rock performance.

Jagger was fairly reserved, and only rarely spoke, 'This is our first time in Albukherkhe…', but the crowd was receptive. It was a coup for the promoters and any other entities who drew status enhancement from the event, and I remember it fondly as a performance where Stevie Wonder did his best even as people swarmed into the seats in front of him. The Stones were comfortable, if not exciting. We can't have it all.

I have footage of Stevie Wonder and of the Stones performing 'Midnight Rambler' and snippets of other songs. It might be time for a digital transfer and to share it with the world.

JOHN RUCKER

I was almost a sophomore at UNM. The good news is I was lucid for the show. I remember wondering if Stevie Wonder really was blind because of the ease with which he moved between instruments. He is such a phenomenal musician. I think I remember the Stones opening with 'Brown Sugar' and closing with 'Street Fighting Man'. I do remember that it was a great concert.

JEFF SIMON, AGE 16

I knew the Stones were coming with Stevie a few months before the concert and I really wanted to go, but I couldn't afford it. My older brother was living in LA at the time and he called one day and told me that the concerts were sold out there, and that if I'd run down to the box office in Albuquerque and get tickets for him and his girlfriend, he'd pay for me and a friend to go too. I got to the box office pretty fast, and was lucky not to get a speeding ticket.

My brother and his girlfriend flew in the afternoon of the concert and I went to pick them up. We drove straight to The Pit (the UNM Arena) and hung out, doing pre-concert rituals and watching the crowd that was gathering several hours before the music was to begin. There was lots of variety in the crowd, which I guess was due to the Stones' wide appeal and the fact that Stevie was with them. There were hippies and Hare Krishnas and cowboys, people under the influence, and women and girls across the spectrum.

When the doors finally opened, it was strange because while people normally rushed in, the crowd stayed outside for a long time. My brother said this was called a 'pre-concert groove'. Everyone was mixing and small groups had formed all over the grounds. We finally got to our seats and the smell inside was pungent from pot smoke. Our seats were off to the left side of the stage a bit.

Stevie did a great set, highlighted by the encore of 'Superstition'. Once he was finished, we figured there would be a long break before the Stones took the stage. But about 15 minutes later, here they came. They blasted from the first note, 'Brown Sugar', and went straight into 'Bitch' without a break. Mick Taylor was more reserved, like Bill Wyman, but he was killing it on both of these tunes. He laid back for 'Can't You Hear Me Knocking', but then really rocked for the next few tunes, including

'Street Fighting Man', 'Sympathy for the Devil' and 'Gimme Shelter'. I was spellbound. During 'Midnight Rambler', my brother nudged me and pointed… It took me a second to realise what he was pointing at, but on the SRO floor were two girls on their boyfriend's shoulders without tops on. At one point, Mick climbed to the top of the PA on our side of the stage and sang most of 'Jumpin' Jack Flash'. A few times, we had our focus on the band broken by joints passing through the crowd.

Keith and Mick did a lot of antics, pretend fighting and arguing, and, of course, Mick did a lot of strutting. The encore was 'Honky Tonk Women', a very extended version it seemed. We tried to get them out for a second one, but I guess we weren't insistent enough. The arena was slow to empty, and we stayed another hour milling around outside, just meeting strangers and reliving the concert.

TERRY WOLLITZ

I worked security that night. I was so loaded that all I remember is the opening song, 'Brown Sugar'.

TOM CARSON

We were parked near, and listened to it. It was pretty bad, actually. I was glad we didn't waste our money on it.

DAVID SANCHEZ

I was there. I set out on a cross country hitchhiking trip the next morning and saw them at RFK Stadium in DC a couple of weeks later.

SUSAN CARR

I had to sit in the back of the stage. Stevie was great. I was less than impressed by the Stones performance. The price for the tickets I will always remember!

BILL ATWELL

I was there. I am not, or ever was, a Rolling Stones fan so I am not the best judge of the show. However, Stevie Wonder was incredible. He played every instrument. I saw Jethro Tull the week before. They were my 'go to' band and, in my opinion, played a much better show.

DAN LOSH

It was an excellent show. The band was at its peak. Stevie Wonder was also in his prime. He was a very hard act to follow but the Stones were definitely up to the task.

ORLANDO MEDINA

Jagger had that emerald in his tooth that looked like a piece of spinach and the band were using those godawful lucite guitars. Stevie Wonder was fantastic as the opening act. He did a bit where he played every instrument.

PHILLIP DOYLE

I didn't see the concert. I was selling hash (five bucks a gram) and acid (Orange Sunshine, for a dollar a hit) under our cover of selling carnations out of ice chests. The cops came and checked us out. We showed them the chests with flowers in them, except for the one I was sitting on – that had our stash in it!

PHYLLIS MORA ARAGON

I stood in line but was on Orange Sunshine so didn't notice the wait. Going inside and seeing the yellow and red dragon floor and then seeing Stevie Wonder was awesome. The Stones were off the hook!

MATTHEW SANCHEZ

A few weeks before the show, I walked into Gold Street Circus Records on Central and bought two tickets for $12. The Stones show was fantastic but Stevie Wonder stole the show with his performance.

MICHELLE HARRIS

I remember someone climbed up on the top of the trusses for the speakers. Because of the huge rush to get in the door, I got separated from my two friends and ended up sitting with people I didn't know, but I had a blast. I thought Stevie stole the show!

ANN STOCKLY-ARMIJO

I was there but had too much Electric Kool-Aid on board from the gallons of it passed around in the crowd outside that hot summer afternoon. I remember Stevie Wonder's great performance more than the Stones. I'd like a do-over.

TODD JAY

It was such a big deal that the Stones deigned to come to little ol' Albuquerque. When the show was announced, the *Daily Lobo* had a huge headline along the lines of '19th Nervous Breakdown on the 15th'.

CHIP MONCK

We carried a fully painted floor with a dragon and griffin on it that was a full 45 feet by 30 feet depth. We had all of our own follow spots. In 1971 in Europe, we carried our own forklift because you never knew what you were going to get, but we fitted comfortably into two trucks.

The lighting system I devised with the mirrors came about because I was trying to avoid the occasional 'phoned in' show. What's the most important focus for Mick and Keith? Themselves. Originally, it was designed for them to view themselves. But then I had a better use for it – fuck them!

I questioned the logic. Why carry those house follow spots up 200 steps or five flights of stairs? Why not just put them on the back of the stage behind the amps? The length of throw was half what it would be from the ceiling and it was going to double my intensity. Blood looks like blood. And clouds look like clouds. So we'd take the lamps out of the truck, put them behind the amps, four feet away. I'd make sure I could reach each operator with a long headset cable, because the carbon arc lamps had a trim that burned for only 42 minutes.

We needed a 30 second changeover, so the supers were pointed upwards. You'd wipe the copper spatter off the reflector with ether and return to the mirror. But you couldn't look anywhere else or you'd lose it. If you replaced them incorrectly, the light source wasn't in the middle of the area that it had to be for the reflector and the reflective lens, and then it would not be bright enough, so it was learn as you go.

You didn't have to turn the lamp off to make these adjustments. Just be careful, if you open the door, not to flood the stage with the light, so you'd point it somewhere where you don't intend it to be. It wasn't a terribly large show but it was certainly large enough for the time. And the impact was at times stunning and every now and then we would just squeeze by.

My intention was to bring the band out of the dark and make sure that everybody saw them and listened to them, and in the right order. The size of the iris from the bottom of the guitar to the top of the head was the circle you were basically lighting your secondary player or primary guitarist. Mick had two lamps and everybody else had one lamp.

Whatever was happening on stage was the emphasis. The directorial finger would be pointing, 'Now, look at this because he's going to do something.' You teach the audience how you want them to react to the show. All it is is color and movement. I would be at the piano. Most of the pianists would be kind enough planning to let me use a portion of the piano surface and I'd run a manual board with eight follow spots. The cable was long enough to get to each one of them.

JOSE CAMPOS, AGE 18

I was there at the UNM Pit. My friend sold me a ticket for four dollars. Stevie Wonder opened the show and performed for over an hour; he had the crowd going. The Rolling Stones performed just a 45 minute set and didn't even do an encore. I heard later that Mick was pissed off that Stevie stole the show!

LINDA ROCKWELL

My first husband, Davis Gauntt, and I stood outside of University Arena with a group of our friends. We were 24 years old and absolutely beside ourselves with excitement. We had been Rolling Stones fans since we were sweethearts in high school in Roswell, New Mexico, and at long last we were going to see our favorite rock group in person. Finally, the doors opened and we took our seat a little to the south of half court on the west side of the area.

After waiting for what seemed like forever in the happy and excited crowd, a person walked out and led Stevie Wonder, the opening act, onto stage. I had never particularly been a Stevie Wonder fan, but I was after that night, and I still am to this day. He opened with 'For Once in My Life', which I had heard before, and I was transported. I do not recall the rest of his songs, except for 'Superstition', but I think he ended with 'I Believe'.

After Stevie's set, the crowd started cheering for the Stones, and when they came out, the arena was electrified. When they opened with 'Brown Sugar', the crowd went crazy. Mick Jagger was jumping and swaggering around the stage with superhuman energy. Keith Richards looked very stylish. Charlie Watts looked calmly out at the crowd. Someone in our group knew Bobby Keys, the saxophone player, and we were excited that there was a person with New Mexico connections performing on stage.

They went into 'Bitch', 'Rocks Off' and 'Gimme Shelter' in rapid succession. The crowd was standing, dancing and singing along. When they got to 'Sweet Virginia' the crowd absolutely exploded. One young man somehow got onto the basketball goal at the south end of the arena, and he was dancing up there and having a great time. Somehow. he managed not to fall, and everyone was cheering for him. Their last number was 'Jumpin' Jack Flash', and again the crowd was dancing and singing along. I think the encore was 'Street Fighting Man'.

I have been to a number of Rolling Stones concerts, but this one was my most memorable. Subsequent concerts that I have attended have been flashier and in nicer venues, but this one was the most fun. We went out for dinner and drinks with friends after the concert, and we could not stop talking about how wonderful Stevie Wonder and the Stones were. 50 years later, it is still a very happy memory.

WALT NYGARD, AGE 22

In June '72 I was living in Albuquerque, New Mexico and working while on summer break from the University of New Mexico and about a year and a half back from the United States Marine Corps and the Vietnam War. I was a Stones fan from when they first came on the scene in the US. I still have all those pre-Seventies Stones albums. Naturally, when I heard the Stones were coming to UNM, I was elated.

I wasn't surprised, even though Albuquerque's kinda off the national radar. I'd seen Cream at the University Arena in '68 – their last tour – right before I went into the Marine Corps. Albuquerque was a seriously hip town and an important crossroad.

The concert: I was with a girl who I barely knew, a former classmate I never saw again and I was concerned when I found our seats 'cause they seemed to be behind the band, but kinda close. The energy was palpable. I don't know how many people were there, but everybody was high speed.

Stevie Wonder was the warm up act and he was great. He was all over the stage. He had a great band but he also played every instrument and finished up strutting around the stage in the arms of two gorgeous black chicks…

The Stones came on like a musical assault team with 'Brown Sugar'. But they didn't waste any time, cranking the electricity through the crowd. Everybody was screaming, singing, waving and weaving. Pot smoke wafted around us like a cloud bank. *Exile on Main St.* was out and brand new. I already owned it but the songs were not yet grooved in my consciousness. That process began that night. One song I really liked was 'Happy' and it was way cool when Mick, in a kidding, disbelieving kinda way proclaimed that 'Keith's gonna sing a song.' And did he ever! There's a lot of songs on *Exile*, but that's my sentimental favorite.

I was hoping they'd play some old '60s stuff, but didn't really have time to worry about it 'cause them just kept that '72 playlist coming. And then they did do 'Bye Bye Johnny' – which I had on a German Stones album and always liked better than 'Johnny B Goode'. For me, that was one of the best songs of the night. When Mick introduced the band – with Mick Taylor in his first US tour with the band – he confirmed what I'd suspected. The skinny guy on piano was Nicky Hopkins, another personal fave from Jeff Beck and Quicksilver days.

The crowd was amped, but very cool. I had a friend who was on duty that night with the campus cops. He had his cop hat stolen off his head. There were a bunch of burly characters in the vicinity of the stage. According to my friend, they were members of the Denver Broncos. Apparently, the Stones wanted a better job done than Hell's Angels had done in '69 at Altamont.

Outside in the night, the Sandia Mountains loomed over the city to the east. Mother Nature got into it and heat lightning flashed along the top of mountains…

It's the best concert of my life.

PAUL KMETKO, AGE 15

I had hair down to my waist and played in a band. We were pretty tuned into the music scene of the day. At least, we thought so! It wasn't uncommon to trek off to Denver, El Paso or Phoenix to see our favorite bands. Tickets were $4.50, which was almost double the amount other bands were charging at the time. Jethro Tull, with Head Hands and Feet two weeks earlier at the same venue, was $2.50. Stevie Wonder played for 90 minutes and put in a great show.

The Stones came out and thought they were in Phoenix. I can't recall if Mick ever even mentioned Albuquerque. Needless to say, they got booed and rushed through a meager 45 minute set with no encore. It was pretty loud and at times hard to discern which song they were playing. We were all disappointed with the Stones show and, though other opportunities arose to see them later on in life, I passed and purchased their albums instead.

Reading about the police action outside and the request to play longer would explain why they were in such a hurry to skedaddle. They were probably afraid there would be a riot and didn't want any part of it. I heard they were in transit before the crowd stopped cheering for an encore. The airport is about ten minutes away from the venue where they played. And this whole time we all thought they just hated Albuquerque…

I still think they are one of the best bands ever. Being a drummer, I was sure sorry to see Charlie Watts pass and hope they continue on.

RICHARD HUGHES

We had a large group and a couple of us queued up early (5pm for a 7pm gate opening). The others arrived later. Once it got close to 7pm, no one respected the nice orderly queue and it was all 'festival seating' so we all arrived on the floor to the right of the stage around the same time. Squish. That summer I saw my first three concerts at age 17, living in Las Vegas, New Mexico (two hours from Albuquerque). The others were Led Zeppelin and Jethro Tull.

ROY MANFREDI

I worked that concert for Albuquerque Police Department. We had six officers and a sergeant. The crowd was huge when we got there, and two hours before there were 7,000 to 10,000 people. Most were already high and we had a hell of a time getting them in line. It was really hot and there were kids throwing up and passing out all over.

I went inside for the Stones' first song and, looking down from the top, I was amazed that no one in the first rows were hurt as the crowd surged forward. It was not my kind of music – it was too loud - and the smoke from the marijuana was so thick that I could not breathe so I went back outside. I worked most of the big names that came to Albuquerque and this was one of the biggest. The crowd was mostly peaceful. They were too stoned out to cause trouble.

SANDRA ASHLEY

I was pregnant and smashed in the front row, but everything turned out amazing.

It was a great concert. 20 something years later, I took my son that I was carrying back then to see them. He didn't have a seat on our trolley and a friend said he'd take him. He ended up riding in a limo with Sheryl Crow and meeting everyone backstage. I will never forget his smile as he came from backstage wearing a *Bridges to Babylon* tour leather flight jacket.

SHARON SAYED KING

My 18-year-old twin sister and I went. We were not stoned. I remember very long lines and it being hot, with lots of people passing out and throwing up because of this. I was exhausted by the time we got in and the 'air' caused me to sleep after the first song, 'Brown Sugar'. It's still my favorite, even though they will no longer perform it.

STEVE SPENSLEY, AGE 18

I went with a couple of lady friends. I've always been a big fan of the Stones. For me, it is awesome to hear the announcer say, 'Ladies and gentlemen, the greatest rock and

Steve Spensley went with a couple of lady friends

roll band in the world, THE ROLLING STONES,' and then the lights come on and – boom! - there they are.

RON ROMERO

My buddy Rich Greene drove us there. But my ticket got wet and was slightly faded so they threw me out, saying it was counterfeit. I had to walk about five miles home.

RICH GREENE, AGE 16

One day, while cruising the streets of Albuquerque in a white Ford Econoline van on my route as a delivery boy for a dry cleaners, I heard on the radio that the Rolling Stones, the World's Greatest Rock 'n' Roll band, was coming to The Pit, more formally known as University Arena, on the University of New Mexico campus. I could not believe my ears — the Stones in little old Albuquerque? No freaking way!

So that afternoon when I got off work, I called my buddy Ron, my best friend since fifth grade (and eventually best man at my wedding) and told him the news. He was as excited as I was.

The first day tickets went on sale, we hustled our butts down to our favorite record store and got ours. If I remember correctly, that precious ducat set me back a whole twenty bucks, and at the time set a record for the most expensive concert ticket ever in the Duke City, and nearly my entire whopping $25 weekly paycheck. But hey, these were the Stones – second only to The Beatles (but of course the Fabs had broken up two years earlier, and stopped touring four years before that) and Mick and the boys were the reigning rulers of rock. No way was I going to miss this concert. I had been to a lot of basketball games at The Pit, and knew first-hand how loud it could get when the Lobos played – 125 decibels according to experts, close to the threshold of pain for the human ear and louder than a 747 jet engine at take-off.

The day of the show, I finished my route about 5pm, drove to Ron's, picked him up and we were off to The Pit in my POS '66 Opel Kadette, a car that we usually had to get out and push through intersections at most red lights when the light turned green. It'd do zero to sixty in about six minutes on a good day.

We thought we'd be smart and get there early, because the concert was general admission and there was always a mad dash to the floor; this one would be an even madder dash because the floor of The Pit is 37 feet and 40 rows below street level. 6pm arrival for an 8pm show should've been no problem. But as we exited the freeway, praying we wouldn't have to push the good ole Opel up the hill to the venue, the traffic started backing up, and we saw that others – many others – apparently had the same idea we did.

The mass of humanity surrounding the building waiting for the doors to open was packed as tightly as cattle being led to the slaughter. We pushed our way into the throng at the southeast entrance and mooed slowly toward the doors, hoping to not get crushed in the process. Once we finally made it in, we thought we were home free and started to make a beeline toward the closest aisle down to the floor.

But all of a sudden in my peripheral vision, I saw a scuffle to the right of me and turned to see a couple of beefy security dudes, no doubt UNM football players picking up some extra spending cash, grabbing Ron by the shoulders and forcibly dragging him along the concourse back toward the doors.

I ran over to him, wondering what the hell was going on, and he yelled they were throwing him out because he had a counterfeit ticket. I thought 'no way!' since we had bought them at the same time. I dug my hand into my pocket, pulled out my stub and tried to show them the numbers on our tickets were consecutive, but our protests fell on deaf ears. He pleaded with them saying his ticket had gotten wet in his wallet when he went fishing the week before and the colors ran. These dudes though weren't buying what he was selling.

Not only that, the concert was a complete sellout, so it wasn't like he could even buy another one. Finally, resigned to the fact he wasn't going to see the Stones that night, Ron turned and said to me, "OK, man, let's go." I stared incredulously at him for a second — thinking, come on, man — you can't be serious! There's no way I'm going anywhere! So I did the first thing that came to my mind – lamely offered him the Opel keys as the gridiron gang tightened their grips on him and unceremoniously escorted him out of the arena.

My conscience told me I should be a good friend and follow him out, but that thought only lasted about a second as I came to my senses and rationalised that if the tables would've been turned, he would have done the exact same thing to me and I wouldn't have blamed him for a second.

After that total bummer of a start, I continued my quest to get to the floor and made it to the nearest aisle leading down, and looked and saw the floor completely full, and the rest of the 15,000 seat arena was too. It happened amazingly fast and I was starting to freak that I might be forced to sit behind the stage.

So I improvised — there were literally no seats left, and I'd had enough of being crushed by the crowd on the way in, and didn't want to go through the same thing down on the floor, so I walked about halfway down the steps and sat down in the aisle like others were doing below me. I did sit far enough over to the side so people could still go up and down the steps.

Then they started making PA announcements asking people to clear the aisles or the concert wouldn't start and the fire marshal would close it down, but no one budged and everyone started booing to drown them out. Finally the lights went down, and the boos morphed into that 125 decibel roar as Stevie Wonder was led to the stage and put on an absolute killer set. Seeing Stevie was an unexpected treat because I had no idea who the opening act was going to be. Most times it's a band or solo artist nobody has ever heard of and the crowd doesn't even pay attention to them because they're impatiently waiting for the headliner.

But when Jagger and company finally hit the stage, and Keith struck those unmistakable opening chords to 'Brown Sugar', the dude sitting in the seat next to me turned with a knowing smile on his face, and passed a joint my way and I blissfully spent the next 90 minutes watching a band play live that I never dreamed would come to my hometown.

The next morning I called Ron, knowing he'd probably be pissed at me for staying. Surprisingly, he actually was pretty calm about the whole thing and told me he walked all the way home - nearly nine miles. I did the math in my head and figured he probably got home about the time the last notes of 'Street Fighting Man', the last tune of the three-song encore rang out.

We heard later that apparently there were a lot of counterfeits that had been sold and many fans suffered the same fate he did. The only problem was, his really was legit.

Now nearly half a century later, we still laugh about that night - and he did eventually get a refund, too. Small consolation, though, for having to go through the humiliation of being tossed out like a two-bit criminal and missing the biggest concert ever to hit Albuquerque to that time.

Over the years we've gotten together to see other concerts even though we now live 800 miles apart; him still in Albuquerque and me in LA. Back in September of 2019, we were going to meet to see The Who in Denver, but Roger blew out his voice two nights before in Houston, and the band cancelled the rest of the tour. It was rescheduled, but then as fate would have it, the pandemic hit. We're still waiting for that one.

YESTERDAY'S PAPERS

CHARLES ANDREWS
DAILY LOBO, JUNE 16, 1972

Bill Wyman didn't move a muscle for 90 minutes. Mick Taylor moved one or two. And Mick Jagger moved everything. He aped with those famous rubber lips and bumped and ground those skinny hips, and moved 15,000 Stone fanatics to a final ovation-roar such as the cavernous Pit has never before witnessed, a roar that was finally ebbing about the time the performers were boarding their jet at the Sunport to head for Denver.

When Jagger hit the stage with his purple-and-silver outfit, purple eyeshadow, two pink stars pasted to each temple just behind the eye, obscenely sucking on a lemon and discarding the parts one at a time, and hopping across the right half of the stage so the glitter in his hair would fly off leaving a sparkling star shower trailing behind him, I knew I was going to enjoy the show.

Jagger's antics during the instrumental break in 'Gimme Shelter' made it what it should be; his duet with seldom-singing Keith Richard on

'Happy' was just great, even if I couldn't hear it very well; the realisation during 'Tumbling Dice' that the Stones are a machine, and that Jagger could damn well still be doing at age 60 what he's doing now (he wears 30 well) – he's got that much gall; finally hearing the piano and horns come through beautifully on 'Sweet Virginia', a generally well done acoustic number; Jagger leaning into the audience, shaking his finger, and really meaning it when he tells everyone, 'You Can't Always Get What You Want'.

But with 'All Down the Line' and everything that followed, there was no possible argument: hard, fast, loud, sweaty, driving, sexy, pure rock 'n' roll. The Best. By the World's Greatest Rock and Roll Band. By the time they finished just after 10.30pm, there could be no doubt left in anyone's mind of their claim to the title. 'Midnight Rambler' followed 'All Down the Line', and Jagger simply outdid himself on this one. Just incredible. I've seen people before who could move well, and those who are totally united with their music. But Jagger surpasses every concept of performance to become an astounding musician whose instruments are his body and soul. It's easy to believe, as you watch him writhing-mugging-kicking across stage, that the music would stop if Jagger did.

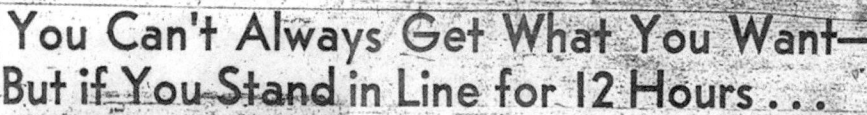

Photo: *Daily Lobo*

Charles Andrews wrote the concert review for the *Daily Lobo*

The roar that followed them up the ramp (and out of the building) was ungodly, deafening. I've been to dozens of concerts but I've never experienced anything to compare with it. I've never heard an audience scream so loud and long for one more number; I honestly believe most of the people would've paid another three bucks for an encore. The tumult did not subside for ten minutes.

What do you do after Rolling Stones concert? Go see *Gimme Shelter*? (You could have, at the Guild that night and the next.) Make long, passionate love to your one and only in the back of your camper? Go home, ingest your best stuff and turn *Let It Bleed* all the way up? What I did was look up at the sky right after I staggered out of the arena, and laugh as I tried unsuccessfully to convince myself that the lightning storm I was witnessing was not the final production number of Rolling Stones US Tour 1972, chapter Albuquerque.

The Stones moved on from Albuquerque, heading north to Denver.

DENVER COLISEUM
JUNE 16, 1972, DENVER, COLORADO

CAPACITY	10,200
SHOWS	2
ARRESTS	75

STEVE CREER, AGE 16

My upper level ticket was $6.50. I saw the afternoon show in Denver. I have very vivid memories of it. There was a lot of Orange Barrel acid involved. 'Gimme Shelter' brought me to my full senses, and 'Happy' was awesome. I've seen them more than 30 times since, but that show brought me to the fold.

PRISCILLA FOOTLIK, AGE 17

In June of 1972, I was a 17-year-old girl who had just graduated from high school the previous month. I had a summer job, a boyfriend, and an exciting future as I looked forward to college in the autumn. When I saw that Barry Fey was bringing the Rolling Stones, it was a no-brainer that we must get tickets. I think they only cost $10 apiece. I attended the show with my boyfriend, his best friend and my best friend. It was sort of a set-up date for my good friend and his. The Coliseum was this huge, loud cavernous building, and our seats were on the floor, but really far back. However, it was a festive atmosphere with frisbees flying and pot smoke wafting all about.

Stevie Wonder opened. It was really cool to see him play the drums, throw the sticks in the air and catch them. Then the Stones came on with 'Brown Sugar' and the place exploded. Our excitement reached a crescendo when my best friend Hillary fainted and my boyfriend's best friend Tim caught her. We were standing on top of our seats at the time, so this was a particularly dexterous manoeuvre. Hillary recovered, and she and Tim did date for a time. I had seen the Stones before that show, and would see them again in the future, but the memory of Tim catching Hillary was what has most stayed with me over the years.

ED HARMS

I saw them in '72 and again in '78. They were not as tight or as good in '72. '78 was outdoors at Folsom Field in Boulder, Colorado and it was the best concert and one of the best days of my life. Thanks for your part, Charlie. RIP.

JAMES PAGLIASOTTI

I was a working journalist in 1972 at a time when the metropolitan newspapers in this country were not commonly carrying advertising for record albums. I came along just at the right time and was asked to report on a few events about what I guess you would call the hippies or the counter-culture at the time, and was criticised by the editors for editorialising. And I said to them, 'Well, I can't be impartial here' – because people were being beaten in the streets for having long hair – 'and where am I supposed to express this?' And out of the blue – I was

23 years old – they gave me a column twice a week in the *Denver Post*, which at that time had a circulation of about 600,000, which for the center of the country was a very influential paper. So it was a remarkable experience. I stumbled into it, literally. I was just out of school. That was 1968. The Summer of Love had just happened. The counter culture was a big thing, and of course the US was deeply involved in Vietnam, which was a huge issue for people my age because there was conscription then and people were being drafted to go fight in this war that nobody believed in – at least, no one I knew, and so it was a very interesting period of history. I felt very fortunate to be in the right place at the right time and to have a front row seat for all this strange activity that was taking place.

I saw the Stones in '65 and maybe '66 and then again in 1969. They opened the tour in Fort Collins, Colorado, which at that time was a little town. It was where Colorado State University happened to be. And that date on the tour came about because the Stones had not planned to play Denver and Barry Fey, who was a pretty prominent promoter by that time, and eventually a partner of Bill Graham and others, was very persuasive and convinced them to do what they called a warm up show. I believe it was the smallest venue they played on that tour. It seated about 15 or 16,000 people. And that tour was the beginning of the really big shows. Bands had obviously toured before that, but that was the first time in my experience that a band was going out with an entourage to conquer the United States and did so very successfully – until Altamont, of course.

In 1969, if you look at any of the photographs from that tour, the thing that strikes me always is there was a change that took place between the '69 and '72 tours that the Stones exemplified. In '69, it was still pretty much face-t-face between the band and the audience. The stage was raised, obviously, but not very high, and actually there were people with their elbows on the stage while the Stones were performing. It was that intimate, and even though they were starting to play to much larger crowds, there was that intimacy. That really changed in '72.

I went on five shows on the '69 tour. Backstage was like a case of beer and some potato chips or something. In 1972, backstage was catered meals and premium brands of liquor and French champagne. It was all done on Persian carpets and it was quite a difference. And I think we saw that in the music too.

The Stones were always great, but they were feeling their way with the music and the production of the music. In '72, everything was first class. It was just beautifully done. I loved both tours. I thought the band were incredible and I still to this day think that the Mick Taylor era was the best that the Stones ever were.

I think back to 1965 when I saw them – I can't remember how many people were there but it was a fairly small crowd of mostly girls screaming, and it was hard to hear anything. And in 2006, when they played at the Superbowl at half-time, they played in front of presumably 90 million people, so that change in that culture was so profound.

In '72, I think we saw the beginning of what we think of as sex, drugs and rock 'n' roll and that change from being the voice of the people to being big-time entertainment and big-time productions.

In addition to working for the newspaper, I did freeform radio at a station in Denver called KFML. The Stones were going to play two shows in Denver and a night off the following night. KFML proposed to Barry Fey, the promoter, that we have a big dinner for them. It was quite an event. It was a 13 course meal for 80 people, with two whole pigs roasted on a spit over an open fire, and goose and duck and oysters. It was a big deal.

They went to Indiana after they left Denver and I wasn't able to get a connection to that city, so I picked them up two nights later in Chicago. They did two shows in Chicago and then went to Kansas City and did one or two shows there. And then went to Fort Worth, Texas and did a couple of shows there. And that was my experience with them.

I saw them again a number of times after that, but not backstage. Things changed a lot too, in the sense that in '72 I had a press pass so I could go pretty much anywhere I wanted. By the 1975 show, when I saw them in Fort Collins, Colorado again, there were layers on backstage. My room mate was one of Mick's bodyguards – Tony Funches – and Tony said to me, 'I'm sorry that doesn't get you backstage anymore.' So things were beginning to be a lot different.

It was wonderful. The finest concert I ever saw, and I reviewed many concerts, was The Who. But I've seen so many great shows that the Stones have done, and I've always been a huge fan, not only of their music and what they've accomplished, but just that sheer endurance to do what they've done over the years.

I remember when the *Steel Wheels* tour happened, and they didn't play Denver. Everyone joked about it being the 'steel wheelchairs' tour because the band were so old. And that tour took place in the first half of their career. These guys are just phenomenal people.

I was such a fan, not only of the Stones and the band but what they represented, that sense of artistry and of doing it the way they wanted to do it. Not the way Elvis and others did it. The Stones captured the artistry and the ability to express their artistry in a way that started with Dylan and The Beatles. Dylan and The Beatles and others really changed the music business, because all of a sudden, the artists were at the top of the heap, instead of doing what the suits were directing them to do. When The Beatles started Apple Records and the Stones started their own label, that's really when the business changed, and hopefully for the better.

In 1972, they played a staggering number of shows in just two months. I was exhausted after being with them for just five shows. It was sex, drugs and rock 'n' roll literally. I was 24 years old at the time I first went on tour with them. After five shows I was absolutely exhausted and they still had most of the tour ahead of them. It was incredible.

JOSETTE BALLERT KOETS

My high school years were spent with weekends at the Grande Ballroom in Detroit seeing the likes of Cream, Ten Years After, Joe Cocker and gang, Muddy, B.B, Albert and Freddie and on and on. The Stones had eluded me...

In 1972, I was a college student in Michigan, and as luck would have it, a friend who had two tickets for the Denver show couldn't go. Lucky me and my boyfriend (now husband)... $6 tickets, sixth row center at the 4pm show. We had to scrape up gas money and, luckily, we knew a person in the area to stay with. (Things have a way of working out sometimes.) Of course, it was a fantastic show and a highlight was my only time watching Stevie Wonder live. It was kind of strange leaving

Josette snapped the Stones in Denver in 1972

the concert and finding that it was still daylight. The set list was heavily centered around songs from *Sticky Fingers* and *Exile on Main St.* as well as some earlier songs.

We were able to visit the tiny Muscle Shoals recording studio a couple of years ago, where *Sticky Fingers* was recorded; unfortunately, it was closed for that day. And I was thrilled to see the Stones again in Minneapolis in November 2021!

YESTERDAY'S PAPERS

SAM MADDOX

COLORADO DAILY, JUNE 23, 1972

The first two-tenths of a second of 'Brown Sugar' hit the fans, and I never in my life have seen a higher peak of mass ecstatic hysteria. Outside of a couple of nasty World War II crowd gatherings scenes in history class movies… Mick and the band work pretty hard for their money. But they were getting off, too. There was no half effort to conserve energy for the late show... How can anybody keep up the pace that the Stones are expected to keep up? When it's all done, will America's youth be the same? Will the Rolling Stones be the same? Will they still outsell Jesus Christ? Think they're using too much coke? I hope everybody has as a good time as we did in Denver, and that nobody gets hurt.

MET CENTER

JUNE 18, 1972, BLOOMINGTON, MINNESOTA

CAPACITY	17,500
SHOWS	1
ARRESTS	10

COLLEEN FOLEY, AGE 16

I was still in high school and went with my high school boyfriend Tommy and several of my pals. I was a huge, huge fan and was thrilled to see them from row 3. My biggest takeaway was that a friend was able to grab Mick Jagger's empty beer bottle and later gave it to me with a rose

Colleen Foley (left) was at the Bloomington show with her high school boyfriend Tommy

in it. Needless to say, security was different back then. I can't remember specifics of the show – I wish!

JIM FISCHER, AGE 19

I was a Bob Sims Usher at the Met. It was a very memorable show as we were big fans. *Ya-Ya's*, *Sticky Fingers* and *Exile* had all come out in high school so we were really excited. We did security for the general admission show and there were lots of counterfeit tickets. The Bloomington police used tear gas to try and break up the crowds outside, but there was no air conditioning in the building at that time so the ventilation system pulled the tear gas into the building. The Stones had spotlights mounted behind the band reflecting off of a parabolic mirror above the stage. There is a DVD of the show and it looks pretty primitive by today's standards. But it was really cool at that time in rock history. We'd had The Who in the summer of 1971. Those were my two most memorable concerts.

JIM REYNOLDS

I was either just about to graduate or had just graduated high school. They played at the old North Stars hockey rink. I went with my brother and our friend, Jeff, who has passed. I'm sure we drank a lot of beers and smoked some dube. I know they put on a great show because we talked about it for years. Concerts were very reasonably priced back then, probably $10-$15.

SCOTT SCHMECKPEPPER

I remember going to the restroom right before the show, and there was a guy passed out in there. He never saw the Stones despite standing out overnight for tickets!

YESTERDAY'S PAPERS

ROY M CLOSE
MINNEAPOLIS STAR, JUNE 19, 1972

Last night's concert was no treat for the connoisseur. It was often difficult to hear. It was all but impossible to move, as the aisles were clogged with spectators. And by the end of the concert, as tear gas from the outside skirmishes between ticketless Stones fans and police began filtering into the building, it became decidedly unpleasant to breathe. But the concert did demonstrate convincingly the excitement the Stones bring to a live performance.

The Stones stayed at the Playboy Mansion as guests of High Hefner whilst they performed at the International Amphitheatre. In his autobiography, Life, Keith Richards says that he and saxophonist Bobby Keys nearly burnt the place down.

INTERNATIONAL AMPHITHEATER
JUNE 19 & 20, 1972, CHICAGO, ILLINOIS

CAPACITY   **9,000**
SHOWS   **3**
ARRESTS   **25**

JOEL MEYERS, AGE 18

The Stones played three shows in two days in Chicago. I saw the first Chicago show. It was 100 degrees inside, and there was a very earthy must in the air due to the Royal Lipizzan Stallions having been the previous show. I was in the mezzanine, but after Stevie Wonder and a half hour wait, the lights finally went down and a shot of adrenaline went through me. Without pre-planning, I jumped the railing to the opening chords of 'Brown Sugar' and went down onto the main floor where I made my way to the front of the stage. Between the heat and the crunch of the bodies, the only escape for those who were overwrought was to be lifted on stage and given a security escort off – including a guy in a wheelchair!

Photos: Joel Meyers

Photos: Joel Meyers

It was a great show and when it was over – 90 minutes and no encore – and as the Amphitheater emptied, we saw all the cheap metal seats in the first ten to 15 rows had been crushed under the weight of the people standing on them. The poor Andy Frain ushers!

I didn't bring my camera to the first show, which was the most chaotic. I didn't intend on moving to the front and being pressed against the stage. I would've had great shots of the show and its aftermath if I had. I did have eighth row seats for the second show, and I took my Instamatic to that one.

Joel Meyers took his Instamatic camera to the second Stones show in Chicago

CHUCK EYERS, AGE 18

I saw the first night and remember Mick saying 'broken strings, broken strings all over the place,' in response to, I guess, lots of broken guitar strings. I also remember the place going crazy when they brought the house lights up during (I think) 'Bye Bye Johnny'.

I saw both shows the second day, and clearly remember large movie cameras being present at both shows. So, somewhere, professional footage exists of both these shows. The house lights came up later in the set in both the second night shows, I think to prevent the chaos that broke out the first night. I did not see film cameras present the first night, which is unfortunate. Bill Wyman's wife Astrid is quoted in Robert Greenfield's *STP* book saying that the first Chicago show was the only one that reminded her of the wild audiences in the early days. I guess she felt fans had grown tamer.

JEFFREY MICHALAK, AGE 16

My friend's dad worked at Sears Roebuck. They were a ticket outlet so he was able to get three tickets in the eighth row center: I think they were like $6.50 a ticket. Stevie Wonder was the opening act. They played about 75 per cent of *Exile on Main St.*

I've seen the Stones six times and only one time have I had nosebleed seats. All the other times we were close up. Ronnie Wood threw a guitar pic to my ex-wife at a show when we were able to get up to the stage. I shook hands with Mick and with Charlie as they came down the catwalk to the little stage at a show in 2006. The best show was a fan club show at the Aragon Ballroom in Chicago in 2003. There were only 2,500 tickets and we were standing the whole show, just ten feet from the stage.

TOM DENHAM

I was in the US Navy at the time, stationed in Chicago. My wife worked at a Montgomery Ward department store. In those days, Ticketron was inside the store so she was able to be one of the first people in line and we got eighth row seats. As soon as the Stones came out – I mean the minute they hit the stage – everybody stood up, and then by the time they were halfway through their first song, everybody was standing on their chairs – for the entire show! It was right after the release of 'Brown Sugar', and I don't believe in my lifetime I was ever so totally immersed in a song like that. It was like that saxophone was my heart.

I am an old guy now and still a musician and I have seen a hell of a lot of shows. But nothing ever matched that Chicago show.

DAVID MATEJKA, AGE 16

I was a Stones fan in earnest from when the *Let It Bleed* album came out in 1969. To me, the Stones epitomised the spirit of rebellion that was finally starting to grip places in the Midwest, plus the Stones were heavily into drugs, which we sort of admired back then. (The joke back then was, 'There is a drug problem around here, we can't get any!') By the time 1971, '72, rolled around, and after *Sticky Fingers* came out in '71, me and my friends were really ready to see them. I was 16 years old then, and had just got my driver's license.

I secured tickets for the early show on June 20th up in the second mezzanine for me and two of my friends, Randy and Roger, which we came to really appreciate. We didn't want to bring girlfriends because of the debacle of Altamont and the unpleasant reputation that Stones concerts had as being near riotous.

1972 was a hot summer, and on the day of the concert it was very hot and steamy. All of the local radio stations were serenading us by repeating the Stones' latest hit, 'Tumbling Dice'. But inside the International Amphitheater, where the concert was held, it was as cold as a meat locker!

Stevie Wonder opened and the crowd was impatient and impolite. There were a lot of chants of 'bring on the Stones' and 'Stones, Stones!' It wasn't a happy crew at first. But when everyone realised Stevie was going to perform his set, people started to get into the music and when he did a song called 'If You Really Love Me', most people were on their feet, clapping along. Then Stevie was over and there was a good hour between him and the Stones.

Finally, we heard, 'And now, the world's greatest rock and roll band, the Rolling Stones!' and the place went up for grabs. Now we saw why those mezzanine seats I bought were so good.

From when the show started until the echoes of the last note faded away, the entire main floor seating was up. The crowd may have sat down briefly for a couple of short periods, but basically if you had main floor seating you were standing for the entire Stones set. Since me and my friends were pretty high from weed and as much beer as we could get down, the prospect of standing wasn't appealing. So I guess it's true that sometimes it's better to be lucky than smart, because I originally wanted main floor seating!

The Stones started with 'Brown Sugar' and 'Bitch' and then 'Rocks Off', which sounded like it needed more work, frankly. In my opinion, some of their songs such as 'Gimme Shelter', 'Tumbling Dice' and 'You Can't Always Get What You Want' suffered and sounded weak because the Stones didn't have female backup singers on this tour. My friend Roger didn't agree, and felt Jagger carried the show well on his own. Randy was so messed up he didn't really express an opinion!

Since this was the *Exile on Main St.* tour, I remember them doing 'Loving Cup', 'Sweet Black Angel', 'Sweet Virginia' and 'Ventilator Blues', and those songs were great. But the highlight was 'Midnight Rambler'. Everyone was on their feet and clapping along. I'll never forget Mick Taylor's fingers flying on the frets. He acquitted himself well that day.

They closed with 'Jumpin' Jack Flash' going into 'Street Fighting Man' and rained confetti down from the rafters on everyone. They might have done an encore too, but I'll be damned if I remember!

THOMAS FILIP, AGE 20

We camped out all night in front of either Wards or Sears – I can't remember which – who had the Ticketron at Woodfield Mall so that we'd be in line to get good tickets. I recall that to pass the time while waiting in the queue all night, we played penny poker. Nobody won as the money kept changing hands all night. We camped on hard concrete with nothing between us and it but a sleeping bag, but as I was a lad of 20, it mattered not one whit! I was seeing the Stones again, having already seen them in '69.

MARY GLUSAK

The International Amphitheater was a dump. They played two shows in one day and my sister and I went to both. They did that several times in Chicago. (Little) Stevie Wonder opened. We were actually in the tenth row, but jammed in. The music was pretty rough because the sound system, or lack of it, wasn't very sophisticated.

YESTERDAY'S PAPERS

DENISE DECLUE
CHICAGO EXPRESS, JUNE 21, 1972

Mick Jagger, the prancing rock 'n' roll peacock, came off like a tired stripper doing his same old tired, bisexual, symbolic and outlandish sex act at the Amphitheater Sunday night. But I don't think it was all his fault. Without benefit of movie close-ups, arty shots, and super sound, the Stones, from the 74th row in the Amphitheater, don't quite make it. The sound was a fuzzy drone, so bad that it was often hard to make out what song they were playing….

Both the men and women in the audience were with him Tuesday night, gyrating, clapping, screaming. It was no 14-year-old faint-a-thon. The crowd seemed generally older and uptight with riot rumors and premonitions, and sometimes experiences lurking in their psyches… I borrowed some binoculars and for a moment the whole scene changed. The small and strutting figure turned into Mick Jagger, wet with sweat, his white open-chested shirt ripped and falling off his shoulder, his face pursed, then petulant, then lusty. His eyes flashed, and he twirled his red sash, his hips quivered, and his pelvis jagged. He was beautiful. Not homosexual, heterosexual, or even bisexual. He was extrasexual.

MUNICIPAL AUDITORIUM
JUNE 22, 1972, KANSAS CITY, MISSOURI

CAPACITY	7,300
SHOWS	1
ARRESTS	0

MARK IRVIN

I was a Stones fan from first listening to 'Time is on My Side'. I was playing in a band with friends. We dressing in blazers in the winter and Beach Boy-looking clothes in the summer. When the Stones burst onto the scene, that was the end of Goody Two-Shoes-looking guys. We were rockers in jeans and chambray shirts from then on. And we played every Stones song. It was the beginning of a 50 plus year love affair.

Photos: Mark Irvin

Mark Irvin was at the Kansas City show

I went to this concert from Warrensburg, Missouri while in grad school. I didn't have a ticket, but I offered a guy 20 bucks (a lot of money then) for one and actually got the best seat I ever had for a Stones concert. I finally got to take my sons to see then in Denver a couple of years ago.

KIRK BOAND

The best thing about the Rolling Stones' 1972 North American tour was the blending of Mick, Keith, Bill, Charlie and Mick Taylor to produce a unified tune that moved fans to a loving, rocking space that we all were caught up in! Many real treats were on the playlist, such as 'Sweet Virginia', 'Starfucker' and the addition of material from *Exile on Main St.*

YESTERDAY'S PAPERS

PEG McMAHON
KANSAS CITY STAR, JUNE 23, 1972

The first appearance of the Stones on stage in Kansas City unleashed all of the energy the crowd had been saving for them. On stage, bathed in blue and yellow spotlights, Mick Jagger was everything Stones fans have come to expect. In a purple velvet bellbottomed jumpsuit, a long purple sash wrapped around his waist, Jagger personified the menacing, ambivalent but open sexuality that gives the Stones music its power... It was a well-conceived, well-organized, well-packaged and well-executed show. What else is there to say? It was the Rolling Stones.

Both shows in Fort Worth were recorded for a planned live album and concert film. The film, Ladies and Gentlemen, the Rolling Stones, was released in 1974 and given a full theatrical re-release in 2010.

TARRANT COUNTY CONVENTION CENTER
JUNE 24, 1972, FORT WORTH, TEXAS

CAPACITY	13,500
SHOWS	2
ARRESTS	0

BILLIEJEAN BAKER-STALCUP

I was there. I was the blonde 22-year-old screaming close to the stage at my favorite, Keith.

PHIL RILEY

I remember the huge silk dragon rug or banner on stage, Mick Taylor was the the guitarist, I believe there were either popcorn or rose petals in nets on the ceiling, they were released at the last number.

DON YOUNG

When I was 13 years old in 1965, I was a paper boy in Fort Worth, Texas. I carried a transistor radio with me on my paper route which I did twice a day, at 4am and again after school. I heard the Stones on that radio as I delivered papers. I bought my first album, *High Tide and Green Grass*, in '66. Before that, I saw the 45rpm singles at a friend's house and was mesmerized by the blue-and-white spiral design of the London Records label. It was different from the orange and yellow-colored labels of the Beatles 45s, and somewhat exotic to me.

Don Young remembers Keith's lucite guitar

117

I think I first learned about the blues from those early Stones tracks. I bought the *Aftermath* album later and loved 'Paint It, Black' but, most of all, 'Under My Thumb'. The vibraphone intro really turned me on.

When I first saw them live in Dallas in '72, with BB King opening, they were a different band. The main thing I remember from that concert was Keith Richard's clear lucite guitar when he played 'Gimme Shelter'.

MARIE HOGAN

I was asked to go to the concert with a fella that I liked and he liked me. The day of the concert I stood him up for a fella I really liked. I've regretted it ever since. But I did get the fella I really liked!

ROGER WOOD

My Dad was the pastor of a growing church. In 1960, he purchased two acres of property with a church and a home on it for $50,000 in 1960 in the area of Rainier Beach, south of Seattle. It was an area that had long been the home of both Italian and Jewish communities, but the African-American community had begun to move from inner city Seattle into Rainier Beach. A lot of the Jewish and Italian families sold their homes and we immediately experienced what was called a 'white flight'.

But we stayed. Dad said, 'Well, I've always been taught that you grow where you're planted. I'm not leaving.' Our church changed. The schools changed. The stores changed. And I became a product of that environment. My first girlfriend was a black girl, and my best buddies were African-Americans. That was just the way it was. I had no problems with it at all. They were my best friends and that's all I knew. It was the opposite of what African Americans often experience, being a minority in a roomful of white people, and it set the tone for my adulthood.

Dad took me and my brother Greg out of school after my seventh and his ninth grades. I grew up with a young African American man, Felix, who became our 'brother' because he lived in our home from the age of about 12. Felix had great musical talent and the three of us just started hobnobbing musically on the black gospel music of the day, starting in 1964, '65.

Dad wanted to be an evangelist. He was a pastor for 40 years. He bought several tents and trucks and trailers over the years, and I travelled in those and learned to drive and to set up tents, and I learned to play the music and sleep on the platform, and sleep in sleeping bags and army cots as security during the nights. Dad also connected his ministry with a very large national ministry out of Arizona called the A A Allen Revivals, a very multi-cultural movement of God. We hooked our hitch to that and touted and played music with that ministry and got to know those guys, who sang and played music very similar to ours. They were maybe eight or ten years older than us, and we modelled ourselves after them.

There was always a healthy respect between the travelling evangelists that would come through the church and sometimes they'd bring organists from back east – Detroit, Philadelphia, Dallas – all guys older than me. I'd sit there behind the B3 on the church stage, aged 13 or 14, just soaking it up and learning to play from that.

It was through this whole concoction of people that we had this opportunity handed to us to go and play with the Rolling Stones. I was almost 17, my brother Greg was almost 19 and Felix, who was under Dad's custody, was almost 20.

Dorothy Norwood called us. Dorothy was an artist out of Atlanta, Georgia who was originally a member of The Caravans, which was really Cesar and Clara Ward, and they were very, very famous, by James Cleveland, so when that band broke up, the Clara Ward Singers went out on their own and Dorothy came into her own as a gospel storyteller. A lot of the stories were about how God can come in the eleventh hour and save and restore, the traditional gospel approach.

Dorothy did not tell us specifically that it was the 'Rolling Stones and Stevie Wonder'. She said it was a 'worldy' tour. This was a term that church people understood to be non-religious – the devil, the dark side. We didn't ask any more questions. We were enthused about it. We thought it would be awesome. We said, 'We'll do it.' Dorothy said, 'I really want you to come but I really don't want it to affect my relationship with your father in ministry.' She was a gospel singer so she'd come to our church several times and concerts. 'I can't tell your dad. You're gonna have to do that one on your own.'

Dorothy sent us airplane tickets. We flew out of Chicago O'Hare to Dallas Love Airport, outside of Forth Worth. The first concert was that afternoon. We hadn't practised. We had done some concerts with

Dorothy over the last two or three years, and there were a few other players from different parts of the country that she assembled. My brother played drums, I played keyboard and Felix was one of her background singers along with two black girls. And there was a piano player from LA called Richard Littlejohn and a bass player out of Atlanta, Georgia whose name I forget. Dorothy was the lead vocalist.

When we arrived in Fort Worth, we had a concert that afternoon. We had two in Fort Worth and two in Houston. We got out of a limousine, got hailed over the speaker in Dallas Love for a limousine and I said, 'Oh my God, Greg, where are we going? Is this royalty or what?' We jumped in the limousine and the limo driver took us to the back of this huge coliseum. I was looking at Greg and thinking, 'Are we in the right place?' The doors opened and there was a bunch of semis and people walking around. We got out and Dorothy was there and she said, 'Hi, you guys,' and we were like, 'Phew, someone we know,' but I was still going, 'What's going on? Where are we at?' She goes, 'We're opening for the Rolling Stones and Stevie Wonder.'

My first impression was, 'Okay, cool!' I felt like we had broken chains and gotten out, not just into freedom, but freedom to do something we really loved to do and had wanted to do for a long time, and that was to express ourselves in a more seasoned contemporary musical way, and not be locked into just gospel music and gospel patterns. It was insane.

That was when I met Truman Capote, who was walking past with Bianca Jagger.

Dorothy goes, 'Hurry up, I got to show you your dressing room. We're due on in about an hour and 45 minutes.' And that's when I first heard that and I was like, 'My God, what are we going to do?' She goes, 'Oh, we'll just do some of the standards,' as she walked us back to the green room she'd set aside for us and herself and the rest of the band. There was beer in the cooler there and I remember opening the cooler and going, 'You guys – look! It's beer.' We'd never in our life been around beer. We'd seen it in the stores when we went to buy sodas as kids, but we knew not to touch it. And so here it was, in front of us, our own in our own room, so it was just very overwhelming.

Before that show, the three of us were introduced to Stevie Wonder. We were standing backstage and he was brought over to us by a manager.

'Stevie, this is Roger Wood,' and I put out my hand and his manager helped him grab my hand, and then he ran his left hand up my arm all the way up to my shoulder, feeling my anatomy and my height. He came to my ear and he felt my ear and my jawline, and he said, 'Very nice to meet you.' And he put his hand out towards my brothers and he did the same thing with Greg and Felix. Later, we were told that was how he gets a visualisation of what you look like. He feels your hair, whether you have any whiskers, and your maturity or whatever. That was quite the experience. He was the typical Stevie and I was like, 'Oh my God, I can't believe this is actually happening.'

We did a 20 minute set, Stevie would do a 45 minute set and the Stones were supposed to round it out each time with an hour and a half. We would sit backstage after our part of the shows were done and Greg and I would go and sit in the shadows behind the Stones' Marshall stacks, peeking around the corner on one of the ends.

We could see the baby grand piano that Stevie was playing. His back was to us and he was at an angle, so you could see the keys. He would play with four fingers on each hand and Greg said, 'Is that braille?' It looked like a metal strip of braille running along the key bed, just below the keys. He had his thumbs on that, and he would check in with his thumbs on the braille.

Stevie invited us into his dressing room. The dressing rooms were huge, with tons of Kentucky Fried Chicken, imported cheese and wine from France and just a bunch of different stuff. And there were tons of different people coming in and out of the room. Stevie and the Stones would go back and forth between each other's rooms, and share and talk and laugh, and we got swapped up into all of that.

We called Dad and told him we had made it to Fort Worth and were at the County Convention Center and when he heard the name of the venue he said, 'What? What would you be doing there? There are no black churches or revivals or concerts there. You said it was the chitlin' circuit, going from storefront to storefront.' He started to smell a rat. He called a Norwegian woman who lived in Fort Worth by the name of Leona Norberg who we knew, and who looked after us when we were young and when Mom and Dad went on little journeys, and asked her to look us up at the stadium.

So Leona came to the stadium, found security and had Greg and I paged from inside the stadium. They opened the door for us. We walked up this big truck ramp and there she was. Greg said, 'It looks like Leona,' and I went, 'Man, it is.' We went, 'Leona!' and she went, 'Boys! How are you? And what are you doing here?' We said, 'We were just playing with Dorothy Norwood.' We knew not to say the Stones or Stevie Wonder or anything 'worldly'. That would have been an admission.

She said, 'It sounds like you're going to have a good time. There's a lot of people there. She's a great gospel artist.' And pretty soon Greg says, 'Well, we're gonna have to go, because we've got one more show to do.' Leona obviously reported back and told Dad exactly where we were, and you could see on the marquee that it was the Rolling Stones.

SCOTT PERRY, AGE 15

I saw the last concert before Stevie quit the tour, in Fort Worth in June '72. The late show. Several clips from this show are included in the movie, *Ladies and Gentlemen*. My favorite is 'Midnight Rambler'.

I had to bum a ride and then waited all day in 100 degree heat for the 8pm show as my driver had tickets to the 3pm show. They didn't play 'Midnight Rambler' at the early show. At the end the cops threw open the doors during the finale of 'Street Fighting Man' and the crowd rushed in. First tune was 'Brown Sugar' and Jagger took off his cap and glitter went everywhere. My best friend was there and he passed away in April. Couldn't believe Keith outlived a doctor. Sent a floral spray of Stones logo to his funeral.

Jerry Hall is from my hometown of Mesquite and is the same age as me. She was rumored to be at the show. It's tough when Mick Jagger comes to your hometown looking for girlfriends.

CONNIE SMITH DOTSON, AGE 18

I was 18 and went with my cousin. It was popcorn. People were eating it out of each other's hair. We had seventh row seats. Five people were standing in our two chairs.

YESTERDAY'S PAPERS

JERRY ZENICK
FORT WORTH STAR TELEGRAM, JUNE 25, 1972

More than 28,000 fans and a film crew flocked to watch and hear one of the few remaining groups from the rock breakout period of the mid-Sixties. What they saw was Jagger – dressed in silver lame jacket, sequinned t-shirt and skintight hiphuggers – prance, slide and literally crawl across the stage for almost three hours. What they heard was an assortment of new tunes off the Stones latest album, *Exile on Main St.*, and a batch of oldies. Best of the lot were 'Brown Sugar', 'Gimme Shelter', 'Happy', 'Tumbling Dice', 'You Gotta Move', 'Sweet Virginia' (an acoustic arrangement, emphasising how mature a voice Jagger has when he's not wailing 'Midnight Rambler' and 'Jumpin' Jack Flash'.

HOFHEINZ PAVILION
JUNE 25, 1972, HOUSTON, TEXAS

CAPACITY	10,000
SHOWS	2
ARRESTS	81

ROGER WOOD

After the second Fort Worth show, we were to hurry up and get to Houston, because the very next day we had an afternoon and an evening show in Houston. Dorothy seemed to be having the time of her life. She seemed to be like a kid in a playground where she had never much been herself. Just by watching her we caught wind that she was breaking a lot of the norms of all of our upbringing and Christian traditions. We weren't judging her in any way. It was just like, 'Wow, okay. I thought Dorothy was this and Dorothy was that and now she's out there drinking it up and partying and having a good time.' Well, she's older than us so who am I to say anything? She was probably twelve or 15 years older than us, in her early thirties.

She had a limousine. It was down in the back, behind the stage with the big folding doors where they let the big semi trucks in and out to unload stuff for the stadiums. We came over to the limousine and couldn't see who was all in it, thinking that was our ride. We had our bags with us. But Dorothy said, 'Oh, I'm sorry,' – and one leg gets out of the back of the limousine – 'we don't have any room in the limousine. But, Greg, you're the oldest – here's fifty dollars, you can catch a Greyhound bus to Houston and I'll have the limousine pick you up at the Greyhound station in Houston.' She gave us a fifty dollar bill.

Our jaws hit the floor a little with disappointment. It was really busy. People were all getting out of there and it was time to go and the trucks were loading up and people were exiting, and at that moment, a gentleman came over to Greg and goes, 'The Stones said you're more than welcome to fly with them on their jet.' I was about four feet away from Greg and I looked at Greg and he looked at me – and we both had that look of fear. And Greg said, 'Oh no, we really appreciate it but we'll be fine, we're just gonna catch the bus.'

I'm really glad I wasn't on that plane. Years later, I watched a lot of footage from the *Cocksucker Blues* video of those airplane rides. Dorothy is in the film. She was about to go on stage and she's snorting coke with what looks like some supplier. He's lining up a couple of lines, and he goes, 'How do you feel?' and she says 'I've never done this before.'

Houston was quite a trip. Taking a Greyhound bus and landing in Waco, Texas at 4am with just a pimp and a couple of prostitutes in the bus station for company. The place was empty and some guy was asleep on the floor and it was a 'what the hell' moment. We had just shared the stage with rock 'n' roll royalty and Stevie Wonder, and here we are, let loose to forge on our own.

YESTERDAY'S PAPERS

JOHN SCARBOROUGH

HOUSTON CHRONICLE, JUNE 26, 1972

The Stones at first seemed dampened a little by the substitution of a soul gospel group, led by Dorothy Norwood, for Stevie Wonder and his band... Apologizing, Jagger promised, 'We're gonna do our best.' It took a while, but they finally did... With the first bars of 'Midnight Rambler', Jagger, sipping from a jug of Black Jack Daniels, caught a little tailwind and took off. A slow guitar vamp by Mick Taylor and Keith Richard found Jagger sinking to his hands and knees, expiring onto the boards, rolling his eyes, then jerking himself up and razor-stropping the stage with a wide gold leather belt. With a nerve-fracturing scream, his lavender eyeshadow moist and spangled temples aglitter, he was up again, trotting jigs on one foot, his other knee bumping, grinding and jabbing. From then on it was the same old freaky Stones everyone had expected to hear (plus saxman Bobby Keys, pianist Nicky Hopkins and brass player Jim Price), churning out the world's meanest rock and roll...

MOBILE CIVIC CENTER
JUNE 27, 1972, MOBILE, ALABAMA

CAPACITY	10,112
SHOWS	1
ARRESTS	12

DAVID WILLIAMS

I saw them in Mobile, Alabama, with Stevie Wonder opening for them.

These are the best seats I ever had at a Stones concert. The auditorium seated around 10,000. I knew people that were still put off by Alatamont and who put some of the blame on the Stones. There were not any issues with the audience. Many were from out of town, as Mobile was one of the few venues in the area. I was used to travelling to New Orleans to see big name acts, and was amazed that Mobile and Tuscaloosa, Alabama had tour dates.

MARIANNE PARKER DEGRADO, AGE 18

I was just the right age for the British Invasion and loved them all, starting with The Beatles, but the Stones were the best for me – plus Mick had a girlfriend called Marianne. I live in Pensacola, Florida, about 45 minutes from Mobile, Alabama. It's a relatively small town and we didn't get a lot of really big concerts very often. In 1972 the Stones were huge, so hearing they were coming to Mobile was unbelievable. Even with tickets in hand my friend and I still couldn't believe it was happening. I drove over with a classmate named Philip. We were unbelievably excited and we made our way to our seats. I still have my ticket stub – all

For Marianne, the Stones were the best

of $7.50! Stevie Wonder opened the show and, as much as I like him, I couldn't wait to see the Stones.

Finally, there they were. Everyone was on their feet from beginning to end and it was just incredible. We were even standing on our chairs. I think I saw just about everyone I knew there. At that point, we'd never seen anything like this. I remember Mick asking us to sing along on 'Sweet Virginia' and Keith broke a guitar string. During 'Love in Vain', someone in front handed Mick one of those trainmen signal lanterns and he took it. In those days they didn't do encores but it was incredible just the same; I thought the roof was gonna blow off the auditorium by the end because people were going nuts. I was just speechless on the way home, and I was so happy. I've seen them several times since and they've always been great, but the first time is still special for me.

After the Stones came, just about everybody came to Mobile and we had concerts every couple of months, so I was able to see Elton John, Eric Clapton, Springsteen and Prince – just about everyone I wanted to.

RON BAYGENTS

It was the day after my 19th birthday. I drove from Gainesville, Florida to get there. It was the first of 23 Stones shows I have seen to date – and the best one!

BILL PETRO

These were the best seats I ever had at a Stones concert. The auditorium seated around 10,000. I knew people that were still put off by Alatamont, and put some of the blame on the Stones. There were not any issues with the audience. Many were from out of town, as Mobile was one of the few venues in the area. I was used to traveling to New Orleans to see big name acts, and was amazed that Mobile and Tuscaloosa, Alabama had tour dates.

ROGER WOOD

We did the Houston show and then we went to Mobile, Alabama and that was where Dad caught us on the phone, after the show back at our little hotel. We three were all sharing one room. My brother got the phone call and he said, 'Hey Dad!' and I looked over and said, 'Aw shit!' Greg was quiet for quite a while. That meant Dad was talking, on and on and on. Greg was trying to speak, 'But… but… but… but…' and then he'd get quiet again, because Dad would interrupt. He was dropping the law. 'You guys are getting out of there.'

Dad nicknamed me 'CC', which I later learned stood for 'Chronical Complainer'. I was always the guy who would ask why. 'Why Dad? Why do we have to do this? I need to know.' That used to hurt him to death. As a man of faith, he didn't have those answers yet, because he was just going by his heart and whatever God led him to do. I was looking for logistics. There's no real logistics in faith.

I got close to the phone. Greg just opened it up from his mouth. He didn't hand it to me but he let me talk. I said, 'Dad, this tour ends up at the Madison Square Gardens in New York. I will probably never ever have a chance to play Madison Square Gardens and this is that chance. Would you please, please let us finish this out? We've been good. We've played. You know us. You have to trust us.'

And he goes, 'No, absolutely not. I've already sent you guys airline tickets in Nashville and as soon as your show's done in Nashville, you're flying right back to Chicago.' He said, 'That's all I want to say about this. So put Greg back on.' Greg was rolling his eyes.

That was a shattering night. We had kids that had followed us back to our hotel. They were slipping joints under the bottom of our hotel room door and milling out in the hallways. So we had every opportunity to be the people that Dad thought we had become in the course of three days; Satan's children. He didn't trust the thing that he had put in us.

That was a great eye opener for me when I really thought about it. Here was a man of faith, who really believed in what he taught, and we were his number one soldiers, with him all the time. He knew our behaviours, yet he could not bring himself to trust everything that he had put into us. He couldn't let it go and let it flourish on its own, to see how we do with it.

YESTERDAY'S PAPERS

KEVIN MCCAFFREY
MOBILE REGISTER, JUNE 28, 1972

The sound levels and mixing were raunchy, which was disappointing. Keys and Price were continually frustrated by mics and monitors which they couldn't hear. Jagger's voice sometimes was fading, and then got too loud. Hopkins was rarely heard. A pity, actually. The entire concert was sensational but could've been better. The sound is what it's all about.

NATALIE CROZIER
MOBILE PRESS, JUNE 28, 1972

Everybody stood clapping and stamping along with the beat and enjoying the performance. Unfortunately, there were some distasteful scenes, like girls dancing frenziedly on chairs, grinding their boot heels into the soft, easily torn cushioning… Jagger closed the concert by throwing kisses to the thousands of worshippers and tossing huge handfuls of red and yellow rose petals to those nearest the stage.

From Mobile, the Stones headed to Tuscaloosa, Alabama, where one Chuck Leavell was in the audience.

MEMORIAL COLISEUM
JUNE 28, 1972, TUSCALOOSA, ALABAMA

CAPACITY	14,000
SHOWS	1
ARRESTS	18

JIMMY BANK

Back in the '60s and '70s, the Memorial Coliseum was the primary college venue for shows. It's where Elvis played his first ever college show, and Jimi and Janis and most of the superstars of the era played

Jimmy Bank worked security at the Tuscaloosa show

there. I worked security at the side of the stage, inside a metal barricade or fence of some type. The security badge or ID that I wore for the show wasn't exactly elaborate! Stevie Wonder was the opening act. While I was

watching him, a man came up next to me to watch and listen. I turned
and looked and it was Charlie Watts. He made a comment to me about
how good Wonder was. We listened and chatted for a few minutes and
then he politely excused himself and said that he had to go get ready for
the show.

The Stones had an enormous mirror hanging over the stage so that
fans at the other end of the floor could see them. We had never seen
anything like that. And I remember Mick, when he came on stage,
doffed a cap he was wearing and sparkly things came out falling to the
floor. Again, that was a stage presence that we weren't used to back in
those days.

ROBERT REGISTER, AGE 22

I worked security at this show for the University Program Council, or
UPC. The deal was that BAMA had a large venue and Birmingham
didn't, so big shows came to the 'new' Memorial Coliseum on the
University of Alabama. Hendrix performed in Tuscaloosa in '69 and he
was booked by the Cotillion Club, a frat-rat BAMA student organization.
UPC booked the Stones in '72. UPC was more freak-independent-
oriented, but for all its counter-culture aspirations, it was just as snooty
and clannish as the Cotillion Club.

I didn't belong to any student organization, but from 1970 until 1972,
my part-time job as a BAMA student was Union Building Maintenance
Man and all student organizations had their offices in my building. I'd
run into most everybody and that's how I ended up working security for
all the concerts, plus I had master keys to every door on the University.
UPC security was trying to make folks behave and follow whatever the
regulations were for a concert. An example was Jethro Tull, where we
closed seating on the floor as soon as all the chairs were full. I was in
charge of that gate at Jethro Tull, and that's how I met my first wife, but
I didn't marry her until 16 years later.

The Rolling Stones show was different. It was festival seating all the
way – 16,000 first come first served so all we did was open the doors and
let 'em pour in. I'll never forget that the late Bob Roberts was the first
person on the floor. How he did it I'll never know, but he had played
football at BAMA so he had practice running over people.

The folks who worked security that night got there in the afternoon and witnessed this incredible production take shape. It was a full Hollywood stage hand union outfit. I had never seen that before. They drove the speakers into the venue on carts and those carts had two pillars that extended somehow and raised the speakers above the stage. They suspended this huge Mylar mirror across the hall and all the lighting was onstage. It was one or two rows of Super Trouper spotlights behind the band, each operated by a union member. The spots were reflected off the mirror so there was no need for security outside the stage. All lighting was on the stage behind the band.

At most gigs, we students got a free t-shirt with the band's name on it. I had graduated in May but was still on the UPC list, so even though I was not enrolled I still worked concerts during the summer and fall of '72. But for the Stones there was no t-shirt. All we got was a name tag with the Stones lips and tongue on it.

I saw this cat who looked just like Bobby Whitlock but he denied it. I still think it was Bobby Whitlock. Bianca Jagger was running around like a chicken with her head cut off. She was wearing this white dress with a wide brim hat, kind of a 'down on the old plantation' costume. I'm pretty sure I saw Truman Capote too. His daddy and granddad had lived in Tuscaloosa so he'd been to town plenty of times.

Chip Monck was the stage manager. My job was to make sure nobody got to him or messed with his cables or electronics so I was on the left side of the stage during the show, not on stage but below. The stage was about 12 feet high so nobody could get up on it.

The stage was covered in formica, with two Donald Duck dragons painted over it. A stagehand came out and mopped it with 7-Up so Jagger wouldn't slip when he went to the edge of the stage. The gospel group wasn't about much, but Stevie Wonder got us stoked.

The show was amazing. Imagine this dark hall and a glowing 'STONES' right in the center with spotlights hitting the mirror and reflecting down. There was no lighting coming from the arena. By 'Midnight Rambler', the crowd was going wild. When they broke into 'Street Fighting Man', the crowd started trying to jump onto the stage from the upper levels and somebody sent me up to stand behind the rail and warn folks that they might get hurt. Some girl fell and started yelling at me so I quit the job. I tore my name tag off, walked into the crowd and enjoyed the rest of the show.

I was bad about eating hash brownies before a big show like that, but I wasn't too buzzed that night because I'd done too much at The Who in the fall of '71 and didn't wanna have a bad reaction at the Stones so I enjoyed the performance. There's a lot to learn about that tour. It was the biggest production I've ever seen before or since.

BILL HULLETT, AGE 23

I was a student at the University of Alabama. That night was truly an experience. I went with one of my best friends, Neil Armingeon. We caught a ride with a friend of Neil's whose name I don't recall. I do remember that the first time he stopped at a red light a half a block from the light, I was told he was tripping on LSD! We made it safely to the show, but we were late and had to sit in the very last row in front of the stage. The smoke was so thick we could hardly see the band and the sound was so loud you could feel it on your skin. I saw lots of concerts in that building – The Who, Led Zeppelin, the Allman Brothers, The Beach Boys and Elvis, but none compared to the 1972 Stones.

I remember reading that the Tuscaloosa airport didn't have the right machine to restart the Stones jet, so they had to leave it running the whole time they were in Tuscaloosa.

BOBBY SNYDER

It's probably the best Tuscaloosa concert I've attended, with Elton John in 1976 a close second. The Stones opened with 'Brown Sugar' and the crowd stood up and never sat down for the entire concert. Jagger was on fire – dancing, singing and jumping everywhere. And Stevie Wonder was great as the warm up act.

GEORGE HADJIDAKIS

I drove with friends from Huntsville to see them. I was at the front door getting squashed all day until the doors opened. At first, we were disappointed we weren't in the first row but once the show got going, our seats a few rows back turned out to be perfect. I remember it like it was yesterday.

BRUCE HOPPER

I discovered the Stones in the Sixties with their first big hit, 'Satisfaction'. That got me into their albums and I discovered their music was based on all the old blues masters. I was already playing music in rock 'n' roll bands at that time and began to cover their music. This has continued to the present day.

The 1972 show in Tuscaloosa was the largest crowd to play the Coliseum. It was very oversold. The capacity was 14,000 but there were 17,000 in there. All of the aisles were jammed and no one could move. Since there was no way to enforce smoking, a cloud began to form. Stevie Wonder was the opening act, but his performance was definitely that of a headliner!

The Stones had a unique light projection setup. The lights were behind them and a huge convex mirror was hung in front of them. The lights were then reflected back onto the performers. It was a great show, with the Stones playing crowd favorites.

In 1980, I bought a local bar, The Chukker. An old musician friend of mine had left town and joined the Allman Brothers. He would come by the bar to see me when he was home visiting his mother. One night in 1981, Chuck came by to see me. The conversation went like this, 'Hey Bruce, you won't believe who I played with last night in Atlanta.' 'Who, Chuck?' He answered, 'The Rolling Stones, and they offered me a job!' That totally blew me away. We spent the rest of the night celebrating his good fortune. Chuck would still come by after that and sit in with the bands I had playing in my club. He is one guy that kept a good head after becoming famous.

CHARLOTTE BLACK, AGE 18

I was eight and a half months pregnant at 18. Hey, it was free love… The show was so great. Pot was being passed around in great quantities, and I imagine the police forces were having a great contact high. People were so excited. The music was great, and I remember people dancing and swaying and singing along… Great, great music in an herbal haze. What times we all had back then. I have seen the Stones three times since, and I made my kids go see them in Birmingham in 1989. They are now glad that they experienced rock and roll history! But this Tuscaloosa show was the best for me. We even saw Mick's wife, Bianca Jagger, on the side of the stage.

CHUCK YOAKUM, AGE 19

I saw them at the University of Alabama in Tuscaloosa. Stevie Wonder opened for them. It was a festival seating show meaning there was no assigned seating, so once the doors opened, it was a chaotic and dangerous dash to get seats. Many people had arrived days early and camped outside the coliseum. It was very hot and the crowd was packed so tightly that you literally could not move or faint or do anything but try to stand and hope you didn't get trampled. There were only a few doors that were opened to let the crowd in, and there were wooden barriers like cattle chutes to funnel us in. As for the actual show, the whole thing was phenomenal.

I was 19 at the time and playing in a band called Nod. All the band members went to this show and we managed to get pretty close to the stage. As I recall, there was a gospel group on first and then Stevie Wonder came on. He did a fantastic set and at one point played every instrument on stage. The Stones came on after a fairly long delay and were in top form. Mick Taylor was especially good and Jagger controlled the whole evening. His back and forth with Keith drove the whole performance and kept the audience in high gear. I think this must've been one of the better shows on the tour.

CONNIE MILES

I was very happy when I went to see the Stones. Everything was going my way – young, happy in love, and going to the University of Alabama. I was rocking a halter top and palazzo pants. My boyfriend let me drive his Corvette from the concert. I wish I had pictures. I should go to some antique shops and look for some of the University of Alabama *Corollas* (yearbooks) to see if any photos made it to press.

DOUG STALLINGS

I just remember red roses being thrown by the band and/or the audience, and Mick Jagger kissing a rose – trying to be sexy? 'Brown Sugar' was awesome. My family and I attended church with Chuck

Leavell and his family. As teenagers, we would go downstairs at his house and listen to him play. His mother, who also played the piano, was friends with my mom. My mother casually mentioned that Chuck's mom had invited her to sit backstage at some concert and that she had refused the invite. I asked her who it was and she said, 'Somebody named Stones or something.' Ha!

DOUG THOMASTON

How I got a ticket I can't tell you, but I did. I was very impressed with the 'new' act they introduced...Little Stevie Wonder. You didn't need to smoke a doobie to get high, you just had to take a deep breath. It's one of the best concerts I ever attended.

DUANE A BLALOCK, AGE 19

Me and two friends drove from Atlanta to Tuscaloosa, smoking joints and drinking all the way. We booked a room at the Holiday Inn. The show was great and I remember Keith Richards was playing that see-through clear body guitar, maybe an Ampeg? After the show, we saw a huge party going on in connecting rooms and wandered over. It was Stevie Wonder's entourage and it was a wild party. There were many comings and goings, with lots of drinks and other substances. My friend says Keith Richards was there, but I don't remember…

Duane A Blalock gatecrashed an after show party Keith may have been at

JOHN HULSEY, AGE 14

It was a sold out show and I sold my $5 ticket for $100. I was 14.

CHRIS W SPENCER

I had to agree with a front page article in the *Tuscaloosa News* the next day. The opening paragraph mentioned that even if you didn't smoke any marijuana at the Stones concert, you couldn't help but inhale some of the smoke that filled the Coliseum.

JANET STEVENSON

What I recall most clearly is being horrified at the rudeness to Stevie Wonder, the opening act. He was booed by many people around me. Despite this, he gave an incredible performance. Honestly, I think he was better than the Stones that night.

JOHNNY SPRINGFIELD

It was a hell of a good show, one of the best ever. My understanding is that the band had made arrangements that no one could be arrested inside for drugs and that that was standard policy on the entire tour. We sat on the third row and lit up with a university policeman ten feet away and no problem. I did hear of several arrests outside the venue.

LINDA SCHAFFER LONGER

I had graduated and had moved back to Memphis. I was in school and working at a restaurant with a bunch of other 20-something friends. We had decided to leave school or work early that day and drive to Tuscaloosa, where I still had friends.

Six or seven of us piled into a friend's car and we made the four-hour drive, met up with the Tuscaloosa crew and headed to the concert. Of course, there were no disappointments.

The music was pure Stones. It was professional, and unlike The Beatles who I'd seen in Memphis in the 1960s, there were no girls screaming in our ears. It was everything that we wanted and more. Music was life to us. I remember the air so clearly. It was steaming hot and humid, and so filled with smoke that you could get high breathing. We were all up on our feet dancing the whole time. We were high and happy. What a great concert it was.

Afterward, we drove back to my friend's house to say our goodbyes. We hopped into the car and started the trek back, only because one person had to get to work in the morning. After around 20 miles, the guy with the car said that he was falling asleep. Everyone else said they were too sleepy to drive. I decided that I would take over. Frankly, I don't know how we didn't all die that night (I assume that I am still alive). It was that stupid time (no interstate, only a two lane highway) when we did things like shut one eye to rest it. I'm pretty sure that I nearly fell asleep more than once and got close to running off the road. But we arrived back in

Memphis around three or four the next morning. So we had driven more than 600 miles in one day. No way we were going to miss that concert.

LUCY KAHLMUS

Cathy Jones Humphries and I went. Some other folks were with us, but I can't remember who. What can I say? They were awesome! They definitely gave you your money's worth. It was one of the best concerts I've ever seen!

MARGIE McCRACKEN CHRISTIAN

My two best friends and I were in our junior year of high school. We loved the Rolling Stones and when tickets went on sale, we were there very early knowing it would be a sold-out show. I can't tell you the level of excitement we felt knowing we would see Mick Jagger!

Concerts were not unfathomable for us; we grew up in a college town and started concert-going young in life. I saw Led Zeppelin, Elton John, James Taylor, Jethro Tull, The Beach Boys, Todd Rundgren, Faces, Alice Cooper, Badfinger and Billy Joel. Percy Sledge was my first concert, at the age of 12. But the Rolling Stones? This was *the* concert.

We wore out our albums and talked daily about what we were going to wear. The day of the show, we got to Memorial Coliseum at 7am and set up camp at the door. The next 12 hours were some of the best times of my life. We met so many people sitting for hours on the concrete, with the smell of pot wafting in the air. So many hippies. There were no cell phones, so we made a lot of human connections that day.

By the time the door opening was imminent, we were all standing up butt to gut, and when the doors opened, I just lifted my feet and was carried in, popping through the door like a baby coming into the world. We ran as fast as we could to the floor. All the seats were general admission and we planned to be front row. We made it to the front! The air was electric. It was a sold-out show, with frisbees flying and people singing. The lights went down and Stevie Wonder took the stage. He was awesome and so good – but we wanted Mick!

Finally, it was time; the Stones came out. Mick had on a white jumpsuit that had little flashing circles on it. The stage was high but we could see so well. They played every song they should have played. Mick danced in only the way he can. He pulled petals off roses and threw them at us. Mine I collected and put in plastic and hung on my bedroom wall, in front of a picture of him leaning over dancing. They stayed there, at his lips, until they disintegrated.

It was amazing. It was crowded. It was the show of a lifetime, and at 64, where I struggle to find my keys daily, I remember it like it was yesterday!

PAUL WHITEHURST, AGE 18

We had many great bands at the Coliseum in the Seventies. Regrettably, I can remember painfully little about most of them, including that one. I didn't smoke pot at that time, but I remember not being able to see across the floor for all the smoke. Over the years, I came to conclude humans attend concerts for the stimulation. As such we're caught in the moment and attempts to reconstruct the events are futile. The girl I took turned out to be going with me to hook up with her boyfriend. That's okay; we were all friends. I also remember getting pulled over for speeding going home.

DAVID S BROWN

In '77 I met a guy at the airport in Atlanta. When he found out I was from Tuscaloosa, he did not mention Alabama football and he didn't ask about Bear Bryant. He asked, 'Did you see the Stones there in '72? I heard it was the best show on the whole tour!'

YESTERDAY'S PAPERS

SCOTT CAIN
ATLANTA JOURNAL & CONSTITUTION, JULY 2, 1972

They performed non-stop for an hour and a half, and could have gone on all night as far as the audience was concerned. Mick Jagger seemed to be having as much fun as the audience, which made the show that much better. So tumultuous was their reception that the Stones performed three numbers after the house lights went up…

In the flesh, Jagger is their strong point and the Stones will stay big as long as he is able to make such a spectacle of himself… His rooster dancing is a sight worth travelling miles to see and, unbelievable as it may sound, he is able to provide enough assortment of movements that he does not seem to repeat himself. Who could ever forget the sight of Jagger lying down on stage and sticking his leg straight up in the air? Or Jagger scooping rose petals from a box, kissing them and scattering them to the four winds?

From Tuscaloosa, the Stones headed 250 miles north to Nashville, Tennessee.

MUNICIPAL AUDITORIUM
JUNE 29, 1972, NASHVILLE, TENNESSEE

CAPACITY	9,700
SHOWS	1
ARRESTS	0

STEPHEN MICHAEL FOWLER

My best friend, Phil Bennett, and I have seen the Stones every time they do Nashville since the 1972 show, and I saw them there on 16 November 1965, which was my 16th birthday. The '72 show was the best the band ever was. They were at the peak of their powers, with the horns, with Nicky Hopkins on piano and with Mick Taylor on guitar. They were young and they had coke. Everything was in place for a show for the ages. They had songs pulled from their great records of that period – *Beggars Banquet, Let It Bleed, Sticky Fingers* and *Exile on Main St.* Only a Chuck Berry nod for Keith to do his Berry imitation, 'Bye Bye Johnny', broke into the list. The Stones were flawless that night. Nashville has been the site of some great Stones shows but this one was the ultimate.

GARY PINKERTON

I had been a fan since 1964, but missed their first Nashville concert in '65. I bought tickets for '72, and on the day of the concert my then wife and I took the day off in anticipation of the show. We were driving around town when we heard a local radio station announce a contest. The first person to show up at the station with a drawing of the Stones' new logo, would win a pair of tickets. I scrawled out the tongue and lips on a scrap of paper and we were at the station within five or ten minutes. I was the first there, so I got my contest tickets. I sold my other tickets to two young ladies from out of state, who had come ticketless to Nashville. The show was so great, but we didn't keep our seats. We walked around behind the stage, up on a balcony level, up behind Keith. It was a great experience, about which we still talk fondly!

BOB DERRYBERRY

My first notice of the Stones came in high school in 1965 with their fuzztone intro to 'Satisfaction'. When they played the auditorium in Nashville, our BCS TV station was right across the street. Fans were camped out in tents and sleeping bags days before, waiting to buy tickets. We also got backstage access to film for our newscasts.

DAVID CHIP HOBBS, AGE 17

In '72 Nashville was still a redneck town, but with a strong hippie movement. I was part of the movement, and soon to be a runaway. There was lots of acid, and lots of counterfeit tickets. It was pretty chaotic. I barely remember the show. It started around 2pm in the afternoon. Stevie Wonder opened and played several instruments. He was dancing around and almost fell off the stage. The whole place filled up with weed smoke. I don't remember the police being a factor at all.

ROGER WOOD

We went home to Seattle after Nashville. The van was locked up and Dad took the keys and locked all the gear up. Greg said he was probably going to move into an apartment with his black girlfriend, Renee, in Elgin, Illinois. Felix said, 'I'm probably just gonna stay with Brother Wood and keep helping in the services and the music.' I said, 'You guys are putting knives in my heart, man. We've spent the last ten years putting our blood, sweat and tears into this stuff. We've sacrificed stuff. We dreamt about which microphones we wanted to buy for ourselves when we were ten, eleven and twelve together. Are you just gonna throw all this away? How can he take that from us?'

I found the keys. I was 18 and a half years old and I called a couple of guys I knew who played with a band and I said, 'Fuck that!' and I jumped in the van and went down and met these guys and started playing in taverns, using the truck and the gear. Dad knew it and didn't confront me on it. He let me go. It was a real transitional moment.

I like to say we stashed our Christian upbringing in a cab for safe keeping at Chicago O'Hare airport, and four hours later we exited a limousine inside the County Convention Center in Fort Worth to hang with the Rolling Stones and Annie Liebowitz, and Warhol and Zsa Zsa Gabor and Liza Minelli and Bianca Jagger, Dick Cavett, Tina Turner and Truman Capote. Even after 50 years, the culture shock still tilts my head.

YESTERDAY'S PAPERS

KATHY SAWYER
THE TENNESSEAN, JUNE 30, 1972

Sound Seventy Productions, in the course of setting up the concert here, received a letter from the Stones management listing 'some of the things we would be very pleased to find in the Rolling Stones dressing rooms'. Among the items considered 'essential to the success of the evening's performance'… were three bottles of Liebfraumilch, with which Bill Wyman always performed on stage, and two bottles of tequila, with lemon quarters and salt, without which 'it would be very strange to see Keith Richards in top form…'.

After Nashville, there was a five day break in proceedings before the tour resumed in Washington, DC. The Stones had played 28 shows; they had 23 left to play in 23 days.

ROBERT F KENNEDY MEMORIAL STADIUM
JULY 4, 1972, WASHINGTON DC

CAPACITY	45,000
SHOWS	1
ARRESTS	70

CLAUDE MELANCON, AGE 15

I was a month shy of 16 and this was my first concert. Tickets were only $8. The setlist was similar to what they just toured, though shorter, less than two hours. At the time, their playing sounded a little sloppy, but I've come to realise that's just their style – they don't necessarily try to duplicate the sound of their albums. 'Happy' is still one of my favorite songs, and that album has always been special.

I had brought several cold cut sub-sandwiches in this ancient ugly cooler that had been in our family for years. And, of course, it was confiscated along with all other coolers that were brought in. Fearing the potential wrath of my father, I went back to try to retrieve it during Stevie Wonder's act and, surprisingly, I was successful.

EMERSON CURLEY O'NEILL, AGE 15

Exile had been released in May. The Vietnam war was in full debacle – young men were coming home in body bags daily – and anti-war protests were constant. The murders of Dr King and RFK, as well as the Altamont disaster and Woodstock, were three years earlier and still ever present in American life. Possession of marijuana was a felony. The threat of nuclear war was ever present and the Cold War seemed pretty hot. Nixon was soon to be resigning. All those dark things were still very relevant in '72. The Stones were at the apex of their awesome creative powers. This was the first American tour with Bobby Keys and Jim Price, and Nicky Hopkins was at the piano. There was zero concept of crowd control. Tickets were $5.50, general admission. There was no way to see the band unless one was down front, as I was. There was a significant risk of being crushed. The people in the upper levels were launching fireworks from the stands, which invariably landed on those of us on the field. And all that occurred before Little Stevie Wonder came on. It was one of the best days of my life. It was epic.

I remember the music clearly. I was very close to stage left – Mick Taylor, Nicky, Bobby and Jim. They opened with 'Brown Sugar' and proceeded to turn Sticky Fingers over for 'Bitch'. 'Gimme Shelter' and 'Midnight Rambler' seemed like the end of the world had come.

The July 4th DC show and July 26th MSG (Mick's birthday) show were two of the highlights of the tour due to the dates and location. The last time I saw the Stones was also in DC, exactly 50 years to the day of Brian's death. As I looked out upon the crowd, I wondered how many people were aware of the significance of the date.

GLENN COLEMAN, AGE 21

I first saw them in 1969 in Detroit and it changed my life. I was 17 at the time and I knew then that I wanted to work in the music business somehow. I also knew I wasn't a very good guitar player, so I thought I would become a recording engineer.

I was going to electronics school in 1972. I was growing up in Ohio. All my friends were big Rolling Stones fans too. I had a map on the wall in the house we were renting, with pins in the cities where they were going to play on that tour, so we planned a trip, starting July 4th in Washington DC and going on to Norfolk, Virginia, then onto Charlotte, North Carolina and back up to Knoxville, Tennessee and home to Ohio. I had asked my mom if I could use her car. Of course, she said 'no'. But that was a month or two before the shows. When the time came, I asked if I could borrow the car to get to school that week and we were on the road!

The shows were great. Stevie Wonder would start at 8.30pm sharp and we would start to move to the front. Back then there wasn't really security to speak of, so by the time the Stones hit the stage we were right in the front, standing there night after night. Later that summer, I also saw them in Detroit, Akron, Philadelphia and Pittsburgh. It was a great tour.

DEBBIE JONES, AGE 19

In high school my friend Becky started dating a football player who really liked the Stones. He was a bad boy type who was kind of intriguing. We listened to the music and I fell in love. We were good Catholic girls and this was the perfect 'bad' rebellious act for us. I continued to enjoy the music and soon married at the age of 18, in 1971. In July of 1972, my husband and I ventured to our first Stones concert. We had no car so we had to hitchhike. We thought it might take a while so we started early in the morning. We were about an hour away from DC. It only took about ten minutes to get a ride from some people who were going to the concert. What luck, plus they agreed to bring us back.

I remember getting there pretty early and sitting on a hill waiting for the gates to open. It was festival seating so when they opened the gates it was a mad rush to get in. We were almost crushed to death and I'm not kidding. People were having trouble breathing, but somehow we made in. I don't remember too much about what we ate or drank. We were not big drinkers but there was plenty of pot to be smoked.

We were sitting on the ground, pretty close to the stage, for hours when all of a sudden everyone was coughing and sneezing. That's when we realised the crowd outside was getting tear gassed. It was very uncomfortable but nobody got up and moved.

When the Stones came on, the crowd tried to rush the stage, which was in the middle of the stadium. We hung back a bit so as to not be crushed again. I couldn't take my eyes off Mick. I had never seen anything like this before.

ESTEL DILLON

Stevie Wonder opened. It was a terrific concert.

WARREN CHERRY

We were packed like sardines on the infield of RFK stadium in Washington, DC, standing where second base would be, in front of the stage. Tear gas was wafting toward us from the outfield, burning our eyes, where police were forcing back fans without tickets from climbing the fences. Jagger came out with a tri-corner Revolutionary War hat lined with fur.

JOHN LAMARTINE, AGE 25

I grew up in northern New Jersey, just outside New York City. By January 1964, all the pop music radio stations started blasting Beatles songs, followed by *The Ed Sullivan Show* appearance, etc. All this, of course, was the start of the so-called British Invasion. At this point, I had just turned 17. As the year went on, British pop was on the radio a lot; The Beatles, Dave Clark 5, Gerry and the Pacemakers, The Animals, Petula Clark and more.

Somewhere in there, I heard my first Stones record, 'Tell Me'. I wasn't particularly impressed – it was okay, but to my teenage ears it was nothing special. 'It's All Over Now' was much better, and 'Time is on My Side' and a few other songs were released in the mix. In 1964 into 1965, there was just a rush of so much new music to listen to – it was hard to keep up. Around March or April of 1965, the Stones released a new single, and this finally got me hooked – 'The Last Time'. I rarely bought singles, preferring to purchase albums. The US album versions were different from UK releases; the US records would include hit singles, whereas in the UK they used a different marketing approach; singles only, or EPs. While I waited for an album with 'The Last Time' to be put out, the Stones released another new single, 'Satisfaction'. Well, that just blew the lid off everything.

Soon after, *Out of our Heads* was released, and both songs were included. I started playing this record..constantly. In addition to the hit singles, two other tracks immediately caught my attention, 'Play with Fire' and 'The Spider and the Fly'. Now I needed more Stones. I found out that three albums had been released previously, so I bought them and they were all fantastic. By the end of the year there was another release, *December's Children*, and from that point on, I just bought every album the Stones released. That has more or less continued to the present day.

Around 1970, I crossed paths with a guy who I found out was as big a fan as me. We spent a lot of time listening to albums and talking about the group, etc. We both missed out going to Madison Square Garden during the '69 tour, which I regret to this day. We did, however, attend the premiere of the film *Gimme Shelter* in New York in 1971. We sat through it twice; in those days, you could stay in the theatre for repeat showings.

By 1972, my friend had moved away and was living just outside

Washington, DC. One day in late June, he called and told me he had an extra ticket for the Stones concert on July 4th. Plans were made, I hopped on a bus to Washington and we met up and drove to RFK Stadium.

The tour was a mix of indoor arenas with two or three outdoor stadiums, where the crowd size could likely be quite a bit larger than the indoor shows. Unfortunately, that led to crowd control problems, which RFK did not seem to be well prepared for. The stadium had several entry points for their normal operation, which was baseball games. However, for whatever reason, for this show there was entry through only one gate, which caused a massive back-up, impatient fans and an eventual show of force from security.

At some point, to counteract the pushing and shoving from the fans, security dispersed some sort of airborne irritant – tear gas, mace, pepper spray, whatever. I heard different rumors and don't have a solid idea of which one was used. However, we all felt the effects. There was much coughing, sneezing, eyes burning and throat discomfort. Fortunately, we were on our way to the upper deck at the time, so the spray was not as concentrated as it was on the lower level.

Surveying the field from our seats, we could see that a stage had been set up in the middle of the infield, covering the second base area, similar to the staging for The Beatles' Shea Stadium concert in 1965. As the evening wore on, and it got closer to the Stones appearing, the field level in front of the stage became quite full – standing room only. The stands also seemed to be nearly full. I don't know if the show was considered to be sold out.

There was an opening act, a gospel singer named Dorothy Ellis, but I don't recall anything about her performance. We might have been walking around to soak in the atmosphere, or beverages. Next up was Stevie Wonder, who put on a good show.

After a time, we noticed that a large gate behind center field had opened and a vehicle of some sort came into view, a Winnebago or other large RV. It may have had the Stones tongue logo plastered on it, but I can't recall. It slowly rumbled onto the field and pulled up behind the stage. Various people emerged, the lights went out for a bit and then we got the opening song, 'Brown Sugar'!

The entire concert is something of a blur. I know I was thrilled to be there, and enjoyed the show, but I wasn't exactly overwhelmed. This was likely due to the fact that we were seated in the upper deck of the stadium, far away from the stage and, it being 1972, the sound amplification was not really sophisticated enough to provide the kind of excellent stadium sound we have become used to over the past 20 plus years. I remember a comment from Mick in the middle of the show. Between songs, he grabbed a bottle of some alcoholic beverage, maybe Jack Daniels, held it up and announced, 'It's nice to be here in your nation's capital on the 4th of July. So, for that, I'll have a drink to your independence.' I was amused, and drank something along with him. The crowd cheered its approval.

So, they performed 15 songs, pretty much straight through, except for band introductions. 'Street Fighting Man' done, they exited backstage, got into the RV and it took off towards the far gate entrance and... that was it!

ERIC CARLSON

This was my second of eight Stones tours. A friend and I drove from Surf City, New Jersey, where I had a summer job as a motel dishwasher. I remember an uncontrolled rush to get into the stadium that turned into a minor riot. The huge crowd outside was funnelled into a row of turnstiles that created an intense crush. I got shoved through a turnstile and my belt caught on one of the metal arms. Luckily the belt broke and I got pushed through without getting trampled. I saw others, who weren't so lucky, get knocked down and run over. I'm not sure what happened behind me but soon there was tear gas in the air and we had to flush our eyes with the canteen I brought.

The show itself was outstanding, second only to my first—one of the *Get Yer Ya-Ya's Out!* concerts at Madison Square Garden. After one of the first songs, Keith took a long pull from a bottle of Jack Daniels and said, 'I drink to your independence!', it being Independence Day and all…

MIKE RUSLANDER, AGE 17

In 1972, I was 17 and a huge Stones fan. My best friend at the time bought two tickets to see them for the July 4th concert at RFK Stadium. One ticket was for his wife who was very pregnant at the time. She didn't feel like going, understandably, but wanted him to go, so he asked me if I wanted to go along. I think the tickets were a whopping $6 each. I was really excited!

Living in Richmond, Virginia, we had a very active rock concert scene and the big names always came to town, but the Stones were a stadium-sized act. My friend had a late '50s or early '60s Volkswagen Beetle and that was our mode of transportation.

Mike was a big fan of Mick

We agreed to take another friend up there with us who was going to hook up with some other mutual friends. So, after stopping by another friend's apartment to get some smokables for the road and show, off we went.

I don't remember a lot about the trip up there, which was about two hours north of Richmond, but I do remember we parked several blocks away from RFK and walked the rest of the way. We went in and sat about half way up in the bleachers, which made the stage seem small, but we didn't care because it was filling up fast. Shortly after we got seated, I remember people from above us setting off a bunch of bottle rockets and firecrackers at the crowd below them, which was where we were sitting.

We all had really long hair, as was the fashion of the time and we were getting hit in our backs. It didn't really hurt, but we were scared that our hair would catch on fire. Of course, it never did. Our passenger had left us for greener pastures (or better drugs), but we were stoked!

The opening acts were Martha Reeves and the Vandellas and then Stevie Wonder.

They got the crowd going and contributed to the party atmosphere. Later the Stones came out and the place came alive. The energy was positively electric. Jagger wore the same white jumpsuit he wore in *Ladies and Gentlemen, The Rolling Stones.*

Way too soon it was over, and it was night time by the time it finished. We walked back to the car, and I seem to remember we both nodded off for a little bit before the ride back to Richmond. Needless to say, it was a great and memorable experience. The Stones were at their peak, and we were deaf after that for a day or two. Good memories.

PATRICIA McSWAIN

Someone was shooting off Roman candles from the top of RFK stadium down into the standing crowd on the field. Mick stopped the show and told everyone to settle down or they would leave. After a couple of tunes, the Roman candle asshat started up again, so the Stones got in their helicopter and left.

PAUL CLAR, AGE 19

I started listening to them when I was 12. I went with my best friend and our girlfriends. Back then they always ended with 'Street Fighting Man' and never did an encore. The stage was set up around second base and the band entered from the bullpen in a white tank. The lid popped open and Mick was the first one out. Since I was familiar with the stadium, we planned to go in Gate F, while most of the fans lined up at Gate A. This put us right behind the third base dugout, perfectly lined up for the stage. They were great seats. I didn't want to go on the field and stand up the whole time, since it

Paul Clar and his friends snagged seats behind third base at RFK

was general admission. It was a beautiful night. We were inside when the teargas happened so we only got a very mild whiff of it. We brought in our own refreshments and party additives. Security was a joke.

STAN BECKER

I was very privileged to see the Stones twice on their 1972 North American tour. The first time was July 4th, in Washington DC at RFK Stadium. It was pretty incredible – that particular line up with the golden Nicky

Hopkins and Stu playing piano never toured North America before or since. They were really going for it.

ALLAN PHILLIPS, AGE 15

I was a complete and utter Stones fanatic. I discovered the Stones at seven years old from my older sister, who had the 45s and albums. By '72, I was obsessed, listening to *Sticky Fingers* and *Hot Rocks* constantly, and had just discovered *Ya-Ya's*, my favorite album of all time. I was visiting my sister in Washington DC. She had tickets to see the Stones at RFK Stadium on July 4 and had an extra one, but she gave it to a friend. I was shattered (pun intended). It would have been my first concert. I had to wait till early '73 for my first concert, and until '75 to finally see the Stones, not to mention missing one of the most notorious tours ever. I held a grudge against my sister for years!

YESTERDAY'S PAPERS

STAFF WRITER
WASHINGTON DAILY NEWS, JULY 5, 1972

The kids in the crowd screamed and shouted, and howled for 70 straight minutes, as Mike Jagger (sic) and the rest of the Stones twisted, jumped and twirled their way through the songs that have made them the collective kings of rock. Girls in halters and tight slacks and guys wearing t-shirts and dungarees, packed so they could barely move, closed their eyes, raised their arms above them and cheered wildly with every song. 225 (police) officers on duty were relaxed with the kids, often letting them toss firecrackers without a word; and apparently turning their back while youngsters smoked and shared marijuana. Some of the dozens of kids who tried to scale the stadium walls were headed off, and others were allowed to try their luck – with only a policeman's warning to 'take it easy… one at a time'.

After the huge RFK show, the Stones travelled on to Norfolk, Virginia.

NORFOLK SCOPE
JULY 5, 1972, NORFOLK, VIRGINIA

CAPACITY	**10,253**
SHOWS	**1**
ARRESTS	**17**

SAM SCHATZ, AGE 15

I was a 15-year-old hippie and the last person to buy a ticket at the box office the day the tickets went on sale. It was a school day and it was 3.15pm when I got there. They only had one ticket left! Stevie Wonder opened, and to be truthful he stole the show. But Keith was great on his solos.

KENNETH BROCK

The Norfolk Scope is a concrete dome designed by Nervi, who was hired because of the dome he designed for the 1964 Rome Olympics. The Stones had Nicky Hopkins and the brass support that was on the *Exile* album. They played 'Sweet Virginia', which I don't think they did elsewhere on the tour, and the oldest song they did was 'Jumpin' Jack Flash'. My ticket cost $12. 'Midnight Rambler' came towards the end of the concert. I sat house left and looked down on the stage sideways, maybe 30 feet away.

Kenneth Brock was 30 feet from the stage

151

JOHN PERSE

There was obviously a great deal of 'buzz' in the weeks leading up to the show, especially with what had happened with disturbances in other cities. Everyone was aware, and a bit excited, about whether those kinds of things would happen in Norfolk. Also, the attitude was 'how in the hell did we score this concert?'. I'm not sure how we got tickets but I went with my parents and several of their friends and their dates, so there were probably six to eight of us. I was by far the youngest of the group.

John Perse remembers the pre-show buzz

One of the friends was Neal Johnson, a six feet eight professional basketball player who played for the Virginia Squires in the ABA. He was on crutches from an injury and I recall watching him hold the crutches aloft all night, bobbing up and down in time with the music. He was also wearing an old army helmet for some unknown reason. Quite the sight.

Our tickets were about midway back from the stage but off to the side, maybe a couple of rows off the floor, so we could see over the people actually sitting and standing on the floor. The first song was 'Brown Sugar' and the crowd went wild. The crowd was electric before, during and after the show. It hit a fever pitch when they launched into 'Sweet Virginia', which we all took as a hometown homage! It was incredible. I also recall being blown away by Bobby Keys (RIP).

People who know music are still amazed to this day that I was actually there. I have seen some extraordinarily memorable concerts over these many years and this one was definitely one the best. The buzz from the show lasted all summer, especially when people would ask, in a reverent tone, 'Were you there? Really? Oh, my god!'

EPES McMURRAN, AGE 16

I bought *Exile on Main St.* when it came out and had been playing it non-stop since. My friends skipped school to go to the Scope box office to buy tickets for the show. On the night, security was tight, with several layers of cops on the Scope concourse. I felt like I was walking into a prison. There was a rumor that the Stones weren't going to show. We had seats behind the stage but still with a good view. Steve Wonder opened and put on a great show. Then the Stones hit the stage and ripped into 'Brown Sugar'. Mick

Epes McMurran couldn't believe he was seeing the Stones

was in the white sequinned jumpsuit and doing the Jagger strut. Keith was playing the intro power chords, Charlie was pounding the drums, Bill was laying down the bass and Bobby Keys was wailing on the sax. And I was going, 'Man, this is the Rolling Stones. This is really the Stones!' Excited is too mild a word to describe how I was feeling. This was the first time I realized how powerful rock and roll can be. It was magical. On that night, the Stones were 'the Greatest Rock and Roll Band in the World'. And I was there!

JINCI CARTER

The music was phenomenal, and it was my first big concert. I was a freshman at Old Dominion University, and my boyfriend at the time worked for a senator in Washington DC. After I picked him up from his parents' home the next morning, we headed to our little

Jinci Carter was at the Scope

local airport in Norfolk, Virginia (now an international airport), and who was at the airport but THEM! I was flabbergasted, but too shy to do anything but say 'hello'! Now that I'm 69, my shyness wouldn't overcome me.

YESTERDAY'S PAPERS

MAL VINCENT
VIRGINIAN PILOT, JULY 6, 1972

Jagger is an amazing, flamboyant performer who has a wild, sophisticated beat to back him. The basic appeal, however, is much more than this obvious bit of showmanship. It is rather, a kind of rebelliousness that thrives on bugging the Establishment… The lyrics of the songs, as much as one could hear, seemed harmless enough, if more sophisticated than in the '60s, or any other time. Their tone, however, is cynicism marked in the spirit of flash bravado. Jagger and the Stones are portable hysteria to their fans. For this country, the 1969 tour signalled the death of the innocent age of rock music, in favor of more socially potent, if vague, imagery. The current tour but drives the nails in the coffin. The age of innocence is over. The '70s speak a different language.

CHARLOTTE COLISEUM
JULY 6, 1972, CHARLOTTE, NORTH CAROLINA

CAPACITY 12,000
SHOWS 1
ARRESTS 31

STEVE WILLIAMS
Counter tickets were sold. Fans were trying to crash the doors.

SUDIE COOK, AGE 19
I remember sneaking into a friend's house one night to hear *Aftermath* when it came out. I was 13. I would have crawled over broken glass to hear the whole album after I'd heard 'Under My Thumb' on the radio. I think I sent off a mail order for my tickets for this show. My friend Laura and I were huge fans and went together. Before the Stones came out, I told her I thought I was going to pass out and sat for about two seconds. We had been drinking and smoking and were hyped to see our idols. They announced Stevie was coming to the stage and one or two people guided him to a keyboard. He had on a blue sequinned jacket or cape. I remember there were bottles of Jack Daniels and George Dickel on the equipment behind Keith and he was drinking from them. They played from a few different albums, *Sticky Fingers* and *Exile*. I was transfixed. I still am.

CONRAD BOOKOUT
The stage lighting with the mirror across the top front of the stage and the lights bouncing off the mirror were awesome. And, of course, the roses…

BARRY SHIRLEY, AGE 19
I was with my girlfriend and friends. We traveled to Charlotte from

155

our hometown of Columbia, South Carolina. I seem to remember Mick's white jump suit and the leather belt he brought out for 'Midnight Rambler', and also the stage was adorned with dragons or serpents. Stevie Wonder and Martha and the Vandellas opened the show, and there was a grand finale with all three bands. It was interesting seeing Mick Taylor as the new member. I've seen them many times since, and I met Bill Wyman in 1995 at his Kensington restaurant, and chatted with him about seeing the Stones in Charlotte 1972.

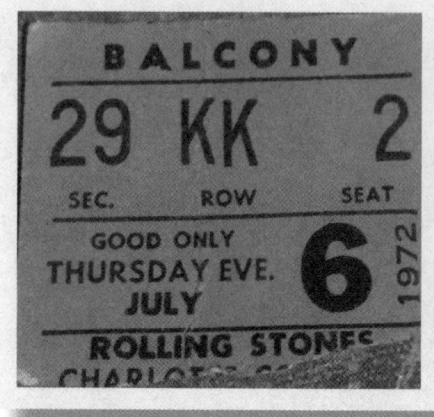

Barry Shirley's ticket for the Charlotte show

STEVEN BURGESS

The Stones were probably at their peak. I remember how massive the show was for the times. I think they had multiple road crews to give them the time to set up the stage from city to city. A friend of mine wandered down to the stage area and the crowd was so jammed up to the stage that, even though he passed out, he never hit the floor. When he came to, he just came back to our seats. He said it was wild. Musically, the support artists helped make the show.

YESTERDAY'S PAPERS

PETE STODDARD
CHARLOTTE NEWS, JULY 7, 1972

Ask any of 12,000 people who were part of a sell-out crowd what was the first number the Rolling Stones did when they popped on stage at 9.20 pm, and none will be able to tell you. But they will be able to tell you that when Mick Jagger, lead singer for the Stones, started to scream the second song, the words were 'Jumpin' Jack Flash, it's a gas'. The gas was an unmistakable cloud of marijuana smoke rolling across the heads of several thousand people on the Coliseum floor who are jumping from the chairs with their hands over their heads…. There are six other members of the group who bring out the drums, bass, sax, trumpet, trombone, and piano for the Stones. But they have changed so much since 1966 that only Jagger and Richards hold the image. When the two step to center stage and crouch close together and begin to scream 'you can't always get what you want', the undulating mob for 50 feet in front of the stage knows that it got what it needs.

CIVIC ARENA
JULY 7, 1972, KNOXVILLE, TENNESSEE

CAPACITY 6,500
SHOWS 1
ARRESTS 8

GARY EPPERSON

On a sunny hot Friday afternoon on July 7, 1972, myself and several of my friends loaded up in my 1960 VW van in Winchester, Kentucky and headed nearly 200 miles south to Knoxville, Tennessee to see the Rolling Stones! Even though we were under age to purchase alchohol, we stopped and bought at least a couple of bottles of either Red Ripple or Boone's Farm wine. We also had some herb to go along with the wine. We got to Knoxville,

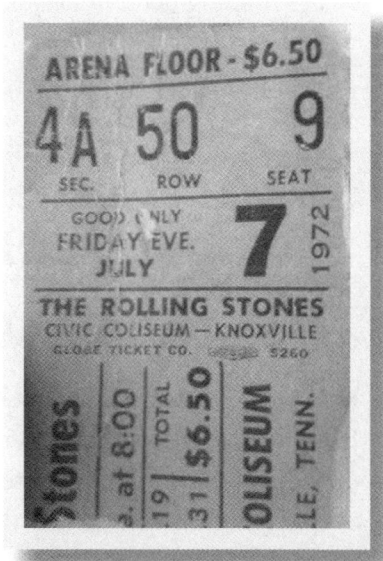

Gary Epperson remembers a wild and crazy crowd

grabbed a bite to eat and I believe we purchased the tickets there at the arena. We didn't have Ticketmaster or credit cards to pre purchase tickets in those days!

The strangest thing about the concert was that, being so close to the 4th of July and the fact that fireworks were legal to buy in Tennessee, spectators in the audience were lighting fireworks and throwing them out into the crowd. It was a pretty wild and crazy crowd. I kept an eye out for firecrackers coming my way, but fortunately I didn't have any explosions near my seat! The concert was great, and I went to see them again about ten years later.

REBECCA TAYLOR, AGE 17

I discovered the Stones as a child in 1963 and have been hooked since. The concert was in our local coliseum, which held maybe 6,000 people at that time. My friend Jill (RIP) and I camped out at the coliseum to get tickets. We were 17 and got to meet people from everywhere. Weed was in enormous abundance and (needless to say) we partied. The concert was great and I was addicted to Keith Richards, as I still am today. I loved them then, and love them still. I saw them in November 2021 in Atlanta. Sadly, gone are the days of getting away with smoking weed and dancing at their shows. To me, there's nothing better than toking and listening to their music.

YESTERDAY'S PAPERS

CHRIS WOHLWEND
KNOXVILLE JOURNAL, JULY 8, 1972

Jagger, looking like the devil in drag, opened with 'Brown Sugar', the song written for his wife. His movements and dancing were in keeping with his image as the epitome of evil sexuality. The audience loved it… A country-flavored song, unidentified by Jagger, with acoustical guitars, featured some excellent tenor sax work by Bob

Keys and some inspired keyboard playing. Also, Jagger's vocals were distinguishable, thanks to the lack of the loud electric guitar work which prevailed in the other numbers.

KIEL CONVENTION HALL
JULY 9, 1972, ST LOUIS, MISSOURI

CAPACITY	**10,200**
SHOWS	**2**
ARRESTS:	**20+**

PATRICIA DOHERTY

I really don't recall much about it. We were pretty messed up. I remember Mick flying all over the stage and throwing roses to those of us in the front row. He was wearing bold stripes, either jacket or bell bottoms. We roasted more than a few brain cells back in the day.

DENIS SNELL POTT, AGE 17

I owe it all to my friend Carole Chunn, who I met in high school. I grew up in St Louis, Missouri. Carole was a year older and a 'cool girl' from California. One day, she asked me to go with her to see *Gimme Shelter*, which was showing at a nearby cinema. I was 16 years old and walked in knowing nothing about the Rolling Stones other than having heard 'Satisfaction' and 'Honky Tonk Women' on the radio. I remember being really excited by the film, and particularly by Mick's performance. There was nothing like him anywhere in my world. It was a revelation. I was so turned on, and all my teenage hormones were going. I walked out of the theatre a brand-new fan. I couldn't get enough; I read everything I could find about them and bought albums – *Through the Past, Darkly* was my first, then *Flowers*.

I was in my junior year when I learned that the Stones were touring, and by some miracle they were coming to St Louis! I persuaded my parents to drive me downtown to buy tickets – that's what you had to do back in the day. Tickets were on sale for $3, $5 and $7. Can you even imagine those prices? I bought two $5 tickets and asked my friend Alan to go with me. I was 17 years old.

When the big day came, we headed to Kiel Auditorium, a large venue. Our seats were pretty good, on what I now know to be Keith's side. I couldn't believe it when Stevie Wonder was the opening act. I was enjoying the crowd sounds and seeing joints being lit, flaring and then disappearing into the crowd, and the smell of incense and pot being passed around. Still, I was really just waiting for the Stones.

Finally, they came on stage. I don't remember which songs they did that day, except 'Midnight Rambler'. I don't know if I even knew what the song was about back then, but – wow! Mick had this big red scarf, and he used it to punctuate the lyrics by slamming it down on the floor. I was mesmerized. I don't know if Alan or I even spoke during the concert. Neither of us could take our eyes off Mick Jagger. After the concert ended, I knew that I had been changed in some profound way by the performance and the music.

My love for the Stones continues to this day. My friend Carole flew in to St Louis to join me for the September 26, 2021 Stones show.

RICHARD MEAD

I went with some high school friends, one of whose moms got us into both shows for free. She was a manager for the food service company. We had seats we snuck into. Back then you could rush the stage and security left you alone and bands didn't care. Stevie Wonder was great. The Stones played great too, for about two hours. Jagger was all over the stage. They didn't say a lot to the crowd, they just played their asses off.

DANNY BLACKBURN

The Stones that day were smoking. They had an incredible light show on 'Midnight Rambler'. I never saw anything like it. Mick had these eight foot long scarves running side to side!

SHERI STEININGER

It was summer 1972, before my freshman year of high school, when my mother saw an ad in the *St Louis Post-Dispatch* with a form to mail order tickets to the Stones. They were going to play an afternoon show at Kiel Auditorium (nobody EVER said 'the Kiel'), so she thought I might like to go with a few friends. My older sister, who was out of town for the summer, and I were huge fans! This kindness was one of the coolest things my mother ever did. We ordered four tickets for me and a few friends.

On the day, someone else's mom dropped us off on Market Street. Inside, it looked like the place was half empty. We were surprised, but they were playing a night time show too, and had done little to publicise this one. We had floor seats center left, probably 30 or 35 rows back – we could see the band just fine, especially standing up. I don't think

Sheri Steininger (in the KSHE t-shirt) was at the St Louis show

there were that many people behind us on the floor. Most were in the seats in the mezzanine.

We were kind of dancing to one number when my friend Tina started boogying in the aisle to our left. We were afraid she might get in trouble, because we were literally the only fans in our area physically getting into the performance at the time. Instead, what did happen was that Mick craned his neck forward and shielded his eyes with a hand over his brow, peering down the aisle at her. Then he raised his entire arm straight up and waved at her exaggeratedly as he sang, as if to say, 'Hullo to the lone waking babe dancing there.' Man, did we ever squeal! I am pretty sure that moment was the highlight of Tina's high school career before

161

it even began. Anyway, after that, a few other people got up and started dancing too.

At home, my sister and I had *Beggars Banquet*, *Let It Bleed* and *Sticky Fingers*. Often, we would stack the albums on our turntable and fall asleep listening to them. I knew every single note and every single scratch by heart.

But in '72, I had only been to a few concerts and didn't realise that artists toured to promote new work, so we were unfamiliar with *Exile on Main St*. Honestly, if I had known, I still would not have had the album because I spent the four or five dollars I had on tickets to the concert. (We were poor kids and often through the years had to decide if we wanted to see a band live or to own the album instead.) We therefore did not know many of the songs they performed that day. But we knew enough to be really happy with the performance. I remember them playing 'Satisfaction', for sure. I hope I'm not making it up when I say I remember 'Gimme Shelter', 'Brown Sugar' and 'Sympathy for the Devil'.

Although Mick waved at her, my friend Tina does not even remember being there. We probably shouldn't have smoked that joint outside!

DEBBY DAUSCH

My friend and I spent the night on the Kiel steps to get a good place in line for tickets. We were successful, about 10 rows back on the floor. The show was promoted as the Rolling Stones with special guest 'TBA'. No one knew 'TBA' was Stevie Wonder. It was a pleasant surprise.

Stevie walked on stage and started playing and he played every instrument on that stage. He was extraordinary! The sound during his show was fantastic. A sold-out show of 99 per cent white kids were sooo pleasantly surprised. People were going nuts over Stevie. He was so worth the money. Standing ovations were in order and he received them.

I think the mindset of the crowd was, 'If Stevie sounds this good, the Stones will be phenomenal.' They were not. The excuse was the sound system, but if so then why did Stevie sound so good? Mick was dressed in his Superman outfit, similar to his Altamont costume. He needed Superman to help him!

The first song they performed was 'Gimme Shelter'. Standing there, I heard people asking, 'What song is this?' Everyone was shaking their heads. Remember, this is the first song of the set, and the crowd started chanting, 'Bring back Stevie!' Mick looked a little taken back by our response. Still people kept chanting. Unfortunately, the show didn't improve but just got worse. The crowd was very disappointed..They should've brought back Stevie to save their show.

Since that day, I've had the mindset that the Stones are a studio band only. It left me with a very bad feeling. I no longer like or listen to their music. It was the worst show I've ever seen and I've seen quite a few. I did buy a few Stevie Wonder albums after seeing him. I owned one Stones album, and the only reason I bought it was because it was a London import and had a resale value.

When the Stones came back in the Nineties, my friend shelled out $200 a ticket to see them. I warned him he would be disappointed. He said, 'But it's the Stones!' I laughed. I saw him the day after the show and he said the sound was bad. You'd think they would've hired a good sound engineer, but apparently not. But my friend said, 'I saw the Stones…'.

To this day, I have a very strong dislike for them. They need to stay in the studio.

PAM BARONE, AGE 14

Back then, you would hear about tickets on sale listening to AM radio and walk down to the post office with your ticket order written out on a piece of school notebook paper. You'd buy a money order and a stamp and mail the order. A few weeks later, the ticket came in the mail. And then it was time to find a ride. I lived 110 miles from St Louis but I got the ride!

Ticket sales were strong and a second show (earlier in the day) was added. I attended the afternoon show. I rode up with friends, although our tickets were not together. I was seated way up in a balcony. The opening act, Stevie Wonder, was fantastic. His set was very high energy. I don't know if much taped back up was used, but there sure was a lot of music coming from what seemed like a small band. 'Superstition' had Kiel Auditorium filled with a lot of feelgood energy.

The Rolling Stones? By 1972, even I felt like they were just playing tributes. It was fun to see them for the first time. What I saw on the stage I remember as mostly yellows and reds. Charlie Watts was always my favorite. He was so handsome, cool – beyond cool. The sound was good,

163

I heard the lyrics and the instruments. Mick was so different from any other front man. I had seen the Stones on TV but – wow! – he moved around a lot and it was neat seeing him dancing all over the place.

I remember someone saying they hoped the Stones would play a Chuck Berry song. They did – 'Bye Bye Johnny'. My future husband saw the tour a few days later, in Kansas City. He was 19, a way better age in 1972. (We would not meet until 1977.) He was in full-on hippie mode, running a bookstore and seeing a lot of great music.

KATY McLEOD

I saw them three times in 1972 – in Nashville, St Louis and Detroit. We never stayed in our seats, no matter where we were. By that time, I was a seasoned Stones fan. All of my friends were Stones fans. When the Stones came to America, we'd call each other up – 'let's get a hotel room, let's get our outfits.' They didn't have much in the way of special effects in '72, but every tour they did they went through a metamorphosis. In 1972 the music was just transformational. They played the old music but the newer stuff was showcased.

My brother's friend was Keith Richards' private guitar tech – Ted Newman Jones – and he came to dinner at my parents' house. I was at the hotel and I had no idea!

I had a bottle of Jack Daniels, which was quite common at the time for me, and walked up to the sound technician in the middle of the floor. He had his headphones on because he was doing the sound for the concert. I said, 'Would you like some Jack Daniels?' He had some Jack Daniels and then he put the headphones on me for a while. They were doing 'Rocks Off' and 'Tumbling Dice' and 'Ventilator Blues'. His relief came and the sound engineer said to me, 'Do you want to go backstage?', and he took my hand and walked me backstage and the next thing I knew we were in the wings watching the show. They were doing 'Rip This Joint'. It was like having a private show. There were 40,000 people there but I didn't even see them. I just saw the Stones, right in my face.

We ran into Mick in the hotel elevator. Someone said, 'What floor do you want?' So we pressed all the buttons to block them all up because we were in an elevator with Mick and wanted it to last as long as possible. I remember him standing there, very quiet and looking very cute, and us all star struck. I saw Charlie Watts in the hallway. He said, 'How old is your girlfriend?' and I said I didn't really know and he said, 'That's a bit shortsighted, isn't it?' I got very stoned with Ian Stewart. And he was such a sweet guy, with six people in his hotel room. We met him at the backstage door and he walked us four city blocks back to his hotel.

We parked our car behind a limousine and followed the car to a restaurant in a high crime ghetto in north St Louis. Mick, Keith and Mick Taylor were in it. Marshall Chess was with them. They parked and then we parked. I wouldn't go to this neighborhood in the light of day. I wouldn't feel safe. But with Mick, Keith and Mick Taylor? We felt safe there. I don't know whether someone told them there was good chitlins there. They were really into black culture.

It was a very small restaurant and we followed them in. There were three booths, a juke box, two long tables and a soda fountain. The menus were tacked on the wall with a nail. It was very cheap. It was exciting to be there but it was so tiny it was embarrassing! None of us had the nerve to get up and talk to them, because we didn't want to disturb them. They ordered their food and Mick got up and put something on the jukebox. We ordered iced tea.

DON CARLO, AGE 18

I went with Steve Peterson. We were working in St Louis, painting houses. It was spectacular. The Stones opened up with 'Brown Sugar' and they kept driving the audience with more and more great songs. The concert was a euphoric experience because of their blues background and them shifting over to driving rock 'n' roll riffs and great lyrics in their songs. Charlie's beat kept the rhythm tight with Bill's bass line. And I don't have to say any more about Keith's magic 'five strings, three notes, two fingers and one asshole' creations. Songs I remember them playing are 'Honky Tonk Women', 'Bitch' and older songs that we grew up with, listening to the band mature.

My son saw the movie of their 1972 tour and took me to see it. I told him what the opening song was going to be and he couldn't believe it. I've been on stage at weddings, singing 'Brown Sugar'.

GARY DYCUS

In 1971 I was in the Army in Germany. A girl from school was writing me letters, keeping me updated on our neighborhood. She wanted to know if I would go see the Rolling Stones. I said, 'Hell, yeah – get tickets!' I asked to go on leave and it was approved.

On July 9th, 1972 we went to Kiel Auditorium. We walked in and the place was packed. I looked at the stage and noticed their Marshall amps plus, on each side of the stage, 16 JBL speakers on hydraulic platforms.

I was wondering why the stage lights were behind the equipment. Plus, hanging above us, was a huge mirror that stretched across the roof. And everyone was wondering who would open for the Stones. They turned the lights off and had one spot light on Stevie Wonder that would turn into a flame as he played. They had the stage lights pointing at the mirror on the ceiling reflecting back to the stage so it would not block anyone from seeing the performance.

It was the loudest concert ever. The music bounced off the walls and echoed inside your head. Stevie Wonder was great and the Rolling Stones tore it up.

GEORGE M KROENUNG

I stood in line for tickets outside the Kiel on a packed sidewalk, but after an hour or more of the line not moving, we went home. Later we heard they had added a second show and so we were able to get tickets for that. And it was a great show!

STEVE WOODRUFF

We waited outside of Kiel for the Stones to come in. We didn't see them but we did see Stevie and his band members enter via the west side door.

GARY HOLDINGHAUSEN

I waited all night with thousands of others to get tickets, but when I got to about ten people before the ticket booth it was sold out. I did meet a girl there in line and we exchanged numbers but I never called. I did get tickets for the second show. I wasn't impressed by Stevie Wonder – I never was a fan. I remember recording the show, but the tape was lost years ago.

MARCIA BAUER HUNT

I had a big crush on my date, who got two tickets that weren't together. At the last minute we shared a seat in about the tenth row. Stevie Wonder was awesome and the Stones were great. It's my all-time favorite concert!

DAN PAUL

I remember you could only purchase four tickets. We spent two days camping out on the sidewalk to get them. It was worth it as we ended up with fourth and sixth row. In my opinion Stevie Wonder stole the show.

RUSSELL TODD

I was there for the afternoon show. Months prior they had folks camping out at Kiel for tickets and then later they announced the afternoon, or 'second' show, which I got tickets for. The people that camped out were pissed. I do remember seeing a 22-year-old named Stevie Wonder open for the Stones. He played every instrument on the stage during his set.

This was the first American tour after Altamont so the Stones show was kind of eerie at first.

ELIZABETH HACKETT

My husband waited in line all night for tickets outside Kiel with many other fans when they went on sale some weeks before the show.

CATHY BATEMAN

At the time this was rumored to be their last tour… My boyfriend waited all night for tickets. I joined the line in the morning. It was my first experience of schmoozing my way to a better spot in line and I ended up with tickets on the floor, while he got nose bleed seats. It was a spectacular show and Stevie Wonder was amazing. I remember a lot of roses being thrown either from or to the stage. I still have a rose petal from the show.

PEGGY FURLONG

As in 1969, Mick threw handfuls of rose petals into the crowd and into the air.

STEVE CAMPBELL

I was there for both shows. I camped out for tickets and got second row for the evening show. And I got fifth row tickets for the day show by mail.

ED SEELIG

I went to both shows on that tour. I distinctly recall running into a guy on the sidewalk after the first exceptional show, and he had great floor seats that he stiffed his friends for, so I bought them and we went back in for the second show!

JOE GARNIER

I had seen them at Kiel Auditorium in 1966 with suits on. In '72, my friends stood in line all night long to get tickets and the box office ran out before they could buy them. They had to give someone four ounces of weed for four tickets. I was sitting front row balcony straight back. We were pretty far away – I took binoculars – but the sound was awesome, with no big echo at all.

Stevie was touring on *Talking Book*, featuring 'Superstition'. His drum solo was off the chain. The Stones were awesome and starting to get more rambunctious!

JOHN ELLIS, AGE 19

I was at both shows. A difference between the two shows was that Mick Taylor played an extended intro solo on 'You Can't Always Get What You Want' at the afternoon show. Taylor, who is as good as any player ever when it comes to developing a long solo on a slow blues, played exquisitely.

I had been going to concerts since I was 14 or 15, so I was already a veteran. The rock concert scene started in St Louis, one year after The Beatles and the Stones came in 1966. After Monterey Pop in 1967, The Who came on a package tour bill with headliners Herman's Hermits and The Blues Magoos. Single headliner concerts in St Louis started when Cream came in April 1968, followed by Steppenwolf, the Grateful Dead, Canned Heat, Jefferson Airplane, Big Brother and the Holding Company with Iron Butterfly, and then Jimi Hendrix and The Doors. But it was mostly serious rock fans who attended. Rock was still underground in 1968.

People started listening to FM rock radio, which started in St Louis around November 1967, and after Led Zeppelin released their first album, and got on FM radio, everything changed. In early 1969, the Rolling Stones were momentarily passe, among serious rock fans. They really had to prove themselves to a new audience.

By 1970, rock music was on the more popular AM radio, and a whole new generation of people started attending rock shows. 1971 had many more rock shows. By 1972, virtually everyone who loved rock music had started going to see concerts. The Stones audience in '72 was a mix of serious rock fans and 'average' concertgoers.

People just assume that the Rolling Stones were always on top, and had nothing to prove. But after Brian Jones got kicked out and Mick Taylor joined, the Stones had a lot to prove. Since they had stopped touring in 1967, much larger amplifiers had become the norm for touring rock bands. The concert scene was rapidly changing, and bands were playing louder and longer. The Stones were used to playing less than an hour at the concerts, but by 1970, headliners were playing for a much longer time. Ticket prices were much higher, and people expected more for their money.

The Stones didn't tour the US in 1970 or 1971, so they had to prove themselves once again. *Sticky Fingers* is now regarded as one of their finest albums, but in 1971 it was 'just another new album', as incredible rock albums were coming out each week.

The same thing happened when they released *Exile on Main St.* The response was lukewarm. Obviously, everyone loved the more accessible songs, but many found the album just too expansive. Of course, it's now considered to be among the best rock albums ever (and easily among the best double albums). So, as we headed down to see them in concert for the afternoon show at the Kiel Auditorium, we didn't really know what type of show to expect.

Very few bands were able to draw the way the Stones did, and since it seemed they only came to the US every three years, the excitement of seeing them outweighed any feelings of concern about how they were going to perform. They hadn't been to St Louis for six years – and it would be another six years before they returned in 1978.

Stevie Wonder opened the show, and the response was polite, but lukewarm. Although he was the opening act, I can't remember if any of the newspapers had Stevie in any of the print ads. He was six months away from releasing 'Superstition', so a lot of the crowd didn't pay attention to him and considered him to be an oldies act. The longer Stevie played, the more restless some people became. At the same time, there was a very positive reception for Stevie, but it was a small percentage of the crowd.

After Stevie finished his set, the anticipation for the Stones was unreal. Virtually none of the 10,000 plus attendees had ever even seen the Stones, but they were already behaving like it was going to be the greatest concert they'd ever seen. The afternoon show was paced in somewhat of a relaxed manner until the last half of the set. Midway through, when they played 'You Can't Always Get What You Want', Mick Taylor was given the spotlight, and it seemed like he took an intro solo that lasted three to five minutes. Jagger used that intro as a way to pace himself. It was some of the best guitar playing I've ever seen in my life. Mick Taylor may be the best slow blues player among famous rockers. He knew how to develop a long solo.

After that, every song got more and more intense. It seemed like they were playing louder and louder, yet I'm convinced they were just playing with incredible intensity.

The evening show was even better, except that Taylor was not given his solo spot on 'You Can't Always Get What You Want'. The intensity from the first show was evident from the very beginning of the second set. The first set was definitely the warm-up set, although it didn't seem like it at the time. Each song seemed to ramp up the excitement. The slower songs were designed to give everyone a slight breather, but when they played something after 'Sweet Virginia', it was at a high level of intensity. They didn't have to 'restart the engine'.

Both concerts remain among the best shows I've ever seen in my life, and the 1972 shows were infinitely better than the other times I saw them – in 1978, etc.

LESLIE LADD

July 1972 was an exciting time for me. I was preparing to leave for a year abroad in Montpellier, France. My Rolling Stones obsession had started a few years earlier when my brother-in-law told me that Mick had written 'Stray Cat Blues' for me. I was 15 at the time (I had never met Mick!). He and my sister, Glenda, were living in St Louis as he was a DJ on the local rock station.

One day my sis phoned me, very excited, to say that they were invited to the press area for the Stones concert at the Kiel Convention Center on July 9th. I was so thrilled and begged to join them. Sadly, my parents wouldn't let me fly up from my hometown of Chattanooga so I had to live vicariously through them.

Sis said it was very crowded (about 20,000) and that she was so excited when Mick came out in his purple rhinestone jump suit with a sash. They were seated next to production

Leslie Ladd wasn't allowed to take the train from Chattanooga to St Louis

manager Chip Monck's area, so they also had a great view of the sound and lighting boards, which fascinated my brother-in-law as he was also a sound engineer.

They started with a popular song, 'Brown Sugar', but she thought of me as they played 'Love in Vain', which was my fave. I still remember driving around with my best friend in her brown Pinto, listening to *Sticky Fingers* on the 8 track) Mick threw the rose petals out which my sis managed to get one of for me.

I was thrilled they got me a poster and I have had it hanging in all my houses since then.

PAUL A STURMA

We camped out on the side walk around Kiel to be able to buy tickets when they opened in the morning. We partied all night with all the hippies 'camping out', sleeping on the concrete with a sleeping bag.

MICK JAGGER

On this tour, the audiences have been good, haven't they? In Knoxville and such it might be a bit quiet, but they have listened and gotten up at the end and responded when we wanted them to... what can you say, good audiences. A bit of crying now and then for 'Sympathy for the Devil', which I can't remember anymore. Of course, we might do a long version of it for Nixon.

YESTERDAY'S PAPERS

CONNIE ROSENBAUM
ST LOUIS POST-DISPATCH, JULY 10, 1972

Poured into a purple, velveteen, rhinestone-studded jumpsuit opened to his waist, Jagger strutted and pranced across the stage, and shook his shaggy hair, straddled the microphone and made boxer-like jabs into the air. Jagger, 28 years old, and aging fast, delivered one of his best tour performances, according to groupies who attended previous shows on the Stones' 30-city circuit... The spectacular lighting arrangement divided the stage into three field depths. Jagger was in front, beaming gold, drummer Charlie Watts was glowing pink, and deep blue enveloped guitarists Keith Richards (who composed with Jagger), Bill Wyman and Mick Taylor.

After St Louis, the Stones rolled on to Akron and an open air show at the Rubber Bowl.

RUBBER BOWL
JULY 11, 1972, AKRON, OHIO

CAPACITY	**48,000**
SHOWS	**1**
ARRESTS	**60**

TOM ENGLEHART

I bought my first LPs, with my own money, when I was 14 years old. In 1964, these first records included the Rolling Stones' first album, called *England's Newest Hitmakers*. Over the next eight years, I bought and listened repeatedly to all 13 Stones albums that were released during that period, except *Their Satanic Majesties Request*. My earliest favorite Stones songs were 'Not Fade Away' and 'Mona', both covers. Included in these albums were two live recordings, *Got Live if You Want It!* and *Get Yer Ya-Ya's Out!* These whetted my appetite to see the Stones in concert. They were easily my favorite band. And their newest album in 1972, *Exile on Main St.*, was in constant rotation on my turntable.

The Stones had already played twice in the area where I lived, in 1964 and 1966. Both shows were in Cleveland, Ohio, 40 miles north of my home in Akron. I was too young to go to either concert. In 1972, when the Stones show was announced for the Rubber Bowl, the football stadium at my college, I was primed and ready to go – along with 50,000 plus other eager Stones fans!

The day of the show was sunny and very hot, in the mid-80s. I went to the stadium early with friends to stake out a good spot on the field to watch the show. The stadium's bleacher seats were too far away from the stage, so we spread out a blanket about thirty yards from the high stage, to the right of center. I wanted to be on the side where Keith Richards had been playing during the tour. One friend had seen them in Tucson several weeks earlier, so the stage layout was well known. The dragon floor on which the Stones played was a work of art.

While it was still daylight, Steve Wonder opened the show. His band was large and very good, stirring a lot of people to dance on the field. I remember them playing 'Superstition', one of my favorites. Some sort of fight developed between the police and fans, on the field, but it was only a temporary interruption to Stevie's set.

The Stones waited until dark to appear, and when they hit the stage there was a huge roar from the crowd. Jagger was a whirling blur of energy from the opening notes of 'Brown Sugar'. For this show he wore the blue-spangled jump suit. But what I remember most was the incredible power and beauty of the guitars, especially as played by Mick Taylor. He was a revelation as he took nearly all of the solos on the night. In fact, I felt some disappointment that Keith had not soloed much.

But it's hard to fault Keith's intense focus on the rhythm lines he played to drive the band. Their version of 'Midnight Rambler', first with Jagger's manic energy, then the slow grind and bluesy harmonica, was a highlight. They played for about 90 minutes, then left the stage as suddenly and dramatically as they had appeared. It took us hours to wind down after this terrific show.

I later saw the Stones again in Cleveland on the 1981 and 1989 tours, but neither concert compared to the great 1972 Rubber Bowl show. Akron was one of the smallest towns they played that tour, but also one of the bigger crowds.

JERRY SESLOW

We got there about three in the afternoon for a 7pm show. It was 90 degrees and hotter than hell. We sat on the infield grass. Everyone was peaceful just having a good time smoking a little weed when all of a sudden in stormed the Akron D Squad, in full riot gear chasing us kids, firing rubber bullets at us and swinging their billy clubs. No one was causing any trouble. My date and I ran up into the stands to safety, but many were arrested. It was very uncalled for, but in 1972 it was almost the norm. Stevie Wonder came on around 8pm and Mick and the boys came on around 9.30pm. It was a great show. My only minor disappointment was that it was one of the few times they didn't do my all-time favorite, 'Satisfaction'. Since then, I've seen them in '89 (*Steel Wheels*), '94 (*Voodoo*

Lounge), and '97 (*Bridges to Babylon*), in Vegas, plus in 2000, 2002 and 2015 in Pittsburgh. A ticket cost $5.50 in 1972 and $100 in 2015.

GREG JOHNSTON

The Akron college team used the Rubber Bowl and also different high schools from that area. It was quite a large stadium, about half a mile from the Goodyear building where they built a lot of the Goodyear blimps. I was living on a farm outside Navarre, Ohio, which was 45 to 50 miles to the show from where I lived. I had just graduated high school, and six of us went. The show must have been sold out as the whole stadium, and even the football field, was full of fans. The opening act was Stevie Wonder, and at that time he was introduced as Little Stevie Wonder!

The show was awesome. They pretty much did the *Ya-Ya's* album, along with a few older tunes. They had big screens on both sides of the stage so we could see better. As a bunch of 16 to 18-year-old kids, we had a wonderful time. And they were very good. Back then, a lot of the other live bands we had seen sounded a lot different from their albums, but not the Stones – they sounded better than their albums. I have only seen the Stones live twice since, in 1999 and 2015. It seemed every time I saw them, they were better!

CHIP MONCK

You are either summoned to see Mick or they know where to find you. Hanging out was definitely not the thing to be done. Let him hang with Ahmet Ertegun and all the rest of the folk from Atlantic and do business. We don't need to party with them, because we were in the hall anywhere from 4am for rigging calls or at 7am for load in or eight o'clock for basically our walk in. Our 'in' was basically four hours. Hang the mirror. The sound system rolled off on cabinets on two eight inch hydraulic ram lifts. The left and the right sound wings were elevated at 32 feet so everybody could see through the eight inch rams or move slightly so they could see through the system itself from way up in the heavens. It only took us four hours to load in and be operative, check all the systems and then go find whoever you want to hang out with, or do whatever you want to do to your health. We had a hell of a lot more fun than the act did. The act was almost in a cage because that's the way these tours work. It's, 'Let's do it, then press, then 'thank yous'…' That regimen is a little restricting.

If I was lucky, Mick's PA and limo driver would hand me a set list if that was possible. If not, or nobody bothered to tell us, I was prepared to just go from one song to another. The moment I hear the first bar, or first four bars, I know what it is. So I know exactly what I want to see in it because I've seen it before.

RONDI VEST

I had been living in Cape Cod for the summer, with two other girls in a rooming house. There were three cots in one room, a sink and a community bathroom. I hitchhiked to Boston airport to catch a plane to Cleveland, Ohio, stayed for a couple of days and then flew right back to Cape Cod. I was way down in the front of the infield. I had bought an ounce to take with me. Once we hunkered down in our little space, I started rolling joints and would take a hit while everyone was passing joints left and right. The Rubber Bowl was a U-shaped bowl. The riot police were lined up, shoulder-to-shoulder, at the top with all their riot gear on.

It was a little tense, but they never came down to the infield up front. Everyone booed Stevie Wonder. They wanted the Stones. When the Stones came on, people around us started shooting up. They asked us if we wanted any and we said no. It really was the first time I saw anyone shoot drugs.

CELESTE DIVITA WAGNER

I have some press cuttings in my scrapbook about the '72 Stones concert in Akron, Ohio. Reading through it all brings back such great memories. I was up in the bleacher seats as we got there late. I wasn't one of the bra-less women on the field! Also, the sucker was

THE PLAIN DEALER, WEDNESDAY, JULY 12, 1972

Police, Teens Clash

40,000 Cheer 'Stones' in Akron

Rock Fans Gather

handed to me as several were being handed out. I wasn't about to eat it then as it may have contained LSD - so I saved it.

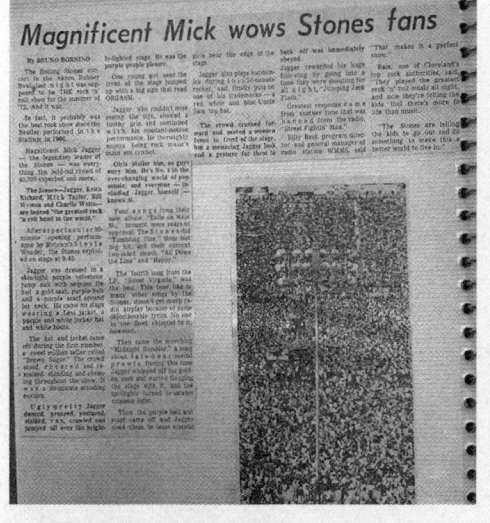

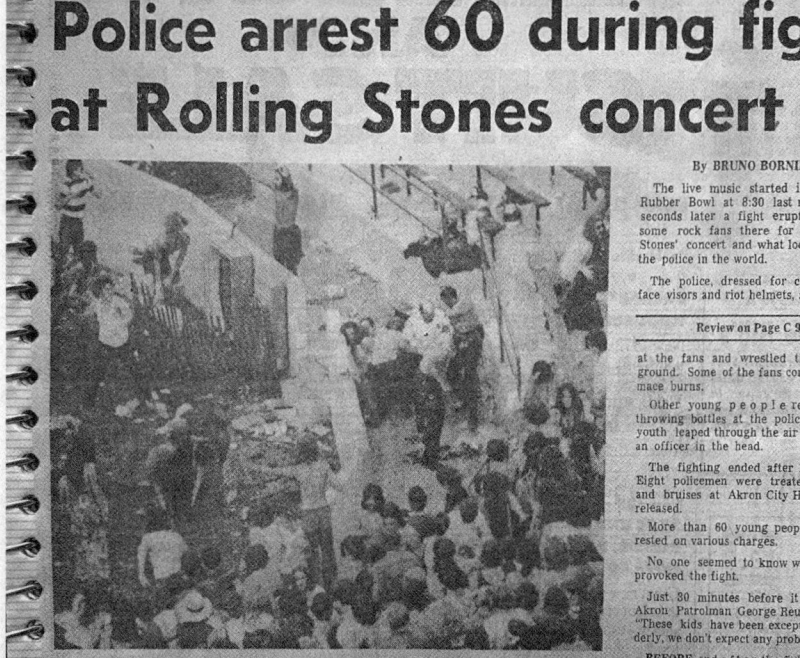

Celeste has kept her scrapbook, and her sucker

CRAIG YOE

The Rolling Stones played the outdoor stadium Rubber Bowl in Akron, Ohio where I lived and where I led a hippie Christian community. I went there with my friends to pass out to the crowd the *Jesus Loves You* newspaper I created and published as they were going in to the concert. I recall the Stones driving within a foot of me to go into the stadium as Stevie Wonder was playing and while a riot went on during his set.

I hung around outside talking to people and giving them the paper as the muffled music inside played in the background. At the end, I went inside when they stopped taking tickets and I continued to pass out the papers as the Stones concluded with 'Street Fighting Man', but I felt a Sympathy *with* the Devil vibe and I quickly trucked on out as the Stones' roadies packed up and fireworks blasted overhead. There's a part of me that wishes I would have heard the whole concert.

KENT ARMANTROUT

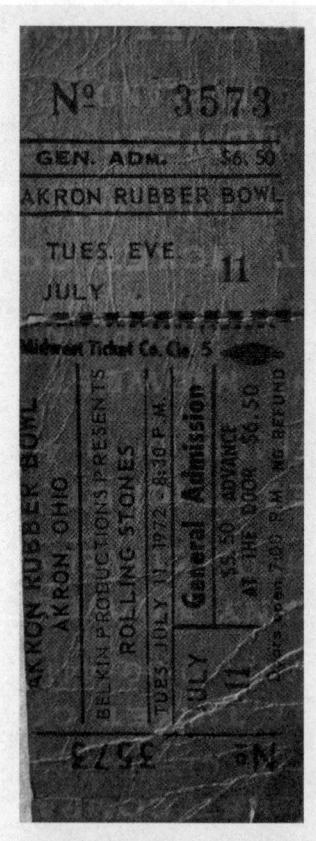

The Hell's Angels rioted that night at the Rubber Bowl. That's why there was a lot of tear gas. The Hell's Angels were security, and I'm not sure how that happened. Those concerts at the Rubber Bowl were very popular. Everyone performed there over the period of a few years. Grace Slick was even arrested for her lack of clothing and trying to entice a riot. Ozzy Osbourne was drunk and trashed on barbiturates. Great show!

Kent Armantrout was at the Rubber Bowl

DAWN LINDSLEY

I was very young and don't remember a lot of details, except it was a great experience and I'm glad I got to see them in their younger days. I still have my ticket stubs.

GARY EDWARDS, AGE 15

Tickets were $5.50 in advance and $6.50 at the door. It was promoted by
Belkin Productions. The Stones were fantastic. The police tried to arrest
a kid for selling pot on the field. This action caused a riot to break out.
People were throwing things. I saw someone throw a thermos jug and hit
a policeman in the head, knocking him off the concrete wall. Then the
police started spraying tear gas into the crowd. This in turn caused Stevie
Wonder to be escorted off stage until the commotion stopped.

GLORIA DEMPSEY

I remember Mick hosing us down with a fire hose as it was so hot out there.

GREGORY J SHERWOOD, AGE 14

My mom told me I wasn't allowed to go, but my friend and I rode our
bikes to the fence and watched it from outside. It was fantastic! I had got
turned on to the Stones by my neighbor Jimmy Hurr, who was four years
older. The album was *Sticky Fingers* and I was hooked. It was the first
album I ever bought and I loved that the album cover had a zipper on it
which actually worked!

When I found out the Stones were coming to Akron, my best friend
and I planned on how we were going to go. My mom overheard us and
said no way were we going to go. The Rubber Bowl was about five miles
from my home. That morning, we got on our bikes, rode to the Rubber
Bowl and locked our bikes against the fence. Stevie Wonder opened
and he was good, but the crowd wanted the Stones. I'll never forget the
opener, 'Brown Sugar'. You can probably figure out that we got busted
and grounded. But it was worth it. The energy was unbelievable. It was
so awesome – I've been hooked ever since.

HUGH WINTERS

It was daytime. I believe Stevie Wonder and the James Gang, after Joe
Walsh had left, were also on the bill. One of the things that sticks out for
me is the way that Jagger was addressing the crowd before he started.
He was kind of having fun or maybe nobody told him how to say
Akron, which is the name of the town. He was calling it 'A-kron', with
the emphasis on the A. It was kind of funny. Americans really enjoy the

179

way the English speak, we're always amazed by that, and love the little differences and what not. It's fun to hear anyway.

I went to Kent State. Somebody was smoking pot out in the field. The Rubber Bowl is a stadium. It's not huge, and somebody got fingered for smoking pot, or something. They never tell you anything but it was a kind of spectacle to see a huge number of police officers basically make a corridor right toward where that person was and then block off all the other people on either side. A couple of officers then dragged the guy out. It was kinda weird, and seemed an excessive amount of effort for one guy doing something that wasn't a danger to others. But it was a long time ago and those were different times.

Ohio was a pretty strait-laced state. That's where the 'four dead in Ohio' came from with the National Guard. I had a friend who was in the National Guard and he said, 'What you gotta realise is that the guys join the National Guard so they didn't have to go to Vietnam.' They were mostly pacifists. They didn't want to go to Vietnam. They were too scared to go. They had the draft back then. They'd grab your ass and put you where they wanted to. So a way out of it was to enlist in something safer, or which better matched your sensibilities. But one way or another you were going somewhere. So these guys in the National Guard weren't trying to hurt anybody, and they probably shouldn't have had live ammunition in the first place. And they shot all over the heads of the protestors. They didn't hit any protestors. What they did was hit people behind the protestors. The campus at Kent State is on a hill, so when they shot over the heads of the protestors, trying not to hurt anybody, they accidentally shot other people. It was a tragedy, no doubt about it.

There had to be 100 officers that formed that corridor holding back the crowds so that they could drag this person out. That kind of marred the whole thing, you know? Maybe the authorities were concerned that it would turn into something bigger. I don't know what.

When The Beatles broke up it started to saw off one of the limbs of my optimism in life. It was a sad thing to me. I was eight years old when JFK was murdered and that was kind of a shock too. Not that I knew anything at eight years old about all these things, but there was so much talk about it. It was on late night radio and everybody had a point of view about it. It was the same thing with the Kent State shootings. There was so much talk and buzz and all that stuff. It seeps into you after a while.

Suddenly you start to get a little bit of skepticism about the world. But for me, where my brain was at the time, The Beatles breaking up was like, 'Whoa! I never thought that would happen.' When Epstein died, they were rudderless. He did a very good job of corralling them and keeping them going forward. With him gone they just didn't know which way to go.

JAMES JOHNSON

This was my first Stones show. I had just finished my second year of college, and I was in a rock and roll band. My friend Tom suggested we go see the Stones at the Akron Rubber Bowl, but I was unsure whether I could afford the $15 ticket price. I scraped it together, and we drove up with a couple of Tom's friends. We got there early in the afternoon, so we could mingle and hopefully meet a few girls. Tom succeeded right away. I never did. Around 6pm, the doors opened and we were swept inside. I'm glad I never lost my balance, because I would have been crushed in the stampede. Tom and I never saw each other again until after the concert. I found a place in the general admission part of the stadium, about 20 yards from the stage. Stevie Wonder opened, and I loved his set.

After what seemed like an hour, the Stones came on. Mick in his white jumpsuit, and Mick Taylor looking incredibly young. Keith kicked off 'Brown Sugar', and I was mesmerized. I watched Jagger prance, and loved the fact that Keith stuck closely to Charlie's drum riser. They seemed so locked in, as if they were a single brain playing two instruments. They played about 15 songs, including several from their new album, *Exile on Main St.* When they finished with 'Street Fighting Man', I was hoping for an encore, since the crowd was going crazy. There never was one. By the time I found my friend Tom, our ride had left, so we had to hitchhike back home to Columbus. It was pretty easy, since there were plenty of Stones fans heading our way. I was a Stones fan for life after that night, and have seen at least one show on every tour since.

MARK JOHNSON, AGE 21

I was just graduated from Hiram College – a great small school about 15 miles from Kent, Ohio where I was living for the summer. Kent State was where four people were killed in 1970 by National Guardsmen. I was on the infield of the Rubber Bowl with my friend from Hiram College. We got there too early, started smoking marijuana and were kind of trashed by the time the Stones came on. There was a disturbance with some bottles flying around. The cops came in in two lines with full riot gear. It was all kind of weird. The Stones played late. They seemed to be a parody of themselves. Jagger was wearing his Uncle Sam hat with the long scarf.

MILAN POTICA

I first took a liking to the Stones when they released 'Satisfaction' and it was played on the radio regularly for months. I bought the album *High Tide and Green Grass* and listened to it often. I enjoyed all their single hits that were aired on the radio, but I really fell in love with the Stones when 'Jumpin' Jack Flash' was released. There's something about that song that is so powerful and driving that I was attracted to it like a magnet. To this day, if someone asked me to pick just one favorite song from rock history, I must say it is 'Jumpin' Jack Flash'.

When the *Let It Bleed* album came out, I was thoroughly sold on the Stones. I listened to the album frequently. 'Gimme Shelter' really knocked me out big time. Then the live *Get Yer Ya-Ya's Out!* album was released and I bought it and listened to it more than any other album. The live versions of 'Oh Carol', 'Stray Cat Blues', 'Little Queenie', 'Love in Vain' and especially 'Midnight Rambler' sounded better than the studio versions.

(I must preface all this by saying right before *Let It Bleed* was released, I was introduced to cannabis and smoked weed or hash most of the time when I listened to the Stones. Most pot heads will agree that listening to music whilst stoned makes the music come alive.)

I bought *Beggars Banquet* and loved many of the cuts on the album. Then *Sticky Fingers* was released and I played the hell out of that album. What a perfect gem of an album, with so many seriously good songs, and the quality of the recording was superlative. With the recording of *Sticky Fingers*, the Stones reached their pinnacle. This is not to say the Stones went downhill after that but I just feel *Sticky Fingers* was flawless. Mick Taylor's guitar playing really added to the quality of their music. He had a style that really enhanced the Stones sound.

Then *Exile on Main St.* came out, another gem. So it was now the summer of 1972 and the Stones were on their 1972 American tour. The city of

Akron was the biggest manufacturer of car tires in the country, so there was an outdoor sports stadium they named the Akron Rubber Bowl. Several of my friends and I drove from Cleveland to Akron the night of the concert. The two cities are about

Milan Potica was at the Rubber Bowl

30 miles apart. We were all drinking wine, smoking cannabis and taking Quaaludes, a typical routine back then prior to attending a rock concert.

Stevie Wonder started off the concert which didn't interest me. Then the Stones came on. There were no assigned seats in the stadium, people were mostly standing on the field watching the concert. I was pretty far away from the stage, but just realizing the Rolling Stones were present there, performing many of my favorite songs, was a magical, mystical experience. It was one of the true highlights of my life.

PAUL McCART, AGE 13

My sister was eight years older than me and she practically introduced me to the Stones from birth. I listened to *Big Hits (High Tide and Green Grass)* as a very young kid, from the age of two onwards. The Stones flew into Akron's Fulton Airport, which was right next to the stadium where they would play. The stadium was a couple of blocks away from my home. I remember my mom standing in the yard waving to the plane as it landed. It had the Stones logo on it.

I went to the concert alone because none of my childhood friends were allowed to go. I was 13 years old and made new friends at the show. When they started playing, their sound was so different from every band I had seen that summer. (I'm a guitarist, and was a beginner guitarist at the time.) I swear they started off with 'Honky Tonk Women', and the sound of that opening chord is something I never forgot. But that's not what history says.

RODNEY PERRY, AGE 20

I have always listened to the Stones since back when they first came out. I liked them better than The Beatles. I've seen the Stones in concert three times now. In 1972 I saw them at the Rubber Bowl, I saw the *Steel Wheels* tour in Tampa and I saw them again in Tampa in 2021. I was 20 in 1972. I lived in Cleveland, right up the road from Akron. Bands tended to play Cleveland when they came through Ohio, but at that time the Rubber Bowl did have some bigger names come to play. It was an open air show and a sold out concert.

It was a good party atmosphere. There were a lot of drugs around but I didn't partake myself as I was driving. But the others with me did. There were a few people with me that don't even remember being there and I know they were because I took them. Two carloads of us went. My good friend who was there doesn't remember how he got there.

We didn't have great seats. If it was an American football game, we'd have been in the end zone opposite the stage. I don't remember a lot of the performance. I remember that Stevie Wonder opened for them. I didn't know that until I got there, so I was kinda surprised about that. I guess I didn't read my ticket or the brochures or whatever. The thing I remember most about the concert is that there was some kind of brouhaha going on and a big long row of police came out and they circled the field. We were up on a second level and they were on a walkway. And some little guy came running through the crowd and jumped up and kicked the cop in the head and we couldn't believe that he could jump that high and kick the cop in the head like that.

I saw the *Steel Wheels* concert with my buddy, Bill Polinsky. That was a good concert. And this last concert in 2021? Because of the great physical shape that Jagger is in, he ran around like a kid. I can't do that, and I'm a little bit younger than him.

RONNIE CRAWFORD

An upstart band opened for them, Stevie Wonder. I could probably go on and on. It's the first time that I saw a cordless microphone and the new Jumbotron screen. The screens were on each side of the stage and unwrapped, bare commercial scaffolding. Mick climbed the scaffolding on the left side of the stage as you looked at it, wrapped his foot around one of the scaffolding pieces and sang 'Monkey Man'. He was hanging out over the crowd, probably about 30 feet above the stage. It was killer.

YESTERDAY'S PAPERS

JANE SCOTT
PLAIN DEALER, JULY 12, 1972

'Ladies and gentlemen, the Rolling Stones,' the announcer said. A scream went up in the Akron Rubber Bowl that would make old-timers think of VJ Day in a boiler factory. Mick Jagger and the Rolling Stones had rolled down into the bowl in a van over the same hill used by the Soap Box Derby… Lights flashed on and Jagger hopped around like a Hopi Indian. He grabbed the mike, fell to his knees, and danced by himself to the front of the stage singing his hit 'Brown Sugar'. He wore nail-studded black pants and blue jacket. He was as mean, moody and magnificent as ever as he rolled into his newer hit, 'Rocks Off'. He sang every song with the energy of an encore.

ALLAN WIGGINS
PLAIN DEALER, JULY 12, 1972

Sometimes it makes you wonder how these youngsters can get enough energy to go out for an evening's entertainment and fight the police when they are obviously so sleepy they can hardly keep their eyes open. To look at the audience it was hard to believe it was taking place in Akron. Most of the youngsters looked as hairy and as elaborately dressed, at least the ones that weren't half-nude, as the rock group which made its name for its sexy performances.

From the Rubber Bowl, the STP headed 300 miles west to Indianapolis.

INDIANA CONVENTION-EXPOSITION CENTER
JULY 12, 1972, INDIANAPOLIS, INDIANA

CAPACITY	12,000
SHOWS	1
ARRESTS	0

DANIEL TEAFOE

I saw the Stones in Indianapolis 50 years ago. Two days later, *Life* magazine came out with Mick on the cover. We got back into town in the wee hours on the 13th, and I went to my mailbox and there was the magazine sitting there, with Mick on the cover and my birthdate on it – July 14. It was just a perfect end to all that experience. It was quite remarkable. I had just turned 17.

In June 1964, The Beatles exploded across America. I was only eight years old. My mum said, 'Oh look, the Rolling Stones are on *The Mike Douglas Show*,' and I said, 'Who is that?' So I saw it live as it was happening, and I was like, 'Oh my God!' My best friend was older than me and she loved the Stones. Her walls were plastered with their posters and pictures and she would play their music all day long. They came to Chicago in 1966 and I said, 'I want to go and see the Rolling Stones.' My mother said, 'You're not going to see the Rolling Stones – are you kidding?' I was only ten, but still…

I finally got to go in '69. Back in those days, you had to send in your self-addressed stamped envelope with a money order for a ticket and hope that you were going to get picked. I think the ticket was $2.50. I got two tickets. My mate's dad drove us into the city and we went to a matinee show. And at the moment they came on stage, my world went from black-and-white to color. I was an impressionable 14-year-old. And after that, you're hot and it's just part of your life. I'm still hooked almost

60 years later. I've seen them many times over the years.

I was vehemently opposed to the Vietnam war. When I was nine years old, I wrote a letter to the President opposing it. I'm gay, so they wouldn't have taken me anyway. I would've used that defence, come hell or high water, even though it was still an imprisonable offence back then. But there was no way I was going to go over there. Call me a coward or whatever. It was absolutely out of the question. 1972 was just at the back end of that. That was when they started having the draft lottery. They picked birth dates out of a hat or whatever. That was how you got picked. I ignored that.

You were supposed to register for the draft and I decided to give it a miss. I went to London

Daniel Teafoe captured Mick in action

in 1974 and I thought, 'I better do this.' I thought I had to clear the air. I remember the recruiting officer said, 'Why haven't you registered yet?' I said, 'I'm just a procrastinator, you know?'

There was a time when 'Brown Sugar' didn't exist, when *Exile* didn't exist. These become your markers in life and you grow up with them, 'That's when *Let It Bleed* came out, that's when *Sticky Fingers* came out, that's when *Exile* came out. That music becomes part of your life.

The atmosphere was certainly more charged than in '69, because what they did in '69 had never really been seen before, with an arena tour and all that and coming out with a great live album. And you've got the political climate and you've got hippies and all of that stuff going on; it was a powder keg in many ways. You had the bombing of arenas. You had counterfeit tickets sold. People crashing gates. Cops beating people up. And you had your parents saying, 'You're not going to see the Stones!' That was the atmosphere.

And they were front page news wherever they went. They still are. Just the other day (in 2022), they were leaving a hotel in Brussels in Belgium and there were hundreds of people standing outside waiting to see them. It's remarkable.

I went to the show with a school buddy. I was the only one in our gang that had seen them before, in '69. I grew up in a very small town. And then in '72 it was like, 'Okay, who wants to go?' I'm like that every time the Stones are touring. Over the years, I've introduced quite a few people to their first ever Stones concert. I had just seen them in Chicago and it was a case of, 'Where are they playing next? We gotta go there.' So you get *Rolling Stone* magazine to get the itinerary. 'Oh, Indianapolis, let's go there.'

But we didn't have any tickets. And I thought, 'If I was a newspaper in Indianapolis, what would I be called?' Remember, this was before the Internet. 'I know, I'd be called the *Indianapolis Star*.' So I called directory assistance, 411 and asked for the number for the *Indianapolis Star*. I got through to the classifieds section where they said, 'Hello, Classifieds, what's your ad please?' And I said, 'No, no, I'm looking for something. Do you have any ads for people selling Rolling Stones tickets?' She had one phone number. 'Give me that, please?' So she did. I called the guy up and I got on the phone and bought the tickets for a reasonable price. I think I paid 20 bucks each, and he gave me his address to get there and we were good to go.

So I had two tickets, but there were three of us. We drove into the Market Square in Indianapolis, where the Stones were playing the arena. One friend had all the money so he gets a ticket and my other friend has the car which got us there, so he gets a ticket. Who doesn't have a ticket? Oops, that's me, who organized everything. Thank you very much.

Everybody was chilling outside, smoking weed and lounging around on the grass. I'm walking around, stepping over people asking them for a ticket. People are laughing at me. 'Hey, you gotta be joking man!' I thought, 'This is not going to turn out well.' I'm all forlorn. My head is down and I'm going back to the parking lot when I saw three people. I said, 'Would you happen to have a spare ticket?' and they said, 'Yes, as a matter of fact we do.' I said, 'All I've got is 20 bucks,' and they sold me the ticket and I was in…

After the show, we drove back into the city at four in the morning and I went to my postbox and there was that *Life* magazine, sitting there with my birthdate on it and Mick Jagger on the cover. I just could not believe it.

GEORGE SCHRICKER

I was so close to the stage that I had to look up at them. As per usual, they were high energy, but the lights were not dramatic. It seems like they were in full light the whole time and there wasn't much variation but I'm not sure if I remember that too well. I like the Stones but, truthfully, I was more into Stevie Wonder's show and music.

YESTERDAY'S PAPERS

JOHN FLORA
INDIANAPOLIS NEWS, JULY 13, 1972

All eyes were on Jagger, thin to the point of looking frail, wearing a skin-tight white jumpsuit, under a Levi jacket and a six-foot-long scarlet sash, his hair full of silver glitter and his eyes made up like a drag queen… A Stones concert starts at roughly the same energy level where most other rock groups peak. From the first note, the crowd was on its feet, packing the aisles and surging against the stage.

After Indianapolis, the Stones had two nights playing in Detroit at the legendary Cobo Hall.

COBO HALL

JULY 13 & 14, 1972, DETROIT, MICHIGAN

NUMBER OF SHOWS   **2**
CAPACITY   **12,000**
ARRESTS   **17**

GARY SMITH, AGE 20

When the tour was announced, I sent in for tickets. Mail order was the only way you could buy them. There was a limit of six tickets per show, so I sent in for six tickets for both shows. Once I got the tickets in the mail, I called my friends and said, 'We scored the tickets for both dates!' This was the first time we would be seeing the Stones live. We were so geeked. The anticipation, the build up to the show, was like a child waiting for Santa Claus to come on Christmas Eve.

Phil Hogan, Bill Adams, myself and some other friends, whose names we really can't recall, went to both shows. On the day of the show, we were so excited to get to downtown Detroit that we set a time that we would be leaving to go so we wouldn't be late. Phil was coming in from Toronto on his Harley Davidson motorcycle and he almost didn't get here on time, but thankfully he got to my house with a few minutes to spare. Driving to the show, we had the Stones blasting over the car stereo and we were all geeked to the max.

Once inside Cobo Hall, you could smell the aroma of the joints in the air. Detroit's own Stevie Wonder and his Wonderlove band was the opening act. When the lights went down, the people went crazy, yelling, whistling and hand clapping waiting for the show to start. Stevie didn't disappoint, but we were there for the Stones!

During intermission, all we could talk about was guessing what song the Stones would open up with and what other songs would be in their set. The lights went down and the place went nuts. Everyone stood up on their feet. The lights came on and there they were, on stage, our favorite band – the Rolling Stones! We couldn't believe we were actually seeing them live.

They opened with 'Brown Sugar' and they sounded great. Mick was all over the stage, strutting his stuff, and the band was jamming. The whole concert hall was electrified by what we were witnessing. Like they say, 'The greatest rock 'n' roll band in the world.' They played an amazing set and the crowd stayed on their feet the entire show. Well, who could sit with the Rolling Stones on stage?

They finished their set with 'Street Fighting Man' and the people were still going nuts.

The lights went down when they left the stage, building up to the encore. Thousands of lighters lit up the hall waiting for them to come back out for an encore.

When the lights came back on, everyone went crazy! It wasn't just the Stones on stage, but Stevie Wonder's band too. The first song they did was Stevie's song 'Uptight', with both bands jamming. We couldn't contain ourselves. Mick took Stevie's arm and walked him around the stage to a drum set and then an organ. It was the coolest thing I had ever seen!

Then for the second song of the encore, they all jammed to the Stones' 'Satisfaction'. The crowd was so into it. I would bet that encore was the best encore of all time. At least it was for me. It still holds true today, after hundreds of concerts I have attended.

The Rolling Stones' *Exile on Main St.* show is at least one of the top five concerts I have ever seen. Then I remembered, I was going to relive this all again the next day at show number two. Two nights of pure rock 'n' roll bliss!

TOM ITCHUE, AGE 18

I had just completed my first year of college when the Stones tour was announced. They would play two nights in Detroit, my hometown, at Cobo Arena. The method of purchasing tickets at Cobo for big events was to send a self-addressed envelope to the box office with postage stamp attached. We got lucky and were mailed two tickets. I went with my college friend Bart, who lived nearby.

The Cobo Arena atmosphere was electric. Stevie Wonder was the opening act, which Bart and I thought a strange choice. He had been a Motown Records star and a child prodigy throughout the 1960s, but he had been a bit out of the spotlight, at least to the Rolling Stones fans attending. But Stevie was brilliant that night, playing several instruments, with two females leading him around the stage. He got a warm welcome from the fans trickling into their seats.

Then the Stones came out to a roaring welcome. I had attended several concerts that year but the Stones filled the arena with a tight sound that rocked the place like no other band I had seen. They had extra horn pieces, including Bobby Keys on sax who really stood out. And they did an encore with Stevie Wonder, who Jagger led out to the stage to the screaming fans.

I can't say I was the biggest Stones fan before the concert. I had seen Emerson, Lake and Palmer, Pink Floyd, Jethro Tull and others that year, and would attend many a concert after including Led Zeppelin, Elton John and Jeff Beck. But the Stones lived up to their reputation as the best live rock and roll band in the world that night. I will never forget it.

KEN KUKLA, AGE 15

I was 15 and starting to partake daily. A good neighborhood buddy just bought a three-year-old Caddy. I was cruising around in style for sure. Reading the morning paper, I saw that the Rolling Stones shows in Detroit were already sold out. However, a couple of days later, another buddy said that a buddy of *his* had offered him two tickets for $10 each. We took them, and several days later I had in my hand my very first Rolling Stones ticket. I could not believe it. I stashed it under a box in the top drawer of my dresser, and I have to admit that ticket was looked at first thing every morning. It was really cool knowing that I had the hottest ticket in town. (I still have the stub.)

The day of the gig started with a trip to Belle Isle, a small island in between Detroit and Canada, to prepare ourselves for that night's festivities, and then it was on to Cobo for the show. I was in Tier B, not too bad, on what was Mick Taylor's side..I remember that, at the very beginning of 'Brown Sugar', Mick and Keith did this little gunslinger-type move towards each other. Very cool. Also, on this night we got an encore with Stevie Wonder for 'Uptight' and 'Satisfaction', which was only done a few times that tour and which made the gig that much more special.

The sound, as I remember, was pretty good. My ears were ringing for two days afterwards. I remember saying that night that the concert was too great for words. I find it really hard to believe that was 50 years ago, and to me the music – *Exile* – and the memories are still as fresh as when I first heard and saw them. Sadly, as a collector I have yet to come across either of the Detroit '72 shows... maybe someday.

JIM HUFF

I saw the Stones at Cobo Arena in Detroit but I don't remember a thing about it – which makes me mad! I sat in the nosebleed section on the left side from the stage. Stevie Wonder opened for them and he joined in on their encore of 'Jumpin' Jack Flash', which I don't remember any of either.

Jim Huff was there but doesn't remember too much

STEVE SYMONS, AGE 19

I had been a Stones fan since 'Satisfaction' came out in 1965. The Beatles were my number one but I couldn't deny the Stones their place. I had a few of their 45s from the Sixties before I bought albums. In the summer of 1972, I had the *Exile on Main St.* LP and had been listening to it quite a bit. Someone at work had access to tickets so I said, 'I'll take two.' I really don't remember what I paid but it seemed like it was only between $25 and $50 each. I had a decent job so it was affordable.

I was recently married to my high school sweetheart and I took her as she was also a rock and roll lover. Cobo Arena in downtown Detroit was only 20 minutes from our suburban home. It wasn't my first big show, as I had seen The Who at Cobo a year after Woodstock. We were excited as we neared downtown Detroit and concert traffic increased. I am sure we smoked some pot as we drove to the show, and maybe even inside the hall back in those days, security being more relaxed. The lines were long and once inside it was quite a Detroit soul hippie vibe, with all kinds of flashy outfits and characters ready and waiting for the Stones to rock out. First though, hometown hero Stevie Wonder opened with his maturing sound of Motown Soul playing oldies and songs from his yet-to-be-released LP, *Talking Book*.

Then the Rolling Stones came out to thunderous applause. We had decent seats on the main floor, maybe 25 to 30 rows back. I remember Mick's new shag haircut looking androgynous and his constant motion – dancing and prancing and doing all his moves in his glittery jumpsuit – and Keith's persona, and the horns playing a big part, as *Exile* songs were a major part of the show.

The encore I've always remembered as a highlight, with Stevie Wonder joining Mick and the Stones for 'Satisfaction' and 'Uptight (Everything's Alright'). That had everybody up and dancing to Mick and Stevie doing their thing together. I had quite the after buzz for some time afterwards.

SHAUN DONAHUE

In 1972 I was a senior at Ferndale High, which is about a half mile from the Detroit city limit and back then was one of the few desegregated schools in the suburbs. At that time, music and cars were king in Detroit. They came together with AM Top 40 radio and FM AOR or album-oriented rock formats. We listened to the music on the radio while cruising Woodward Avenue. We could not afford hot rod cars like many of the kids had, so we borrowed the family sedan to go 'cruisin' Woodward'. This pastime is now remembered every year in Detroit in August at an event they call the Dream Cruise.

Obviously, Detroit is known for Motown, but it also has a rich music history in rock, jazz, pop and gospel too. We were big rock fans and we listened to local bands Bob Seger, Grand Funk, Alice Cooper and Mitch Ryder and the Detroit Wheels. Music was just part of life in Detroit in 1972. We were also huge fans of the so-called British Invasion. At the time, there was a rivalry between The Beatles and the Stones and you were kind of one or the other. The Stones were considered more outlaw than The Beatles. I was more of a Beatles fan. In grade school, I had purchased a Beatle wig and my favorite Beatle was John. My best friend, Mitch, was for the Stones all the way. He had a Mick Jagger haircut and he bought a velour blazer. When his parents were out of town, we would blast the Stones on the family console stereo and Mitch would lip sync an awesome Jagger imitation.

Every week, we waited eagerly for the ad in the *Detroit Free Press*, the local newspaper, for the announcements of the upcoming concerts at Cobo Hall in downtown Detroit. 'Cobo' as we called it, was a basketball arena and home, at the time, to the NBA Detroit Pistons. (It's now called Huntington Place and has been repurposed as a convention and meeting center and no longer has an arena for concerts.) In 1972, the advertisements in the *Free Press* were just tiny announcements way down in the bottom corner of one of the last pages of the paper. Earlier that year, I went there to my first arena rock concert ever and saw Joe Cocker. They did 'Delta Lady' for an encore and it was wild, with Leon Russell dancing on top of the piano in his white top hat and tails.

A few months later, we saw the ad in the *Free Press*. There it was – the Rolling Stones were coming to Cobo. My friend Jim said, 'We have to go!', if for no other reason than to honor Mitch's Jagger imitation. Also, in the ad, it said 'special guest Stevie Wonder'. So the three of us got tickets. I think they were going for around $10 or less each.

Back in 1967, the Summer of Love was big in Detroit and the hippie movement was in full swing. I turned 13 that year and my bedroom was adorned with black light posters, incense and scented candles that I bought at one of the many local 'head shops' that were springing up all over suburban Detroit area. In high school, me, Mitch and Jim began to identify with the anti-establishment hippie movement and grew our hair long. Of course, along with that, came the drug culture.

So, the three of us went to the concert. We smoked pot on the way, and I think Mitch and Jim did something stronger. Mitch got a little sick and spent some time in the bathroom. He missed a lot of the Mick Jagger performance that he loved to imitate.

In 1972, Stevie Wonder was a legend in Detroit. However, although he had a string of Motown hits, he still wasn't yet 'Stevie Wonder' the international star that we know today. We did not think Stevie, or 'Little Stevie' as he was previously known, was actually on tour with the Stones. We thought that he was just invited to play one time because it was a Detroit concert. We were proud as Detroiters that the Stones had recognized Stevie's talent and had asked him to perform.

The concert was fantastic. Most acts gave it their all when playing Detroit because of the music history of the city. The Stones were no exception. Stevie Wonder played first, obviously, and he was unbelievable. He played all of his hits and the place was totally rockin'. At one point, the band left the stage in the middle of a song and Stevie went around the stage and played every instrument as well as singing and playing the harmonica. I have still never seen anything like it. It was obvious that we were witnessing something special. The Stones came on and played all their hits as well and it was fantastic. For the encore, the Stones invited Stevie on the stage with them and they played together. I could tell that the Stones had tremendous respect for Stevie, Motown and Detroit.

It is the best concert I have ever seen. To witness two of the greatest legends in music history together on stage was a once in a lifetime event for me. The Stones, from Europe, and Stevie Wonder, from my hometown, performing on stage together, was such a joyful experience for me. I will never forget it and it is the best music experience of my life. Looking back objectively, I would have to say that Stevie Wonder outperformed and upstaged the Stones. In 1972, *Innervisions* and *Songs in the Key of Life* were just on the horizon. We were witnessing the transformation of 'Little Stevie' into the enormous adult talent he would soon become.

A couple of years ago, I was fortunate to see Stevie Wonder perform the entire *Songs in the Key of Life* album, live, in concert, at the Forum in Los Angeles. To me, it is one of the greatest albums of all time. It amazes me that both Stevie and the Stones are still performing 50 years later, and that I'm still here too.

RICHARD McMAHON

Hometown Superstar Stevie Wonder was magical as the Stones' opening act, and a good choice as Jagger and company owed much to black musicians, especially in their early years, as they searched for their own unique sound. Wonder was in great form that night, both on piano and in voice, and he pleased the anxious crowd with hit after hit in a seamless flow of smooth jazz and danceable songs. Physically moving from instrument to instrument on one song, Stevie demonstrated his

196

musical prowess and range despite his blindness. When he finished, his set seemed too short, but that was by design for the Motown Genius.

A long intermission followed as roadies readied the stage for the next act, and the crowd grew restless, although by Stones standards they were well behaved. I began to smell marijuana from below as we watched from the edge of the upper level in Cobo, when the lights suddenly dimmed and a roar issued from crowd as Jagger led the Stones as they raced onto the stage and into the spotlights.

As he ran, Mick kicked a beach ball from the stage and into the crowd. Pausing for a moment, he acknowledged the huge audience and said it was great to be back in Detroit before the band launched into 'Brown Sugar', the crowd instantly recognizing and reacting to the opening chords. Concert on!

TOM HAGERTY, AGE 17

I was just out of University of Detroit high school. I went with Debbie Hoffman, who I was dating at the time. She got tickets. We went with another couple and he drove a Plymouth Duster 340 if memory serves. I remember Stevie Wonder kicking ass on the opener. He played drums on one song.

The Stones were coming off my favorite LP, *Exile on Main St.*, and were truly the greatest rock and roll band in the world, having released four classic LPs in a row. What other artist had such a run of excellence? For me the highlight of the show was Keith's playing on Chuck Berry's 'Bye Bye Johnny'. The band was tighter than a shrunken t-shirt and Charlie kicked ass (as always) on drums. For me that was the highwater mark for the Stones, the place where – as Hunter Thompson would say – you could see the wave breaking roll back. I have never seen a better concert.

RANDALL NOLLIN, AGE 16

My brother was going to the University of Michigan and I went with him and some of his friends. I really don't remember how we got tickets, but I know they were in very high demand. There were a lot of bogus fake tickets being sold at what were very high prices for that time. The tickets had three colors of paper that would show when torn. I knew of some kids whose parents had a printing company. They had access to that special paper and they printed up a whole bunch of fake tickets.

This was a wild time for concerts and this was a huge concert to go to, as the Stones hadn't toured in some time in the United States. What I remember the most was that I observed a lot of drugs being used by my brother's friends and then we drove to Detroit from Ann Arbor. I was not sure how – or if – we would get back as they were all crazy high and drunk. It was a little scary for me, but I had to see the Stones!

We got to Cobo Hall where the concert was and it was a madhouse of craziness. There were large crowds with people trying to get tickets. We got into the concert and the main floor had mostly been taken over by motorcycle gangs, who controlled their territory. So we went up to the first level, dead center, which was a perfect view for the show.

Before the show went on, there was basically a riot going on outside with people breaking huge windows and doors to get in. There were riot police and I think the National Guard was called out as it was out of control. You could smell tear gas and lots of fighting going on.

Martha Reeves and the Vandellas opened the show and played a short set. Then Stevie Wonder came on. He was from Detroit and he was great, but the crowd, and especially the main floor, wanted the Stones and they did not make Stevie Wonder welcome. I think he cut his set short but I really don't remember much about that.

There was a wait for the Stones and the crowd got moodier and crazy. Some fights were going on and the bikers were causing trouble. Then the Rolling Stones came on and they were just the best band in the world. Jagger was incredible and Keith and Mick Taylor were phenomenal. Bill Wyman and Charlie Watts were at their peak and the Stones just rocked. *Exile on Main St.* had recently been released, and *Sticky Fingers* before that, and the Stones just were the greatest rock 'n' roll happening.

Once it was over, we walked out and found all the glass walls to the building were mostly broken, with litter everywhere and police and National Guard military taking control of things. There were more people than tickets for seats and a lot of them had seen the show as it was jammed packed inside. There were a few cars on fire and smoke going around. We found our car and got the hell out of there.

YESTERDAY'S PAPERS

DAVID FENTON
ANN ARBOR SUN, JULY 21, 1972

It's a long way from 'Satisfaction' to being self-exiled on Main Street in the French Riviera. (The tunes from the latest album were the low-points of the night.) They seem to have even less of a positive charge than ever before, with their cynicism and their distance from their audience growing greater and more frightening all the time… The Rolling Stones made it clearer than ever with their latest extravaganza that they just don't care about much more than getting people's money and using it only to pursue their own decadence.

From Detroit, the Stones headed for Canada and shows in Toronto and then Montreal.

MAPLE LEAF GARDENS
JULY 15, 1972, TORONTO, CANADA

CAPACITY	17,000
SHOWS	2
ARRESTS	13

GUY HOWELL, AGE 16

They did two shows and we were at the late one. It was 32 degrees Celsius outside and a sweat box inside. For a 16-year-old, it was quite an eye-opener!

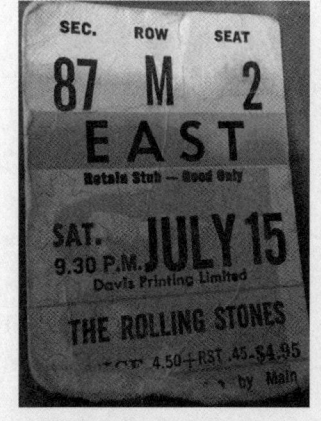

Guy Howell remembers it was hot

ANNA PETTI

We were kids, and best friends at 15 years of age. The show was sold out.
I had been trying to get through night and day for weeks on end. Q107,
a radio station out of Toronto, was having a contest, and the 107th
person to call in would win a pair of tickets to the Stones at Maple Leaf
Gardens. I remember that it was late and I was cooking eggs in a frying
pan with my ear to the phone (as always) when they actually answered
and I was the 107th caller! I remember flipping an egg so high that it
splattered against the wall. We won!

My friend's dad drove us to Toronto from our home in Niagara
Falls. I'll never forget the impact that show had on me. Jagger and
Richards exuded a magic that has not to this day been duplicated by any
other musicians. We were mesmerised for the entire show and thus began
the soundtrack to my life. I've been to 19 Stones concerts since and
have every album they have ever made. Never have I ever experienced
anything close to the emotions that band awakens in me. After 50 years I
feel as though they are family.

JAMES McMANUS

I started listening to their second and third albums through my older
brother when we lived in Arden, about 20 miles south of Asheville,
North Carolina. He was three years older than me. He seemed into them
more than he was The Beatles; this would be 1964. This fascination
continued through the Sixties as they began having hit singles.

The Rolling Stones were part of the British Invasion and were as
popular as The Beatles. We loved buying records and the Stones were
always a great buy when a new album came out. *Aftermath*, *Between the
Buttons* and *Got Live If You Want It!* were the mid-Sixties choice. We moved
back to Rochester, New York and the hype with the counterculture
was in full swing. My brother was now into the newer Rolling Stones
material like *Beggars Banquet* and *Let It Bleed*. It seems his musical interests
were getting into a more protest-oriented music, like the MC5, Moby
Grape and Frank Zappa, but also the Kinks, starting with *Face to Face*
and *Something Else*. The Beatles were always on the radio and TV, and
everyone was tuned into them.

Going to college opened up new doors of music appreciation for me. I went to school with a bunch of people from New York City. One guy had got to see the Stones at Madison Square Gardens in 1969, but another guy was into the Fillmore – The Allman Brothers, etc. – while others had been to Woodstock in 1969 and one girl saw George Harrison's *Concert for Bangladesh*. I realised that the Stones weren't the only thing people listened to.

In the summer of 1972, a friend of my younger brother went to Toronto to stand in line for tickets to the show on July 15th. They were there for eight hours waiting early on so they would get tickets, which they did. He was apologetic because the tickets that were available were in a mezzanine area behind the stage, maybe ten rows from the very front row, which was directly above the band. The reason he thought the tickets weren't any good was because there was a metal post sort of near our seats, but it was nowhere near blocking our view. I was shocked, because I thought they were going to be bad seats but not at all.

We got in to the Gardens and to our seats quickly, because everything was being monitored by RCMP. But they were cool and friendly and almost pleased at what was happening. Canadians are a lot more friendly! The audience was really buzzed with excitement but still pretty much reserved and peaceful. I was extremely comfortable and relaxed with the whole scene.

CHUM FM was the promoter of the show and they were playing music through the sound system for quite a while – Argent's 'Hold Your Head Up' and Jethro Tull's 'Locomotive Breath' are two songs I remember. Finally an announcer – a popular DJ at the time – came out and announced Stevie Wonder, who wowed the audience and had them dancing and jumping around after a few songs into his set. But while he got a good response to his music, I don't think the Canadian audience was seriously into him so he only got a lukewarm reception.

I remember we smoked some pot and someone passed a bowl of hash over to us. Like I said, the audience seemed kind of laid back. After Stevie Wonder, there was a long break before the Stones came out, but when they did the crowd really got loud and jumping and getting really into it.

Bill Wyman and Charlie Watts came out on stage first and next was the horn section, with Bobby Keys being the most animated performer of that group. He stepped up to the front of the stage and said something that got quite a response from the audience. Bill Wyman went up to him and said something to him and they laughed. Next out was Mick Taylor, who seemed really quiet but said something and waved to the audience. Next, of course, were Keith and Mick who came out arm-in-arm. Keith, in typical Keith fashion, was really loose and animated, walking up to the front of the stage and bowing or making a 'hey, everybody here I am' kind of movement. He appeared to be very loose and taken by it all.

Mick was in one of those one-piece suits – white with spangles just like Elvis used to wear. He was very all over the stage, and bantering in a way that only the front of the stage people could hear. They started playing and the audience really went nuts, like loud clapping and moving around and shouting, etc. They did the de rigueur hits – 'Bitch', 'Brown Sugar', and then they did a bunch of songs from *Exile*, including 'Rip This Joint' and 'Rocks Off'. The crowd was really into it and the band was really tight and awesome. They played all their hits and then Keith did 'Happy' and I thought that was one of the highlights of the show. His voice was clear and easy to hear and it just rocked! The band was really tight and awesome and I was overwhelmed how easy it seemed for them to perform this music. They were at the peak of their career and they were so perfect and just rockin' away, with the chicks in the front row going crazy.

I remember Mick and Keith royally drinking booze and a couple of times Keith signalled to someone in the back part of the stage, like an assistant who was wearing a cowboy hat, that his bottle was empty and that he needed another one. This happened three times – he was seriously liquored up! But they played like it was their skin; it was so incredible and loud and just hittin' the note that the whole place was buzzing.

We had these glow sticks which, when you twist them they light up, and in the darkness you can see them from anywhere. My brother shook that glow stick and then threw it on stage and Mick Jagger picked up and played it like a harmonica and then threw it into the audience; the crowd ate it up royally, really making a lot of noise.

The Stones really put on one hell of a show, and considering what we paid for the tickets – $18 to $20 – it was so amazing, better than any show I had ever seen. They just cranked out all their great songs. 'Midnight Rambler' went on for a long time and Mick was actually crawling on the stage like a snake.

They got to the end of the show and in the backstage area this really old black guy started moving around, moving things and doing something. I really could not figure out what he was doing, but then he shuffled out to where Mick was and gave him a Coke and handed him a basket, which Mick started spreading red rose petals on the front of the stage group and eventually threw the whole basket out into the audience. I think someone threw it back on stage and the black guy picked it up. Strange huh?

The Canadian audience was a whole lot different than American audiences!

They did a couple of encores – I'm guessing - but the crowd would not stop clapping and stomping. I'm not sure what they played. I know from seeing them other times that this show and this tour had to be them at their best and just doing it as if it was second nature – just as tight and on note for every song. The horn section was just cranking it out and having the time of their life.

BILL McPHERSON, AGE 19

We lined up overnight and got great seats on the floor. I was 19 years old, it was only rock and roll and I liked it.

PAUL B (AKA RUBY BEGONIA)

I was a young man at the time, on my own and struggling. I could not afford a ticket, or even the subway fare to get there but for some reason I felt compelled to go to where they were playing and hang around outside. I didn't normally go to concerts that I could not afford just to stand outside and hang around, but this was pretty big and, in all honesty, I was probably looking to get laid. I walked down there with a friend who was equally destitute, but he had no money or anything better to do.

About ten minutes after our arrival a young professional man dressed in a suit asked me if I needed two tickets. He said his girlfriend had cancelled their date and he did not want to go alone. I told him that I had no money whatsoever and he just gave the tickets to me! There were dozens of people looking to buy tickets from scalpers, who were charging and getting outrageous prices so this man could have easily sold his tickets at face value or doubled his investment but he just gave them to me. I thanked him profusely, went and found my friend – who could not believe my luck – and we went in and saw the entire concert.

Our seats were on the main floor, so they would have been considered good seats. We were center to the stage, about 35 or 40 rows back. Maple Leaf Gardens was built and used as a hockey stadium that seated maybe 12,000 people, so this being 1972 and it being the Rolling Stones, this was big stuff!

The sound was horrible as this was in a hockey arena and I always thought of the Stones as a band I would rather see in a smaller venue. Because of the horrible acoustics, Stevie Wonder, who had a huge entourage, actually sounded better than the Stones and put on a better show. Regardless, I had a wonderful time and I will never forget the kindness and generosity that this man displayed. It was a magical evening for a very poor young man who was in need of a break.

This may have been my first concert in a large arena. The acoustics were terrible in comparison to somewhere like the Easttown Theatre, an old movie theatre that was converted into a rock and roll venue and where, growing up in inner city Detroit, I saw many bands perform. But the Stones were in fine form. Mick Jagger pranced around like a petulant school girl and Keith Richards and the band put on a great show.

SCOTT MEYER

As youths of 14 or 15 in 1966 and '67, we were divided into two groups – Stones or Beatles. I was firmly a Stones guy, although I liked The Beatles too. It's just that we could identify a little more with the Stones, being the 'bad boys' ourselves. I saw three shows in five days on the '72 tour – Akron Rubber Bowl, Cobo Hall in Detroit and my then current home in Toronto, at Maple Leaf Gardens. I started in Cleveland (Akron show), then hitchhiked to Detroit, then on to Toronto. I got in each show free... one way or another – but was given a twelfth row seat ticket in Toronto from a friend who wasn't going.

All of the vocals were pretty much Jagger and Richards, and maybe this tour was the ultimate in musicians, with Nicky Hopkins and Ian Stewart along with the Stones' horn guys, Jim Price and Bobby Keys. Richard's' harmonising was spot on, even in the raw and unrehearsed live shows.

The slide work of Taylor was right on… he quietly stood there hitting all his ins and outs and pretty much duplicated his guitar parts in each of the three shows that I saw. The band was fronted by Jagger's high energy, but was deeply supported by Richards' driving force coming through and the Watts/Wyman rhythm… with Taylor coming and going on time and on key.

This wasn't a choreographed, much-rehearsed show with little gimmicks that the Stones eventually morphed into, but more like being in a huge club with the band on stage shooting out an unrelenting wall of sound, and ebbing and flowing on key. Richards wasn't exclusively using his open G tuning yet… and he played his Telecaster on many songs. Taylor was mostly playing his Les Paul, I think. Anyway, it was a comparably much more traditional act, although there were some guitar changes. Watts never missed a fucking beat! At all three shows he was a phenomenal force, and totally unassuming. Wyman stood there seldomly moving anything but his hands, but he was always smiling. It was a raw, powerful sound fronted by Jagger's infinite energy and Richards' precision.

The show I actually remember the most was Maple Leaf Gardens. It was the second of the two shows they played there and I was stage center left, about twelve to 18 rows back. It was bold and raw, and Mick Taylor was on it, as they all were. I've still got this little 8mm reel in my brain of the show – quite used, a little frayed… but it's there.

YESTERDAY'S PAPERS

URJO KAREDA

TORONTO STAR, JULY 17, 1972

The most memorable of many astonishing moments came near the end when, suddenly in mid-song, all the lights in the audience blazed on, exposing a writhing landscape of bodies utterly under the spell of Jagger's rock magic incantations. An enormous crowd – estimated at 17,000 for each concert – moved as a single inhabited being, arms waving, clapping, swaying, completely submissive, without a fragment remaining of its own will. This was the greatest, most ferociously stylish, most fearful-exciting rock concert in memory, a staggering hour of total theatre...

After Toronto, the Stones headed to Montreal.

MONTREAL FORUM
JULY 17, 1972, MONTREAL, CANADA

CAPACITY	20,000
SHOWS	1
ARRESTS	13

JAMES MALLOCH, AGE 13

It was my first real serious rock concert and I was there with my dad, Archie, who was the coolest dad ever. He and my mom had already seen the Stones before, in 1965 at Montreal's Maurice Richard Arena. My earliest musical memories of life were watching the Stones and Beatles become famous on *Top of the Pops* and *Ready Steady Go!* before either band had even begun to tour North America.

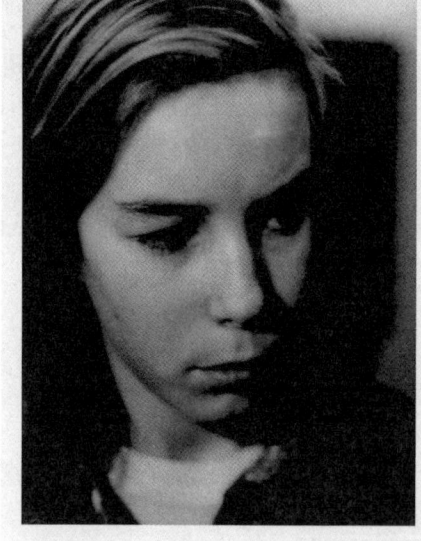

James Malloch's family were all listening to Exile ahead of the show

We were eager to see the show, as our whole family was playing the hell out of *Exile on Main St.* On the day of the show, someone planted a bomb under the Stones' equipment truck as the crew was setting up, so the promoter Donald K Donald had to arrange to have a whole new PA system flown in from LA at the last minute. They managed to do it in time.

There were also riots outside the Forum because of forged tickets and there were too many people with tickets for the number of seats inside, so a lot of disgruntled fans ended up missing the show.

I remember how hot it was inside. So hot, in fact, that a number of ladies took their tops off and bared their breasts to the crowd. A photographer got some shots of them and actually printed an explicit photo in the Gazette newspaper the next day. The ladies tried to sue the paper for invasion of privacy but lost the case.

And it was LOUD! My ears were ringing for a few days afterwards. The band sounded great, though. Jim Price on trumpet and Bobby Keys on sax fortified the sound. Mick Taylor was wearing a sequined tank top t-shirt, and Jagger was in his white body suit. I read later that he was asked to leave the restaurant of the Ritz Carlton Hotel they were staying at because he wasn't wearing a jacket and the maître d' didn't recognize him.

I feel so lucky to have seen them on that tour. I feel like they were at the height of their musical prowess then. I've seen them several times since, but that tour had a special feel.

ANDRE ISSA

Counterfeit tickets were sold for the concert and people were unhappy and this caused a riot. You can see part of the riot and the Stones arriving in a camper in a documentary called *Station 10* by the National Film Board of Canada, about life at Police Station 10 in Montreal. The Forum is located in the Station 10 section of town.

MARLENE DIETRICH

That summer was the summer of the Stones. When tickets went on sale it was the first time that people ever started waiting in line two days before to get tickets. I was trying to think of a way I could lie to my father so that I could stay out all night to try and get a ticket. He called me from work before I had the courage to ask for tickets. He said, 'What are you doing at home? You're not standing in line for the Rolling Stones tickets?' I was like, 'Oh my God, thanks Dad.' We did get tickets, and very good ones, so the whole summer was spent waiting for this show.

The Stones were not just about music. They were (and are) fashion icons. We walked like them, and were daring like them. The words to their songs led into all kinds of mischief. We created our fashions because of them. I will never forget the day before the show. It was almost cancelled because their equipment truck got blown up as part of some union thing. But the city knew better and the show went on. There was rioting outside as the show was taking place. There's a video of them in Montreal at that show, and a video of the riots outside.

BILL WYMAN, THE ROLLING STONES

'When we found out (French separatists had blown up a tour truck), Mick got pretty agitated. 'I don't want to go on tonight,' he said. 'After that, I don't want to go on.'

MAURICE RAYMOND

My life and history with the Rolling Stones go in step since the age of seven, from when I saw their first appearance on *The Ed Sullivan Show*. I'm from Canada, Montréal originally. My older sister was a Beatles fanatic and as such was enthralled with anything British Invasion-ish. The Stones appearance marked a change for both of us. Their rough-hewn swagger and pouting attitude was exactly the prescription for both of us to feel armed with restless angst. I'm three years younger and she, Lynne, was an outgoing precocious young lady. By the age of 13 in '67, she was a fully developed hippy radical. I followed her, both musically and socially. Protests, sit ins, leftist political rallies. She worked as a volunteer for Pierre Elliot Trudeau in '68. I passed out pamphlets door-to-door. Heady times, and all the while, hand-in-hand, were the Stones and their music, antics and influence.

First the blues activism and the music of Howlin' Wolf, Willy Dixon, and Muddy. Then 'Satisfaction', 'Have You Seen Your Mother…', '19th Nervous Breakdown', yadda yadda yadda. Then Brian's passing and the subsequent evolving into the greatest rock and roll band in the world with the Jimmy Miller years of *Beggars Banquet*, *Let It Bleed*, *Sticky Fingers* and *Exile*. All this led me to not only admire and, for lack of a better word, worship the band but, I also found myself performing their music. At the age of 12, I started my first band, Jade, and we played almost all blues, Berry and Stones covers. I have now been a touring musician and lead singer with the Blushing Brides since 1979 (42 years running).

I had obviously been over the moon at the fact that I was going to get to see my idols play the Montreal Furum. Problem was, I had purchased a scalper's ticket that was one of the counterfeit tickets. And I was not the only one. Hundreds of us were turned away and, as we realised that we were in fact not getting in and that we had been scammed, things got pretty ugly pretty damn fast. Bottles were flying, and cops were brandishing billy clubs and riot shields, forcing us away from the front of the Forum. A police car was set ablaze and I was almost run down by a motorcycle police side car. It was both terrifying and exhilarating.

Making our way around to the side of the building, we could actually hear the music faintly, which crushed our hearts even more so. Needless to say, although I did not get to actually see the gig that night, I lived a part of it, as a real-life Street Fighting Man.

I finally saw them live in Toronto for the first in 1975. It was one of the most precious memories I carry with me. It is attached to my DNA… it is part of me.

CATHERINE RICE, AGE 13

In 1972, my best friend Bernadette and I had the chance to get Rolling Stones tickets for $15 each to see the Stones in Montreal, Canada for the July 18th show. We bought the tickets with babysitting money we had saved up, hoping our parents would let us go. We were 13 years old, full of piss and vinegar and excited to have the tickets. We were planning on taking the Greyhound to and from Montreal, but this did not go according to plan. Our parents told us that under no circumstances were two 13-year-old girls allowed to take a 1,400 mile bus trip from Winnipeg to Montreal to see the show without an adult present. I remember being so pissed off.

It felt like our world had ended, so we figured out our brilliant plan. In the wee hours of the morning of the show, we snuck out of our bedroom windows with nothing but our back packs and $25 between us and were on our way. We hitchhiked the 1,400 plus mile trek to Montreal, arriving around 4pm that afternoon, and got to the Forum in Montreal. This was the rock and roll concert of the year in Montreal.

I don't remember the first opening act but the second was Stevie Wonder. The Stones were late in starting as there was a tiny bomb that went off earlier in the day and some of their equipment was trashed, but no harm came to the band members. After Stevie, the magical words we had waited to hear were uttered, 'Ladies and Gentlemen, the Rolling Stones,' and I went into a hysterical scream of seeing Mick Jagger strutting his stuff on stage. I was in awe of what was happening in front of my eyes.

After the concert, there was bottle throwing and a few fist fights and we were a little bit scared of the huge crowds outside, but we were happy and we survived. We were totally exhausted by our long journey and couldn't stand the thought of hitchhiking home. We just wanted our homes and our beds, so we mustered up the courage to call home and our parents sent us air tickets to get home, but only after we heard how much trouble we were in and how the police were looking for us, etc.

We finally made it home and sat through a three hour long lecture of how bloody stupid and inconsiderate we were and so on. But in my mind, I was really reliving the concert and our journey to see the best rock and roll band of all time.

Since then, I have seen them 36 times but still that night of July 18, 1972 was my favorite concert of all time. And in case you're wondering, the month of grounding and no phones calls was well worth it. I often wonder if the Stones knew back then the impact they would have on rock and roll and on the world. 60 years and counting. If I could talk to any one of them, I would thank them for being a part of my journey through life and being with me every step of my life and for helping me on my musical path.

YESTERDAY'S PAPERS

DAVE BILLINGTON
MONTREAL GAZETTE, JULY 17, 1972

In the top galleries of the Forum the temperature must have reached 120 degrees... The fans lolled listlessly like sated lizards... barely able to snap their fingers or tap their toes. The steamy atmosphere even prevented the

familiar heavy wave of 'pot' smoke from penetrating the upper reaches…
After the simple announcement, 'Ladies and Gentlemen, the Rolling
Stones,' the whole Forum shook physically to the great heaving roar of
emotion. The rolling, sweating animal of a crowd was about to be fed…
It ended as fiercely and as noisily as it had begun, to the crashing chords
of 'Street Fighting Man'. The Stones bowed and fled the stage, leaving,
for a moment, no void at all. It was almost as if the crowd had taken
over. It made one of the most fearsome noises I've ever heard. A single,
one-note roar that lasted for a full seven minutes.

Boston was the next stop on the tour. It should have been a routine stop…

BOSTON GARDEN
JULY 18 & 19, BOSTON, MASSACHUSETTS

CAPACITY	**15,509**
SHOWS	**2**
ARRESTS	**41**

BRIAN NELSON

At age eleven, my parents bought a house on Adams Avenue in Ryal Side
in Beverly, Massachusetts, a blue-collar working neighborhood. A couple
of streets over, on Elizabeth Avenue was Allen Paulino, a small but feisty
kid with a mop like a rock star. We rode our Schwinn Stingray bikes, the
ones with the high handles. We were inseparable. Allen had the Rolling
Stones *December's Children* album and we listened to it over and over. That
was to be the first Rolling Stones album I purchased.

My mom, while at the breakfast table in 1962, had told me of a new
British band called the Rolling Stones. Move forward to 1972 and the
Rolling Stones had instituted a lottery for ticket purchases. Fans were
told to send in postcards and my mom sent in a postcard in an envelope

marked as 'registered' mail. Her strategy was successful and we received two tickets to the sold-out July 18th concert, the infamous night where fog detoured the Stones plane to Warwick, Rhode Island.

Keith Richards was arrested when he took a belt to a photographer taking their picture. Mick then jumped on the police officer's back and he too was arrested. That's when it got interesting. Mayor Kevin White, fearing the potential for riots and violence to break out if the show didn't go on, made the call and used his pull to get the Stones released and even given a police escort to the Boston Garden.

The Garden, sans air conditioning, was a sauna. Stevie Wonder had long left the stage. The fans were getting hot and restless, including my ride home. He had enough and said he was leaving, I told him, 'I'm staying.' He was obviously concerned but I told him I was staying. Although I had no idea how I was to get home, I was happy. Sometime later, as the crowd was now showing its angst, on comes on stage, the mayor of Boston, Kevin White. Angst turned into hero worship when he told the steamy Garden crowd that he had bailed out the Rolling Stones and provided them with a police escort to the Garden. It got even better, as he announced the MBTA would be running for concert goers, no matter what time the show finished.

This was the age before cellphones, so a concerned mother was at home, I thought. The word on what Mayor White did made the local newscasts, assuring all concerned that their sons and daughters would have a ride home via mass transit.

As the concert ended at 2am, I recall the sheer joy of the crowd as we all walked slowly to the train, exclaiming along the way, 'Can you believe what we witnessed on this night?' Sometime around 4.30am, the train pulled into my stop at the Beverly Depot. I exited and started the hour walk home, wearing my Rolling Stones shirt with a smile on my face. I walked through the door at dawn and Mom greeted me as a mother does, with a hug. She stated the news kept everyone updated but she was sure relieved when her son walked through the door at 12 Adams Avenue.

CINDY BABAIAN

I turned 16 just six days before I saw them in '69. I went with a neighbor friend. The show just blew me away. I had never really been to a big concert like that before. I had great seats overhanging the stage and I could not believe what I was seeing. They came back to Boston in 1972. It was impossible to get tickets, and I would have done anything to get tickets, so I bought tickets out front from a scalper for $20. The face value on that ticket was six dollars and fifty cents. I still have them. The seats were on the floor, 18 rows back. I went with a friend.

It was so hot. Boston Garden had poor ventilation. People could smoke all the time, so it was smoky. There was no air conditioning to speak of. I don't even know if they had air conditioning. Stevie Wonder opened and just did his regular set. There were some reports that he played longer. He didn't. People just waited and waited. It was a tough time in Boston. There were race problems and the venue was filled with what we called the Tactical Patrol Force. They were dressed in face shields, they had clubs, they had the dogs and it was pretty tense in a lot of the spaces around the Garden. The dogs were straining at their leashes.

But people were pretty calm considering what was going on. People were just exhausted and tired. Of course, at that time there were no cell phones, so many people lined up in front of public telephones, of which there were a few in the Garden, just to call home and to say that they were okay and they were going to wait it out. I was pretty young still, and I'm sure my parents were worried. When I finally got in touch with them, they said they'd seen it on the news.

After a while, the Mayor of Boston, Kevin White, took the stage and explained what had happened. He was quite a showman himself, and he really played it to the hilt. He did a great job. He had his shirt sleeves rolled up, like he was the mayor of the people, and he came out and explained that the Stones were arrested in Rhode Island. Everybody booed, and then he said, 'But then I got them out!' and everybody cheered.

But the race problems in Boston were pretty intense. There were parts of the city – I don't know if there was rioting but there was quite a bit of fighting going on – and he was concerned that this was going to turn into a problem. So he pulled some of the police from the Garden that night and that got a big cheer. And everybody just behaved. The trains stopped running around 11pm in Boston. And the mayor kept them running so that people could get home.

When the Stones finally came on, it was just intense. It just felt like they were incredibly fired up, or we were all fired up, because they took the stage very, very late. They hit the stage around one o'clock in the morning and they still played a full show, 16 songs, one after the other. It was really high energy.

There are almost no words to describe that '72 show. How could they have been better than they were in '69? But they were. It was one of my favorite shows, because *Exile* was just coming out. And buying tickets on the day of the show, having tried so hard to get tickets, made it all the sweeter.

GARY STUART

It was a Boston hot summer night in July when I got my third chance to see the Rolling Stones. I had been a fan since I was 12 years old and, now 21, I was thrilled to get a ticket for $4.50, very affordable. More exciting was the chance to hear another favorite, Stevie Wonder, who was their opening act at Boston Garden in North Station, Boston, Massachusetts. I had seen Jimi Hendrix there.

Stevie Wonder was great and then there was a big problem. Logan Airport was fogged in and the STP couldn't land. They were over an hour away in Rhode Island, but Keith decided to punch a photographer and got arrested. Boston Garden was filled to capacity when we heard of the news. The local police were afraid of riots if the band didn't play and the Mayor of Boston intervened on stage to calm us down and let us know 'the boys' were on their way after some legal finagling, with a police escort to Boston Garden.

About three hours later, after the roadie had placed appropriate spirits on the amps (Jack Daniels for Keith and Courvoisier for Bill Wyman), we started to get excited to hear *Exile on Main St.* live! Well after midnight, they roared onto the stage, Mick in his glitter jumpsuit with a butch denim jacket and Keith with a satin white ruffled shirt.

They blazed into 'Brown Sugar' at lightning speed followed by 'Bitch' and then right into 'Rocks Off' before even taking a breath. Their fire and fury were palpable. They slowed down a bit for 'Tumbling Dice' and Keith got his moment with 'Happy' midway through. Of course, Boston was the perfect place for 'Midnight Rambler' to take center stage, bathed in blood red spotlights and highlighting the Boston Strangler's infamous murders… 'I'm going to hit and run and rape her in anger…' The crowd went wild.

Then there was a new song off *Let It Bleed* from a few years earlier, and after introducing their 'new' guitarist Mick Taylor (who played exquisite blues), they blasted through 'All Down the Line' off *Exile* and then 'Jumpin' Jack Flash' and the closing showstopper of 'Street Fighting Man'. The house lights went up and Mick had buckets of water and roses to douse the crowd. He started blowing kisses and I was on the far-right corner of the stage, and felt he blew me a kiss as our eyes locked for a nanosecond!

My first impressions left me dazed and happy beyond belief as I strolled into the night of July 19th, 1972. I was so crazed that I went back for the following night's show and got another ticket for the scalped price of $10. That made their *Exile* tour a two-fer in 24 hours.

BRUCE WHEELER

This was my first Stones concert. I got my ticket and one for my buddy via a lottery, and we ended up in the nosebleed section. (Boo!) Stevie Wonder opened the show. (Great!) I was in a psychedelic state at the time, and I went for a walkabout during the break. At the time I was a roadie for the rather eclectic band Seatrain, and while walking near the backstage entrance, I spotted a friend who was with a local sound and light company we used. He asked if I'd like to go backstage. Duh!

Problem was, I didn't have backstage credentials, which meant I'd have to maintain a very low profile if I wanted to stay there. Right. Me, on acid, wearing a bright yellow long sleeve t-shirt with a large embroidered rainbow on the front. Okay.

This was the show where the Stones had to fly into Providence, Rhode Island's T.F. Green airport, because Boston's Logan was fogged in. They were coming from Canada, and they had to go through customs. Boston's customs was ready for their arrival, and had set it so the band and crew could get through with minimal scrutiny and delay. Not so in Rhode Island. Along with other issues the tour party experienced there, Keith and a roadie were found to have drugs on their persons. Not good. Stevie's set ended at around 9pm or so. The Stones, never ever really 'on time', were expected to take the stage at something after 10pm. But at

10pm they were still at the Providence airport.

Boston Garden was an old hockey rink, and it wasn't air conditioned much, if at all, and it was July. The audience of some 16,000 was hot, and getting restless. (I'm still trying to hide backstage as best I could.) So, the Mayor of Boston showed up, to explain what was going on, and to hopefully calm the crowd.

He related that, at the urging of the Massachusetts governor, the band and crew were being released (pending further action later) so they could get to Bean Town for their show, and help prevent 'a riot'. They were driven the 61 miles in a police-led motorcade, arriving at the Garden close to 1am. Once there, they got it together fairly quickly, and hit the stage at perhaps 2am. To make up for it some, they played the longest set of the tour, substantially longer according to one source, with the sun coming up when it was finally over.

Earlier, as they were taking the stage for that show, I was standing in a corridor as they walked by, Mick and company not more than three feet away. Their road manager, and Woodstock stage manager, Chip Monck, looked at me as he passed, smiled, and said, 'What's up, Rainbow?' (Me, thought I?)

Anyway, I went to the guest viewing area, stage left, to watch the concert, along with a number of others. Mick Taylor was about ten feet away, and I had a decent view of everyone else for the duration. It was quite an amazing night, all in all, and definitely one for the books! (The friend who came with me had no idea where I went, but he was able to bum a ride home okay.)

I'd often used the 'professional courtesy' ploy – complimentary passes for fellow music biz types – to get backstage at other concerts put on by that show's promoter, Don Law (Elton and Sly Stone among them.) Unfortunately, I had 'worn out my welcome' with the woman who issued such passes, so there was no way she was going to accommodate me for this show. Anyhow, she was the one person I didn't want to run into that night. But, as it turned out, she eventually did see me, during the show – eye contact from a little distance away – and while I know she couldn't account for how I got there, she didn't bust me, and I never saw her again afterwards. (I fantasised she may have thought I was, perhaps, a guest of the band.)

My sound company friend, who got me backstage, later said he could do it again, this time with credentials, for the second Boston show the following night. But Seatrain had a gig and I couldn't take him up on his offer.

The Stones played Madison Square Garden the next week, and Seatrain's road manager and I were in New York on business, having to get 'stuff' from their management's mid-town office (They were managed by Albert Grossman/Bennett Glotzer Management. Grossman managed Dylan, Joan Baez, Peter, Paul and Mary and The Band, among others.) We called the office in advance, to see if they could call in a favor and get us into one of the MSG shows. Their effort came an hour too late, sorry to say.

The other Stones shows that I did see were the two they did in San Francisco in '75, both 1981 San Francisco shows, the '81 concert in Oakland and the '98 show at Honolulu's Aloha Stadium.

CHIP MONCK

The Stones arrive in Providence on a plane, and for some reason they're going to take a couple of limos up to Boston. Providence, Rhode Island to Boston isn't too far but, unfortunately, they were a little sloppy and the security or the police (or whatever they were) got to the aircraft and found stuff. So the Stones were being held until such time as Kevin White, the mayor of the city of Boston, called the guy in Providence and said, 'Come on, I've got 28,000 people here and I'm going to have a terrible time if you don't get them released.' So they got released and they came in about five hours late.

Stevie Wonder did at least two shows. *Jonathan Livingston Seagull* had just been published and I sat on a stool and read half of that to the audience while they threw frisbees and beachballs around. They were quiet and attentive. Then it was time to introduce Kevin, the mayor, to them. My introduction was, 'Ladies and gentlemen, okay, I need your attention please, because I have somebody to introduce you to who has a gift for you.' And then it got to be, 'Shut the fuck up. Sit down or stay still. This is Kevin White, he is your mayor and he wants to tell you some things that you need to know.'

He thanked them for being silent for a few minutes and he said,

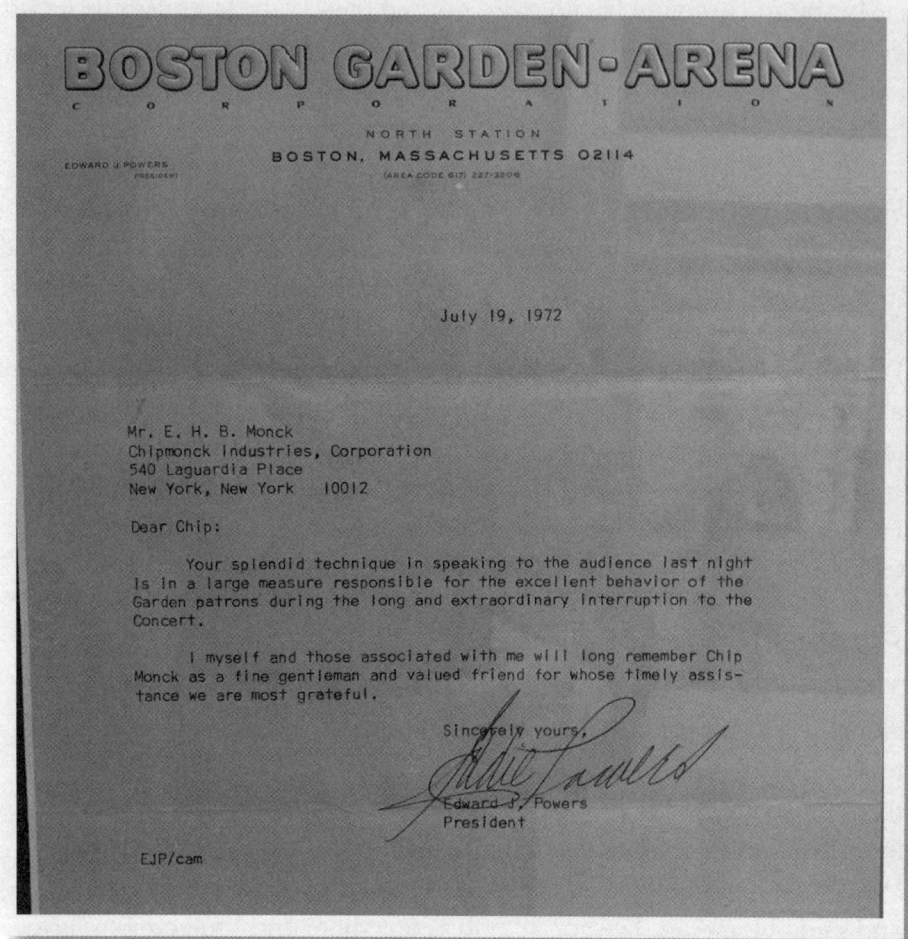

Chip Monck was praised for the way he handled the audience at the much-delayed Boston show

'There's free transportation for the next 24 hours. Anything you need from us, just ask,' so it turned out wonderfully. It just took a little bit of being hard-nosed and hard arsed to tell folks what to do. In such gatherings, it's normally pretty easy to throw a net on them and guide them all into something like that which they're not quite expecting. You can start slowly but once you get hard, you'll get their attention and get it to the place you wish it to be. And first it was the mayor and then it was the act. Eddie Powell was one of the most difficult arena management people you could ever possibly hope to meet. He was stone cold. That letter of thanks is a nice letter.

There was no additional cost for the band as a result of showing up late. The cost is met by the promoter; the act walks away with a guarantee. But you want to stay friends with the promoter. You had promoters like Don Law in Boston and Frank Fried in Chicago who knew their markets very well and exactly what they could get away with and how to fill the house. Live Nation has broken that down, and now all those guys have just gone away, because their homeland, to all intents and purposes, is now owned by somebody else.

ERIC ERICKSON

Mick and Keith fight photographers in Warwick, Rhode Island, get sent to jail and Mayor White pardons them and gives them a State Police escort from Warwick to Boston. After two hours in the roaring crowd, they rip up the Garden and we get buckets of iced water and real roses from Mick from the stage. Excellent. Mayor White saved the show. (Mick and Keith are still avoiding Warwick, Rhode Island!)

KEITH RICHARDS

Mick and Bobby Keys and Marshall Chess demanded to be arrested with me. I've got to give that to Mick.

Mick and Keith were arrested

TONY MILLS

The Stones didn't make the stage until 12.45am. Their plane had to land in Rhode Island due to fog at Boston's Logan Airport. Jagger and Keith were arrested for an altercation with a photographer. Stevie Wonder played twice that night. A local young guy came out and sang. He was good. There was concern that there would be major problems for the city, which was already experiencing problems at an event in the south end of the city, that could turn into a riot. Mayor White came out around 10pm to us that he got the Stones released and would be coming into the city soon. He pleaded with us to remain cool. We were young, and waited for about two hours with the house lights on. I only saw one guy and police officer go at it – the young guy lost. The Stones were nothing less than excellent. They played for us until 2am. It was nice to be young.

DEBRA JOHNSON

I had tickets for the July 19 show, but we must first visit July 18, 1972. The Stones plane was grounded in Warwick, Rhode Island because of heavy fog. Keith got into a fight with a photographer and landed a punch, and Mick and Keith and company ended up in jail. There was a huge crowd waiting at the Old Boston Garden, in Boston, Massachusetts, a very restless crowd. If it weren't for the Mayor, Kevin White, pleading with the police to release them, well, we can only imagine what would have happened back in Boston. It was after 2am when the boys finally burst onto the stage. I had a friend who went to that show and she said it was bedlam, but happy bedlam. Thank goodness for Kevin White or it would have been ugly!

I was watching the late news, planning what to wear to the show the next evening, when it came on the TV... 'BREAKING NEWS – STONES ARRESTED, IN JAIL IN WARWICK, RI...' I instantly felt ill, and I did not recover until hours later when the news came back on reporting the band's release. A sleepless night followed.

Flash ahead to the family's trip to Boston in a VW bus. The boyfriend and I were in our seats, watching 'Little Stevie Wonder' warm up the crowd. The two guys next to us were warming up with Jack Daniels. They shared their powerful binoculars with us, and out came a joint, which they also shared... None for me, thanks... I wanted to see the show!

It was 9.30pm, the Stones were introduced and they ran onto the stage. I'd never heard crowd noise like that before. Mick was dressed in a gold jumpsuit, jean jacket (which he quickly tossed aside), pink sash around his waist, pink scarf around his neck and glitter all over his chest. They opened with 'Brown Sugar', complete with original lyrics (they've since edited the lyrics to be more politically correct).

Mick Taylor was brilliant and Mick Jagger was on fire, leaping, jumping and strutting across the stage. 'Bitch' followed, and then songs from their newly released album, *Exile on Main St.*, their best album ever! 'All Down the Line' was very fast, then 'Happy', with Mick and Keith sharing one microphone... the good ole days! Then four more *Exile* tunes in a row, 'Tumbling Dice', 'Sweet Virginia', with Mick on harmonica, 'Rip This Joint' (one of Charlie's favorite tunes) and 'Rocks Off'.

We noticed early on that the two guys next to us were passed out cold... what a shame...so we borrowed their binoculars. I could see every drop of sweat on Mick's chest, and the glitter flying off in all directions as he twirled around like a ballet dancer in his white Capezios. Our seats were stage left, right over the stage, very close and those binoculars had us right up on that stage! Next came 'You Can't Always Get What You Want', a stripped down version compared to how it's been done in later years complete with a choir. One of the highlights of the show was 'Midnight Rambler', a very menacing version, unlike today's more subdued approach. Mick was bathed in red light as he crawled across the stage like a cat, harmonica in his mouth, whipping the stage with a studded belt. The crowd answered his howls... brilliant and dramatic, a show stopper!

Mick Jagger was, and still is, sooo good on harmonica. He told the crowd, 'You're a beautiful audience,' and later, 'It's HOT IN HERE, open a window, open THE ROOF!' It was very humid inside the Garden that night, and made so much hotter by the Stones. Mick went off stage but I could still see him, wiping the sweat from his face with a towel. I recall Nicky Hopkins being amazing on piano and the brass section adding much to the overall sound, especially on 'Brown Sugar'. Next up was 'Johnny B Goode' and then the crowd pleaser, even back in 1972, 'Gimme Shelter'. 'Street Fighting Man' followed and then Mick Taylor, in all his glory and keeping the band true to their roots, did a blues-inspired 'Love In Vain'. His lead was perfection.

Suddenly, all of the house lights went up and they ended with a blistering 'Jumpin' Jack Flash', with Mick jumping high into the air, prancing to our side of the stage as he looked up to our section. I swear he waved at me and threw kisses in my direction.

'Bye bye,' the crowd cheered wildly, and we all clapped with our hands above our heads. Then, as they made their way off stage, Mick was still bowing low and thanking the crowd. He was still bowing when Mick Taylor affectionately shoved him off stage! It was over... and we were all as sweaty as Mick. There was no encore. Everyone seemed numb and energised at the same time... and sad that it was over.

I'm certain that Charlie was perfect, he always was, and Keith was Keith... adding harmonies more frequently during that tour. The show did not run two hours, it was more a 90 minute plus set, but for me, it was a slice of heaven. My first Rolling Stones concert – 39 others would follow.

JIM SHEA, AGE 18

I just graduated from High School. The concert was sold out. So, I took my graduation money and with three of my friends hopped a train to the Boston Garden to try to buy scalped tickets. This is 1972, tickets were like $7.50 and we were all able to buy Scalped tickets for around $35.00. Can you imagine that? We weren't sitting together. I ended up sitting in the balcony right on the rail in an area that normally had a TV camera. There was so much pot going around you didn't have to take a hit to get high, but that did not stop me from taking hits.

Opening act Stevie Wonder was fantastic! Then the wait for the Stones. First, they revealed a giant snake painted on the stage as they set up. Then we waited and waited and waited for over 90 minutes, but finally the concert began. I had waited to see my musical heroes since I was ten years old and they did not let me down. They were great. Mick Taylor added such a new dimension to the band and 'Sympathy for the Devil' was mesmerizing. When they played 'Midnight Rambler' and Mick sang 'you heard about the Boston Strangler', the crowd went crazy. It was the Stones at their peak. Between the end of the show and the encores, every one lit a match for tens of thousands of lights. It was a new phenomenon.

What a show and what a night. I have seen the Stones many times in the 50 years since and that was still the best time I ever saw them.

JOE POTENZA

I was able to get scalper's tickets for floor seats at $25 each. I live in Rhode Island, about 50 minutes drive from Boston. The tickets were for the second night of two scheduled for the old Boston Garden. The previous night had seen the Stones' arrest debacle in Rhode Island. They'd landed at the main airport in our small state, a zealous photographer had taken some flash pictures and Keith responded by swinging his belt. Keith, Mick and Bobby Keys were arrested and detained.

So I'm listening to the news thinking I'm going to miss the show the following night! Meanwhile, in Boston, the first show was now delayed. Fearing a riot, the mayor of Boston pleaded for the Stones' release. They got a police escort to the Garden.

Joe Potenza saw the second night at Boston Garden

My date and I took the train to the Garden the following night, a sweltering July night. I was unaware that Stevie Wonder was opening the show, so I was floored even before the Stones came on. They were ragged and loud and triumphant after their brush with the Rhode Island authorities. Raw, barely polished and at their peak with the horns and Nicky Hopkins joining the band.

I found the ticket stub (along with others from Hendrix and Cream shows) during an attic cleanse a few years ago.

JOE MINVILLE

I sent away for tickets to their show at the Boston Garden. You had to actually send a money order with your request. I was not one of the lucky ones. My money was returned to me and my dream was crushed at 15 years old.

YESTERDAY'S PAPERS

ERNIE SANTOSUOSSO
BOSTON GLOBE, JULY 19, 1972

At 12.45am, some three hours and five minutes after Stevie Wonder had completed his act, the Rolling Stones, led by Jagger, clad in a purple jumpsuit, studded with enough rhinestones to keep a Minsky chorus happy, bounded onto the stage and were greeted as warmly as if it was 9.45pm. The stage was beautifully illuminated as six varied-color spots to the rear of the stage played off a 14 x 40 foot Mylar mirror suspended in front. The sound was indistinguishable but who cared? The Stones were back in Boston after too long a wait. For all that crowd cared, Mick Jagger could've sung three pages from *The Fannie Farmer Cookbook*.

The tour was now reaching its conclusion, but there were still eight shows to play in seven days, starting with three in Philly.

SPECTRUM
JULY 20 & 21, 1972 PHILADELPHIA, PENNSYLVANIA

CAPACITY	15,472
SHOWS	3
ARRESTS	25

PATRICIA PRADEL
Steve Wonder had opened for them, and when they did the encore of 'Jumpin' Jack Flash', Stevie came out and did it with them. I had run up to the stage and was scared that Stevie was going to get hurt. There were a lot of large cables running across the stage. Mick and he were jumping up and down and I was afraid since Stevie couldn't see, he would trip on one. But he did fine!

GEORGE BRADY
Stevie Wonder opened up. The Stones came out and opened up with 'Brown Sugar'. I was blown away the rest of the night. At the end of the show, Stevie's band and the Stones were on stage doing each other's songs.

JEAN SCULERATI COTNER, AGE 27

I fell in love with old blues in the early to mid-Sixties. I followed both rock and folk blues groups and I was a very early Stones fan. I was one of those that picked the Stones over The Beatles, at least early on. The very first Stones single released in the USA was Buddy Holly's 'Not Fade Away', and I loved them from that time on.

I went to the concert with my then boyfriend. We didn't have tickets as they sold out before we could buy them, so we ended up buying tickets from some guy for $30 each, which was highway robbery for tickets pretty far from the stage and on the second level. Philadelphia was the second to last stop on that tour and they played two nights. We went the first night, July 20th, which was good because they didn't do an encore on the 21st. Then they went off to NYC for four final shows.

Stevie Wonder was the opening act. I didn't have good seats but the music was really a pleasure. The Stones were really tight then. My best memory is of the encore (which they were rarely doing that tour). It was a jam with both bands doing a song with lots of jamming among the group. That's something to always remember. I've only heard bootlegs from that concert. The sound was very poor.

GEORGE KEAHEY

I grew up in the Philadelphia area and attended both shows at the newly-built Spectrum in 1972. I was just shy of my 16th birthday so car pooled with an older neighbor. I slept out for tickets a few months before, in like February – I remember it was very cold. I bought tickets for both shows as I remember going to see them with a friend's older brother in 1969 and he had informed me that you needed to go to all the shows, because they'd play different songs at each.

I scored tickets in the upper level for both shows, which were on consecutive week nights. They played a lot of selections from *Exile* but still mixed in some older selections and I was surprised to hear them play 'As Tears Go By' at one of the shows. I was very impressed with Bobbie Keys and Jim Price, who were featured prominently on horns, but disappointed that they didn't play any real early stuff like 'Come On' or 'It's All Over Now'. But they ended both nights with 'Bye Bye Johnny'! Finally, Stevie Wonder opened both shows and, on the second night, he joined the Stones on stage for a great rendition of 'Satisfaction'. At the close of the second concert, I purchased the ubiquitous bootleg t-shirt from one of the parking lot guys.

ROBERT KLUGER

I've been playing the guitar since 1966. Two songs made me decide to learn to play the guitar – 'I Can See for Miles' by The Who and 'Shapes of Things' by The Yardbirds. It was called the British Invasion but it was just great music, with The Beatles and the Stones. I had a jukebox in my bedroom as a kid growing up, with a collection of all The Beatles, the Stones and the Kinks' 45s as well as Simon & Garfunkel, Buffalo Springfield, The Byrds and all those major, influential '60s bands.

Unfortunately, on June 22, 1972, Tropical Storm Agnes came through where I lived in Pennsylvania and flooded the entire valley so I lost all my records, all my 45s. The house was not destroyed but we had ten feet of water on the first floor. I spent the month before the Rolling Stones concert cleaning up our home. I had to take an axe to my piano to get it out the door. I was ripping up carpet. I was doing everything you have to do to prepare a home to be repaired after the waters have receded. And after doing the house, I had to do the office buildings that were part of my family's business. I worked almost a full month of 15 to 18 hour days, only taking time off to sleep.

I was between my junior and my senior year. My friends from college knew what I was doing and how hard I was working, and they sent me a ticket to go and see the Stones at the Spectrum. It was my only day off that summer, so I drove to Philadelphia from the Wilkes-Barre area, which is about an hour and 45 minutes by car, and went to see the show. I travelled on my own. The friends who took pity on me and bought me that ticket didn't go to the show.

My seat was close to the stage, but side on and towards the rear of the stage. My view was partially blocked by amplifiers. The show was amazing. Stevie Wonder was great. I was not a Stevie Wonder fan at that time but I liked his music. I was certainly aware of his singles. His keyboard playing and how he handled the harmonica was incredible. And there were some really standout songs, like when he did Marvin

Gaye's 'What's Going On' And he sat in with the Stones at the end on the two encores, 'Uptight' and 'Satisfaction'.

Mick Jagger is no slouch when it comes to playing the harmonica. He is an amazing harp player, and very underrated. But for me the whole focus of the show was Mick Taylor, who did some absolutely outstanding guitar work, especially during the middle of the show when they let him take a couple of steps forward and actually play solos. Their version of 'Love in Vain' was incredible, and 'You Can't Always Get What You Want' and 'Midnight Rambler' stood out.

It's probably in the top 20 of all the shows I've seen. They were playing some of my favorite Stones songs. The band was tight and the encore with Stevie Wonder was just incredible. The synergy between Mick and Stevie on the stage was absolutely incredible to see.

For me that was the peak of the Stones performances. I'm not a huge Ron Wood fan as far as him being a lead guitar player. He fits into the band socially, but musically I don't think he does a whole lot to advance the band. Keith Richards, obviously, is amazing but he's not really a lead guitar player. He's a great rhythm player in the Chuck Berry tradition. 'Happy' was an amazing performance. I remember that because it was first time I had seen Keith get up and do the vocals.

I saw the Stones later on, on the *Steel Wheels* tour. That was okay; it was a good show and my wife loved it. But it was in the Giants Stadium, and we were sat a long way from the stage. It was nothing like this experience. At the Spectrum, I could probably have hit Mick Jagger with a tennis ball if I wanted to. I was mostly hearing the monitors in '72, and from the side of the stage I could hear a lot. I could pick out Stevie Wonder's harmonica and keyboards. Mick Taylor was as clear as day on guitar. The sound system was good enough.

DOUG POTASH AKA STONESDOUG

The summer of 1972 was peaked with the news that the Rolling Stones would be touring again, and that we would get to hear some songs from one of their greatest albums, *Exile on Main St.* Seven of my friends wanted to go and asked me to get tickets. I was only allowed to get four, so I took my 11-year-old brother, Chris, to Ticketron to stand in line for the chance to get the tickets.

Photos: Doug Potash

Doug Potash had floor seats and got some great photos

The day of the show, we all gathered at my parents' home for a couple of beers. I mixed up a pint of mint juleps to take to the show. As we entered, I was frisked and the police took the pint bottle away from me, but they gave me a receipt. At the end of the show, I went to this truck that was full of liquor bottles and they gave me my pint back. We had floor seats and I was able to get some great pictures. We all stood on our chairs, except my ex-girlfriend who was dizzy, and I couldn't understand how she could do this.

Whenever I go to a Stones show, I go into a sort of trance and don't remember most of the show. We did get to see and hear the band bring out Stevie Wonder for the encore of 'Uptight'/'Satisfaction', the first time on the tour this was done. And, after the show, I went home and basked in the glory of a great evening.

MICHELE E BURTULATO, AGE 14

It was awesome. Friends' siblings took us. They took us to see everyone. I remember they did two shows on one of the days, a matinee show and an evening one. Tickets were $10.50, a little more than the usual $4.50.

TOM GALLAGHER

I saw the Stones in 1972 in Philadelphia, at the Spectrum. It was a great show, as they were in their prime and at the height of their writing prowess. Mick Taylor was outstanding. There was a jam at the end with both bands. I saw them later on the *Steel Wheels* tour, at the Ohio Stadium. The Philly show was an Electric Factory production. They later produced full tours for the Stones.

YESTERDAY'S PAPERS

ROD NORDLUND AND MIKE LEARY
PHILADELPHIA INQUIRER, JULY 21, 1972

It wasn't exactly Woodstock… Nor was it the violence-scarred tumult that erupted at Altamont in California barely five months later. What it was was (a) joyful and high voltage mixture stirred by the masterly wand of His Satanic Majesty, Mick Jagger… Jagger spun around ten or 20 times at the end of the set, grabbed a handful of confetti, kissed it and threw it, some on the band, some on the audience. Then quite politely he said, 'Thank you good night, you all.' The lights went down and, as they say, the fans went wild. It was a gas, gas, gas.

The final stop off before the end of the tour was in Pittsburgh.

CIVIC ARENA
JULY 22, 1972, PITTSBURGH, PENNSYLVANIA

CAPACITY	13,911
SHOWS	1
ARRESTS	70

REX NORRIS

I saw the Stones at the Pittsburgh Civic Arena in '72, which has since been torn down. As a young guy from West Virginia, walking up to the venue and seeing the people going to the show was absolutely amazing. This was my first concert of any kind, except seeing John Denver singing 'Country Roads' on the Capitol steps in Charleston, West Virginia. My cousin was a disc jockey at the local radio station and it was this great guy who had turned me onto the Stones. We'd ride around in his Plymouth Duster listening to the AM radio trying to catch them playing 'Brown Sugar'. I mean, literally all night!

Rex Norris (left) was turned onto the Stones by his DJ cousin

ROBERT BUELLER

It was the summer of 1972 and I just graduated high school. Stevie Wonder – Little Stevie Wonder, they still called him – opened for them. He joined them on stage for the encore medley of Wonder's 1966 hit

'Uptight (Everything's Alright)' and '(I Can't Get No) Satisfaction'.

It was awesome how Mick Taylor and Keith Richards jammed together. It was like hearing these songs for the first time, even though I'd listened to them I don't know how many times. There was so much energy coming off the audience, and the lighting was spectacular. The lighting was done by these mirrors above the band, kind of behind them in a row, and they rotated so the lights would hit the mirror and then come onto the stage. I have never seen anything like it, before or since. Songs like 'Midnight Rambler', 'Sympathy for the Devil' and 'Gimme Shelter' totally blew me away. Mick's voice was so strong and the way he played the harmonica was unbelievable. I was on the floor so we stood for the whole concert, sometimes even on the chairs.

KAREN CERCONE, AGE 16

It was the first concert I was permitted to attend, and I was on my very first date. I had a red and white striped shirt on with my denim bellbottoms. It was a long concert and they played most of my favorites. We were seated in the first section to the right of the stage, in the second row. It was love at first sight. I have been in love and obsessed with the Rolling Stones ever since.

I saw them most recently at Heinz Field in October 2021. My daughter, China, finally agreed to go with me because she wanted to understand my obsession and love for the Stones. Every time I attend one of their concerts, I always end up crying; but the tears are from joy, happiness and love. It takes me months to come down and get back to normalcy after seeing them. This time was no different with the exception that China had the same experience. We never sat in our seats. We danced, screamed and cried throughout the entire show; never wanting it to end. My heart was and still is very heavy. Charlie is gone and I may not get to see them again. But I have to say, I'm so lucky to have seen them quite a bit throughout my lifetime and the only regret I have is that I never had the privilege of meeting these Masters of Rock.

LAURIE KING

My late dad was a local TV and radio celebrity and had gotten four complimentary tickets to the concert. I was too young to go on my own,

232

so my late mom's secretary said her 18-year-old son would love to go. I went with him and a friend of his. (I guess the fourth ticket went unused). We had great seats on the floor, about 100 feet from the stage. It was my first-ever rock concert experience. I wish I'd taken photos.

YESTERDAY'S PAPERS

MIKE KALINA

PITTSBURGH POST-GAZETTE, JULY 24, 1972

Jagger sang, pranced, shouted, strutted and danced across the arena stage like a poor man's Nureyev, as the four other Stones played behind him: bassist Bill Wyman, who rarely moved more than a foot from his station at stage right and who cast only nonchalant glances at the audience; sinister-looking Keith Richard, who looks like an advance man for a tidal wave, using his guitar as a weapon to complement Jagger's histrionics; baby-faced Mick Taylor, the rhythm guitarist and newest Stone whose Bobby Vinton looks seem out of place, and ashen-faced Charlie Watts, who beat out frenetic rhythms on his drums… The only bad vibo (sic) came when a spectator threw an empty bottle to the stage, just in front of Jagger, who shouted, 'Don't go throwing your bottles up here at me…'. Jagger was a decade off when he told the crowd Saturday night, 'It's nice to be back in Pittsburgh. We haven't been here since 1956.'

The tour wound up in New York, with four shows at Madison Square Garden and the Stones performing to a total of 80,000 fans. Demand exceeded supply more than ten fold, with an estimated one million applications for tickets mailed in.

MADISON SQUARE GARDEN
JULY 24 - 26, 1972, NEW YORK, NEW YORK

CAPACITY	20,000
SHOWS	4
ARRESTS	15

CHIP MONCK

I had eight crew with me, and twelve local crew, plus the Teamsters loading in and out. Most of the shows went off like clockwork. A few small problems with non-union labour always present themselves. There's always somebody wanting more money. They say, 'Oh, that's something popular. They must be making money. I want some of it.' Madison Square Garden was always the ball breaker because of the division between the stage itself and all the area around it, in which you hang so many different things. There were two unions, the IATSE (the theatrical union) and the IBEW (electrics only). The IA had jurisdiction on and over the stage. The IBEW ruled everything else, and both the upper echelons were balanced for unions rule.

You've got somebody hanging over you, saying, 'You can't tap into that electrical service,' and you'd say, 'I'm terribly sorry, I've done it for the last month and a half. And that's exactly the way we're going to do it, so get your electrician over here and he and I will have a conversation.' And you just go from one step to another and it always works. It has to. Otherwise, you're of no use to the act. And then, unfortunately, you won't be there.

We became the first, and only, music tour to become a IATSE Yellow Card show, and we had the pick of elder craftsmen from around the country as heads of department. A 40 foot, 4,200lbs mobile mirror hanging over the public was not a shoe-in, but it was worth it!

If you play with Meccano a lot, swallow all the nuts and bolts, and keep ordering parts you do have a certain love for mechanics and building stuff and that's what I loved. That's what I really enjoy. And that's what I did.

The act is the spearhead or the energy or the culmination of all of these wonderful things. What they become is what makes it well worthwhile working with (if not for) them. Mick is probably the best front man in the business. It's quite a craft and he's very good at it. I take my hat off to him. He is wonderful.

DAVE KAUFMAN, AGE 19

I was at sleepboy camp and 'Get Off of My Cloud' was all over the radio. That was the breakthrough song for me. I said, 'These guys are good. Who the hell are they?'

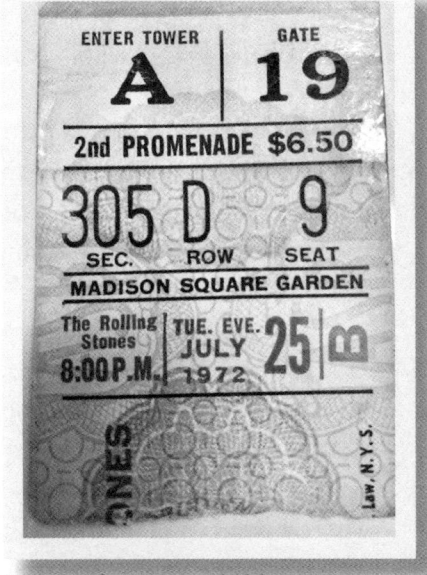

'72 was the only time I got to see them. My friend said, 'Hey, I got tickets for the Stones at the Garden,' and I said, 'Yeah, I'll go.' He said, 'I gave my ticket to another friend but he can't go. But his friend gave it to somebody else.' So he had to piss off his friend to get the ticket back to give to me. My friend still reminds me of that today.

Dave Kaufman was at MSG

Going to Madison Square Garden, where the New York Knickerbockers basketball team played, or the New York Rangers ice hockey team played, was a real big deal. It was a happening. It was one of those things. And then at the last minute I found out Stevie Wonder would be there. 'Stevie Wonder. Oh my gosh, oh my gosh. Little Stevie Wonder.' *Inner Visions* was coming out. *Talking Book* was coming out. *Music of my Mind* was coming out. And everyone knew his greatest hits.

Back then at Madison Square Garden, it was a crazy, wild atmosphere. In the fire stairwells, people were lighting up and getting high. There were people walking up and down the fire exit stairwells selling loose joints and rolling papers and bongs and it was kind of a carnival environment. There were cops inside the Garden but they didn't care.

There was a certain point where, when I was younger, I would go to Ranger games or Knicks games and between the periods of the quarters people would go into the stairwell and get high. This went on up until, I guess, the mid-Seventies. Then, all of a sudden, the police and the authorities said, 'You know, it's a family environment and we should stop this nonsense.' And they did. I wasn't getting high going to shows.

Just to be there. The excitement and the electricity. The lighting. Mick Jagger was in his prime. Now he's an old man. He waves his arms a lot and that suffices for dancing. But, gosh darn, he's amazing on stage. It was a religious experience back in those days. Of all the shows I saw, the Stones were number one.

When my friend in Texas told me she was going to the Stones concert down there recently, she said she had paid a hundred and something dollars for it. She sold the ticket to somebody else, who resold it for like two hundred dollars. It reminded me to pull out my ticket stub. I paid six dollars and fifty cents.

STEVE RUBIN, AGE 19

To have the opportunity to hear the Rolling Stones at Madison Square Garden in 1972 in New York City, where I lived, was a thrill. My brother, who was three years older than me, had gone to see them in 1969. In 1972, *Exile on Main St.* came out. Inside the album was a postcard and other material. In order to handle the number of requests coming in for the concert, Madison Square Garden asked people to send in a postcard. And if your postcard was selected,

Steve Rubin was at MSG

then you were able to purchase four randomly selected seats. I mailed in the postcard that came with the Rolling Stones album. Interestingly enough, I actually won twice so I won the opportunity to go two times.

I thought *Exile on Main St.* was their hippest, hippest album. I went to the show with my brother and my friend Robin. We lived in Queens and took public transportation and the New York City subway system to get to Madison Square Garden. We were pretty excited. That first night we had really good seats. I wouldn't say they were extremely close, but they were close enough to have an unobstructed view of the band, and of course the sound was terrific.

Robin brought some weed and we smoked a little bit before the concert. In those days, you could do that unofficially before the concert even though you weren't supposed to. I was thrilled to hear Stevie Wonder's set.

When the Rolling Stones hit the stage, I thought it was something incredible. I had quite a bit of experience of going to the Fillmore East in New York and seeing rock bands there. I was a writer on the college newspaper and a self-made record critic, principally for the purpose of getting free tickets. I thought the staging, the way it looked and the lighting, just looked a cut above all the rest of the shows I'd seen.

As terrific as the Fillmore East was, there was something very dramatic about the staging at the Garden. The lights were unusual. The light changed from behind the stage. The light then came back down off mirrored reflectors onto where each lead Rolling Stone would stand.

I remember thinking how smart they were to be so contemporary in their sound and to have Mick Taylor in the band, because all the rock bands then coming from England were all featuring classic guitar players, who were the focal point of rock 'n' roll bands at the time. I thought, 'Well, here's the Rolling Stones reinventing themselves and not only having that kind of guitar player in their line-up but a great one. And I just thought the way they did the material on *Exile on Main St.* sounded terrific.

Seeing them two nights later, all the way in the back of Madison Square Garden, was not the same effect. Mostly because when you've been to a big arena concert you're just not caught up in the rock 'n' roll drama if you're too far away. I remember them doing 'Rocks Off'. I remember them doing 'All Down the Line', 'Happy', 'Brown Sugar', 'Satisfaction' and 'You Can't Always Get What You Want'. When they left the stage after one encore, they had a very mellow acoustic Rolling Stones number playing over the PA. I forget which one it was, but it was a very soothing effect, to have everybody exit Madison Square Garden to a very mellow Rolling Stones tune. I thought that was also a very nice dramatic effect.

I just remember being in awe. Emotionally it was very satisfying. I'm now thinking it was the greatest thing I'd ever seen at that time. I've listened back to the recordings that are on YouTube and my sense of how good they sounded then still how old is good today.

They sound a little sloppier to my ears now than they did to my 19-year-old ears then but that's not a criticism. It's just an observation. But that's the Rolling Stones. That's what they are.

I saw the Rolling Stones again in 1997. That was not as satisfying an experience as that was a very large athletics stadium. When people went to rock 'n' roll concerts in the '60s and '70s they really focused on listening to the music. But if you go to a rock concert now it's an event. People are busy on the phones, they're getting something to drink, the focal point isn't the music anymore. The focal point is being able to say you were there. You can't connect to the music and the experience if you're not listening to it.

And I was a little disappointed when they went on tour with Mick Taylor in 2015. It felt like he was there as a bit of a novelty. He wasn't really integrated into the band. Musically it's not quite as together as it was despite all the extra musicians. It's a little bit past its time.

I feel they could be a better version of what they are today. If they let other people make the music, there are plenty of bands can do the Rolling Stones better than the Rolling Stones. They're doing a little bit of 'riding the waves' of many years of knowing that all they have to do is be there. There isn't a critical listening audience that is discerning the difference between what they're playing as musicians and the fact that they are at the event. And that's not just a critique of them but a critique of the times we live in.

Keith strikes me as a lazy musician now. He acts like, 'I can do what I want.' I don't know if this is a function of his physical limitations, but as much as I enjoy the spectacle there's got to be substance. I saw Emerson, Lake & Palmer and Ten Years After and Santana at the Fillmore East, but when I saw the Rolling Stones at Madison Square Garden, I thought, 'Wow, this really tops it all.' There is no question in 1972 that that was a spectacular performance.

I still think the sound is better live in 1972 than they sounded in any subsequent years. I don't think Ronnie Wood was a big step forward.

If you look at the way Keith Richards played the guitar back then, he physically played with such obvious involvement. He was much less involved in his persona and was much more involved in what he was contributing musically. Maybe, and it's through no fault of his own, he's been made aware of what his personality is.

I keep the CD of *Exile on Main St.* in my car, alongside the John Coltrane CDs and the Miles Davis CDs. When I just want to listen to some rock 'n' roll, that sure does it.

CLIFF DVORKIN, AGE 20

They did four concerts and I went twice. I went with my girlfriend, my sister and her boyfriend to one show and to the second concert with a close friend. Stevie Wonder opened for both concerts. I was 20 years old and lived in North Jersey. Every song was great but 'Jumpin' Jack Flash' was exceptional. I played 'You Can't Always Get What You Want' repeatedly for my son. He's now a huge Stones fan, having just seen them in St Louis in 2021 for the twenty-first time.

CAT CLARK

I went. I saw. They conquered NYC. I was in high school. I remember the hippie kids in the audience and the anticipation as we waited for the lights to go down. It was a basic stage and they had that raw young energy. I'm still a huge fan. I saw Charlie's last show, in Tampa.

JERRY SCHEIN, AGE 18

We had the draft on then, and in February I got a high lottery number which meant I was going to be drafted. So I wanted to have fun that summer. I was in college and I loved rock 'n' roll music; The Beatles foremost, but also British Invasion and Motown. Music was always in my house. My parents never said to me and my sister, 'Turn that junk off.' They never said that. They had their own music – Sinatra, Nat King Cole, Benny Goodman.

I only saw one show before the Stones. That was January 1969, also at Madison Square Garden, where I saw The Doors. I went with a friend, Howard, who I also went to see the Stones with, and we paid five dollars for tickets. And I tell people that today and they go, 'What are you, nuts?'

The whole rock 'n' roll touring concert scene changed after the Stones toured in '72. That was the first modern rock 'n' roll tour, and everything that came after that sort of patterned themselves after that tour in terms of stage shows, media presence and so on.

It was the *Exile on Main St.* tour. I don't know when the tickets for New York went on sale. I went with my friend, Howard, and his girlfriend at the time. I don't know how much the tickets were. But we were looking at the ad and it said 'two shows' on either Wednesday or Thursday. I said, 'Two shows?' I didn't understand it.

At the Garden at the end of July, around Mick's birthday, they did four shows, and on one of the days there were two shows. There was an afternoon show and a night show, so I said to Howard, 'We're never going to get tickets for the night show. Maybe we could get tickets for the afternoon?' This was before Ticketron and all this. We went to the box office and there was a medium-sized line of people, who didn't know about the afternoon show, so we got three tickets. All our friends were jealous. They said, 'How could you get tickets to the Stones so easily?'

We went to the afternoon show. We showed up at one or two o'clock and people were milling outside. It was an older crowd. I was very intimidated because of all the types of women that were there. There were a lot of women in their late twenties and in their thirties, either with their boyfriends or on their own. The only girls I knew at the time were girls I knew in college and girls in my neighborhood. And this was 1972 and girls had started to dress a different way, with no underwear and tight jeans, and they'd all come to see the Stones. I remember standing outside saying, 'Look at this. Look at all these girls.' I didn't talk to them or anything. I was too intimated.

At the show I remember 'Brown Sugar', because that's my favorite Stones song, and I remember 'Gimme Shelter'. They had to have played 'Satisfaction', but I don't remember it. I remember the general atmosphere of the night. There was such intensity. You felt like the stage was going to lift off the platform because the fans were all into it, and here were the Stones in New York. The Beatles broke up two years ago. The Stones were the kings of rock 'n' roll and Mick was probably at his peak then as a performer. It was an electric night. I only remember flashes and bits and pieces but it was a highlight of my growing up and being a music fan.

I don't know what time the show ended. Maybe five o'clock? We were hungry so we went to a diner not far from the Garden and it seemed like everyone in the diner was coming from the show. And this was before the big business of t-shirts at shows, to show off that you supported the Stones. I don't think anyone had souvenirs. We were just sitting there talking about this show and everyone it seemed had come from this show.

Mick Jagger was on the cover of *Life* magazine that week, or maybe the week before, and the story was 'The Stones are rolling again'. I went to a newsstand around where my sister and her husband had lived on 24th Street in Manhattan and they were all sold out. I walked uptown to Penn Station, where they had a few newsstands, and they were all sold out there too, so I never got that issue. It was a classic shot of Mick in make-up and wearing a sequinned thing. I can still remember it. I can get it on eBay now, but I don't want a 50-year-old magazine.

I saw them in 1989 at Shea Stadium. They did five shows and it was a 50,000 seater stadium and of course it was electric and they were in good form, but nothing's the same as going to see a rock 'n' roll act when you're 18 years old. Especially in '72, because everything was still new.

I don't remember Charlie Watts saying a word on stage. Mick would talk to the crowd and try to make funny jokes and banter back and forth with Keith, but Charlie was a total professional. He just kept the beat. I'm sorry that we've lost him.

RANDI MARKOWITZ

Around March of 1972, maybe a little earlier, a full page ad in the *New York Times* announced the upcoming tour dates at Madison Square Garden; three shows in July. This was great – tickets would be available only through a postcard lottery! The idea was to mail in as many postcards as you wish. 'Winners' would be selected from a giant mountain of postcards. Problem: I was 14 years old (and already a seasoned concert-goer – a great thing about growing up in NYC), and the months of July and August were spent at a summer camp in the Catskill Mountains. Never mind that – I was a clever NYC girl and so about 100 postcards were mailed in. I think postage was two cents. About a week into the camp season, the results of the lottery were announced and one of my pack of friends had won the golden ticket.

We were able to secure four tickets for the final NYC show, on July 26, 1972. I believe it was a Wednesday. A scheme to attend the show, even though I was away at camp, was hatched.

Luckily, my dad was a music fanatic, so he understood my very profound need to attend this concert. He arranged for the camp director to take me to the bus station in Monticello, New York, where I boarded a Greyhound bus to the Port Authority in Manhattan. I was 14. My parents were so permissive. I would never have allowed my own two kids to attempt something like this!

On the day of the show, my friends and I took the subway to MSG and we somehow made our way down to the front. I spent a magical two hours or so with my heroes, and came home with my pockets stuffed with the rose petals that Mick showered on the crowd. It was probably the greatest moment of my whole 14 years.

I got back on the bus the next day, and my summer at camp continued on.

The coda to this story is that I took all my memorabilia with me, wherever I went, including of course my precious rose petals! Two summers later, in July of 1974, a fire started in the dining room at camp. My bunk at that time was attached to the dining hall. Nobody was hurt, but all of my belongings, including my clothes and my Stones memorabilia, were destroyed when the entire structure burnt to the ground. A profound loss to my young self.

JIM KEARNS, AGE 20

In 1972 my wife Lillian and I had just started going out. We were both big into the Stones. We were 20 years old and living and working in our 'hometown' of The Bronx. The Stones had been part of our adolescence, always with provocative hits on NY AM radio stations WABC and WMCA, and then later on FM stations like WNEW. By the time '72 rolled around, demand for Stones tickets was at a fever pitch, as they had not played the States since the disaster at Altamont in '69. Within those two and a half years, interest had only grown with the release of *Get Your Ya-Ya's Out!*, *Sticky Fingers* and *Exile on Main St.* and the film, *Gimme Shelter*.

We were both quite bummed about not being able to score tickets as the end of July approached. Miraculously, on the day of the first show at MSG, my friend Gus somehow obtained four tickets and included me in. I was on cloud nine! My most vivid memories of that first night are the excited anticipation of the audience on the escalators inside the Garden, and the elated buzz of the same crowd on the way out. The place was bursting with youthful exuberance and a clear, focused energy. The audience was primed and the Stones met and exceeded all expectations.

The next day, Jagger's birthday, I called my girlfriend at her job (she worked in the back office at a Chase branch) to see how her quest for a ticket was progressing. She had a line one through a girlfriend at work, but it was going to necessitate tracking down some guy in the north east Bronx who had a drug habit and a single ticket that he intended to sell outside the Garden for maximum profit.

As soon as Lillian got off work, we hopped in her friend's car and headed for the upper reaches, eventually locating the guy walking down a side street. After much cajoling and negotiating, he finally let the ticket go for three times face value. I agreed to accompany Lillian down on the subway; since we had friends going to the show, she'd have people to hang out with once she got in. But I was gonna give getting myself a ticket a shot too. Prospects looked grim when we passed a really tough looking middle-aged woman muttering that she had tickets for $300. But then we met some entrepreneurial hippie guys who had an arrangement with one of the ticket takers. 40 dollars and I was waved in! We were ecstatic, locating our friends and squeezing into the row of seats with them.

And of course, just like the previous night, the Stones were magnificent. I was thrilled to see them a second time, but even more thrilled that Lillian got to see them for her first time (of many).

NEIL LAVEY, AGE 14

I was 14 years old and went with my 18-year-old brother. We greatly enjoyed Stevie Wonder's opening set, during which my brother consumed a pint of Southern Comfort. By the time the Stones hit the stage, he was passed out.

Mick strutted across the stage wearing a denim jacket and white jumpsuit, and spinning a cane to a thunderous version of 'Brown Sugar'.

The highlights were 'Sweet Virginia', 'Midnight Rambler' (complete with Mick whipping the stage with a leather belt) and 'All Down the Line' towards the end. Witnessing Stevie Wonder join them for their encore with his hit 'Uptight' and for 'Satisfaction' was also sensational. Amazingly, my brother revived himself by the end of the show. I spent most of the night dancing in the aisle behind our seats. I have also seen the Stones seven or eight times in total, up until 2005. Maybe because it was my first time, no other concert has made the same impact on me.

STEVE BEDNEY

I went to the July 25 early show, my first Stones show. I didn't win the ticket lottery, so I got my ticket from a scalper... for $30! The whole thing went by in a blur, but I remember most of the set in every detail; Mick dancing and prancing, the super trouper lighting, Mick Taylor, Keith, Charlie, Bill never moving and Bobby Keys wailing, 'Tumbling Dice' (a brand new song then) rolling on, Mick and Keith duetting on 'Happy' (yep, Mick sang it then), 'Street Fighting Man' blowing the roof off MSG and 'Love in Vain', with Mick moving in slo-mo as if parodying the slo-mo in 'Gimme Shelter', but oh so well played. There was no encore.

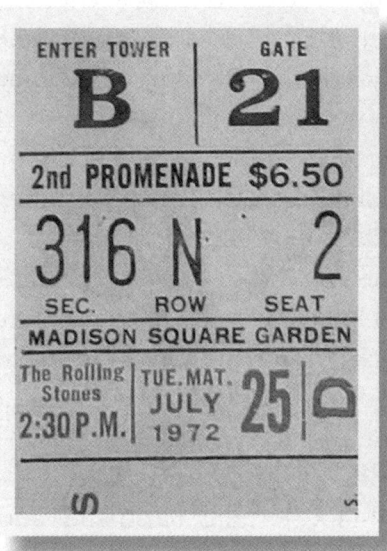

Steve Bedney was at the afternoon show

KATHY FRIERY, AGE 16

I acquired my ticket from the man who lived across the street who happened to work at Madison Square Garden. When the second show was added at 2.30pm in the afternoon due to demand, he got enough tickets for the whole neighborhood.

We were allowed to take the train from my hometown of Perth Amboy, New Jersey into New York City since the last stop was Penn Station. All we had to do was take the escalators up to Madison Square Garden and never set foot outside the building. Our parents considered us safe doing that, given the crime rate at that time.

I had a seat on the floor, halfway from the stage but with a direct view. It started with Stevie Wonder and then out came The Ike and Tina Turner Revue. Do ya think we were fired up by then? After the break, the sound that changed my life came blaring out from the speakers.

Kathy Friery remembers the Stones at the Garden

The sound was that of a 747 taking off. I was literally blown back in my seat by the sheer volume. It was like nothing I'd heard before. My jaw dropped… it was a religious experience in that my heart and soul were never the same.

Which only led me to downtown Manhattan, where a music scene was birthing on the imitation of the Stones, with David Johansen trying to be Mick and Johnny Thunders trying to be like Keith. It all came together with my ear up against those speakers once again, for the volume I craved given the 1972 tour.

In 1975, Charlie came up with the idea of promoting the Stones 1975 tour of the US by having the band play 'Brown Sugar' on the back of a lorry as it drove down the street in Manhattan. That street was 7th Avenue, past Madison Square Garden, where I was standing in a crowd, waiting for them to go by.

OTTO ANDRIADIS

It was called the STP tour. Being young at the time, I thought they did that purposely to relate it to the drug, although I think it was coined from Stones Touring Party. It was wild, with lots of rowdiness and celebrities everywhere. The Studio 54 crowd was all there, plus many other notables. It was four shows in three days and I know people that managed to attend all four sets. I only did the last night. I saw the Stones again in 2018 and 2019, and I think they play a much tighter set today than they did then.

Back then I used to think that bands were supposed to sound just like they do on their records. I remember thinking them to be a little too relaxed, maybe tired because they just didn't sound their very best. But these were the Rolling Stones. And they were great. The local TV and news media went wild. The Rolling Stones at Madison Square Garden was a big deal. This wasn't their first roll around at the Garden but it was certainly the time when arena rock was really taking off. I remember the personal stuff, like who I was with, the coke I had, the champagne I drank and the clothes I wore. Oh, and also that, even though I wanted to be Keith Richards. I wasn't!

KEVIN FITZPATRICK, AGE 20

I became a lifelong Beatles fan as a 12-year-old and was hooked after seeing them on *Ed Sullivan*. And, of course, the Stones were all over the radio as well. I'm actually a drummer and was heavily influenced by both Ringo and Charlie. I really became a Stones fan later on as I loved the *Beggars Banquet* album. Their reputation as a live band was becoming legendary and I was so lucky to get to see them at Madison Square Garden on Mick's birthday to boot. The demand for tickets was so great they had a lottery. You sent your name in on a postcard and if you got picked you were allowed to buy four tickets. I was in college and, as luck would have it, my girlfriend at the time got picked.

I remember the excitement in that building as being electric, for lack of a better word. I'd never felt that before, where you could actually feel it. I mean MSG and Stevie, Mick Taylor and Keef, Charlie and Bobby Keys? On Jagger's birthday? Come on!

Stevie was just great. I think he was supporting *Music of my Mind*, which I loved. And Stevie plays a mean trap set, which he was happy to share with us. I remember having a bet with friends on what the opening tune would be in the Stones set. I just knew it would be 'Brown Sugar' and I won the bet. 'Brown Sugar' was my favorite song and I was good

246

after that, as anything beyond that was another bonus. But I remember 'Midnight Rambler' as truly an amazing standout in the show. We got the white-studded jumpsuit from the birthday boy that night, and he was really on his game. He gives so much of himself with each show, it's truly amazing. As Charlie once said, 'He's the best frontman ever.'

The encore was 'Satisfaction' and Stevie came out to join them. As Keith played the signature lick, stage hands wheeled out this huge, monstrous cabinet which had cream pies in each shelf. To celebrate Jagger's birthday, they began throwing those pies all over the place during the song. Everyone was having a blast. Everyone was covered in pie except Stevie.

I'm so lucky to have been there that night. I'm almost 70 years old now and the memory tends to slip a bit. But who could forget that?

RICK DOSTAL

MSG, NYC. It was unreal. A birthday cake food fight! I met Bobby Keys in Hong Kong one time and we talked about it. He said the best part was when he hit a New York cop in the face with a piece of the cake. We laughed!

HOWIE ALTHOLTZ, AGE 18

I remember seeing The Beatles on *The Ed Sullivan Show*. I remember seeing the Stones on *Ed Sullivan* too. If someone asks you to describe smelling your first flower it's hard to put into words. The same is true of seeing the Stones on *Ed Sullivan*. It was so powerful and overwhelming. It was a complete sensory blow out. Seeing The Beatles made me realise there was another path here, different to the one I'd been watching my parents follow. It was comfortable and safe-ish, even though it was a little rebellious. But when the Stones came it was like – 'wow!' The energy there was a little more in your face. The Stones gave you permission to be a bit more different, and also be edgy. I've seen them maybe 15 times, including several times in Boston at the Gillette Stadium and at Boston Garden. And I was 18 when I saw them at Madison Square Garden in '72…

You take the attitude and energy of New York City and the attitude and energy of the Stones in '72 and you have a perfect storm. It was the pinnacle of the counterculture revolution. It morphed a little bit from flower power into 'fuck the establishment'. The Vietnam war was going crazy and Nixon was resigning and there was so much going on. The Stones didn't seem overly political, even with songs like 'Street Fighting Man' and 'Satisfaction'. They never got out front, marching and holding rallies like John Lennon. But the attitude and energy said, 'We don't respect the establishment,' which was captured in Mick's reaction after they were fined for urinating in public: 'We piss anywhere, man.' That attitude is really what you felt. You were on that side of the counter culture. And you were looking for an opportunity to go from flower power to 'Street Fighting Man'. There was no holding back from the Rolling Stones.

Altamont was dark. I think the Stones were still trying to come to terms with it in '72. There was a lot of recklessness and negligence and probably they weren't paying attention, and I don't think they conceived that things like that could happen, especially after Woodstock and all that. You can't say the Stones were to blame for anything, but it was chaos. I think we were all in denial about Altamont, no one wanted to digest that. We didn't have social media like you do now, so those things didn't stay with you that long or that deep. I don't remember any shadow of Altamont over the tour. I didn't sense any danger. But Frank Zappa got beaten up on stage around that era, and was hospitalised for six months, and Lennon got shot dead in 1980. There's always been crazies around.

I don't remember how I got tickets for Madison Square Garden. My uncle was involved with Warner Brothers and they had Atlantic Records. Ahmet Ertegun, who brought the Stones to the label, worked for my uncle so it's possible my uncle helped me get tickets (he's the one who got me the Beatles tickets). I think I got tickets just from hustling around. I probably went to the show with my friend Dennis, who played bass with me for many, many years. I do remember seeing the movie, *Ladies and Gentlemen, the Rolling Stones.* I was tripping out of my mind. It was a wild experience. It was a great movie which really captured the essence of the band.

The production gets better. '72 was before the days of mega-production. It was really more straight ahead and not over-produced. In those days it was just get out and play, pure energy and sweat. I don't think anyone could accuse the Stones, and especially Keith, of being over rehearsed in those days. But now, if you're going to charge $250 a ticket, people want something more than the straight ahead show they can get at the local bar. Not that I've ever seen the Stones play one of those local bar shows, much as I would love to!

Keith lives near me in New England, in Westport, Connecticut. I had the opportunity to jam with him once. Someone I knew had done some shows with him or worked with him in the studio. They set it up for me and, unfortunately, I was committed to visit my ex mother-in-law with my ex-wife. I was trying to patch up the marriage and I needed those brownie points. I had to blow off Keith for this stupid dinner with my mother-in-law. That marriage never worked out anyway, so I lost on both counts.

RUSS ROWLAND, AGE 14

My father took my brother and I. We had amazing seats, fifth row in the center, and the tickets were a whopping $6.50 each. It was Mick's birthday and the last night of the tour. At some point, they wheeled out a cake and champagne. Mick took a swig of one of the bottles and handed it down to someone in the front row to be passed around. I was hoping the bottle would get to me but, surprise surprise, I never saw it.

The Stones were amazing. I was in heaven. I recall people standing throughout most of it and I had to stand on my seat so I could see. For some reason, I recall thinking Mick was a little hoarse but I've listened to bootlegs of the show and they don't really support that memory, so there you go. It was a highlight of my young life… and still is.

Russ Rowland had amazing seats

Ironically, many years later, the Stones were playing a show at MSG that would have been some anniversary of the show I saw. I couldn't get anywhere near the fifth row and the tickets were $450. Time marches on.

JOE ELLROTT

In the summer of 1964, I had just finished my freshman year of high school and Beatlemania was thriving. I was somewhat into it as… who wasn't? I liked many of the British bands and my hair started to creep out bit by bit. However, for the most part it was just background music to my daily day-to-day as a young teenager. My friend and I always had a transistor with us and played it quite loudly, but most likely it was just to get girls' attention in our immature way. Then one morning it happened.

As I was leaving my room to meet my friend, a song came on the local AM station that made me stop. As the song continued, I found myself staring at the radio and fearing that once the song ended, the disc jockey would start another song without saying who the artist was or what that song was. It was something I never experienced before over a record. You see, my parents ran a bar and grill. We lived above it for a good part of my early life and my bedroom was almost directly above the jukebox, so every night the bar was open I fell asleep to a booming bass and early rock and roll. It never really registered with me. I mean, there are songs I would sing as I walked to my grandparents' farm, but it was just time filler, I guess. This song was different. It was raw, it rocked and it just grabbed me. The song? 'It's All Over Now', by the Rolling Stones. That was it. I was hooked. The Beatles? Who?

The excitement I felt from this new British band was undeniable. Yet, coming from a small village, there weren't many who felt the same as I. Even my friend Billy, who was a huge Elvis fan, humoured me somewhat but never had the same feeling for this band, but that was cool. I enjoyed going to the Elvis films; they were corny but something for bored teenagers to do. But now the worries would start. On Top 40 radio you were only remembered for your latest hit, and I was afraid the Stones would fade away as quickly as they appeared in my life.

That feeling would ease once I would hear the DJ say again, 'Here's the latest from the Rolling Stones,' and everything would be fine again, at least for the next four to six weeks, and then it would start all over again. How foolish that looks now in hindsight but, hey, who knew?

We would gather at the family farm at Christmas. One uncle would get us kids the greatest gifts. We always looked forward to what it would be. Now that we were teens, we got to tell him what we would like, and for me every Christmas for the next couple of years, my gift was square and flat. Yep, the latest Stones album. He always came through for me.

My musical knowledge was broadened and awakened through the Sixties courtesy of Mick and company. (My favorite was Brian, and when boys said that they were sporting Beatle haircuts, I always said mine was a Rolling Stone haircut. It was depressing when Brian was fired from the Stones in 1969 and died later that summer, close to the day of my birthday. Mick Taylor may be the best guitarist the band has had, but Brian and his ability to play multiple instruments just seemed invaluable to me, and I consider Brian's time in the band to have created the best of the Stones music. My oldest son carries Brian as his middle name in honor of Mr Jones. When he was a youngster with his long strawberry blond hair, he bore an uncanny resemblance to Brian.

I absorbed the various musical forms as 1964 turned into 1967 and '68, and blues and psychedelia and FM radio took hold. The music became more thought provoking and inspiring. Going to see bands like The Who, Led Zeppelin, Canned Heat and Steppenwolf, etc., live, was great. I saw and attended many memorable concerts and thoroughly enjoyed myself, getting high or tripping and hanging with so many like-minded people. It was 'groovy', but there was just one thing missing.

Back in 1964, the Stones came to the city outside my village but I could find no one who wanted to go, and not wishing to attend alone I passed, a decision I still regret to this day. (Years later, I found out that a slightly younger kid I knew and who only lived a couple of blocks away had tickets to the show but he passed as well because he could not find anyone to attend with him. I never figured him to be a Stones fan.)

And thus the infamous '69 tour was never in reach, and that slid by as well. I watched the *Gimme Shelter* film a number of times, but it was not the same as actually being there. Which brings us to 1972. It was announced the Stones would be playing Madison Square Garden and tickets would be issued via a lottery drawing of postcards. And, not wanting to miss out again, I went to the post office and bought 22

251

postcards, filled them out and mailed them in and waited. And waited.

The wait was dragging me down, especially after I heard that three guys I knew sent in one postcard each and all three had their cards pulled and would receive tickets. Hearing this, while ironically the Stones song 'Happy' came on the radio, was more than I could take. How was it possible that I sent in 22 postcards and hadn't heard a thing, yet these three could send in one each and score? No, no way – it wasn't right.

Feeling my chance flickering away as the dates drew nearer, it was a warm day and a pleasant sunny bright afternoon as I went out to check the mail, as I had each and every day since mailing those postcards. I was not really expecting anything, but once again I was hoping that this was the day. As I pushed open the lid on the mailbox, a yellowish envelope peeked out at me among the mail. Up in the left-hand corner was the image of, and words which read, 'Madison Square Garden'.

I froze and then immediately grabbed the envelope and the rest of the mail and ran back to my apartment. My mind was racing, thinking 'yes, finally!' but also filled with dread. Maybe this was a condolence letter saying, 'Thank you for entering but sorry...' I slowly opened it and read the beginning.

'You have been selected to purchase four tickets for the afternoon show of July 25th.' Wait, what? An afternoon show? There were only supposed to be three shows, but by sheer luck and possibly an overwhelming number of requests, they added a fourth show. I couldn't believe my luck but if that show wasn't added, does that mean I would have been shut out? I didn't care, it didn't matter now, I had the golden ticket. I screamed and grabbed the phone. I called my (now) wife and rambled something incoherent but she understood. The Beatles were still her band, but she wasn't going to miss this and anyway she was my wife so I had to take her.

I had to go to New York and the Madison Square Garden ticket window, present the letter I had received and then purchase my tickets. With the promise of a ticket, my friend Tim agreed to drive me the couple of hours into New York City in his MG convertible to collect the tickets on the allotted day and off we went. Arriving in plenty of time, we parked somewhere near the Port Authority and walked to the Garden, immersing ourselves amongst the others who were waiting their turn.

Finally, there I was, standing at the window clutching for dear life the letter, and handing it over and receiving the envelope with four tickets for the second level, just slightly left of center stage. I heard someone complain because they got tickets that said 'back of stage'. I guess I could see their point but my thought was, 'Hey, who cares? You still got tickets.' Would those tickets have bothered me? Hell, no, as long as I was in the building in eyesight of the stage and band it would not have mattered at all.

So now I had four tickets and only three were spoken for. I was about to become very popular. Back home I was getting questions and requests for that fourth ticket. But I remembered how, before I knew I had secured the tickets, a group of us were sitting around talking about the concert and my buddy John had said, 'Man, imagine getting to be there. How great would that be?' And the look on his face and in his eyes just stayed with me and I knew that the fourth ticket had to be his. He was stunned when I told him. And so that was that.

On the morning of July 25th, Tim, John, Patty and I boarded a Greyhound bus for NYC. I had another uncle who happened to be a driver for Greyhound and so we travelled for free. You can't beat that, and off we went for one of the greatest experiences of our young lives. Walking from the Port Authority to MSG, I don't think my feet ever touched the ground.

The excitement was building, and we saw the large crowd outside waiting for the doors to open. It was the big city, the number one city, the number one rock and roll band, the big concert. Far out man, far out.

Once inside and in our seats, we just sat there and took it all in. The atmosphere was electric and the place was buzzing. To know what was going to happen in a few long minutes was an incredible and unbelievable feeling. The lights went down and out came Stevie Wonder. He did a short but fabulous set. It's Stevie Wonder we're seeing as a warm up? The guy's a legend. What a great start!

The lights came back up and now we waited. I had to remember to breathe. We waited for what seemed then like an eternity and then the lights dimmed and the PA reverberated. 'Ladies and Gentlemen, are you ready?' Repeats. 'Are you ready? I think we're ready, are you ready? The Rolling Stones, the Rolling Stones,' and I believe it was repeated again, a third time. Who knows? I was numb.

Bam! The lights came on big, bold and bright and there they were, live and in person, and off we all go on the ride of a lifetime, dancing across the stage with Mick flowing through the fingers of Keith, Mick and Bill, our hearts beating in time with Charlie.

In all honesty, it was a blur, a flash, and the only clear memory I have is of Mick in the 'Street Fighting Man' finale, teasing us with a basin of water he grabbed from the stage, mimicking throwing it a few times until we screamed for him to throw it and throw it he did, releasing all that pent up energy pulsing through the building. What a climatic ending.

Spent, we were now sitting there and questioning ourselves, asking if the concert really did indeed happen. Or was it just our imagination? It seemed like no sooner had the lights come up that the last note was struck and they were gone. Then off we went down the stairs, mixed in with the arriving crowd, answering the perpetual question, 'How were they?'

'Fantastic, man, fantastic.'

I waited and bought a tour shirt from the gypsy vendors outside the Garden. It was a much nicer and cool shirt than what they were selling inside, and also cheaper in price, but you had to be quick because the cops were rounding them up and putting the vendors on the back of a large flatbed truck and the arrested vendors just stood there, smiling and waving at the crowd. After all, it was New York City. How cool was that?

SEVIGNE GALINDO-WILICHINSKY

I remember camping out at Madison Square Garden to get tickets, and my friend giving someone some hash to get further in the line. I actually have a picture of Bob Dylan sitting at the concert. I asked him why he didn't get better seats! The concert was great, as always, but I was probably pretty stoned to remember too much.

Sevigne Galindo-Wilichinsky
remembers being 'pretty stoned'

STAN BECKER

I've been telling people for decades – this was the best rock 'n' roll show I've seen in my life. Growing up in Brooklyn, New York I listened to ABC FM. That transistor radio was broadcasting, not 'narrow' casting. It was years away from FM stereo but we got it all, so I was a big fan of rhythm and blues years before the British Invasion. But there was something about the Stones that I didn't get until I was a teenager. I was a kid who read a lot and I was intrigued by their lyrics, but I wasn't an experienced person and they were talking about some hard blues shit. It wasn't until I started having girlfriends at 16 and getting heartbroken at 17 and going through some shit and then, when I was 18, started listening again to the Stones albums that I already had that I went, 'Holy shit!'

I missed the Stones when they were here in '69. Then I heard the album, *Liver Than You'll Ever Be*, a bootleg of the Oakland '69 show which so many people had that they ended up having to release *Get Yer Ya-Ya's Out!* I knew where Mick Taylor was coming from, because I knew The Yardbirds, but as much as I'm a Taylorite, I heard Keith's winding lead in 'Sympathy for the Devil' and that was it. I went, 'Holy mackerel, I gotta see the Stones!'

In '72 when they came around, it was very hard to get a ticket. I had to win a lottery. I had to send in hundreds of postcards to even get the privilege of being able to buy tickets. But I had heard *Let It Bleed*. I had *Beggars Banquet*. I had *Sticky Fingers*.

Nothing was going to keep me from seeing the Rolling Stones live in 1972. I saw them at RFK Stadium on July 4th in Washington DC. I turned 21 on July 12th, and on Mick's birthday, with the cake fight and Stevie and that jam, I saw them at the last show of the entire North American tour, at Madison Square Garden. They were hot as a pistol.

Today they have this two hour and ten-minute extravanganza and it's very professional and I say, 'God bless them and God bless their second line.' But 1972 was a whole different story. It was 70 minutes from start to finish. They opened with 'Brown Sugar', a song with the energy that some of the best bands in the world could only muster in their final encore. That's how these bitches opened up. That's how these hardy, dirty, whorehouse music motherfuckers opened up their act in New York City. And we went nuts. It was just incredible, man, and I'm still not over it. And I'm a cynical 'show me' New York City kid, not a 'I'm gonna scream at you' kid.

So I'm all watching Bill. I'm all watching Stu and Nicky. I had taken piano lessons before I got into folk guitar as a kid. I'm watching this shit like the reporter I grew up to be. And I'm loving it, man. No big screens. 70 minutes including the encore, and you didn't want one minute more. You didn't feel ripped off in the slightest.

It cost 15 bucks a ticket. I got to buy four tickets and I didn't get to pick what night and I didn't get to pick what section. And I got the last night of the tour and floor seats. Do you know what that means? It means Jesus is real.

The Stones were a brilliant amalgamation, even the breakdown into the acoustic thing, and the virtuosity of Mick Taylor. The brutal intensity of Keith Richards. And Charlie. We all loved Charlie for his grace. We've all seen this classy, powerful, wonderful life, but in '72 he was pounding those things. Charlie was very propulsive and very amazing. Those guys were very serious rock 'n' rollers in 1972.

I saw a Rolling Stones nine-piece band that never toured anywhere in the world before or since that particular tour. It was Bobby Keys' first tour, which was incredibly significant because that was right from Delaney and Bonnie.

I saw the Stones in '75, which was one of Ronnie's first eight or nine gigs with the Stones while the Faces were still active. I had seen the Faces close up at the Fillmore East in 1970, which was a very small theatre comparatively, and contemporaneous with *A Nod's as Good as a Wink*. I had been a huge Small Faces fan since Steve Marriott was in the band, and I adored Rod Stewart in the Jeff Beck Group, and there was Nicky Hopkins. And I adored The Kinks, and there was Nicky Hopkins again. So when I saw the Stones in '72, I knew who the hell Nicky Hopkins was. To me, it was about Nicky Hopkins as much as it was about Michael Philip Jagger. Not that I'll say anything critical of Mick, because he's brilliant, he's charismatic, he's funny, he's sardonic, he's probably a damn good dad – I love him. But I was also watching Nicky and Stu as much as our funny, wonderful, costumed, fantastically charismatic, physically thrilling lead guy up front. Of course, I appreciated Mick's energy and enthusiasm and beauty. But – holy shit!

– what a gift to see Nicky Hopkins and Stu at one point banging on the same piano. I nearly wept.

I'm trying to keep from weeping telling you about it now, and it's over 50 years later. Those guys came to play.

RFK was a stadium show in a big outdoor sports stadium. I had great seats, sitting on top of the home team dug out. I had clear sight lines to the second base area of the stage. And the sound was great and it was fun and all that, but it was a stadium and I'm not so much of a stadium guy. Whereas Madison Square Garden was the end of the tour. The end of the tour was reputed to be an extremely hot performance period for them. A lot of critics say they were a lot hotter than in the excellent *Ladies and Gentlemen* film, so this was hotter than Texas. It was the last show. There was a lot of tension coming off. And it was a party and Stevie Wonder was going to join them on stage with the hand percussion members from Wonderlove, so things were going to get extremely fun and interesting and polyrhythmic, and it was – relatively – a theatre show. Of course, Madison Square Garden is a 16-17,000-seater basketball stadium indoor kind of a thing, but it's very different from an outdoor baseball stadium. And having floor seats, I had the sound from the stage and the sound from the PA. It was a real gift to actually have the sound from the stage. That was extremely thrilling. For me, it was a much more musical performance rather than a big celebration like you get in a big baseball stadium. And New York's a different place, and they're willing to listen. At least, they were back then.

I think it took the Stones a while to realise that they really lost something when they lost Bill Wyman. They didn't take proper care of that. I'm very happy to have seen Bill Wyman live and to have heard him and felt him. I loved him as much as any of the others that night.

JULIA SALINGER

For as long as I can remember I have loved the Stones. I think it was Keith Richards who really attracted me to the band. The whole rebellious gypsy persona was potent. I can't remember the first time I heard their music, but I was drawn to it because of the blues roots influences. I always loved the blues. You got tickets by lottery. I sent in about 50 letters and I got twelve tickets. I went every night and brought friends. I didn't scalp one ticket. I went with my friend Arthur and some other guys from art camp.

The Garden was great then, because there wasn't security like there is now, and there was much more of a mix of concert goers and performers and what we now call 'celebrities'. I remember Dick Cavett sitting next to me at one of the shows. Those were great NY days. Outside of MSG was a fantastic party, we were all so excited to be seeing the Stones. It was summer and hot and we were passing joints (when pot was illegal, a much nicer time) and everyone was in a great mood. There wasn't that fear of cops so much then. They were friendlier and if you had a 'hood story, which I often did, you could get backstage. The crowd was wild in '72 and the energy was intense. *Exile on Main St.* is my favorite Stones album. It reads as a beautiful dream or story.

SAM KURSHAN

It was Mick's 29th birthday. During the encore they brought Stevie Wonder back on stage and everyone sang happy birthday to Mick. A cake was brought out and a massive food fight broke out where everyone but Charlie Watts ended up covered in cake. Mick even put one in Stevie Wonder's face. An insane night where Wonder did his hit at the time, 'Superstition'. There was a lottery to get tickets and half a million people sent in postcards. But once again my wealthy Cousin Aaron, rest his soul, got me two tickets through his friend, Irving Mitchell Felt, the owner of Madison Square Garden.

TOM MILLER, AGE 13

I remember the British Invasion. I was a kindergartener. My sister had the 45 of 'Satisfaction' and we had a teenage babysitter who would play it on the hi-fi and hint at forbidden mysteries in the lyrics that I was too young to understand but was fascinated by anyway. When I was in sixth grade, my mother happened to walk into my room just as the automatic record changer slid the *Let It Bleed* platter onto the turntable, the tone arm swung over, the needle dropped and the haunting opening strains of 'Gimme Shelter' started ringing out. She was so startled to hear something that beautiful coming out of my little plastic speakers, instead of what typically sounded to her like just a bunch of harsh noise, that she asked me what it was. At first, she didn't believe me when I said it was the Rolling Stones. She had a newfound respect for the kids' music after that, even though I assured her the whole record didn't sound like that. (The next album she heard me playing was far more dissonant, a modern classical LP by Edgard Varèse which worried her about my state of mind so much that she begged me to turn it off, even though it was being played by a very respectable symphony orchestra.)

Then I had the original Andy Warhol *Sticky Fingers* album cover with the real metal zipper fly that I would zip and unzip when I was bored in Sunday school. I peeled back and separated the sleeve to see if there was anything else to see behind the zipper. And there was, a full Warhol photograph of a male torso! Naively, I wrote my name all over all my Rolling Stones records and album covers so nobody would steal them. Even more naively, I sold them all when I went to college and got more into jazz, foolishly thinking I'd outgrown childish pleasures. Maybe someone out there still has my name written in 19-cent blue Bic ballpoint in the corner of the octagon-shaped jacket of *Through the Past, Darkly*.

I played the organ in Ramrod, a junior high group put together by my friend M Scott Young, a drummer who was the number one Stones fan in our school. We were later convinced by Sid Albert, a very hip local music impresario in our small suburban town with a big Afro, little rectangular shades, a turtleneck and a psychedelic record store called Sight 'n' Sound, to change our name in order to get even the possibility of an actual gig. We mostly covered Rolling Stones songs, especially deep cuts like 'Citadel', along with some Doors, Jefferson Airplane and T.Rex.

At one of our only gigs we banged on a cowbell and did 'I'm a Man' as if it were the truth, never mind that our voices hadn't even changed yet. Another time, before a football game, we were supposed to play the national anthem with some of the horn players from the junior high school band but the sheet music blew off the stands, so after a short drum solo, the rest of us launched into 'Volunteers' with its call for revolution in the streets, much to the school's displeasure. Later, when a few of the horn guys actually joined the group, it became less rock oriented and more into Chicago Transit Authority or Blood Sweat and Tears, and that's when I lost interest.

But, at first, we were just this little three-chord combo and the cowbell part in 'Honky Tonk Women' was what everybody was going crazy over. I remember we sat there scratching the needle back and forth on the opening 'identiriff' of 'Jumpin' Jack Flash' and Scott being convinced that it was either overdubbed or played on two guitars, because nobody could possibly play those chord changes that fast. We couldn't figure out how they did it. It was about 50 years later when I learned that Keith Richards was playing most everything in open tunings. One time, when I was a university student waiting out a flight delay at San Francisco airport, I tuned my guitar to an open chord, took out a slide and played 'No Expectations' to a surprisingly receptive audience of stranded airline passengers whose only other source of amusement was trying unsuccessfully to avoid a pack of Hare Krishna devotees pressing leaflets on them.

In 1972, the Stones tour was the biggest rock tour yet. In my memory, it was the first time that there was a lottery for tickets for a concert. It was a big event, and the odds of getting a ticket were almost impossible. But M Scott was such a Stones fanatic. I think he had some kind of portable tape recorder, and he had managed to get an advance copy of 'Wild Horses' that had been leaked before the record came out, and which he would play little bits of surreptitiously in math class. Madison Square Garden was the hardest ticket to get, and most people didn't stand a chance.

You had to write into a random drawing and send a self-addressed stamped envelope, then hope you were one of the lucky few who beat the odds. Some people decorated their envelopes with elaborate hand-drawn designs. I don't know if he entered the lottery multiple times or what, but amazingly Scott scored two tickets out of I don't know how many people trying to get them. Almost as amazing was that he convinced his parents to let him go. He would play the tape of 'Wild Horses' over and over until his father was like 'Okay, okay, whatever.' He invited me as his 'plus one', maybe because of our band repertoire or maybe because I was the only other kid whose parents would let him go to the city unchaperoned. I was 13 going on 14.

When I saw the envelope with the tickets, I was so excited. I can still remember standing in my parents' bedroom to show them. The ticket had been mailed to me and it was the most beautiful thing I'd ever seen, an art object with multicolored designs, Peter Max-style, sort of psychedelic and elaborate so it couldn't be easily counterfeited. It was like the Holy Grail. I couldn't believe I had it. I was showing my parents how special it was so they would let me go. I'm sure I kept the stub; maybe my mother finally threw it out, or maybe one day it will magically appear at the bottom of an old storage box.

When *Exile on Main St.* came out, the controversy among the fandom was whether they had gone in the wrong direction by adding not just Bobby Keys on saxophone, but a whole horn section and that sort of Memphis soul sound. I was one of the sceptics. I didn't like what had happened musically in our little so-called band when the horn players moved in, and this seemed like the same thing on a far, far grander scale. A lot of Stones fans initially thought *Exile* was overblown, or even not rock and roll enough. Hard to believe, because now it's considered their greatest album by so many critics and fans. But M Scott, who was the true Stones aficionado, just said, 'Tommy, have they ever let you down with a bad album?' I was like 'no'. Not that I knew all their albums, but he convinced me. Even *Flowers*, which was rumored to have been cobbled together from singles and outtakes because the group was having legal troubles over drug busts and couldn't record any new material, held up as a solid LP listening experience. After all, as the saying went, who breaks a butterfly upon a wheel?

The concert was actually the last performance of their US tour, a now famous event with Stevie Wonder opening, on Mick Jagger's birthday, July 26th. I remember at one point the lights went down and they brought out a birthday cake. It was the first of two shows on the last night of the tour. The whole evening was this big New York society event that was in all the gossip columns and newspapers and magazines, with Truman Capote and Andy Warhol having an icy standoff backstage and Bianca Jagger partying with Princess Lee Radziwill. Dick Cavett was there, interviewing Mick, and he featured the spectacle on his national late-night TV talk show.

There we were in the new Madison Square Garden, which was only about four years old and already the world's most famous arena. Our seats were on the side about halfway back, stage left, first level up by the railing. I'd been to sporting events but had never been at such a big rock concert before. As cavernous as it was, I was astonished that we were in the same room and breathing the same air as the Rolling Stones. I didn't see anyone else there who looked as young as us without an adult accompanying them.

Stevie Wonder blew the roof off the Garden in his opening set, playing all the instruments on stage with a beautiful tall woman leading him from one to the next. He was 22 years old and at the height of his powers. I distinctly remember the huge clavinet and Minimoog bass sound on 'Superstition', which was then a new song, not yet released. It would come out four months later and kick off his classic three-album run of *Talking Book*, *Innervisions*, and *Songs in the Key of Life*.

The Stones were either just past their classic three album run of *Beggars Banquet*, *Let It Bleed*, and *Sticky Fingers* – I learned that *Get Yer Ya-Yas Out!*, the live album I had bought and memorised, didn't count in the canon – or else they had just topped it with *Exile on Main St.*, depending on who you asked. It took some time for the fans to completely warm up to *Exile*, but from then until now there's been a nearly unanimous opinion that their next LP, *Goat's Head Soup*, was in fact the mythical bad album that M Scott had assured me they were incapable of delivering.

I remember the excitement building and growing impatience during a long changeover before the Stones came on. The lights finally went out and a recording of the opening to '2000 Light Years from Home' played, a strange and interesting choice given that it was so different from the style of music they were playing now. It really built up the anticipation. They came out and fired up 'Brown Sugar' and it was off to the races. It was a great show, one of the best I've ever seen. The fans like myself who thought maybe the new album was too flashy, too big, too polished, were won over immediately. Seeing and hearing the film footage shot by Robert Frank for *Cocksucker Blues* now, it was so primitive! It really looks and sounds raw and primitive, the antithesis of polished or overproduced. It feels the same way watching *Get Back*; The Beatles were so technically stripped down to the basics in 1969.

So they did this great high energy show. There was a big wide stage that seemed like it went all the way from 7th Avenue to the Avenue of the Americas, and Jagger spent a lot of time and energy running back and forth and up and down and climbing these tall scaffolding structures on the sides, getting a real workout. All the while you were half expecting him to trip over the incredibly long microphone wire, which must have been strongly grounded or there probably would have been a massive hum.

There was a long stretch of 'Midnight Rambler' in the second half, which seems like a song nobody else could possibly sing now without getting cancelled, a song told from the point of view of a serial rapist, even though the Stones still do it and get away with it, and they only dropped 'Brown Sugar' from their setlist in 2021. I mean, this is the band that got away with 'Let's Spend the Night Together' in 1967 (except on *The Ed Sullivan Show*, where they had to change it to 'Let's Spend Some Time Together') and 'Jumpin' Jack Flash' in 1968 (everyone knew they were really saying 'shit's a gas gas gas'). I'm pretty sure no one else could have gotten 'Start Me Up', which includes the lyric, 'You make a dead man come,' not only on Top 40 radio but featured as the theme song of an ad campaign for Microsoft in the early 2000s.

So anyway; great concert, great show. About half the songs were from the new album, which made me an instant believer, and a generous helping of the required classics. Keith sings 'Happy', we're happy, and then for the encore, Stevie Wonder and Mick Jagger duet on a medley of 'Uptight (Everything's Alright)' and 'Satisfaction'. I remember it so well, it's burnt into my burning brain and my personal 'best of' lists. Okay, musically maybe it's not quite the very best I ever saw, but it's up there. For years, when people would ask, 'What's the best concert you ever saw?' I would say, 'The Rolling Stones and Stevie Wonder,' just to watch them go, 'Wow!' And then I would say, 'Playing together!' and they would kind of stare at me in disbelief. I would tell them that Stevie Wonder upstaged Mick Jagger even though Mick was dancing all over the stage. Seeing that sequence in *Cocksucker Blues* now, it's exactly how I remember it. Just exactly. The only difference is that it's filmed from the other side of the stage. I'm pretty sure we noticed the camera operators all over the stage that night.

I remember, when the house lights came on after the encore and people started filing out of the Garden with this sort of pleasant murmuring buzz, they played 'Coconut' by Harry Nilsson over the sound system and I just stopped to listen and watch the people. It sounded so good, some others did too. As with the intro music, this outro was a complete shift in mood from the concert, a totally different vibe but a groove nonetheless. It was very interesting. I wondered if maybe Keith or Charlie, someone in the group with eclectic tastes, was choosing the intro and outro recorded music; which is why it was so different, like cleansing the palette. I wondered if the late show would be even more supercharged. Lots of bands did two shows a night, and for 13-year-old me, getting to stay out late enough to go to a second show became the new Holy Grail.

I only ever saw them play live one more time. It was in 1981 in the Seattle Kingdome, when Mick Jagger was wearing the football jersey for each stadium. He actually did some London School of Economics-type market research with the crowd, asking for a show of hands. 'How many of you came down from Vancouver? How many of you came up from Portland? If we added a show in Vancouver, how many of you would still drive to Seattle?' It was a very impressive bit of putting the business into stage business. It was like the episode of *The Simpsons* where Mick is running a rock camp, and he has his green accountant's eyeshade and adding machine. But he had such charisma in that show, it was as if he were the Reverend Sun Myung Moon and the audience was a full-blown cult, the way the energy of the crowd focused on him and he radiated it back. He was absolutely mesmerizing.

The only other performer I ever saw who was the focus of that much crowd-driven intensity was Captain Trips himself, Jerry Garcia. His onstage demeanour, self-effacing and unadorned, was the opposite of Jagger's preening and prancing. But Jagger could just reflect the crowd's energy and control them with an almost totalitarian charisma. Thousands of people and nobody could take their eyes off him. Has anyone ever done that better? Seeing what was going on behind the scenes in the footage of *Cocksucker Blues*, I'm amazed the band and the crew could even stand up without nodding off.

I might have seen the Stones one other time, or at least some of them, close up and personal in a little hotel coffee shop when I was about six or seven years old, around 1965. I was with my mother and my sister eating lunch on the east side of Manhattan, all dressed up to go somewhere or other, and there was a big scene over these British Invasion rock-and-roll stars with long hair and suits in the booth next to our table. They were sitting there eating breakfast, looking kind of hung over, when suddenly all these teenage and preteen fangirls rushed in shrieking and asking for autographs, along with a horde of trench-coated press photographers popping off flashbulbs. The English rock stars seemed sort of bemused by it all, sheepishly half-grinning and playing along. I've always believed it was Mick Jagger, Keith Richards, and Brian Jones – as I recall it, one of them was blond – but my sister, who was older and already an actual record collector, would know better. She insists it was in fact three fifths of the Dave Clark Five. I like to think it was Mick, Brian and Keith, or at least maybe Bill Wyman and Charlie Watts. That way I don't have to explain to anyone who the Dave Clark Five were. I rarely even tell people anymore that I saw The Beatles on *Ed Sullivan*, since it automatically gives away my age. It's like saying, 'I fought in the First World War.'

MEREDITH SCOTT YOUNG, AGE 14

On March 17, 1965, I saw the Stones on Clay Cole's TV show for the first time. I liked them immediately and felt no need to choose between them and The Beatles. I thought they were cool. At nine years old, I tried to emulate their look, and particularly that of Brian Jones. I was only semi-successful. I borrowed my cousin Bonnie's *Got Live If You Want It* when it was still pretty new, and loved the intensity and pacing of it. I finally gave it back to Cousin Bonnie in my mid to late twenties.

In the summer of 1969, I was at camp when Brian died and I didn't find out until October. I mourned by buying up every Stones album I could get my hands on. Somewhere around its release date, I bought *Let It Bleed*. It was at that point I realized how much more there was to the Stones. Keith's guitars were intense, raw and beautifully blended. Mick, vocally and lyrically, was on fire. As an aspiring drummer, Charlie's playing, particularly on *Let It Bleed*, became my bible. I spent many hours trying to copy the intensity of his beats and his fills, as well as his overall drum sound. As an 11-year-old, I was just a bit too young to convince anyone to take me to see them at Madison Square Garden for the 1969 show.

I spent the next three years analyzing and emulating pretty much everything from Bill's (and occasionally Keith's) bass to Mick Taylor's slide playing and fluidity and Keith's mysterious open tunings. My friend

265

Tommy and I decided that Keith's riffs and rhythms had to actually be two guitars, where the second guitar played the middle notes and chords. Obviously, we needed to learn a lot more about what Keith was able to do with those open tunings.

Pretty much all I thought about was the Stones and whether I would ever get to see them live. Tickets for most 1972 shows went on sale early spring. It wasn't until early June that it was announced that there would be a lottery for the tickets to the Madison Square Garden shows. Fans were to send in postcards. If your card was chosen, you were given a time to come in and purchase your tickets. I might have cheated a bit by sending a card in under my dad's name, but also one for my Uncle Steve using his address over on the other side of Mamaroneck.

A few weeks later, I received a call from Uncle Steve asking me about a letter saying he had won the right to buy four tickets and when to go down to the Garden to buy them. Immediately, there was a giant lump in my throat and I could barely talk. My uncle laughed and offered to go down to the Garden and pick the tickets up. Coincidentally, he had other business in the city that day. I became convinced that someone would try and steal the tickets from him. I repeatedly asked my uncle to be careful. But the whole thing went very smoothly. The scene at the Garden was pretty mellow, and I had the tickets by dinner time.

For the next six weeks, I looked at those tickets many times a day, still not believing I had 'won' the lottery. I read later that each postcard had a one in 22 chance of being selected. Man, was I cool…

The day of the concert, I had to take care of reality before we could leave. I had a summer paper route. Fortunately, the papers came early. I raced through the three apartment buildings. As I rounded a corner in one of the buildings, I heard the words, 'This is a stick up!' My heart jumped into my mouth and I froze. As I looked up, I saw my next customer laughing. He was just joking. It took a while to calm down but I did and I finished the route. There were no stick ups and I didn't get hit by any cars while finishing the route by bike on the Boston Post Road. I spent about an hour getting ready, into the clothes I had pre-selected weeks ago. I had to look just right…

It was obvious that my friend Tommy would be going. I had gotten a call from another friend's older sister's boyfriend, offering to drive us down to the Garden if they could buy the other two tickets. After giving it some thought and consulting my parents, I agreed. As it turned out, they wanted to go to dinner first so I'm pretty sure my dad and uncle drove us down.

We were in loge 47C, row C. 50 years later, how could I forget? We were about two thirds back but pretty level with the stage. It was a great view but I wished we had been a little closer. All in all, though, they were pretty great seats and pretty lucky for a 14-year-old going to only his second real concert. We arrived about an hour early. As time went on, seats started to fill up. I was so nervous and so excited.

Stevie Wonder was just transitioning from 'Little Stevie Wonder' and his set reflected that. While the set had a few of the old Motown hits, it was clear he was adding more mature material. He was also now a band leader and not a child pop star anymore. The set was enjoyable and interesting. It calmed me down, at least temporarily. Feeling much more like a fan than a cool guy, it was getting to be the main event.

Suddenly the lights went down. A giant lump took over my throat. From the opening riff of 'Brown Sugar', everyone was on their feet and clapping along with the beat. I couldn't believe I was there. I tried to calm down and soak it all in. Mick Taylor was so fluid. His lead lines added so much. Besides sounding great, for 1972, it added a lot of jammy street credibility. It was hard to know where to look. Keith was strutting and moving to his riffs. Mick was like a rocket that had just taken off. He threw himself into the music with an intensity that I have not seen since. In 1972, Charlie was still young and a pretty hard player.

As an aspiring drummer, watching Charlie Watts live was like being given the keys to the kingdom. (That was the last American tour before Charlie cut his hair and developed his fashion sense. Actually, he was pretty appropriately dressed for 1972.) Bill Wyman was his solid, steady, unmoving self. He looked cool and got the job done. Mick Taylor didn't move much either, but his hands more than made up for it.

The set focused mostly on what at the time was newer material. Besides a cover of Chuck Berry's 'Bye Bye Johnny', 'Jumpin' Jack Flash' was the oldest Stones song. Everything else during the set was from 1969 and *Let It Bleed* or later. There was a clear sense the Stones were showing that they were still very relevant and able to hold their own against the newer, louder, jammy bands of the day.

After 15 songs, which is short by today's standards, the Stones were gone. While people were screaming for more, there was movement on the stage. The lights went back down and all of a sudden, an intense backbeat came in. At that point, the Stones and Stevie Wonder along with his band were gearing up for a wild medley of Stevie's 'Uptight' going into the Stones oldest song of the night, 'Satisfaction'. Mick and Stevie traded vocals on both songs. My favorite part of the encore was when Mick held Stevie's hand and they started jumping as high as they could in unison. The intensity level just kept going up. Then it was over.

After the show, we were drained and didn't want to leave. They announced that the Stones had left the building so we slowly left the Garden. Once outside, the teenage couple realized they had no idea where they parked. We walked around the area for well over an hour. Things got tense between the couple. The rest is a story for another day....

JACK WEISS, AGE 20

In the summer of 1972, I was 20 years old, living in an illegal basement apartment in Brighton Beach, Brooklyn without heat, but with plenty of cockroaches for company. Although I was a registered full-time student at Brooklyn College on a full NY State Regents scholarship (Brooklyn College, as was all of the City University of NY colleges at the time, was tuition free), I had long shoulder-length hair and gladly used the stipend for purchasing pot and record albums. I loved listening to the Stones on record (along with Jefferson Airplane, Creedence, Dylan, Hendrix and the rest of the rock bands of my era; I didn't care much for folk, but loved blues, soul, and jazz, which I didn't know much about) and the news of their first tour in three long years was heaven sent. I read that the deal was a maximum of four seats per request, postcard lottery only, at $6.50 per seat at Madison Square Garden, with Stevie Wonder and Wonderlove as the opening act.

I purchased 100 postcards and spent a weekend smoking pot and addressing them. None of them hit the mark; I was dejected until a phone call from a sorta girlfriend (let's call her Sally; we hung out a lot, I raided her mom's abundant fridge, we got high and we didn't fuck, to my regret) that a girlfriend of hers, who knew nothing about music, had sent in a single postcard and bought four tickets. She offered two to Sally and Sally in turn offered me one. I was a made man.

We got high on weed before the show; it was at 1pm, an added show inasmuch as the three evening shows had sold out almost instantly. Honestly, they could have sold out every night for months. They were at the height of their popularity, with a string of smash albums since they hooked up with Jimmy Miller in '68.

I brought a small pencil and notebook in my pocket so I could write down the song list. Wonderlove was a fairly large band with great material but loud and, to my ears, with an unbalanced sound. I had a headache; if it was any other group, I might have left. As much as I had looked forward to checking out Stevie in person (I loved his albums and TV appearances the rare times I would see him), I couldn't wait for him – and my headache – to vanish. He left, finally.

There were a few minutes of excited chatter; the 20,000 seat Garden was sold out and the air was ripe with reefer smoke. Suddenly, the lights dimmed. The opening bass notes of '2000 Light Years from Home' sounded through the PA and the catcalls and whistles from the crowd, standing in anticipation, began. I looked forward to hearing the opening fanfare for 'Brown Sugar', when suddenly the Stones were on stage and blew straight into 'Brown Sugar', minus the fanfare.

They were much louder than Stevie, but balanced. I could not hear the sound of my own voice when I turned to say something to Sally. Keith was wearing a silver lamé shirt, jeans and boots. Charlie was wearing a t-shirt, but from the distance I couldn't see the logo on it (I saw later in the newspapers it was Three Ball Charlie from the cover of *Exile*). Mick Jagger was dancing and singing wearing his white and gold jumper, Bill Wyman was solid as a rock, but I don't remember anything he was wearing, and Mick Taylor had some sort of fringed handbag over his shoulder.

The crowd was dancing its ass off; I remember two young men, one with hair like a '50s greaser, the other wearing a then-fashionable hippie jeans overall with long, long hair, their arms locked and doing a round-and-round deranged Western square dance. The octogenarian MSG ushers, wearing their jivey suit and cap ensemble, had emerged from the tunnels and were taking in the crazed scene. Joy reigned supreme.

I have seen hundreds of rock, blues, soul and jazz concerts in my life. I have seen Jimi Hendrix and the Band of Gypsies, Jeff Beck (seven times), Miles Davis and the On the Corner band, CSNY, The Beach Boys, Joni Mitchell, The Band (at the time of their second album), Eric Clapton, Mike Bloomfield and Al Kooper, Billy Cobham, Mahavishnu Orchestra, Les Paul and many, many more. But no one, *no one*, was musically tighter than the Stones that afternoon. If all of the others were on the top floor, the Stones with Mick Taylor were the penthouse suite.

Forget the bullshit sour grapes from Keith and all his baloney about guitar weaving; with Mick Taylor, Richards was chording like crazy; he was the Ultimate Rhythm Guitarist whose chords rang out. Ian Stewart was introduced to a rousing round of applause as the legend played piano for a blues number, and then back to Nicky Hopkins. Jim Price played tambourine during the songs that didn't require his trumpet.

I was stunned by Mick Taylor. Nothing had prepared me for his fantastic lead playing; he never repeated himself. Dave Mason will trot out his wah-wahed triplets over and over again; every guitarist has his favorite licks. Mick Taylor was unbelievably fluid and never repeated himself. I walked into the concert saying to myself, 'Mick Jagger, Mick Jagger'. When I left, all I could think was, 'Mick Taylor, Mick Taylor.'

The Stones had the famous Jules Fisher mirror behind them; no chick back up singers, no lasers, no balloon cock. Just fantastic music that lives in my mind for as long as I walk this Earth and breath this air. Simply, the greatest concert I have ever seen or heard. And no encore.

I saw the Stones when they returned to MSG in '75 with Ron Wood in lieu of Mick Taylor; the rest of the band was still fantastic but Ron Wood, pleasant though he might be, is a journeyman compared to Mick Taylor; the Stones had become the Stones Lite as far as I am concerned. Although I dutifully bought their albums, I have never wanted to see them again. I have been to the peak of the mountain.

CHARLES 'CHUCK' FARRELL

I recently read a quote from Keith Richards. He stated that in 1964, many American fans of the Rolling Stones thought that they were an R&B band. That was me, except that I was eight years old and had no

idea what R&B was. I only knew I loved the Stones sound. I discovered
the band on my transitor radio when 'Time is on my Side' hit the top
ten. Soon after that were television appearances on *The Ed Sullivan
Show*, but more importantly for me, *The Clay Cole Show*, a local music
show in New York (our version of *American Bandstand*, only better). The
Stones played much of their *12 X 5* album over two of Clay's shows in
consecutive weeks. Move over Beatles, I had a new favorite band. My
love for their music has never waned since those days. I see people who
I have not seen in 50 years and they say to me, 'Do you still like the
Stones?' I'm a bit of a fanatic, to say the least.

So. fast forward to 1972. *Exile on Main St.* was released in May, right
around my sixteenth birthday. I was incredibly excited when I heard that
it had arrived at our local King Carol Record Store. I ran home to get
the money that I had saved for it, while my good friend Steve, another
big fan, went to beg his mom for some money. I ran to the bus stop – no
Steve. I ran back to Steve's house. 'Steve is not coming out.' I ran back to
the bus stop. One of the neighbors inquired if someone had been hit by
a car (Did I mention that I was excited?). Steve did not make the trip, but
I got my copy of the album that day.

Soon after, news of the tour hit the New York newspapers. We heard
from our favorite FM radio station that we would need to send postcards
and hope to get chosen to purchase tickets for Madison Square Garden
from July 24th through July 26th. Thinking that the band wanted an
audience that was familiar with the songs from their new album, I mailed
all 12 postcards that were included with the *Exile on Main St.* LP to the
address that was given. I told all my friends to do the same. We waited.
Eventually, I received a notice in the mail that I had four tickets waiting
for me to be picked up at MSG on such-and-such date. I was over the
moon. Now, I had to pick three friends to go with me.

Steve, of course, was my number one choice. When I told his girlfriend
that I wanted her to keep it a secret, she twisted my 'you-know-whats'
for a ticket. 'Chuck, you know Steve will want me to be with him!' Okay,
one ticket left. I chose another friend, Paul, who was a major music fan
and who also loved the band. He eventually became a DJ on a major FM
station in New York.

I was too excited to keep the secret, so I told Steve about a week later and he came with me to pick up the tickets at MSG. We got tickets for the final night of the tour, and it fell on Mick's birthday. Unbelievable!

The tour had begun and the media was reporting every step of the way. Mick and Keith were busted in Boston, which gave us a temporary scare. Reporters started asking Mick about the last show. This was the official beginning of Mick being asked about his age, which would go on for the rest of his career (and still does). He was going to be 29. Next up 30. Would he feel strange still singing rock and roll as a 30-year-old? Would he still sing 'Mother's Little Helper'? Then they started asking him if he would do anything special for his birthday show. He said that he might just stand on his head (he did try). I have been around for many Stones tours, but I really feel that none reached the level of excitement that North America '72 did.

While I was anxious for the concert to come, it was a difficult time, because my family was moving from my beloved neighborhood five days after the show. Leaving all my friends would be bittersweet, for sure.

The night finally came and I don't think I need to tell you how the four of us were feeling. We had seats in section 208, not bad; a good view of the stage and out in front of the speakers. I think that I can confidently say that most core Stones fans have seen the movie *Ladies and Gentlemen, The Rolling Stones*, so you have a pretty good idea of what we saw and heard.

Believe it or not, I was surprised that they played 'Jumpin' Jack Flash', as the newspapers had not mentioned that tune in their reviews of the first night's show. And was that 'Johnny B Goode'? It sounded like it, but different (I found out later it was 'Bye Bye Johnny').

The show's finale is what made this night different than other shows on the tour. After 'Street Fighting Man', the audience sang along with a recorded version of 'Happy Birthday' for Mick. His wife, Bianca, came out with a stuffed panda, and a huge cake also came out. We cheered for an encore, but as the know-it-all Stones fan, I told my friends, 'They don't do encores.' Well, guess what? Not only the Stones, but Stevie Wonder and his band (the opening act) came back for more. They started with Wonder's song 'Uptight (Everything's Alright')', with Stevie chanting 'happy birthday, Mick' a few times. Finally, the band segued into 'Satisfaction'. Everyone bowed, and left 19,000 smiles on the faces of everyone in attendance. I had no voice for two days after singing along all night. It was a quiet ride home on the subway and the bus. Moving day was five days away now.

So, fast forward to 2021. Although my family moved away, it was not that far away. Steve and I are still good friends. I saw him recently as he and his wife attended my daughter's wedding. His old girlfriend is a friend of mine on social media and we chat about things often. We lost Paul to leukemia in 1991. We think of the night of July 26, 1972, as a special night in our lives; as the best concert we have ever or will ever attend.

MICHAEL GALILEO, AGE 21

The first I heard of the Rolling Stones was after we'd heard of The Beatles when the whole British Invasion was starting. I was 12 years old. My parents were just going through a divorce. I was usurped from the home that I lived in and ended up with my single mom, not living in the best of circumstances. Kennedy had just gotten shot in November '63, but at 12 years old I was already into music. I'd started buying records a couple of years prior. One of the first records I bought was 'Sherry' by The Four Seasons, but I go all the way back to 'Does Your Chewing Gum Lose its Flavour on the Bedpost Overnight?' and 'How Much is That Doggie in the Window?'. My mom played a lot of music in the house. She would play albums so I would constantly be listening to Tony Bennett, Frank Sinatra and Johnny Mathis and all the records of the Broadway shows – *Oklahoma!* and *Carousel*. I have Asperger's which means socially I have difficulties, so having a difficult home environment and being on the spectrum and falling through the cracks meant life was challenging for me on a regular basis. I didn't have a lot to hang onto but I found a lot of joy in music.

We had transistor radios and the music was very cool and that was something I could identify with. When The Beatles came out, for me it was one of the biggest things that ever happened. I was in middle school in Long Island. I remember going into a candy store which sold magazines and leafing through all the magazines and seeing on the cover this new group called the Rolling Stones. And I was like, 'Oh, what are these guys?' I started looking into it and then I started telling everybody at the school. I said, 'I know about these new guys that you never heard

273

about.' That's when I became a fan. All the way through the Sixties I was a Stones fan as well as a Beatles fan. I loved their experimentation, just as I loved what The Beatles did.

When *Beggars Banquet* came out in 1968, we had the benefit here in New York of a radio station that was probably one of the best in the world which was WNEW-FM. They were a very cutting-edge FM station and they played music that nobody else played, so I would hear lots of the good stuff that most people on the top 40 stations weren't hearing. I remember hearing a little thing with Mick Jagger talking about how *Beggars Banquet* was going to be a return to the blues and their roots. I was very happy to hear that, not that I understood that 'Crossroads' by Cream was a Robert Johnson song and that we were being resold all the music that originally came from here from the black guys.

On July 4, 1972 I was involved in a pretty bad car accident. I was driving a British Triumph GT6 that I had bought brand new in 1970 and I ended up in a head on accident with a much larger American vehicle, a Pontiac GTO. I wound up in hospital with all kinds of broken bones. But while I was in the hospital, I was able to listen to my favorite radio station, WNEW-FM, and they said the Stones were going to be playing in Madison Square Garden and that the only way you could get tickets was to fill in individual postcards and send them in, from which they would randomly pick out cards and if your card got picked then you were able to go and get tickets to the show. My then girlfriend and I sat in my hospital bed and filled out between 50 and 75 postcards and put stamps on them and she mailed in. While I was still in the hospital, we got notified that I was able to get tickets.

The only problem was… I was still in the hospital! I had broken bones and stuff but nothing was going to stop me, and so I told the doctor I had to be released. He said under no circumstances could I be released from the hospital. I said, 'If you don't release me, I'm leaving of my own accord.' One thing led to another and sure enough he let me out.

We had to go and stand online and pick up the tickets from Madison Square Garden. I had been on my back in the hospital for like three weeks, getting shots of Demerol every four hours, and here I was all of a sudden vertical in about 95 degree heat with about 95 per cent humidity, standing online outside of Madison Square Garden. I didn't think I was going to make it to the door. But I didn't pass out and I managed to get the tickets. I arranged to go to the show, taking my girlfriend. A friend of mine had a 35 mm camera. I had never taken 35 mm shots before but I said I would like to take the camera with me to the show if at all possible and he loaned me his Yashica 35mm camera. I bought three rolls of high speed Ektachrome slide film and I went to the show.

We got there early and of course the Stones always used to delay their entrance, whether it was because of Keith or whether it was planned – as it was in '75 – to build up the audience's sense of anticipation. When I got there, my seats were literally all the way up in the top row at the far end of the arena. You could not have had worse seats. They were as far away and as high up as they could've been. I was satisfied for a short period of time, while things were getting going, but then I got antsy and, being 21, I just walked out of the door I'd gone in and worked my way down closer to the stage, outside of the auditorium where they normally have people going to the different gates. I walked in through this door and found myself at stage level. A guy let me in. I guess he must've assumed that, because I had a 35mm camera, I was there taking photographs legitimately and so I started taking 35mm slides. I got some fantastic shots, about a hundred of them. I even had a couple of pictures where Jagger looked right into the lens of my camera and gave me his best look. I had those shots hanging in my living room for years. I would give slideshows at my house to my friends for years afterwards, in which I would play the set list along with the slides of the whole show. It was quite phenomenal. Unfortunately, when I left my first wife, she destroyed all of that stuff.

The show itself was, of course, fantastic. It was probably the pinnacle of rock shows for me at the time. I remember 'Midnight Rambler', with the stage drenched in red and Mick in the cape. It was very surreal. I couldn't tell you song by song what they played, but they had just released *Exile on Main St.*, which I think is the best album they ever made in their lives. I played *Exile* to death.

Musicians were like surrogate fathers to me. I loved everything about these guys. I was addicted to music and the poetry of rock 'n' roll because it guided me through my life. I watched what all of these guys did. I watched how they lived. I watched how they dealt with everything.

I watched the words that they played. I watched their commitment. Probably John Lennon was more of a surrogate father to me than anybody else. But I could do a Mick Jagger like nobody's business on the dancefloor.

Mick and Keith are the epitome of, 'Don't let it bring you down, just keep going'. They were just feeling their way. It's been an incredible journey to watch. The guy I feel the most empathy for is Brian. He has so much to do with the origination of the band and their original attraction because of his musicology. He seems to have just got lopped off. He's not even on the stamps over there in the UK.

I was lucky to be born in 1950. The Earth's been around for four billion years and to be here when all this creativity took place? It was just an incredible time to be alive. The Stones represented everything so cool it was unbelievable.

I saw them in '75, and on the *Steel Wheels* tour in '89 and again in 2019, when I thought they were better than they have ever been. I could not believe that these guys, who are closing in on 80 years old, were playing music that is so incredibly inspiring. And I was thinking, 'If you guys can keep going, I can keep going.' They're going to be like the old blues guys who die on the road. Me too. They've been role models for better or worse. They've been heroes. They're still inspiring me, 50 years later.

ANDREW GREENSPAN

My first concert. What I remember most vividly is the palpable sense of anticipation before the show.

CATHY DEUTSCH, AGE 16

I will never forget the first time, at eight years of age in 1965, when I heard *'Satisfaction'*. I was in an after-school arts and craft class with other pony-tailed girls when the song came on the radio high up on a bookshelf. It was a fitting introduction, considering that this song is about hearing something on the radio…

To this day, I remember with great vividness how I put down my papers mesmerised, staring at the dropped ceiling panels above the radio. Of course, at such a young age I had no idea of the meaning of the song, but I was moved, almost hypnotised by its rhythm and urgency. From then on, I was inexplicably attuned to their music. Luckily the radio was always on and their songs became the background of my life as I turned from a girl, to a teen, and eventually into the woman I am today. They, through their music, helped me to define myself, to accept my bigger than the box personality and to embrace my love of R&B, soul and rock and roll. The music and performances of Mick gave me permission to be bawdy, to be all up front, to be sexual, androgynous – and to not be afraid to shake it!

As I got older and could go to concerts, I saw the Stones in New York whenever they toured. In 1972, my first concert, at the age of 16 when there was no Ticketron, we had to send postcards in a ticket lottery. All duplicates would be removed. With my Stones freak friend Susan (who looked a bit like Bianca) we sent in around 100 postcards with the names of all our family members and pets, hoping to get tickets to all New York shows. My aunt's dog Coco, a brown French poodle, got two tickets. ID would have to be shown at the box office, so I just walked into the library and asked for a library card under the name of Coco Benjamin. When the librarian questioned my unusual name, I said my mother was French and named me after Coco Chanel.

Score! Two tickets closer to success!

By hook and by crook we got seats to all the shows at Madison Square Garden, where we slowly but surely made our way to the front row every night. It was there that I lost my shoes, and would have lost much more given the opportunity! Mick was the focus of my adoration, and remains a life long fascination, but I didn't until I was older learn to listen to the music as a band and not just the lead singer. When this happened, it was an expanded experience of what had already become my second heartbeat.

I appreciated each of them as the perfect pieces that made the group what is considered The Greatest Rock and Roll Band in history. Keith was Keef, raunchy, dark, bad boy playing wild and brilliantly, always a cigarette hanging out of his mouth. Bill Wyman, then Ronnie Wood – both the bookends that added texture. The former members Mick Taylor, Brian Jones, were before my time.

Charlie, *dear Charlie*, was always steady, the inside of the music hidden in the back that drove everything without flash. Demurring, humble, taking a small blushing bow at the end of the show. He was the good boy, a consummate professional, the beat that gave them life. He was a brilliant drummer, primarily a lover and player of jazz, whose ever-steady rhythm kept the band musically together. He was the backbone that let Mick sing it to his primal beat, and gave the space for Keith to let his guitar freak fly!

In August 2019, I took my then 26-year-old daughter to her first large arena concert in New Jersey. I saw it as her initiation as she has had the songs as her secondhand smoke all her life, as I play and talk about them probably too much. We exuberantly danced and danced all night, never sitting down once. She even commented upon seeing people seated, 'Do they think they're at a freakin' James Taylor concert?' It was impossible to *not* move. She was mesmerised, and fell into the tribal power of thousands dancing and singing under the stars. It was joyous, and remains one of the best nights we have ever had together, and we have had many. At the end, she said of Mick, 'Mom, he's a freak of nature, I get why you love him so much.' This from a 26-year-old girl captivated by a 76 year-old man. That is the power of the Rolling Stones.

My love for the band will always live on but it will never sound the same. This band of brothers has given the world a tremendous musical legacy. I've seen them around twelve times and will unabashedly say they have been some of the most exulted full body moments of my life.

Contrary to lyrics, the Rolling Stones have given me satisfaction and yes, I can always get what I want.

RIP Mr Charlie Watts, a brilliant elegant gentleman who gave us a legacy unrivalled.

PHILIP SIMMONS, AGE 18

I was living in Canarsie, Brooklyn, NYC when my buddy asked me if I wanted him to get me a Rolling Stones ticket for the Garden. I had seen them play at Madison Square Garden in 1969, and that was a phenomenal show, so I said, 'I'm in.' By then I was a very experienced rock concert attendee, having seen about 30 shows at the legendary Fillmore East, as well as many others, including the Allman Brothers, the Grateful Dead, Pink Floyd and *The Concert for Bangladesh*. The Rolling Stones stood out as one of the best live rock shows I had ever seen until then, and still does now. By '69, the great Mick Taylor was in the band

and he was still going to be playing in '72, so I was more than eager to see them again.

I went with the same childhood friends I had seen the Stones with in '69. The band were once again at the top of their game. The opening act was the great Stevie Wonder, who at that time was starting to get a large rock audience. He had just written 'Superstition' for Jeff Beck but had made it his own, on the advice of his manager.

After Stevie's set, they announced, as they always did, 'The greatest rock and roll band in the world, the Rolling Stones.' For me, they really were. When they came out along with their touring backup ensemble, they started to crank it up. The set list was great. Having just released one of my favorite Stones albums, *Exile,* they did several tunes from that album along with their great later songs from that time period. The live versions of these took on a new life, with some of them extended and embellished. They were smokin'.

That's the essence of a great live rock show, in my humble opinion. They weren't just playing the note-for-note shows like in the Murray the K, three minute song days. Of course, times had changed and the Stones were an absolute powerhouse at this peak period in their career.

The band was almost in its original form except Mick Taylor had replaced Brian Jones. On this tour, there was the addition of the great pianist Nicky Hopkins who was absolutely phenomenal and my favorite rock piano player. Also, they had a great horn section and backup singers.

Jagger was in rare form, trying to lighten it up a bit since the last tour and the disaster at Altamont. They did not perform 'Sympathy for the Devil', and he acted a bit more clownish than devilish. Mick Taylor played phenomenal extended solos. At that time, he could go toe-to-toe with any other guitarist in the business. Keith was great but I always felt there was no comparison between him and Mick Taylor's virtuosity, especially in '72. The late, great Charlie Watts, along with Bill Wyman, were fantastic, as were the whole ensemble.

Having seen hundreds of shows since, including the Stones in 1975, 1989 and 2006, the 1972 show still ranks as one of the best live shows I ever saw. They weren't kidding in those days when they called them 'the greatest rock and roll band in the world'.

MARSHALL CHESS, ROLLING STONES RECORDS

(Stevie) and Mick were dancing on stage together, then somebody came out and put a whipped cream pie in Mick's face. It was crazy. The building was actually vibrating. You could feel it in the concrete.

(as told to *Uncut* magazine, December 24, 2020)

WALTER DONACH, AGE 14

1972. The Greatest Rock 'n' Roll Band in the world. I was 14 years old. I was fortunate growing up in the Sixties, with a sister four years older and a brother two years older, as I got to listen to a lot of the great music of the era, first on AM radio, then on freeform FM in New York – WNEW, WOR-FM and WABC-FM, which later turned into WPLJ. Buying 45s and LPs, the first Stones LPs we had were *Let It Bleed*, *Sticky Fingers* and *Get Yer Ya-Ya's Out!* We wore out the grooves. Then *Exile* was released and the '72 American tour was announced. Four shows at Madison Square Garden. Everybody wanted to go, but you had to send in postcards to win the chance at tickets. Who didn't send in cards?

I followed the tour exploits in *Rolling Stone* magazine – was it Hunter S Thompson writing? The mail comes one day, and there it is… pick up your tickets at the MSG box office. I was ecstatic. I'm not sure who went to purchase them but – holy shit! – we got four seats, orchestra, row 24, for the last show of the tour – July 26, Mick's 29th birthday! We'd been to a couple of concerts by this time, but nothing of this magnitude. The Rolling Stones!

Some 'friends' offered $100 each for our tickets. Inflation adjusted, that would be around $700 today, but no way. We subwayed into Manhattan, found our floor seats and waited. Stevie Wonder opened. He was okay, but everyone wanted the Stones. As the first chords of 'Brown Sugar' rang out, we were on our feet, on our chairs, and we stayed there for the entire show. It was mesmerizing to see and hear them, live and loud right in front of us. Then they ripped through 'Bitch' and 'Rocks Off'. The place was beyond electric. 'Tumbling Dice', my favorite at that time, was awesome, as was the entire show.

'Midnight Rambler' really stands out in my memory, with Mick using a red scarf like a whip in the slow middle section, then the song building to a raucous ending that was so beyond the album version. When they got to the encore, 'Jumpin' Jack Flash' and 'Street Fighting Man', the house lights were up, the crowd was wild and Mick was throwing buckets of rose petals and then water into the front rows. It was a transcendent experience.

Then… Stevie Wonder and band came out, singing 'Uptight', into 'Happy Birthday, Mick'. The Stones came on with them and segued into 'Satisfaction', while a giant cake was brought out. A huge teddy bear presented by Bianca was dropped onto the cake by Mick, and pieces of cake, and pies, were flying onstage and into the audience as they kept playing 'Satisfaction'. When they finally finished, we felt as spent as they looked, an experience like never before. I remember people with pie and cake on their clothes as we made our exit.

This show made me the diehard Stones fan I am to this day. And having seen most tours to date, this first one was truly life changing.

YESTERDAY'S PAPERS

GRACE LICHTENSTEIN
NEW YORK TIMES, JULY 25, 1972

Although the Stones show had an almost impromptu look, every gesture had been carefully rehearsed and the audience's response seemed equally practised and carefully engineered. Jagger almost seemed to be manipulating the vast audience as he invited them to pound their hands together high above their heads during 'Jumpin' Jack Flash'. The lighting too seemed carefully geared to elicit a frantic, blood-pounding response…

SUZY SAYS
NEW YORK DAILY NEWS, JULY 28, 1972

The wildest craziest best party of the year – so far – broke up at 6am a couple of hours after a young lady with about five pounds of silicon in each breast had popped out of a huge cake to say hello there to Mick Jagger (whose birthday it was) and a crew of dancers from Harlem had tapped their way into 500 hearts. After that, there just didn't seem to be much left for an encore. It was the Ahmet Erteguns' supper dance in honor of the Rolling Stones at the St Regis Roof, celebrating the final performance of the Stones' triumphal American concert tour which rocked Madison Square Garden to the rafters and mesmerised 20,000 fans. The electrifying performance by Mick and the boys, ending when they rolled the first enormous birthday cake on stage and began hurling lemon meringue pies all over the place, was sensational and deafening. The way to hear the Stones is with two sets of earplugs, if you value your hearing.

AFTERMATH

LLOYD BARDE

I saw them again in '75 at Fort Collins. And I saw them twice in LA. But after that they were stadium shows and you'd end up watching the screen more than the stage. I figured I'd already done it at the absolute max. When they came out on the stage for that first show in '72 it was really heavy rock 'n' roll. I saw a lot of really fantastic groups, but when I make my best all-time concert list it's the Rolling Stones first with Bob Marley a very close second. Back in Greeley, Colorado, 'See the Rolling Stones!' became the motto of our little record store – on our t-shirts, on our ads on the wall of the store. Everywhere it said, 'See the Rolling Stones.'

TOM SCHUTZ

I remember watching through binoculars as they left the stage in San Diego, feeling completely satisfied after having skipped school to see the Stones on the West Coast five times in 1972. Arriving home, my parents were not so happy with my choice, but they got over it. And I will never forget it!

GLENN COLEMAN

I have seen them at least once on every tour since 1969. I become a studio electronics tech and worked at Atlantic Records in the Eighties. I even met Mick Jagger there twice. Now I build recording gear and have sold equipment, through my dealers, for their tours. They had it on the *Bigger Bang* tour.

HUGH WINTERS

I'm really surprised the Stones have held together with so much tragedy they've had, Brian Jones and Bill Wyman leaving, and all that stuff. But they've just kept going. Mick doesn't have a great voice. It's a British intonation of an Alabama soul singer type voice. It would probably be comical if you looked at it analytically. But I grew up with the Stones. Jeez, we used to play their records. We used to have 35 cents worth of nickels stacked on top of the tone arm in order to keep it in the groove. Those were fun times after school. We'd always play some rock records and, 'I got this record... Let's go to his house...'.

GARY STUART

I've seen them many times since. In Los Angeles at the Staples Center in 2013 over 40 years later, they were on fire as they were that night. I posted that the Stones were 'on fire' in LA and, as luck would have it, that term stuck for the rest of the tour Down Under. Coincidence? Hmmmm...

DEBRA JOHNSON

The frantic pace, and the crazy energy given off by Jagger, are captured in the film *Ladies and Gentlemen, The Rolling Stones*, which I've watched dozens of times since then. They were – and still are – the world's greatest rock 'n' roll band. No one comes even close. I'm eternally grateful that I was lucky enough to have seen them live... and I have reviewed every single show I've seen... all 40 of them. God speed the Rolling Stones.

CHIP MONCK

In 1967, when I did Monterey Pop, I had a bust. I went to Canada to see Habitat, a new housing development which sounded pretty interesting. I had a joint behind my ear and forgot that I was changing countries, so I ended up doing seven days in Bordeaux Prison in Montreal, which was pretty hard edged. Alan Crossman and Peter Rudge got me out, because they were ready to tour and the Stones were my act. But I couldn't get a working visa in Australia. The 1973 Los Angeles Nicaragua Earthquake Benefit concert was about the last show I did with the Stones. I built everything that went to Australia, but I wasn't able to go there personally.

AFTERWORD

In 1972, the Rolling Stones played 51 shows in 54 days to a combined audience of 750,000, grossing somewhere in the region of four million dollars. This sum is of course dwarfed by the economics of a single Rolling Stones show in 2022. (The 2022 *Sixty* tour played to 712,000 people across Europe and grossed five times as much, even allowing for 50 years of inflation.) But at the time the 1972 tour set a new record.

1972 put the Rolling Stones firmly back on the map as rock's greatest live exponents. It established a new model for touring, with bands in future bringing their own versions of the Stones Touring Party and crewing their own shows. And the shadow of Altamont was quickly dispersed by the Californian sun of those early West Coast shows. The tour wound up in New York and was considered a triumph for all concerned.

The enduring myth of the Rolling Stones, from the group of scruffy teenagers learning the chords of blues records whilst living in a crummy and freezing cold apartment in London, through to the act that continues to be box office more than 60 years later, is in part built on those 51 shows and the trail that they blazed across North America back in 1972.

Mick Taylor left the Rolling Stones in 1975.

Bill Wyman left the Rolling Stones in 1992.

Charlie Watts died in 2021.

Mick Jagger and Keith Richards are rumored to be making plans to take the Stones out on the road again in 2023…

YOU GOT TO ROLL ME AND CALL
ME THE TUMBLIN' DICE

ABOUT THE AUTHOR

Richard Houghton lives in Manchester, UK. He divides his time between writing books about music (and especially collecting fan memories of seeing classic bands in concert), walking his dog Sid, watching Manchester City FC and Northampton Town FC and… listening to the Rolling Stones and going to their concerts.

You can reach Richard at *iwasatthatgig@gmail.com*. Or check out his website at *richardmhoughton.com*.

SPECIAL THANKS

Special thanks to:

Mike Gaffrey
Karen Cercone
Thomas Schutz
Johanna Dempsey
Steven Van Booven
Joe Ellrott
Thomas Schutz
Jack Weiss
Philip Simmons
Joseph Potenza
Pat Thomas
Janice Higginbotham
Gary Epperson
Michael Ruslander
Erwin Hoetjes
Donna Meller
Sandy Spickler
Donald Stone
James Kearns
Jonathan McLaren
Rich Greene
James Johnson
Lori Chavez
Julia McKinnell
Wayne Gaddy
Curt Angeledes
Ira Knopf
Gary Tufel
Steven Butcher